I0846619

FAIRYTALE HUNTER CAIN

Book I
by LlazyLlama

ISBN: 979-8-88993-081-5

Edited by Darien Aris Kirst
Art by Fernando Granea

Published 2025 by MoonQuill
Arlington, VA

www.moonquill.com

Table of Contents

Chapter 1

Big Bad Night

My brain pounded in my skull, each pulse wreaking havoc on my mind. Some idiot sang in the distance, like a dying cat clawing at a chalkboard.

"Make it stop... please," I muttered.

My breath hitched as something stung the right side of my chest. Sliding my hand forward, I winced as my fingers grazed a sore spot.

With a gentler touch, I tried to find the source of the pain and brushed against an extended cut.

I cracked open my eyes and shielded them from the blinding light.

What the hell?

My hand was coated in blood—my blood.

I took in my surroundings and tried to raise my head but banged it against something solid and collapsed to the floor.

My side throbbed. It was a minute before I was strong enough to move again.

This time, I brought myself to my knees. I raised my head again and gently lifted it until I met hard metal.

Okay. Don't panic. Someone is probably playing a prank on you.

My instincts screamed, telling me I was an idiot, but I clung to the hope that this was a crappy joke. Because if it wasn't? I'd face either death or torture—the kind of fate you'd expect from a psychopath who locks humans in cages.

A quick glance told me I was outside. Inside some unknown forest in the middle of nowhere, I was locked in a cage with only moonlight to help me see.

Reaching my arm out slowly, I gripped the metal bars in front of me and tried to pull. "Urggh." My side spasmed, and I dropped to the floor.

I'm going to die. Some maniac is nearby preparing to eat me or something! What the hell did I do?! How did I get in here?

I bit my lip to stop myself from screaming and alerting my captors. Even on the verge of freaking out, I knew *that* would be a stupid idea. I had to think.

Closing my eyes, I tried to recall what I did the night before, but my mind came up blank. I squeezed them tighter and tried to retrace my steps, but all I got was a load of nothing.

Why can't I remember?

My fingers closed around the cage bars, and a moment later, I froze in realization.

No more singing.

I dropped to the floor and lay still, easing my breath.

"Oh, Wolfy! He thinks he can pretend to sleep," a little girl said.

The wolf let out a sound akin to a scoff.

"Silly man. I can hear your heartbeat!"

My thoughts froze. The last word was whispered right next to my ear. Hot breath caressed my skin, making the hairs on my neck stand tall.

An insane fit of giggling burst from the girl's throat. It reached a pitch so high it became a cackle. The sounds of screams and laughter mixed in as the wolf beside her howled.

Screw it! I need to know!

I cracked my left eye open and flinched. My back hit the bars, and my head bumped into the top plate.

A little girl in a red hood stood in front of me, unmoving, with a grin fit for nightmares. Her eyes glowed crimson, and she had a mouth filled with razor-sharp teeth.

"No more sleep. It's time to eat!"

The glow in her eyes faded, and they transitioned into a striking blue. Soon, her teeth morphed into more human-looking ones, squared and perfectly straight.

"Wh—" My voice was hoarse and shaky, so I swallowed and tried to speak again. "Why am I here? Let me go, p-please!"

She shook her head and held out her arm. I didn't know what she wanted, but something impacted the cage from behind. I whipped around, but a large shadow blocked my vision.

No, not a shadow. It's a monster!

I trailed the black figure's form until I saw gray teeth attached to a wolf's maw staring back. It snapped at the bars, causing me to squirm away. The little girl cackled again, the sound driving me mad.

"Bleed, oh bleed, a sight to see! Your crimson gift is pure glee!"

I wouldn't have noticed the blood coating the cage if her words hadn't rung in my head. I no longer felt pain; the adrenaline in my veins kept me from feeling my new injury.

Blood and gore trailed from my arm to the wolf's bloodstained teeth, and I screamed. "Stop! *Stop!* Let me go! Let me out of here!"

A lone wolf howl met my plea, and tiny fingers ran down my back. I screamed internally and stayed still as the demonic child petted me like a dog.

"I'm going to miss you when you're gone, silly man." She moved her head closer, and I caught a glint of crimson in her crazy eyes. "So, let me take a bite or two."

Her teeth sharpened back into points that gleamed in the moonlight. I couldn't take my eyes off them as she slowly leaned in.

Not once did she lose her demented smile. And a pointed tongue licked the back of her teeth.

"Amara! Playtime is over," an older female voice commanded from behind the demon. "I thought I told you not to disturb the volunteers."

The little girl's face returned to normal, and she pouted. She slowly stood and joined the white-haired woman wearing a matching crimson cloak.

The shadow wolf sunk into the girl's shadow.

"I'm sorry, Granny Elspeth. But his fear smelled sooo delicious!"

"I know, little one. Only a bit longer, and we can enjoy ourselves." The older lady stroked the girl's hair. "Go see Granny Aylona, all right? She's ready for you and your sisters to join the circle."

The girl giggled and squeezed the lady's leg. If I hadn't been tortured by the demon child and hadn't seen the monster underneath that human skin, I'd have thought they looked sweet—a loving grandmother scolding her grandchild.

"Let me out of here!"

I knew I shouldn't scream. They were demons, and I was an idiot for antagonizing them.

Screw them! They're monsters! Why? Why am I here?!

Seeing the little girl skipping away while the lady proudly smiled made me sick to my stomach. Vomit tickled my esophagus as I suppressed a scream. I wanted to run, but I was trapped in a bloody cage.

The woman sighed and approached me with silent footsteps. When she was closer, she leaned down, revealing a set of crooked teeth. "I'm so sorry, dear. The little ones have trouble controlling their hunger."

The wrinkles and liver spots on her face made her feel far less threatening—loveable, even. However, pure malice filled her eyes. They didn't glow but were just as monstrous as the girl's.

My stomach dropped, and I wanted to rage and beat myself bloody in order to escape.

I didn't.

I couldn't.

Those eyes told me everything I needed to know.

I was going to die.

The old lady stood up and hummed a playful melody as she snapped her fingers. From her shadow, a wolf the size of a bear stepped out and pushed its nose into her palm. She stroked its fur and then pointed at my cage.

The beast padded over and casually latched its jaw around the bars. It raised my prison into the air, sending my body crashing against the back end of the cage.

"Try not to move, dearie. We need to keep the rest of your blood in your body. But don't worry, the others are only a short ways away."

She traveled deeper into the forest, the wolf in tow, as she escorted me to my doom.

We exited through the trees and entered a clearing. I heard several voices, both young and old. The wolf placed the cage on the ground, and I could finally see where I was.

Inside the clearing, blood covered the ground in swirling lines. It formed a pentagram on the stone, and each quadrant held several runes.

There were five "grandmas" positioned at each point of the star, each separated by a young girl in a red cloak.

They danced in place or sang along to a tune only they could hear.

I'm going to be sacrificed. An insane cult kidnapped me, and now I'm going to be eaten!

Someone sobbed to my left, and I noticed my cage was not the only one placed inside the circle. There were four others like me; bloody, beaten, bruised, and afraid. One woman stared into the forest, unblinking and unmoving, as she wept.

"Let me out!" a man screamed repeatedly.

The demons ignored his wailing.

A loud, bassy thrum rang throughout the clearing, popping my ears and vibrating my bones so intensely that it aggravated my chest wound.

The elderly woman from before spoke, her voice cutting through the chaos. "Sisters! Little ones! It is time!" She clapped her hands, and another pulse passed through my body. "Tonight is the night our coven grows in power. These brave volunteers before us will grant us their energy and grow our Lore."

A few of the girls squealed in delight as the women nodded their heads in perfect sync.

"To the court!"

"To our fate!"

"For the coven!"

"For the children!"

"Avenge the fallen!"

As one, the five women chanted and raised their arms to the sky. Even the girls stopped their chaotic ramblings to join in. My fellow prisoners fell silent, shaking in their cages.

It started as a single hum, then they all sang in unison. The sound, alien to my ears, made my skin crawl. The hums shifted to low, guttural growls that shook the earth.

In my head, I knew this was it. Nothing could save me, and I would never escape. But my body didn't accept that. I punched the bars and ignored the pain. My knuckles split, and my hand was bloodied. I pressed my back against the bars and kicked forward with all my strength.

Hot tears ran down my face as I punched the metal ceiling.

It did not dent.

The chanting rose in pitch, and something scraped at my skin. It felt as if burning nails were scratching my limbs, forcing me to yelp in pain.

I tried to maneuver onto my stomach, but the feeling of hot needles pressed into my legs, leaving them immobile.

The agony grew, each new pain weaving itself into my nerves.

I fought and failed to keep my eyes open, letting the void consume my thoughts.

Make it stop...

As a new pressure crushed my chest, a loud howl cut through the haze of misery. Screams erupted, and the burning pain disappeared.

My eyes shot open, and I looked around just as a large wolf carried a screaming grandma by the leg and charged into the woods.

An eruption of blue flames blinded me. When I opened my eyes again, the clearing looked like a war zone.

One of the grandmas elongated her limbs and lifted a snarling wolf into the air before launching it away.

Wait... That's not a wolf!

One of the girls pressed her back against my iron bars, screaming as she cowered.

"Get away from me, you naughty wolf! Get away!" she shrieked.

A tall man with broad shoulders, wearing a familiar red cloak—albeit one more ripped and torn—came stalking closer with a bloody axe in hand.

He was silent as the demon child yelled at him to back away.

He raised his weapon, and the girl's feet shifted.

She was going to dodge, and *I* wouldn't let her.

My hand shot through the bars and seized her ankle in a death grip. She stumbled and tried to break free, but my other hand held her still. Her screeches of terror brought a maniacal grin to my face. Now *she* knew what it felt like to be scared and hopeless.

The man severed her head from her neck in a single stroke. Together, we watched it tumble to the floor in a fountain of black blood.

When a drop landed on my hand, it sizzled against my skin. I pulled back as the man kicked the corpse away from the cage. He looked at me with glowing orange irises that caught the moonlight's radiance.

He raised his axe again. I closed my eyes, accepting my fate. Then, I heard metal cut through the lock.

Huh?

I peeked through squinted eyes to see him offer a hand. Hesitant, I stared, unable to discern if I were still alive or in some twisted afterlife.

When I didn't react, he reached in and lifted me by the shirt. I winced as he grazed my right side but forced my mouth shut.

"Wake up, kid. You're still alive." He had a voice fit for radio, deep and smooth.

"I... What's going on?" I asked.

He sighed and kicked the severed head away. It flew into the trees, crashing with a wet thunk. "There's no time to explain. Just shut up and come with me. Follow my orders, and you'll live to see another moonrise. Sound good?"

I had no time to answer before he clapped me on the back, pushed me forward, and broke into a sprint.

Chapter 2

Escape the Reds

Sounds of screaming and fighting filled the air as the Hunter led us deeper into the woods. I ran, scared out of my mind. I would have looked back to watch the horror show like a fool, but he made me run at a dead sprint, so I didn't even have the option if I wanted.

"Please! Wait! Don't leave me behind! Get me outta here!" came a cry from our left.

Against my better judgment, I turned my head just enough to watch a twisted granny rip the top off the cage and bite the captive's head off. Crimson blood sprayed the air, and the demon let out a high-pitched trill.

The deceased's body slumped to the floor, blood spurting from his neck.

Oh crap! Oh crap!

I kept running. My feet hurt, and my limbs were still sore and twitching from the burning needle sensation. This was misery—no—this was hell.

Have to move; keep running. Don't stop, Cain!

We ran for what felt like forever, and I wanted to kiss the Hunter's feet when he held out an arm and stopped. I collided into him, bouncing off of his muscular frame and falling to the ground. It felt like running into a brick wall, and what little air I had left in my lungs was knocked out of me.

"Urgh! Why are we stopping? We need to get out of here!" I asked through deep breaths.

My head turned on a swivel, but we were alone. The forest stayed silent, absent of the wolf howls and demonic screams. It was dark, and I could barely see, even with the moonlight pushing through the canopy.

I was about to speak again when the Hunter cursed.

"Damn, Reds. Kid, get up. We can't stay here."

Though I wanted to demand an answer, I figured it was best not to question the man who battled demons. So instead, I clamped my mouth shut and moved behind him.

He sniffed the air like a hunting dog. It only hit me a second later that the Hunter who saved me was most likely a werewolf. Why I hadn't made that connection when I saw other werewolves fighting the grannies, I couldn't say.

The man who saved me is a monster.

Something inside my lizard brain panicked, but another part couldn't care less. Two sides of me warred with each other, but the one fried and overwhelmed to the point of inaction won.

So what if he's a werewolf? He's a kind werewolf who saved me—a werewolf who chops off demon children's heads.

The small part of me that dealt with logic understood that even if sticking with him had its pros, it was, frankly, still insane. He could have killed me or left me for dead at any point, but instead, he was keeping me safe.

He stopped sniffing and grabbed my wrist. We moved at a brisk jog further away from the grove. Occasionally, he would stop and sniff the air again, only to turn us in a different direction.

Three minutes, then five, and finally, a dozen minutes passed as we maintained our routine of moving, stopping, and adjusting before moving again.

My adrenaline wore off, and the pain in my side flared with each new step. I couldn't complain; I couldn't force my mouth to form the word *stop.* Stopping meant death.

We came to another, smaller clearing before he released my arm. The sudden change in routine left me confused and forced me to process what happened. He no longer moved nor sniffed the air.

"Hey, kid. You have a name?"

"Cain." I panted. "Y-You?"

"Elias." He pulled his axe from the strap on his back. "Whatever happens, Cain, do not interfere. If you do, you will die. Do you understand?"

Not in the slightest.

I nodded. "Yes."

"Good, at least you can follow orders. When the fight happens, stay out of my way. Right now, you're a walking meat sack to these things."

I bobbed my head like a chicken as my heart raced.

Silently, I stood waiting for more instructions, but Elias kept quiet. He scanned the dark forest for something, and I had no idea what.

Suddenly, a blur of living shadows launched at me. It happened so fast I couldn't even scream. The missile came from my right, and I tried to turn, but it moved too fast. Sharp teeth aimed for my throat, but Elias swung his axe.

The shadow wolf rolled away and growled as it sank into the ground. Before it could escape, Elias extended his arm, and fire erupted from his palm. The sudden light exposed the creature, causing it to hiss.

With casual ease, as if tossing a coin, the Hunter flicked the fire off his hand and punched through the creature's head. A loud screech came from somewhere deeper in the woods, and the shadow wolf burst apart.

Holy crap! That was magic.

"I'll have to thank Astra later. I owe her a drink for forcing me to learn the words." When Elias spoke, it was done with perfect calm, as if the wolf hadn't been mere seconds away from tearing out my jugular.

"Kid, move closer. That was too cl—"

A massive shadow wolf bit his arm, pulling him to the ground. He swung his weapon, and the wolf leaped backwards. Scrambling to his feet, Elias hastily raised his hand again.

The wolf didn't like that.

In an explosive jump, the wolf became a blur. Elias used his axe to intercept the attack, forcing the monster back, but it wasn't quick enough. The result was a long, bloody gash across his forearm.

I froze. This was out of my league.

Move! Do something! Get away!

My legs shifted, but the wolf dodged another swing of the axe by pouncing toward me. A single smack of the enormous tail sent me flying several feet, and I felt something crack.

"Fuuuu—" I gritted my teeth and held in my whimper, the battle continuing on without me.

Elias threw a few fireballs, and one successfully blasted apart the giant shadow wolf's front leg. The injury forced the creature to fall, and a quick downwards chop severed another limb.

The wolf tried to stand up, but Elias had had enough. He threw himself at the beast and sacrificed his blade to keep its jaws occupied. With his free hand, he shoved his arm into its shadowy body.

The flames poked out from the shadows, and Elias growled. The wolf's eyes widened before there was a sound of air sucking inward. Its body bubbled and promptly exploded, bursting into pieces of void particles that coated the forest floor.

Elias raised his head and let out a howl that matched the scream echoing from deeper in the woods. "You dare send a pup against a Grimm? Fight me yourself, cowards!"

When he faced me, his glowing eyes paralyzed me the same way the little girl's had. The glow faded, and he flashed me a pearly white smile.

He stopped smiling when he noticed me rooted in place. "Can you get up?"

I pushed myself off the ground, powering through the pain. My arm trembled, and I stumbled. Without thinking, my hand shot out to brace myself, and I had to bite my tongue to contain the scream in my throat.

"I'm... up."

"Good." He turned his back to me. "Sorry, kid. I didn't expect to get caught in their spell. Whatever happens, run. I can't keep you safe anymore."

My head throbbed, and I couldn't contain my anger. "What spell? What's happening? I don't... I don't want to die!"

"Bad night, I get it. But if you stay here, there's a good chance you'll have your head bitten off just like the guy in the cage."

I wanted to argue but stopped. I hadn't acknowledged it before, but he was wounded. Blood dripped from his arm, collecting into a small pool at his feet.

"You're injured."

He didn't acknowledge my statement, but his grip on his axe tightened, turning his knuckles white.

He pointed behind us, and I turned to leave. I couldn't do anything. Monsters, demons, fireball-slinging werewolves—this was too much.

My foot shifted one step and then another. Within seconds, I was running away.

Chapter 3

Fight or Flight

Before I had gone even a dozen feet, a voice cut through the eerie silence, stopping me in my tracks.

"Oh, naughty wolf! You killed my pet." The annoyed voice of a little girl bounced between the trees. "Granny Maybel, we need to punish him."

"We will, dearie. And when we're done, you can capture the mortal that's running away. What do you say, a nice little pet as an apology?"

"Oooh, yes, Granny! Maybe he'll make a better pet than the stupid doggy."

My heart pounded in my ears, and I bolted. I couldn't look back, even as two demonic trills pierced the quiet.

Must get away.

I went deeper into the darkness. My shirt clung to my body, with my blood acting as a binding agent between the linen and my skin.

Tears streamed down my face, and I had to stop and wipe them away.

Elias had been my only hope. The demon child wanted to keep me as her pet after feeding on him; I didn't want that!

I tried to push my legs forward, but I stumbled over a root and crashed onto the forest floor. A sharp rock met my stomach, puncturing my skin.

The same hopeless line kept repeating itself in my head.

I'm going to die.

I lay there curled up into a ball, a cold tree trunk digging into my back.

By the cacophony of sounds around me, the chaos grew more chaotic—something I didn't think was possible. A flare of orange light penetrated the unnatural gloom but quickly faded, returning the forest to its void-like darkness.

I'm going to die.

There was a shriek so chilling my breath paused, and the sound bounced around my head, knocking aside my thoughts.

"I'll rip you to shreds!"

Another trill echoed between the trees this time, and a distinctly male shout followed.

I ignored the pain and got up.

I'm going to—No! Screw this! If I'm going to die, I'll do it on my feet! Elias didn't hesitate to look death in the eye, so I'll fight!

I spat out blood that pooled inside my mouth from biting my tongue. With a grunt, I forced my feet to move toward the ruckus. My logical side begged me to run—to hide away and stay far from the monsters.

Shut it out; ignore the thoughts. You'll die anyway. Ten... twenty... It doesn't matter how many minutes it takes.

I stumbled on another root but used my good arm to grab the nearest tree and hold myself up. My broken rib creaked, and I spat out more blood.

Stabilizing myself, I pushed onwards and didn't stop until I reached the small clearing. The monstrous mockery of an old woman stood over a beaten and bloody Elias.

He looked like crap. His left arm ended abruptly below the elbow, and claw marks ravaged his chest.

On the left, a girl's disfigured body lay dead, her head twisted the wrong way. Her lifeless blue eyes stared through me, terror plastered on her face. It sent a chill down my spine, but I continued on.

Granny Maybel ripped the man's axe from his hands and tossed it aside. "You Grimms and your precious iron. Without your claws and weapon, all that's left is a pathetic mortal."

Elias spat blood at her. "I'd rather be a pathetic mortal than have your ugly mug. The best glamours in the Nexus wouldn't be able to hide that melting abomination you call a face."

The woman wiped the blood off her chest and held her hand up to the light. Drops of blood dripped into her open mouth, and she extended a serpentine tongue to catch every last one. When she was done, she licked her fingers and cocked her head to the side. "Werewolf blood tastes the sweetest. Did you know that?"

She raised her foot and stomped on Elias' chest. He yelped, but the granny dug her heel deeper. "I'll consume your corpse whole and grow a new coven. Be proud; your tainted soul will be of use to me."

She twisted her foot, and a sharp snap rang out. The man gasped for air but gritted his teeth and stared the demon dead in the eyes.

I needed to do something—she'd turn him into paste if I didn't.

I looked around the clearing, searching for something to aid me, until my eyes skipped over the iron axe partially hidden in the dirt.

My gaze narrowed in on the fallen weapon. Images of the little girl's severed head flashed through my mind.

There is something I can do.

Another snap, another groan, but my pounding heart helped me silence the horror.

With the woman's back turned and the Hunter too engrossed in his torture, I crept across the clearing unnoticed.

I stopped and paused until there was another snap. This time, two snaps caused a feral growl to rumble past Elias' lips.

Hold on—just a moment.

I grabbed the axe with one hand but nearly toppled over. Panicked, I dropped low and spread my feet wide apart.

Holy crap, it's heavy!

Slowly, I reached for it again—this time with both hands—and barely managed to lift it. The weapon strained my muscles, but I raised it above my head and rested it on my shoulder.

Only one thing left to do.

My body slowly turned toward the torturer and torturee.

"I'll preserve your head. It'll make a nice trophy for my hut. Whenever one of my precious grandchildren asks me to tell them a bedtime story, I'll tell them of you. 'He was one of the great Grimms and became a decoration piece for my wall.' I can't wait!" Maybel sang, her voice almost human.

"Your breath stinks," he said.

Crunch!

Another limb went limp in her grasp. "Can't forget to add how mouthy you were. It'll help teach the kiddos a lesson."

I snuck up slowly until I was only a few feet away. My arms shook, threatening to give out at any moment.

Elias saw me. There was no way he didn't. My legs trembled so badly, I feared the demon would hear me.

Do it. Raise the axe. You're going to die.

I screamed in my head to drown out the noise, but it didn't work.

You're going to die.

My muscles strained, and I raised the weapon high into the air.

You're going to die!

I begged my arms to swing, but I couldn't.

Elias met my eyes and smiled through bloodstained teeth. He looked up at Granny Maybel's sadistic grin. "Do you know what's the most annoying part about hunting your kind?"

Snap!

He threw up blood and vomit in equal measure as Maybel crushed more of his bones to pieces.

"Stupid wolf. So big and bad until you try to hunt one of us. Our powers cancel yours, turning you into a whimpering pup," she replied.

He flashed a smile again, and something within me snapped. "You're right. But you know what? It works both ways, bitch."

I screamed. Whether it was in my head or out loud, I didn't know. With a downwards swing, the metal axe bit into leathery flesh. There was a moment when it hit bone but continued its momentum less than a heartbeat later.

The clang of metal against compacted dirt cried out, followed by a wet *schlunk*, and I stopped screaming.

My ears rang, and my chest hurt. My legs wobbled and gave out, sending me to my knees as Maybel's body crashed in a lifeless heap in front of me.

The man watched me carefully before lightly shaking his head and letting out a slow, pained laugh. "Cain, I told you to run away."

I met his eyes and then turned away to throw up, my vomit mixing with his. When I wiped my mouth, I looked him in the eye. "I did. I couldn't stay away. Was going to die, anyway."

My words came out as short quips as I tried to regulate my breathing. Erratic heartbeats made that almost impossible, but I tried, nonetheless.

Elias laughed again and ignored the blood oozing from his gut. "You're insane. That's good—you'll need it."

What?

"What do you mean? Why would I need it?" I demanded.

My nerves were too fried to deal with new things, especially those unknown.

"Kid. Stop freaking out. It's over. The Labyrinth spell is fading now that the Reds are dead. The others are coming, and I don't have much time left."

My head cleared, and my eyes shot open. I'd ignored it in the heat of the moment, but Elias should've been dead. One side of his chest was caved in; Granny Maybel had been systematically breaking his ribs to prolong his agony.

The man was a zombie—barely alive yet still talking. Nothing made sense, but that was frighteningly normal given the situation.

"You're dying."

"I am." He coughed up more blood and smiled as best he could. "Perhaps my regeneration could save me, but I doubt their suppression spell will wear off quick enough for it to kick in."

"W-What do you need me to do? *Can* I do anything?"

"To save me?" He shook his head. "No. But you need to know something before I offer you a choice."

He tried to sit up but gave up when he could barely shift his leg. He banged his head against the tree trunk with a sigh. "You can return home. After some healing, we can erase your memories and make you forget about tonight. You'll be banged up for a while, but you'll be alive and none the wiser of the horrors you experienced."

Say yes!

I punched my leg and silenced my desperation to leave this nightmare.

"And my other option?"

"Can't tell you. You choose it and accept the new life you'll be stepping into."

I didn't answer him immediately, and he was content to let me think. Every instinct inside me pleaded to take option one. Who wouldn't choose to forget the insanity that had unfolded?

But Elias had saved me. He fought, tooth and axe, to free me from torture, just to be caught and dismembered himself. Now, even on his deathbed, he was offering me a choice—a choice to live or to forget him—and I didn't *want* to forget him. It felt wrong. And every passing second made it worse.

He was going to die, and I was going to live. The decision was easy, or so I thought. I felt a stab of guilt deep in my gut. I tried to open my mouth and demand the first choice, but my tongue betrayed me. Having been bitten a few times, it probably wanted revenge.

"Option two."

"Very well, Cain. Extend your arm."

I did as instructed, and he grabbed it with a grunt before gripping my wrist so tight it creaked. "Tell the others this: 'It's the last moonrise, and the metal returns to the earth. Hunt on, for I join the endless pack.'"

I etched his words into my memory. When I gave a nod, he gradually slumped forward.

"To my sister, Alice, tell her I'm sorry, and not to blame the others. She'll make a great Hunter—greater than I had ever been." Elias' mouth hung open as he struggled to breathe. He was so close, I felt bloody saliva splash against my skin. "And when you meet Biggs himself, deliver this message for me, please. Tell him, 'The stars knew us well. Keep howling, dear friend.'"

Another tear ran down my face and fell into the man's hair. It was chestnut, streaked with thick strands of pure white. It was an odd thing to notice, but it helped me anchor myself.

His face brushed against my arm as he breathed so infrequently that I was sure he'd pass on at any moment. He moved his lips slowly, and I felt something happen. More bones snapped, and his lower face morphed into a muzzle.

Before I could pull away, he sunk his teeth into my arm, and a burning sensation raced through me, bringing my heart to a stop.

In slow motion, his face changed back into that of a human before his head landed in my lap.

He breathed in, and I breathed with him. As he exhaled, I matched his final breath. As Elias died, my world turned to fire.

Chapter 4

System, System, Knocking on Your Soul

I screamed until my throat turned raw, and I could no longer make a sound. A coppery taste coated my tongue, and I barely registered my skull hitting the dirt.

My insides burned like magma, forcing me into a personal world of hell.

When I tried to breathe, fire met my lungs. The feeling was so intense I couldn't close my eyes, yet I only saw black.

An eternity later, something shifted, turning the lava into ice. Cold agony replaced the previous pain. It felt good, and I didn't want it to end.

Slowly, breathing became easier, and my muscles relaxed. The pain receded to just a few spots until even those disappeared. Just as the cold faded for good, the urge to throw up overtook me, and I pushed myself onto my side.

One hurl wasn't enough. I did it again four more times, with less and less coming up each round.

I sputtered and flopped back to the comforting ground.

It's over. I'm alive.

Then, the mother of all migraines hammered inside my skull. I groaned and was surprised to hear my own voice.

I reached for my throat. That simple action made me pause, and I slowly ran my fingers gingerly across the edge of my wounds only to find nothing.

Ignoring the migraine, I sat up and checked for any bleeding or scars.

Gone. They're all gone. What the hell?

Another pulse across my brain caused me to groan and massage my temples.

Suddenly, a melodic chime rang loud enough to deafen me. The migraine disappeared, and in its place, a prismatic dot appeared in the corner of my vision.

What?

I focused on the dot and jumped backwards as it expanded.

System Assimilation complete.
Welcome, Cain, to the G.R.I.M.M. System.
This system is more than it appears, and your role is not simply to survive but to change the very fabric of these tales.
Your actions will echo; your choices matter.
You've been called to the wild hunt. Raise your head and find your prey.

[ALERT] You have been given an inheritance from Elias Ironhart.
Lore Strain detected.
Strain identified: ΔΩ-Lycan-Skö
Commencing synchronization with the Lore Matrix...
5...
4...

"Wait! Stop!" I yelled at the air.

3...
2...

"I said stop!"

1...

There was a sickening feeling in my gut, and my chest squeezed as my jaw stung, but strangely enough, the pain hurt far less than I had feared.

A minute passed.

I tried breathing in and out, but nothing hurt. In fact, everything felt better—better than it had been all night.

Placing a hand on my chest, I felt warmth radiating from my skin, and I paused to feel my heartbeat. It sounded crazy to my ears, but my heart sounded stronger; I could feel each thump clearly through my skin.

Running my tongue across my teeth, I felt the sharpened points of my canines resting strangely in my mouth. They were sharp enough that I could puncture my tongue on them if I got careless.

Suddenly, the prismatic notification appeared, and I hesitantly selected it. The strange, game-like interface popped into view, the glowing text typing itself into existence.

Lore Matrix Synchronization complete.
Soul Integrity: 100%, perfect compatibility.
Running body base capabilities…

My body vibrated, and I clutched a thick patch of grass to try and stabilize myself. After thirty seconds had passed, another message popped up.

Base capabilities established.
…
[ALERT] You have initiated the First Kill event: Slaying of the Elder Red, Granny Maybel
Calculating… 1/1 xLvl-15
Rolling Reward…
Applying Strain Modifier: -25%
Calculation complete.

The screen winked out and then came back online with completely different text.

Congratulations on achieving a feat few Hunters have ever accomplished, Cain.

Title granted: Crimson Hunter
Ability granted: Summon Shadow Wolf
You are now level 2.
Bonus Stats: Agility +2, Intelligence +3, Wisdom +2, Luck +3

More vibrations shook my body, and I collapsed as hot pokers stabbed me intermittently.

How many times is this going to happen? What's even happening to me?

There was a final chime in my head, and I scrambled away from Maybel's corpse. All of a sudden, it started to glow a shimmering barrage of colors. Fascinated, I couldn't look away as the body melted into rainbow sludge, evaporating and emitting sparkling particles into the air.

Using my bloodstained shirt, I covered my nose. At this point, my brain was numb to all the mystical nonsense. The rainbow cloud slowly drifted toward me before picking up speed.

I flinched for a moment, prepared to roll out of the way, but tiredness gripped me.

Maybe it was the continuous bouts of weird body sensations, or perhaps my brain had finally given up, but I stood still and waited for the next round of magic shenanigans.

Instead of entering my body, the rainbow cloud swirled around me. The thick haze made me crinkle my nose at the smell. It filled my olfactory senses with blood and cinnamon.

Disgusting.

As the energy swirled and thickened, it solidified again. A flash of light appeared and blinded me; a weight dropped onto my shoulders and extended to the ground.

When I was able to see again, I lifted my arms and stared at the crimson cloak draped over them. The material felt like heavy silk, and it drew my attention toward it.

My mark. Protection. Mine.

Those words entered my thoughts as I pulled the garment tighter around my body. The fabric was comforting in a way that made me cling desperately to its edges. The cloak, despite its tattered ends, felt strong and sturdy. And the strangest detail was the connection I felt with it. It was deeper than a misguided sense of ownership. It was *mine.*

With the magical cloth around my shoulders, I surveyed my surroundings. The corpse of the demon girl lay by the trees, the same as before.

I tried to picture this as a nightmare—one from which I would wake up. However, the heavy weight of Elias' head in my lap told me otherwise.

Defiantly, I stared at the dot sitting in the corner of my vision.

I'm ready.

Congratulations, Cain. You've been rewarded with a cloak of your own. Wear it well, and strike fear in those you hunt.

[ALERT] You have acquired: Cain's Red Cloak

I expected the system to reveal the cloak's purpose. However, the screen closed, and another blip appeared.

With a sigh, equal parts frustration and weariness, I waited. The magical text did not disappoint.

Name: Cain Veldman

Title: Crimson Hunter

Level: 1 (+1)

Stats

    STR: 12

    AGI: 10 (+2)

    CON: 14

    INT: 10 (+3)

    WIS: 10 (+2)

    LUK: 10 (+3)

Skills

    Summon Shadow Wolf
Passives
    Ember Soul

Skills unlocked? Luck? What the hell is an Ember Soul? I didn't know what any of it meant.

Instead of answers, the glowing text flashed once and disappeared.

System Error: Admin Override
[ALERT] Code: X93F2, Z01L7, G66Y8-Dm-Scry%-Dr Msg%
%%Err%%-Ω-FK-OB-%%Err%%

And so the pack gains another. Will this pup surpass the others? When in my court, call my name; for your destiny is not a simple game.

The message flashed red, then rainbow, and vanished. That last message didn't feel normal; something about it hurt my eyes, causing another headache.

I pulled my cloak tighter while awkwardly resting my hand on Elias' head. He said others would come and that the maze spell was ending.

I want to go home. I want my bed, and I want to go home.

Yet, I made this choice. I made the decision not to forget. My idiotic self said no to the easy way out. So now I sat with a corpse on my lap, waiting for some mysterious Hunters to find me.

I waited, letting the eerie silence comfort me: no more howls, no fighting where iron clashed with leathery flesh.

It was peaceful.

* * *

"Kramer, keep them back. Adeline, prepare the portal; we can't stay here."

My eyes fluttered open as a commanding voice said something about a portal.

Hunters?

"Devon! He's—" A sob cut off the woman's words. "I'll get the portal ready. You do what you need to do."

"Thank you, Ald," the man whispered as the sounds of footsteps grew distant.

A man with long blond hair splattered with blood approached. His amber irises had a red tint.

"So you're awake. Good..." he said. He glanced at my hands that I instinctively moved to protect Elias' head. I couldn't tell what the stranger—Devon—was thinking, but a hint of anger gave way to sadness. "Thank you, kid. You didn't have to stay with him."

That's a lie. He's a pack member. He deserves to be around kin, even in death.

Slowly, I removed my hands from atop Elias' head and recoiled. Those were not my thoughts. Or they were, but I hadn't meant to think them.

A sympathetic look crossed Devon's face, and he smiled. "You'll get used to it—I promise. Most pups have trouble tapping into the bond, but it looks like you're special." He let out a sinister laugh. "Sorry, I know this has been one hell of a night for you. Do you mind setting him on the ground gently?"

The last words were more of a command than a question, but I complied. With solemnity, I lowered Elias' head to the bloodstained grass and backed away.

Blood had drained from his face, and he looked ghastly in the sparse moonlight. I knew he was a corpse, but something about the sight of him with ghostly white skin reinforced that fact.

Still, even with his corpse as brutalized as it was, he had died with a smile on his face. The long canines he had shown before were fully displayed, drawing my attention.

He died happy, defiant of the death that claimed him.

That knowledge made me feel better. A small part of me was proud of a man I barely knew. At this point, I didn't question it. My emotions were all over the place, and keeping up was impossible.

Devon bent and pulled a small black stone from his pouch. When he placed it on Elias' chest, the moonlight briefly caught onto the object, and I realized it was a crystal.

Illuminated for only a second, golden lines lit the sides. Then, Devon backed up a step and held out his hand.

"Ek kalla til myrkr hjarta, hlífa þú innan rót þinna."

Each word scratched the inside of my ear, and my mind went into a whirlwind of thoughts, trying to parse out the syllables.

It sounded vaguely familiar, perhaps from a song I may have heard that carried the same tone.

As he finished, the crystal chimed with a low ding. Black roots as thick as my wrist burst forth from the tiny crystal's underside. I watched silently and waited until the roots finished wrapping Elias' body.

Where he once rested, a creepy mummy now lay in his place.

Devon carefully lifted Elias into a bridal carry, the black roots glistening in the moonlight like shimmery oil. "What's your name? I can't keep calling you kid, kid."

"Cain. Cain Veldman."

He let out a long sigh and motioned to the axe on the ground. "Grab that. We can't leave it here."

But iron returns to the earth, it's proper.

Again, a strange thought entered my mind, and I frowned. These thoughts were definitely mine; I sensed the wrongness of the request—like someone was shaking their head at me.

Devon waited silently, his eyes piercing the gloom. I swallowed and pointed to the axe. "It... feels wrong. Shouldn't we leave it?"

"Oh, your connection is stronger than I thought," he said. "Listen, just grab it. We'll bury it with Elias afterwards, but we can't leave it here. It wouldn't be right. We don't leave the pack, and that was a part of Elias."

The strange feeling of wrongness disappeared, seemingly sated by his words.

With a nod, I grabbed the weapon, expecting it to strain my muscles, but was shocked when I felt little resistance.

What the hell? It's lighter.

The iron axe still weighed a lot, but my arms didn't struggle as much as before. Instead of screaming for release, they merely winced.

Clutching the axe close to my chest, I followed Devon.

My eyes lingered at the spot where the blood and vomit had pooled, mixing with the black tar that was the granny's blood.

I'm glad it's over.

Chapter 5

Meet the Hunters

It wasn't long after our journey started before we met the other Hunters. There were ten people in total; all of them wore matching red cloaks.

Amongst their flock, I spotted iron in every sheath. Blood marred their clothes, and ripped threads exposed scarred skin.

The woman, who I assumed was Adeline, chanted in the same strange language that Devon used to activate the crystal. The air behaved weirdly, and her cloak whipped around as if caught in a gust.

"Og til stiganna þarf ek ferð þinni, því veiðimaðr hefir komið aftur frá villtu veiðum!" she shouted.

The winds howled across the trees, and a flare of colorful light formed between her hands. It floated outwards and then expanded as the fallen leaves and dust collected into a swirling maelstrom.

Bubbles of light expanded until thick, brown thorns emerged from the ground and formed an archway. The light stuck to the edge of the arch and flattened until an actual portal appeared.

Then, rainbow light gave way to a fiery void. Eventually, the colors sharpened, and slowly an image formed of what looked like a cave with torches lining the walls.

Adeline slumped forward but managed to remain upright as she stared at the portal. Under her breath, Adeline muttered incomprehensibly.

Is that what the strange words are, incantations? Is she a witch?

I wanted to ask questions, but I held my tongue as I followed Devon toward a man holding back the crowd of Hunters. He stood silent, unbothered by the growling and snarling mob.

Another man, about three inches shy of Devon's six-foot-seven height, looked to be the main aggressor of the group. With his fingers splayed out, I saw sharpened claws instead of nails. The hair on his arms stood straight, and he had a near-feral glint in his eyes.

When he spotted Devon approaching, his eyes darted toward Elias' covered body. His hands dropped to his sides, and his eyes grew wide with grief. "No, Devon... tell me that's not—"

"You already know, Garret," Devon said. "I'm sorry, but we'll have to mourn back at the Warren."

The rest of the Hunters quieted. Most grimaced in horror, while others bared their teeth in anger. The rare few—the two oldest of the group— shared a look between them, their eyes sad and their lips pressed thin. They showed no animalistic anger, simply a grim acceptance.

Suddenly, Garret rushed forward.

"Let me through, Kramer! I want to see Elias!" he shouted, as another Hunter blocked him.

Garret tried his best to barrel through but struggled in Kramer's grip. His feet created a divot in the dirt, but no matter how he thrashed, he could not move closer.

Kramer remained silent and looked back at us.

No. Not us. He's looking at Devon. He wants permission.

Devon sighed. Garret quit struggling as his face went through a whirlwind of emotions. Most notable was the anger as he bared his sharp canines. His eyes were hard, but they wavered, the red glint in them flashing.

"Everyone, gather up! The portal closes in three ticks. Start crossing over." Devon pointed to the two older Hunters. "Any other survivors?"

The older woman motioned to where a familiar face had been hiding. It was the captive woman from before who had cried motionlessly during the ritual.

So she survived. That means we're the only two survivors.

That knowledge made me feel hollow.

Only two people…

Devon shook his head. "Two is better than what we hoped. Make sure she enters after you. She'll most likely pass out once she crosses through."

He turned to a man with a graying mustache and beard. "What about the cloaks? How many are usable?"

"Only two elder cloaks, poor condition. The rest were too torn up to be of use. We collected the scraps and kept them separate from the little girls' cloaks. For the little cloaks, we have four," he replied. His voice had a gruffness that spoke of a harsh life.

"That's an amazing haul. She'll be happy."

I didn't know who "she" was, but it was clear that the cloaks from the demons held importance to these people. Why else would they be wearing them?

Without thinking, I pulled my cloak tighter, drawing the attention of the two older Hunters. They gave me strange looks as they examined me from head to toe.

Devon rescued me from further scrutiny by subtly nudging me toward the portal. Another Hunter, one who kept his hood up, took the axe out of my arms and carried it through the swirling void.

Two Hunters, Kramer included, helped move Garret along, nearly dragging the listless man.

I waited with Devon and Adeline as the others crossed over, leaving only the three of us and Elias' corpse behind.

"Time?" Devon asked.

"One click. Any longer, and I'll pass out," Adeline replied, her voice heavy with exhaustion.

Devon nodded and turned to me. "Cain. When we cross over, Adeline here will take you. Don't speak to anyone, and don't do anything stupid. I'm sorry, and I know you want to rest, but that'll have to wait. For now, listen to what she says as if it were law."

Nodding, I tried to show I took his words seriously. "I understand."

"Good. Let's go. Be careful when you cross over. Keep your eyes shut and exhale before your head pushes through."

He gave no further instructions, his body distorting briefly before appearing on the portal's other side.

I glanced at Adeline, and she motioned to the archway with a grimace.

Into the fray, once again.

It was a simple saying. The words strangely fit the situation and brought me a modicum of peace.

I stepped closer and felt a strange energy tugging at my skin. My cloak reacted and tightened around me.

It provided a feeling of safety and trust. It was a strange thing to feel from a piece of clothing, but it was magic, so what did I know?

After exhaling, I pushed through the energy, and the world dropped from beneath my feet.

Something pulled me, and then again; soon, my entire body was being assaulted from all directions until another strange pulse of energy emanated from my cloak. It grew, and for a moment, the cloak felt bigger than it really was. It felt more like a cocoon than a piece of fabric on my shoulders.

The moment passed, and my feet touched the ground. The assault on my body disappeared as I sucked in a deep breath.

"Strange. He seems fine," said a feminine voice.

I opened my eyes and found myself in the torch-lit cave. A woman with shocking neon green hair hovered near me. She grabbed me by the arm and firmly moved me to the side of the circle where the portal stood.

There was little point in resisting, so I complied and waited. A part of me wanted to be excited, but I couldn't bring myself to be.

Soon, Adeline stepped through and nearly collapsed to the floor. The portal behind her shrank and disappeared with a loud pop. With the glow from the strange magical portal gone, the cave had only the torches lining the walls to provide light against the gloom.

The green-haired woman helped Adeline up before offering her a drink. Adeline sighed and accepted the flask. "Thank you, Neina. Damn, the spell takes too much to run, and Devon really pushed it."

Neina patted Adeline on the shoulders and headed to a large wooden chair. A table stood nearby, supporting a worn, dusty tome. "I saw Devon carrying a preserved. Do we know the story?"

Adeline stopped drinking. A look of disgust crossed her face before it faded. "At least pretend to care about others' feelings. Everyone's running hot right now, and you can't afford to make them angry."

Neina waved her off. She picked up the book before slouching into the chair with her legs resting on the arms. "I'll win, or I'll lose. It's not like injuries matter much. Not to us."

"You need help."

Neina laughed. "Maybe." She briefly lowered the book to point at me. "What's with the kid? I don't remember his smell. He smells like Elias."

My smell? Right. Werewolves. I shouldn't be surprised.

"We don't know yet. Devon found him next to Elias. He's..." Adeline sighed heavily. "I'll tell you later after we get more information. For now, he's a pup; you can smell it on him, so be nice."

The look Neina gave me sent a chill down my spine.

"Fine. But pup?" She met my eyes, a yellow glint tinting her chocolate irises. "I expect a good story from you once you're settled in. Your smell is too interesting to leave alone."

I clutched my cloak, feeling marginally better after doing so.

Adeline grabbed my shoulder and forced me out of the cave and down the tunnel. "Ignore her for now. She'll at least wait until you come to her before messing with you."

"That's not comforting," I replied.

"Maybe not, but dwell on it later. Throw your hood up, and don't say a word. Most of the pack should be focused on Devon, but you never know."

"Is there a problem with me being here?"

Adeline looked like she wanted to say something, but instead, she shook her head and kept guiding me.

I followed her instructions and flipped up my hood. The cloak felt like wearing reflective neon; the bright red was nearly impossible to miss, but with every other person wearing the same thing, I had a decent chance of blending in.

But not olfactorily. I smell new.

We kept walking, passing different tunnels and side rooms. The Warrens were mostly empty, maybe a person every once in a while, but even they continued moving.

We were about to exit into a vast cavern when I was not-so-gently slammed into a wall. Adeline dragged me backwards, her movements slow and stiff.

While I let Adeline drag me down a new path, my anger bristled, but I felt no pain. I raised a hand to where my temple had smashed into stone, and I could *feel* there was an injury.

That's... weird.

I might have been frazzled, but I knew better than to slam headfirst into a wall. My legs hadn't failed me. And there was only one person around to throw me off-balance.

She definitely jerked me hard enough. There's no other way. But why?

Eventually, Adeline flipped me around. She knocked my hand aside and pushed my hair out of the way. Whatever she was looking for, it wasn't there, and she cracked a slight smile. "Good. Your constitution is already doing its work. Sorry about that, but I couldn't let her see you."

I frowned, still somewhat annoyed by the rough treatment. "Who is 'she'? And why can't she see me?"

"Don't worry about it. Devon can explain later. Now, come on. Let's get moving. We're nearly there."

Feeling miffed but not enough to care, I followed her through more side paths.

At the end of the tunnel, Adeline stopped and placed her hand on the wall. She complained about something under her breath and moved to a small indent.

"*Afhjúpa,*" she said.

The stone lit up with hidden runes that glowed bright green. They flared once and then twinkled out of existence. The stone faded and turned transparent, revealing a comfy-looking room the size of a studio apartment. There were no torches inside, but in the back corner of the room, a small pool with luminescent water bathed the space in bright blue.

Adeline turned and held out her arms. "Be happy. Most pups aren't shown the hidden rooms until after their second year. Now get in."

She kept a tired smile on her face as she gestured for me to enter.

Okay, either I'm about to be interrogated, or I get to hide away for a while and get a nice nap on that couch over there.

I stepped into the room, and Adeline entered behind me. As she crossed an unseen barrier, the stone wall reappeared.

She led me to the couch and forced me to sit. Adeline stood, keeping her arms crossed as she regarded me from a few feet away.

"Now that we're alone..." Adeline snapped her fingers, and a stone chair rose from the ground. She sat and crossed her legs, her arms placed on the sides with her claws digging into the stone. "Explain what happened to you and Elias. I'll know if you're lying to me."

Why couldn't I get a nap instead?

Chapter 6

Explain Yourself

By the end of the story, Adeline cried. Though tears stained her face, she didn't acknowledge them, and neither did I.

From what I learned about Elias in the short snippets Adeline added as commentary, he had been well-loved—the kind of guy everyone got along with and looked to as friend, leader, and brother.

Each new comment was a twist of the knife. They may have helped her cope with her grief, but they murdered me inside. Elias, the renowned Hunter, sacrificed himself for me.

I already knew I would hurl if I had to explain this to everyone else. The expectations of some grand telling—a deliverance of reasoning—as to why I lived and Elias died? I couldn't handle that. Not if everyone reacted the same way Adeline had.

At the end, when I explained how he laughed in the face of the granny and delivered a one-liner fit for cinema, Adeline cracked and excused herself to stare at the glowing pool.

My eyes wandered to the stone chair she had summoned from the ground. It had claw marks so deep I could push my fingers up to the second knuckle.

That could have been my flesh.

The thought chilled me to my core in a way completely different from the demons' soul-draining fear. These people, these Hunters that looked human, were not. They were monsters in human skin, the same as the Reds.

Pack... Acceptance... They are kin.

An even more terrifying reality dawned on me when I ran my tongue against my sharp canines.

I'm one of these monsters.

That fact left me unsettled, so I tried to shake it from my thoughts.

Eventually, Adeline returned, and she stared at me silently before finally speaking. "I... I want to resent you. Looking at your perfectly healthy body, without a scratch on you while Elias looked..." Her voice cracked, but she locked her jaw and reined in her emotions. "I don't blame you, and most others won't. Certainly not the older Hunters. With that said, many will look at you and feel the same anger."

She delivered her words in a way to soften the blow, but the reality of the statement spelled things out clearly. Others will see me as the one who got Elias killed.

I gripped the edges of my cloak. "Screw them—all of them. The Reds took me out from my home and threw me into a cage. Some creepy demon child petted me like a dog and played with me like a psychopath. I didn't do anything to deserve that!"

I don't know when it happened, but I stood up at some point during my rant and found myself snarling. That realization made me pause and clamp a hand over my mouth.

What the...

Rather than lash out, Adeline slowly placed a hand on my chest and guided me back to the couch. After planting my butt on the ragged cushions, I waited for her to speak. Her gentleness dissolved my anger, and I wasn't sure what to feel.

"I'm sorry."

My eyes locked on to hers, my mouth agape in shock. "What?"

She sighed. "I owe you an apology. I'm angry at how everything went down, but that isn't your fault. This was probably the worst night you've ever experienced, and I made it about how I'm feeling."

"I... Um... Thanks."

She bowed her head, her blonde hair cascading over her face. "Thank you for going back when you did. To face something like that as a mortal couldn't have been easy. I'm glad he offered the choice to you, pup—even if he broke some rules to do it."

Though I didn't feel it was entirely appropriate, I decided to mention what happened after I had been bitten.

"After Elias bit me, some weird screen popped up. There was an achievement, skills unlocked, and it mentioned something about a Lore Strain. It said I inherited it from Elias. Lycan-Skö? There were some symbols, too. A triangle and... I forget the rest."

Adeline stared as if gazing into my soul. Eventually, she came out of her thoughts and said something in a foreign language. It sounded angry, and the pound of her fist against the chair reinforced that.

"Pup, promise me something."

"Uh, sure? What's up?"

"When the others ask, don't mention anything other than the first kill details, along with your skill. Keep the stuff about the Lore Strain and the message at the end to yourself." She leaned forward, her eyes showing a hint of red. "Swear that you'll only reveal it to Devon or someone higher up."

"Can you tell me why?"

"No."

Oookay. This is getting weird.

"I swear I won't reveal it to anyone except who you mentioned."

Seemingly satisfied with my promise, she leaned back and closed her eyes. There were even more questions I wanted to ask, but I decided to hold my tongue and enjoy the temporary peace.

There was a knock that echoed inside the room, and Devon walked through the stone wall. He looked haggard. His face had stress lines, and his eyes spoke of a weariness that begged for a long sleep. Even his hair looked more disheveled than the last time I saw him.

"Did anyone see you?" he asked while nudging Adeline with his boot.

"No, only Neina, and there's no avoiding her," Adeline replied.

"Good." He moved to the couch and flopped down on the other side, letting out a small groan as he did. "We have maybe an hour before they start knocking at the gates."

"Elias?"

"We'll have a funeral, most likely in a few weeks."

"First moonrise?"

"Yes."

Devon sat up, revealing a long tear in his shirt, exposing clean bandages underneath.

"Kid, listen, there is less time than I'd like, but the others are already asking questions. I'll keep you protected. None of them would hurt you, but there are more than a few hotbloods scratching at the walls. It's unfair, and you deserve some rest, so we'll try our best to give you that. For now, explain everything you know from the very beginning. Don't leave anything out."

I swallowed and sank into the cushion. Retelling the story was exhausting, but it was better to get it over with.

After being stopped multiple times to explain specific details, it took me nearly twenty minutes to wrap up the story. I watched Devon's face, looking for any sign of emotion, but he was a statue. He held a perpetual frown, and his eyes stayed hard and unwavering. Whenever he asked for clarification, he kept a calm tone.

In a way, it helped to ease the tension—that was most likely intentional. I may have been handling everything to the best of my abilities, but I came close to erupting when I relived my run-in with death.

My breathing turned ragged. Only Devon's pillar of calm and the strange reassurance from my cloak kept me from shutting down.

He reached out and firmly squeezed my shoulder. "Take a breath, you're safe. The forest is behind you, and right now, you're relaxing on a couch."

Pack is stronger together... To guide the young is the elders' duty.

Again, the foreign thoughts were both mine and not at the same time. I ignored the intrusion and finished telling the rest of the story. When I got to the part about the weird system screen, he grimaced.

"Cain, don't repeat this to anyone else."

"I already made him swear," Adeline interjected.

Devon nodded and slowly relaxed. "Good. The others don't need to know."

I finally braved a question. "Why is it so bad if I tell the others about the Lore Strain? Is there something strange about it? What does it mean, anyway?"

Devon glanced at Adeline, but she kept her eyes on the ceiling with her hand over her face. He sighed and turned back to me. "I can't explain it all right now. Maybe later."

"I wish I didn't know," Adeline said. "I can't even process this right now." She tapped her foot in a staccato rhythm.

"I'd like an answer," I demanded.

Devon searched my eyes for something and eventually nodded. Whether that nod was for himself or me, I couldn't tell.

"Well, the problem is that your Lore Strain doesn't match any of ours. In fact, it doesn't match any Grimm right now."

My eyes narrowed, and I tried to understand why that was such a big deal. "I don't follow."

Adeline leaned forward. "It means Elias lied to us. Every Grimm is inducted through the rite and gets... infected with one of three Lore Strains. Every single person I know has done it. I've watched several over the last few years. I even watched Elias' ceremony."

"And because he acquired something different, that is a problem... *how*?"

An actual growl escaped her throat, and my eyes widened as she dug into the stone chair with her claws. "The pack does not lie to each other! We're all we have against the other worlds, and it turns out he wasn't even pack!"

When she said pack, I felt it—a sense of hurt that stung deep. It didn't feel good, but a part of me wanted to defend Elias. To me, he *was* pack.

"I won't claim to understand the issue," I said, facing Devon. "And right now, I have no solution, nor the capacity to find one. In the final message, the system said, 'When in my court, call my name; for your destiny's not a simple game.' What does that mean?"

"Don't mention that to anyone else. I'll need to talk to someone, but it's usually not a good thing if the system takes a personal interest in you," Devon said.

I didn't know what to say. With little time left before I'd be forced to meet the others, I decided that the only thing I could do to help myself was get some sleep.

My mind went blank not long after I closed my eyes, the cushion under me drawing me in.

Chapter 7

Speak Up

I don't know how long I rested, but it wasn't sufficient. My brain felt fuzzy, and I was worried, but my cloak offered me comfort as I rubbed at its threads.

Are you alive? Can you speak?

It didn't answer back, and I didn't expect it to. To be honest, the idea of a sentient cloak would be off-putting.

As I got up, I glanced at Adeline. She was calmer, and she seemed indifferent to everything now. Even her posture was straight yet not stiff as she stood by the door with her ear to the wall.

"I can hear them scrambling already. Won't be long," she said.

I heard nothing. All I got was silence and the sound of my own breathing.

Devon nodded and straightened his cloak. "Let's get this over with." He turned to me and gave me what he may have thought was a reassuring grin. "Only answer questions as directly as possible. If you need help, Adeline or I will step in."

"It sounds like you're dragging me to a public trial," I remarked.

He smiled for real this time. "I'm not, and I won't. But, there *could* be problems later on if things get too rowdy. Just stick to the script, and we'll have you back here in no time."

I tried to return the smile but failed. Instead, I pulled up my hood and set my eyes forward.

Devon stepped up to the secret wall and touched the stone. Unlike Adeline, who had to use a weird phrase to get the magic to work, the stone door simply faded away for him. He took the lead with Adeline behind, leaving me sandwiched in the middle. It felt uncomfortably close to being escorted like a prisoner. We passed the first tunnel and the empty side rooms within.

We traveled east, spiraling toward what I guessed was the center of the cave system. The peace didn't last. Three men donning all black—and no red cloaks—sprang from one of the side rooms. They bombarded Devon with questions before they laser-focused their sights on me.

The man's green eyes roamed across my body, stopping frequently on my cloak. "He has a cloak, why?"

Devon's eyes flickered for a second. "The system granted it."

That brought silence, but the rattled men stuck to us like glue.

They seem young—younger than me. Are they Hunters, too? No cloaks, so maybe not.

We continued deeper into the Warren, and by the time we reached an auditorium, the crowd following us had grown to eleven people. The main hall held another group of thirty-plus people waiting around, talking amongst themselves.

As one, they turned as Devon stepped into the room. Almost all had red cloaks, marking them as Hunters, but a few wore simple black shirts. Most of the people without cloaks were young, ranging from ages fifteen to eighteen.

I briefly stopped under the weight of their stares, but a hand on my back gently pushed me forward. Devon walked up to the podium while Adeline guided me behind him. Nobody spoke, which surprised me, but he had a commanding presence.

"Anyone who is not a Grimm, leave."

A small uproar erupted from the teenagers, and a cloaked woman stepped forward.

"They deserve to know what happened to Elias. He was close to most of them."

More yells followed her statement. Eventually, Devon smashed his fist on the podium, causing a shrill whistle to ring out. Everyone covered their ears. Strangely enough, I heard the sound, but my hood muffled it.

The Hunters in the crowd were the most affected. They recoiled at the chimes, each one causing them to shirk away.

"Enough. Those who are not currently a Grimm can find out later. I'm sure the information will spread rapidly, whether I prefer it contained or not," Devon ordered, his tone brooking no argument.

There were a few grumbles, but in the end, everyone except the person without a cloak departed. That reduced the crowd to fewer than thirty.

I wonder why that one guy isn't wearing his cloak. It seems pretty important.

Devon removed his hand from the podium. "Now, let's set a few ground rules. Number one: this is not an interrogation. This is a courtesy offered to help bring some peace and enlightenment. If you have issues with that, you are free to challenge me, but don't expect to win."

He paused and waited while a few of the Hunters glared but kept silent. During the pause, I noticed Kramer standing next to Garret, who stared at me with unveiled anger.

"Second: this pup is a Grimm now; there will be no arguments. Despite the fact he hasn't undergone the rite, Elias gave the choice, and it has been accepted and acknowledged by the system."

Whispers filled the room, but they were quickly silenced when Devon raised a threatening fist over the podium.

"Third, and you will acknowledge this or leave." He lowered his fist and stared menacingly at the crowd. "Do not interrupt his story; he will tell it once, and then you can ask questions. Both Adeline and I have heard it. Less than two hours ago, this poor kid was locked in a cage without a clue about the ritual, the Reds—everything. You know what most people are like when they're summoned and imprisoned. It's only through sheer willpower that the kid has lasted as long as he has. We'll respect his right to rest when this is done, and that is final."

Again, nobody spoke up. Even Garret eased up a little.

Devon gestured for me to stand at the podium.

Let's get this done with.

I crushed my fear and tried to avoid eye contact. Slowly, I dragged my feet forward and stopped once the podium stood at my chest. I hesitated for a moment, unsure what to do with my arms, but decided to keep them tucked into my cloak. That small action brought a moment of comfort that faded the second I opened my mouth.

"Hello. Umm... My name is Cain. And until recently, I didn't even know monsters existed."

Silence.

All right then. Here we go.

As I retold the story, some people smirked while others lowered their heads. I felt like every word and expression was being critiqued. I wanted to melt into the ground. "Uh, there's one last thing he told me to say before he... passed."

Heads snapped back up. Adeline turned to face me for the first time since I started talking. She narrowed her eyes. Devon did too, probably worried I was about to go off script.

"It's the last moonrise, and the metal returns to the earth. Hunt on, for I join the endless pack."

A collective intake of breaths followed. Faces shared looks of sadness and surprise, and I wished I had more context for what Elia's final words meant.

A rumbling growl grew from the center of the room.

"That's it?! You come in here thinking your sob story means anything? He died for a pathetic fool like you!" Garret screamed.

His eyes glowed red. Kramer held him back, but he struggled.

"Garret! Calm—"

"We traded Elias for a nobody!" He slammed his head into Kramer's chin, forcing him to let go. "Why are you alive and he's not? Answer me!"

Garret's back arched, and his legs rippled. The sound of snapping bones echoed inside the room.

I raised my hands as he launched toward me like a rocket. His arms were longer, clawed, and wolf-like.

I ducked and closed my eyes, feeling something fast whip through the air beside me.

CRACK!

My hands raced to cover my ears as a loud chime pierced my eardrums.

Aagh!

I paused, waiting, but nothing touched me.

Opening my eyes, I found five people surrounding Garret. He had shed his human form and now struggled on the stone floor as a snarling werewolf.

Kramer and four others had their boots on his limbs and back. One person for each appendage, they pressed him to the floor despite his wailing.

Holy crap. This is insane.

Bright red blood dripped from Devon's knuckles, and four lines sliced into the back of his hand. In seconds, his skin closed and healed.

"Adeline, get him out of here."

Firm hands grabbed my shoulder and forced me to the exit. I had enough time to look back and watch as Garret reverted to his human form while Devon whispered something I couldn't hear.

I slipped my fingers underneath my shirt. My skin radiated warmth like a furnace burning in my chest.

Adeline continued guiding me toward the tunnel with the secret room.

When she spoke, I was so caught up by the new sensation in my chest that it took me a second to register her words. "What?"

"I said you did good. You didn't have to, but changing up your speech like that helped ease the others. Elias helped a lot of them in one way or another, so hearing about his bravery gave them some peace of mind," Adeline explained.

"Oh," I replied, unsure what to feel. "They seemed troubled. I barely knew Elias, and I'm an outsider, but I owe him my life."

Adeline stopped and turned around instead of activating the door. "No."

"What?"

"No, you don't owe him anything. You gave him an ending worthy of a Grimm—taking down our greatest foe before his final moment. And you're mistaken about that other part."

"What do you mean?"

She shook her head and opened the door. Once the wall became solid once more, she plopped onto the couch and stared directly into my eyes.

"You're not an outsider, Cain. You're a Grimm now."

Chapter 8

Food First, Talk After

Run with the pack; must keep up. Can't fall behind. Must keep up. Battle erupts, chaos ensues. Brother runs the opposite direction. No choice; must follow my path.

Day and night in a relentless cycle, chasing the sun, the moon, the guiding stars.

Howl, scratch, bite, claw, pounce on the prey. Rip its throat, drink the blood, grow stronger.

When I run alone, I set the pace. Always behind, yet never truly ahead. This is the hunt I chose.

I bolted upright, my heart thumping in my chest. When my eyes adjusted, the light from the strange pool reminded me where I was. My hands clenched the couch cushion, and I felt rough, scratchy fabric.

I stood up slowly and stretched. My back popped a few times, and my neck got some relief after sleeping in such an uncomfortable position. Letting out a pained growl, my stomach informed me that it was time to eat, but upon looking around, I saw that they had left me nothing to eat.

Maybe drinking water will help...

I grabbed a cup from the small bar and filled it with water from the pool. As I tipped it back to drink, I nearly spat when I noticed my reflection.

I squeezed my eyes shut and centered myself—a deep breath in, a deep breath out. Repeat.

After finding my inner zen, I opened my eyes and slowly leaned closer to the glowing pool and stared.

Ignoring the blood stains on my hoodie, I rubbed at the dried splotches along my cheek. Brown lines marred my skin as dried bits flaked and fell away. Intermingled with the brown were streaks of gray, resembling ash.

I looked like this in front of everybody, and not a single person said a word.

Then again, most of the Hunters sported blood stains of their own; I probably fit right in. Whatever hang-ups I had about my gore-splattered appearance were mine and mine alone. But the blood wasn't what made me choke.

My gaze wandered up past my chin and to my green eyes. The sight of them used to bother me, but not anymore. It may have been stupid, but I always thought color was strange since neither of my parents shared the same color. Teenager-me eventually got fed up with my childhood insecurities, and nobody I met thought they were anything less than pretty. So why would I think differently?

I continued my gaze upwards and stopped at my hair. Most of it was the same brown I've had all my life.

Most of it.

A streak of white clashed against the darker brown on the right side of my head. I doubted the psycho grannies had dyed my hair for the ritual; that sort of idea seemed crazy and implausible. The only person with dyed hair out of all the people I saw last night was Neina. And honestly, with magic and weird rituals going on, I wouldn't have been surprised if neon green hair was natural.

My thoughts flickered back to Elias's head resting on my lap. He had several streaks of white striping his chestnut hair. Could the new dye job be because of the Lore Strain? I didn't know, and I doubted I could ask the others.

Shaking off the thought, I used the remaining water to clean off as much blood as possible. Hopefully, Adeline or Devon would return soon, and I could get a shower. One sniff underneath my arms told me all I needed to know about my current hygiene.

I wonder if they have soap.

* * *

Devon knocked thrice before stepping through the wall. He curiously eyed me and motioned for me to join him outside. After being trapped alone with nothing to do, I was eager to escape.

Following behind, I waited until we started walking down the tunnel system before questioning him. "What happens now?"

He kept walking but didn't answer for the longest time, and I worried he wouldn't. We entered the mess hall with several tables and chairs set up like a cafeteria, and toward the right side, smoke drifted from a large cast-iron pan with strips of meat sizzling away. My mouth watered at the smell of bacon, and my stomach growled louder than it had earlier.

"We can discuss things afterwards. For now, we eat. I'd rather not deal with a hungry pup this early in the morning."

I kept silent after that. Devon sounded exhausted, more so than last night. It was the kind of bone-weary tiredness that kept you in a deep sleep for several hours if you gave it a chance.

He must have been dealing with everything while I slept. Probably hasn't had a chance to lie down yet.

Before I realized it, I had taken a few steps toward the food and was promptly grabbed by the collar. "Sit. I'll grab you some food."

I nodded, embarrassed over losing control of myself so easily. That didn't usually happen, and I loved bacon as much as the next guy. I wondered if Devon's insistence on food first was for a reason.

Soon after, Devon came back with two plates. One had three eggs, half a loaf of bread, and ham. The other plate—the one Devon sat in front of me—had six eggs, two loaves of bread, and a mountain of meat piled high.

I stared with my mouth agape, my eyes bulging at the ridiculous amount of food. "Umm, thank you, but I'm pretty sure I'd explode if I ate this much."

He grunted and sipped something that was decidedly not water. "Pups undergo a period of extreme hunger to fuel the rapid stat changes to their body. This'll last you a few hours, and then you'll be just as hungry again. Trust me, and eat the food."

I hesitantly picked up the fork sandwiched between the meat. With dead eyes, he watched as I ate. Once the meat hit my tongue, I went into a frenzy, scarfing down more food.

It wasn't until after I had finished that I finally regained my composure. I placed a hand on my stomach to check if I had a bulge.

I didn't, and that felt wrong.

"What just happened?" I asked, my eyes looking away from the empty plate.

"I told you—pups are hungry after the change. Usually, we have some time to prepare for when one of you gets access to the system, but..." Devon shrugged. "Volto can deal with it. Just be prepared for a lot of grumbling and complaints."

I nodded and took in the room. It wasn't a cavern, but it was massive. Smokeless torches lined the walls, and a candle chandelier hung from the ceiling. I watched, waiting to see a single line of wax drip down, but none did.

"Hey, kid. What are you doing?"

My eyes darted to Devon. He had been watching me over his mug.

"The torches, they don't produce smoke. Are they... magical?"

He raised a brow. "I wouldn't say they're magical, more like enchanted. Eternal flame, simple enchantment. Keeps a smokeless flame lit unless you purposely snuff it out."

So they are magical! Awesome!

My excitement must have shown on my face because he shook his head and pointed to one of the tapestries lining the wall. "They don't look like much, but they're enchanted too. I'm not sure who made them. You'd have to ask Neina; she probably knows. Still, they absorb the air in the room and purify it every thirty clicks."

He mentioned "clicks" again. Does he mean minutes or something else?

"Can I ask a few questions?"

"Sure. We got time, but be quick."

"What do you mean by pup? And what are clicks? In fact, where are we? And why did I get kidnapped? What happened to my world?"

I closed my mouth and lowered my head. "Sorry, I didn't mean for all that to come out at once."

Devon stood up and waved at two Hunters eating at another table. To my embarrassment, they were staring right at me.

I followed his example and awkwardly waved at the duo.

Once we were alone in another room, he finally spoke up. "I'm sorry."

"What?"

"I'm sorry you went through everything you did." His footsteps sounded heavier after hearing his apology. "Clicks are sixty seconds. Don't ask how it started, but you'll hear it used a lot."

"That's easy enough to remember. Guess I'm just glad I bumped into portal-hopping werewolves that all speak English."

He chuckled. "We don't. We speak Ealden. Don't ask the origin of that either. The moment you crossed the Nexus, your language got replaced with this one."

"So... some mystical force reached into my world and helpfully installed a language pack before shoving me into a cage. What use would I have understanding the Reds if they were going to sacrifice me anyway? I don't get it."

He shrugged. "I don't claim to understand the system or its intricacies."

That's fair.

"As for your other questions, I call you pup because that's what we call fledglings here. Newborn werewolves. You won't like the reason you got kidnapped, and you'll like the answer to your last question even less."

I frowned and let my thoughts settle. "Go on."

"Cain, you didn't get kidnapped for a special reason. The Reds' rituals randomly pull from other worlds. It's not picky about who it chooses other than finding healthy individuals under thirty years of age."

My jaw clenched. "I suffered through all that because of bad luck? I got someone killed and nearly died because some cosmic dice roll picked my number?! Elias, he..."

Devon kept his expression blank and waited until I calmed down enough to breathe.

In, out. In, then out. Repeat.

"I'm sorry... You didn't do this to me."

"I don't blame you, Cain. Most people we rescue experience the same thing. We may be a little rough around the edges, but we can understand what you're going through."

I wiped away my tears. Everything felt wrong. I was an emotional wreck, yo-yoing from one state to the next. I didn't know how to handle it. Suddenly, a private room seemed like the best place to be.

It's too late for that now. Get it over with.

"And my final question? How do I know if my friends and family are in the same situation? Is there any way I can check?"

"You can't."

My legs felt weak, and my heart sank. I breathed in and exhaled slowly, but the closeness of the walls felt suffocating.

"I'm not allowed to leave because I agreed to the contract Elias placed on me?"

He shook his head. "Yes and no. The next available time to return someone home is about a month from now. The process takes time, but we can do it for the victims rescued from the Reds. When you gained access to the G.R.I.M.M. System, you tied yourself magically to the pack. The system would force you to stay anyway. It controls the Nexus, and you'd never find a way back. Not unless your world gets integrated."

"What does that mean?"

He shook his head again. "I'll refrain from explaining that; it's not my expertise. But it would be best if you gave up on gaining closure. It'll cause you misery otherwise."

I didn't know what to say. There were so many questions, and Devon made it clear he couldn't answer them.

I'm trapped in a different world... People back home are probably looking for me. Maybe they're trapped too... That's too much to process right now.

Devon turned, and I followed him down the tunnel.

"What are we doing now?"

"Now? We're going to teach you some sorcery."

Chapter 9

SEEKING KNOWLEDGE

"I received some skills during the initialization. Something about summoning a wolf, and another—Ember Soul—listed under passive. Is that not magic?" I asked.

"Not exactly the same thing, but sure. You should have access to mana now that you've been inducted into the system. If you think about it, the knowledge of how your skills work should come to you. But if you can, please wait until Astra can explain better."

I must have hit my limit of questions because Devon refused to speak for the rest of the walk.

We turned down a dark tunnel and stopped before an iron door. It had no visible locks or keyholes.

Devon placed his palm on the middle of the door and waited. It reacted quickly, and the thick metal lit up with previously invisible runes. When it opened, a room with dim, purple light was revealed.

Devon and I stepped across the raised threshold, and when the door shut behind us, the runes turned a golden yellow before fading away.

That was cool. I wonder if everything in this place runs off magic.

I didn't have long to dwell on this thought when menacing growls reverberated around the room.

"Astra, calm down. It's me. I brought the new pup," Devon said.

Suddenly, the room lit up bright pink. There were no torches lining the walls, and I couldn't figure out where the light was coming from.

"Devon? New pup? Oh. Ooooh!" a female voice said.

Once my eyes had adjusted, I noticed bookshelves lining the room. Some were packed with thick tomes, while others held slimmer, more delicate volumes. The air carried a scent of parchment with a hint of lavender.

Beside the bookshelves were tables stacked high with scrolls, each bound with strings of varying colors. Some appeared so fragile they might disintegrate upon being touched, their strings faded. Others seemed brand new, with parchment crisp and bound by clean, vibrant threads.

Devon cleared his throat and shoved me toward a tall lady dusting herself off. She was stunning. Her black dress contrasted with her pale skin. Thin chains of silver were draped over the sleeves of her dress and around her waist, sparkling under the pink light.

Surprisingly, the chains did not clink, and the fabric of her dress swayed with each step, yet I heard nothing in her approach.

No cloak. Not wearing it, or not a Hunter?

"Astra, this is Cain; you remember him from last night. I saw your spider on Wyatt's shoulder."

Astra swept up the hems of her dress and curtsied. "Hello, Cain. Welcome to the Grimms! I know it's been a rather unexpected night, but you're here now, so you might as well make the most of it!"

She was... not what I was expecting. Given her dress and outfit, I anticipated someone more reserved or gloomy. Nevertheless, her friendliness was welcomed, especially if that was all I could get.

I placed my right hand over my heart and bowed. "Pleasure to meet you, Astra."

Devon yawned, bulldozing through the polite atmosphere. "Astra, I need you to explain his skills to him. I'll be back in a few hours after I get some rest."

She lazily eyed Devon, the happy smile washing away. In its place was a sour sneer topped with furrowed brows. "Why are you rushing for him to learn his skills? It hasn't even been a full day."

"You know why, Astra. That raid cost us an experienced Hunter, and now we'll have to pick up the slack."

The lights turned purple again, and strange energy made the hair on my arms stand up.

Astra's eyes shifted to amber. "You plan on sending him out on a hunt. He's a pup, Devon. Are you insane?"

"Yes. If I don't prepare him, he won't stand a chance against what's coming. You know that as well as I do."

Sparks flew; you could have cut the tension with a knife. Neither growled nor bared their teeth but looked ready to fight.

Astra forcefully lowered her shoulders, her movements strained and unnatural. "Fine. But if you're more worried about Elias' sister than Cain's safety, I'll make it hurt, Devon. I mean it."

He flexed his fingers but remained silent. Eventually, he looked at the ceiling and exhaled before meeting Astra's eyes. "You know I would never. Now, please, I need some rest, or I might bite someone's head off."

He patted my shoulder and left the room. With him gone, I could leave the cramped corner and relax.

Astra stared at the metal door before shaking her head and smiling at me. "Sorry about that. He's usually easier to get along with, but he's under a ton of stress right now."

"Oh, uh, it's fine. He's been nice so far and even got me some breakfast. I'm sure he has a lot to handle."

"More than you know." She motioned toward the back of the room. "Let's get out of the archive, and I'll show you something cool."

She led me through the maze of bookshelves and brought me to a wide alcove with a table surrounded by chairs. She gestured to the chair opposite hers after adjusting the folds of her dress.

That looks uncomfortable to sit in, especially with those chains.

If the dress bothered her, Astra didn't show it. She maintained a soft smile and placed her hands on the table, palms up. Unsure of what she wanted, I slid my hands over hers.

"Ah, good, good! Trust is important between an instructor and their pupil!"

I waited to see what she would do. She looked like the type to do palm readings, but with magic being real, I hoped it was more than a parlor trick.

"Soft, warm hands. Not too delicate, has nice flexibility in the fingers. Great."

She caressed my palms and flipped my hands over. Curling my fingers into a fist, she pushed them toward me. "Well, is there anything you'd like to ask before we begin our lesson?"

"Yes!" I nearly shouted before realizing my voice came out in a yell. "Sorry, but the idea of magic is so fascinating. Uh, let's see... I think I have a skill, but how do I use it?"

"Ah, so you've undergone your first kill initiation, then? Good. What did the notification say?"

I closed my eyes to recall the notification, but the exact words eluded me. Unfortunately, I *could* remember the smell of blood and rot mixing with fresh dirt and grass.

A hand on my arm made me open my eyes. "Stop. It's okay. It's best not to relive trauma until you're ready. For now, imagine the rainbow of colors when the notification popped up. Focus on it. Make the dot expand into your status sheet."

I did as she asked, picturing the prismatic dot shifting through shades in an ever-spinning wave. The image expanded, slowly growing until it stretched across my eyes.

The status sheet appeared.

Name: Cain Veldman

Title: Crimson Hunter

Level: 1 (+1)

Stats

    STR: 12

    AGI: 12

    CON: 14

> **INT: 13**
> **WIS: 12**
> **LUK: 13**

Skills

> **Summon Shadow Wolf**

Passives

> **Ember Soul**

The screen felt disjointed with the harsh reality around me. Golden text written in the air described my stats; being personified in numbers felt wrong.

Without a reference point, the stats meant nothing, but the skills sounded exciting.

"I take it you've managed to pull up your status sheet," Astra said.

"How did you know?"

"Most people try not to stare at the air randomly. And your eyes were moving side to side like you were reading something. It's a very *pup* thing to do, so don't fret over it." She giggled and raised a finger. "But remember to work on that. Others will judge you as inexperienced otherwise, and a few years down the line, with dozens of hunts under your belt, that's a social death sentence."

I immediately tried to do as she instructed, forcing the text to adjust to where I looked rather than moving my eyes.

That's surprisingly difficult to do.

I didn't know how to close the status sheet, so I thought of the process in reverse. To my surprise, it worked.

Chapter 10

Playing With Magic

"I have more questions now."

"Mmhm... Ask away."

"The numbers next to my stats no longer have a plus sign, but I have a plus sign next to my level. Does that mean anything?"

She blinked. "Well, that's surprising, but I suppose not entirely, considering what happened. Let's see. Let me demonstrate."

She lifted a metal chair above her head as if it were made of paper. Her arms showed no visible strain despite the effort.

"After becoming a Grimm, I had a STR stat of ten. All Lore Strains increase our STR by two, so I had a base stat of eight before the initialization. When I completed my first hunt, it was for a monster called an earth knocker. It's generally a friendly spirit, but this one had been separated from the earth and became corrupted. It murdered a family of six by the time the Grimms were informed. I killed it, granting me a title and stats. I got a plus one to STR, and it took a night of rest for my body to adjust. The next time I opened my status sheet, the plus was gone."

Throughout the explanation, she had kept the chair lifted in the air, her arm steady.

That's impressive and scary.

"I think I understand. What about the plus to my level? Does that mean I can level up?"

She placed the chair down. "Yes. You should get a notification if you open your status sheet and focus on the plus. Try it."

I did as she instructed and then felt something tingle inside my chest. My status sheet temporarily disappeared and new words appeared.

[ALERT] New Lore acquired. Lore Matrix upgraded.
You are now level 2.
Stat points gained: +2 from Lore Strain, +3 from an upgrade.

I looked up and found Astra waiting again. "Do I place these now? I don't even know what the stats do."

"The first level should place your stat points into STR, AGI, and CON, those being important for new pups to survive. Same with your second level, though sometimes people get one placed in INT or WIS if they're learning sorcery like I did."

I frowned. From how she described it, it sounded like the stats were automatically distributed for Grimms according to their specializations.

But that's not true for me...

    Level: 2
    Stats +5
    STR: 12
    AGI: 12
    CON: 14
    INT: 13
    WIS: 12
    LUK: 13

It looks like I get to choose where to place them.

"Can you explain what each stat does? I think I understand, but I want to be sure."

"With pleasure. You saw what strength does. It determines how strong we are and how much force we can generate. Agility helps with nimbleness and speed."

"Like moving my fingers faster or something?"

She giggled. "If you want to keep it simple, yes. Try some stretching exercises when you can; you'll find yourself a lot more limber." She reached over and lightly poked my skin. "Constitution is one of our most important stats. Care to guess what it does?"

If it works the way I think it does...

"It makes us tougher?"

"Vastly oversimplified, but when you boil it down, yes. It boosts not just our toughness, but a high-level Grimm recovers from most wounds within the hour, sometimes minutes. It also helps resist diseases and curses. More so diseases, but many curses have a physical affliction that our bodies can resist. It's why we have such a stringent requirement for hunts involving witches and hexers."

"That sounds terrifying. I see why it's important."

"Don't worry. You almost always get a point in it, especially in the early levels." She raised her hand and tapped the side of her head. "Mental stats like intelligence and wisdom are a tad indirect."

"Does it make you smarter? Because that's very weird unless it deals with mana."

"INT helps memorization rather than make you smarter like some foolish pups like to believe. It also increases the amount of mana available to you."

So, it's not superhuman intelligence. That's almost disappointing.

"And wisdom works separately from intelligence. It helps mental fortitude and magical perception. Someone like me with high WIS can easily detect active spells or the presence of mana in the air. And more directly, it affects how fast you regenerate mana."

It was a lot to take in, and I felt a headache begin to form. None of the stats were surprising in their effects. Modern Earth used similar stats for MMOs and RPGs.

"What about luck? How is that even a stat?"

"Ahh, the infamous stat." She shrugged. "Don't worry about it too much. It's nearly impossible to place a stat in LUK, and generally, that's only through special rewards from the system. As for what it does, that's also hard to answer. Ask any Grimm who hunted a monster with high LUK, and they'll tell you it's real. It's a thing of frustration. Things happen that shouldn't, and sometimes things hit harder than they should."

"That's... okay, I think I get it."

"It's frustrating, but few get enough points assigned for it to matter. Twenty LUK can be just as useless or helpful as ten."

That's not ideal. I'll ignore the stat for now.

I thought about how to distribute my stats. It would be good to put a point into the basics; it seemed important and expected.

One point went into each stat. I had debated adding another point to CON instead of WIS but decided against it.

They're basically extra points, right? So, I'm ahead of the curve.

Only after I confirmed the final stat point did I remember the agony of fire inside my veins. I clenched my jaw and prepared for misery.

"What are you doing?"

I opened my eyes and realized that the hellfire didn't come. To Astra, I had tensed for no reason.

"Sorry... I suddenly remembered how painful the last time was, and I thought it would happen again."

Her face softened. "It's okay. Only the first initialization hurts. You get a sudden injection of stats, and the Lore Strain integration is what messes you up. Now your stat points will be distributed over the course of a day or two."

She squeezed my hand and let go, allowing me to collect myself.

"Thank you."

She clapped her hands and stood. "I know the perfect distraction!"

I joined her. She began moving the tables and chairs to the side, so I helped and waited as she stepped back until we stood five feet apart.

The lights in the room dimmed dark purple, and something touched my cloak.

Astra's hair lifted, caught in an invisible breeze. Her eyes glowed yellow, cutting through the gloom. She raised her hands, and the silver chains around her wrists untangled and fell away.

The chains caught the light, gleaming a bright purple in its reflective sheen. I stared, transfixed. They expanded around us like a cage. Throughout it all, a radiant smile brightened her face.

"It's amazing," I whispered.

Astra spread her arms wide, and the cage shifted with her movement. "This is my skill, Silver Manipulation."

"How does it work?"

She seized my arm, setting it around her shoulder before placing my other hand on her waist. With a tap of her foot, a low melody played. It sounded like a chime from a music box.

The chains weaved in and out as she guided me through a dance. They swirled in beautiful patterns, never touching us.

My excitement bubbled, causing me to laugh. "This is amazing."

Each step was a new chime, every turn filled with the clinking of chains. We spun around and around, Astra leading the waltz.

When the music came to an end, the chains tightened around my arms, forcing one high and one low.

Astra twirled, dragging the chains with her. They spiraled like a whip, creating a gust, and she finished with a deep curtsy.

The lights glowed pink once more, and I clapped in applause.

Chapter 11

Incite the Incantation

"Thank you!" Astra shouted.

I stopped clapping and saw the chains adorning her dress in a new light.

That's beautiful and terrifying all in one. I wish I could control chains like that.

"How long did it take you to master? Your control is amazing," I gushed.

"Something as intricate as the dance? A few months. I used my skill a lot, so I experimented often. When I first acquired it, my control was way worse." She clapped her hands together. "Are you ready to try your skill? If it's a projectile, please aim it at the floor."

"It's a summon. How do I do this? Devon mentioned thinking about it, but I don't know what that means."

Her eyes lit up. "A summon is rare! It's been a few years since someone got one as a skill. And non-skill summoning magic is a tricky ritual that can turn fatal with the smallest mistake, so good on you. Try to picture using your skill, and the details should enter your mind."

All right. It's a shadow wolf... like the Reds used.

I paused. It didn't occur to me that the creature I'd be summoning would be the same as the one that tried to eat me and played a part in Elias' death.

No. Stop. It's magic. You get to do magic. Don't let them win. The Reds are gone; they won't take this away from you.

I spent a moment breathing until I felt ready. When I said the skill name in my mind, a series of instructions expanded.

"I'm going to try summoning now."

She nodded and stepped aside.

Closing my eyes, I let the mental download of instructions guide my actions. I pictured a pool of energy inside my chest and willed it down my arm. Strange words flashed in my mind—runes that glowed crimson—each glyph twisting into spell lines.

My chest burned, and it felt like fire in my veins had rushed to the center of my palm, condensing into a ball of magma. The summoning circle in my mind lit up, and I pictured a beast armed with fangs and claws.

Opening my eyes, a low, drawn-out howl filled the room, and a connection similar to my cloak snapped in place.

I froze as a shadow wolf met my sight. The endless void that made up its form whipped like black flames mimicking the wild fur of a wolf.

"Wulf!"

The creature let out a sound that not only reached my ears but also resonated inside my mind.

Oooh, I don't like that.

It moved closer, and I tried not to move. Its snout sniffed the back of my hand. The wolf's jaw gaped wide, and I braced myself for a bite. Instead, it dragged its frigid tongue across my hand, sending shivers down my spine. The sensation was like a wet cloth soaked in ice water. Seemingly pleased, it nuzzled its head into my palm.

Good... wolf? Apparently, shadow monsters can act cute.

I scratched its head and moved my fingers behind its ears. The wolf barked once, causing me to jump. It continued to stare at me with a wagging tail as it sat on its haunches.

"I think it likes me."

I expected Astra to say something, but when no reply came, I looked over and saw her black talons pushed into the chair's metal frame.

She looked away from the shadow wolf and gave me a strained smile. "Ah, you didn't tell me the skill was for a shadow wolf."

"Oh. Oooh! I'm sorry. I got so caught up in doing magic that I didn't think about how you would react. I can, uh... dismiss it, I think?"

She shook her head. "It's good to treat summons right. If you don't, you'll struggle to use your skill properly."

"Oh..." I looked at the shadow wolf cocking its head, looking adorable. "Is there anything I need to do now?"

"Well, you summoned it. That's pretty good. For now, tell it your name and dismiss it. Creatures summoned through a skill are prevented from dealing you harm directly. So it's safe to give your name, and in doing so, you'll have a higher chance of the same creature answering your call the next time you use your skill."

I knelt and brought my fingers to its nose. It licked it once and pushed its snout into my neck. A smile split my face, and I ran my fingers through its fur. "Thank you for answering my summon. I'm Cain."

"Wulf."

I closed my eyes and pictured the energy inside my chest returning to my center. In my mind, the spell circle rotated in reverse, and the runes inverted.

I locked eyes with the wolf as it melded into the shadows, its black gaze lingering until it vanished into the floor.

With the wolf gone, I finally breathed, my body quivering. Those eyes were unlike anything I'd ever seen. And I had seen more than enough wolves in a twenty-four-hour period.

I checked my hands. *They're dry.* Despite the wet sensation, the wolf left no trace of saliva.

"That was weird. Does mana always feel like that?"

"Yes, the cold takes some getting used to, but you hardly notice after a while. Just don't overdo it. Running low on mana sucks, and using it too quickly can leave you numb." Astra plopped down in a chair. "So, what'd you think? Exciting, huh?"

Cold... Yeah. But what about the fire in my veins? Is it supposed to feel like a bad case of heartburn?

"It's not too bad actually. It hurt for a second, but that was it. I'm excited I got to do real magic! That's the best part."

She smiled. "So many Grimms focus on their ability to swing an axe or jump higher and punch harder. Skills are great, but sorcery is where it's at!"

"Are skills and sorcery not the same thing?"

"Hmm... No, they're not. But that debate is useless to you right now. For now, think of skills as ready-made spells with shortcuts. We Grimms learn incantations and other casting forms to help us on our hunts. However, those are much harder to learn without the system guiding you."

"What do you mean?"

She raised her hand and pointed it at the stone floor. "Observe and try to listen. *Ek kalla heiðarloga.*"

Her hand glowed brightly, flames erupting from her palm. The fire swirled and blasted through the air, crashing into stone with a small *woosh*. The miniature fireball burst apart and turned into cinders.

That's what Elias used!

Except, that wasn't what he used. His flames were bigger and brighter. The fireballs he shot at the shadow wolf were much larger than these tennis-ball-sized ones.

"That chanting—I keep hearing it, but it sounds strange, like it's scratching my ears. What's it called?"

"We call it Wyrdtunge. It's an old language predating the Grimms, so we don't know where it originated. Everyone describes hearing it the same way: a tickling in the ears and a scratching inside the mind. Since a lot of our sorcery is rooted in this language, it's essential for pups to learn the basics."

"Can you teach me?" I couldn't hide the desperation in my voice; I *really* wanted to learn how to shoot fireballs.

She tapped her chin. "The language can be pretty difficult. It'll be a challenge."

"Please."

I sound so uncool right now, but I don't care. I need a fireball spell!

"Well, since you said please, it'd be my pleasure."

"Thank you! Do I just repeat the words?"

She laughed and wiped a fake tear from her eye. "Oh, it's much harder than that. You are learning the old way without the system's help. So there are no shortcuts. You need to picture the correct image, imagine the runes in your mind, and pronounce the spell perfectly—all while guiding your mana."

I tried not to let the requirements dampen my mood. Magic was magic, and learning it would be even better, difficult or not.

"All right, it's difficult. Where do I start?"

* * *

Over the next hour, Astra turned into a strict instructor. First, she had me practice drawing—focusing exclusively on mastering the fire rune. I learned how to sketch it and add lines that meant 'creating' and 'heat.'

"Are you sure I should be skipping over the alphabet?"

She clicked her tongue. "I'd prefer you didn't, but we'll have to make do with the time given to you. You can learn the rest when you get back from your hunt. For now, focus on perfecting this rune; you want it perfect, or you'll struggle to form the spell."

Another twenty minutes passed, and all I did was learn to recreate the fire rune perfectly with every scratch and squiggle appropriately placed.

Magic is a lot more boring than I thought it'd be.

I kept that thought to myself. Astra continued to help me and pointed out every detail incorrectly drawn while offering tips and tricks. She devoted her effort to helping me learn, and I wouldn't be so rude as to complain.

Once she approved of my drawing, we progressed to the incantation. Learning to pronounce the words took another twenty minutes. The syllables left me tongue-tied, but I had to power through.

"Wait a second. This is a different incantation. What's up with that?"

"So you are paying attention. I was starting to think you wouldn't notice," Astra teased. "It's different because you're learning a different spell."

Why show me one thing and then teach me something else?

"The spell I'm learning is longer. Wouldn't that make it more difficult?"

"Yes, but what you're learning is the proper incantation. What I spoke earlier was a modified, shorthand version. Care to guess why?"

She waited for my answer as she wrote something on a piece of clean vellum. Her black-feathered quill dipped into a blue-black inkwell beside her. Since she obviously intended for me to give a serious answer, I tried to think things through.

She keeps emphasizing proper mental imagery and pronunciation. Does that mean the shorthand is something she can do because she's more skilled? That probably means modifying an incantation is difficult and harder to work with.

Can longer incantations be shortened once I can do the spell faster? Let's go with that.

"I'm learning the longer version because I'm not skilled enough to shorten the incantation."

"Correct!" She finished a long scratch, creating a line of ink at the bottom. "Most Grimms focus on a single spell or two that they favor and learn to shorten it. If you're really good, you don't even need to say the verbal component of the spell. Simply imagine the rune and will your mana and *ta-da*! Flames."

"Huh."

Other than the effort required to get to that level, that sounded very convenient.

"I think I'm ready. What about the mental image?"

"I'll guide you. Get in whatever position you think is proper and aim at the floor," she instructed.

I closed my eyes and aimed at the ground toward the center of the room. I relaxed my shoulders and held my palm outwards, fingers straight.

"I'm ready."

"Very well. Start with a spark. You need fire, but start small," she whispered into my ear. Her breath tickled the back of my neck, smelling like crisp mint and juniper. "Visualize the flame in your mind. Feel its heat, sense its warmth, and picture the shadows fleeing from its light."

I tried not to squirm, but the hot breath blowing against my skin made it difficult.

Despite the distractions, I did as she asked. I thought of a matchstick and kept the flame, letting the burnt wood fall into the void.

It was a tiny thing, barely a flame—pushing at the void, forever battling its advance. I raised a mental hand to the spark, picturing its tendrils licking my fingertips.

"I have the image in my mind," I whispered back.

"Good. Now, picture the rune inside the flames. Let it burst to life. Sear the lines into your mind."

The spark grew a tad larger. The rune became a new flame inside the spark, one deep red contrasting the yellow, increasing the heat that spread between my fingers.

I didn't wait for the next set of instructions; I did what felt right. I kept the mental image crystal clear as I tried to recall the burning energy moving from my chest and down my arm until it reached my hand.

Something thumped in my chest, and I let the words dance across my tongue. "*Heita'k á hyrupp heiðarloga; um mér at orna.*"

The heat in my chest erupted, pushing my control aside as mana surged. It was like cracking the floodgate—searing hot and unstoppable.

Runes in my mind flickered to life, turning the inner void into a sunlit blaze. I opened my eyes to see flames dancing between my fingers, my skin encased in fiery light.

What shot out was no baseball-sized fireball—it was more like a basketball that exploded on impact, sending fire licking up the walls.

Flames grazed my leg, but my cloak did *something*, and the heat vanished.

My arm throbbed, making me grunt as I clenched my wrist. I turned my hand and saw charred skin, the center of my palm a bleeding, black mess.

"I don't know what happened, I swear," I said.

Instead of yelling, Astra moved to a small table, pulled open a drawer, and rummaged around until she found a small vial and a stack of cloth.

She opened the vial before pouring a few drops onto my hand. The bright green sludge tingled, making my muscles twitch before the tingling shifted into a cool, numbing sensation.

"You did nothing wrong," she said as she wrapped the cloth around my hand. "In fact, you did amazing."

"I don't understand. I nearly set the room on fire."

She finished tying the bandage. When I looked up, her eyes were a bright, piercing yellow. "And it was explosively fantastic."

Chapter 12

Arm Yourself

Devon entered the room, looking more refreshed than he had a few hours ago. He had brushed his hair, and his eyes had lost their previous lifelessness. When he walked, his movements flowed smoothly, a contrast to his stiff gait from before.

He stopped and sniffed the air before staring at my bandaged hand and raising an eyebrow. "What happened?"

"He has a gift for fire incantations," Astra answered. "You should have seen it; should have smelled it!"

I frowned. "She tried to teach me the firestarter incantation, and something weird happens every time I try it. We found out why, though! It's my other skill."

"Other skill?" His eyes narrowed. "I recall you mentioning you gained two skills. It's a passive, right?"

I nodded. "Yeah, it's called *Ember Soul*. I'm not exactly sure what it does, but the weird information I get when I think about it goes something like this: 'Blaze eternal, forever light the way to repel the dark.' Whatever that means, it boosts my affinity for fire, though!"

"And that's why you have bandages on your hands?"

"Yeah, this whole regeneration thing is insane. The burns healed so fast, it felt wrong—like that's not supposed to happen. Since my hand healed, I tried the incantation again; the same thing happened: bigger fire, more heat, and a burnt hand."

Devon shrugged. "Perks of being a Grimm. When you increase your constitution, you'll heal even faster. I take it the reason the room smells like burnt flesh and ash is because of you self-immolating?"

"Umm, yeah. That sounds really bad when you word it like that."

"You'll get used to it. A few wards we use require our blood as a component. You can't be a porcelain doll if you're going to be a Grimm."

The excitement I had felt for the last three hours dropped. Astra kept me thinking and distracted; I partly suspected she did it intentionally. Even if my hand looked horrifically damaged, the wonder of magic had made everything fun.

I didn't blame Devon. He probably wanted me to know that the job wasn't all rays of sunshine and cool fireballs.

"I understand," I replied.

Astra clapped her hands. "Don't ruin the fun, Devon. He's had enough bad things happen in the last day to fulfill your weird need for balance. Let him enjoy himself while he can. You're already about to drag him off to a hunt."

"Fine," he grunted. He tossed something in my direction. "Pin that to your cloak."

I caught the small, silver object. Inside a crescent moon sat a howling wolf's head above a slanted lumber axe.

"What's this?"

"It's your emblem. We all have one, so never lose it. If you ever go missing, we use these pins to help track you down. And it's enchanted to open some passages inside the Warren."

I placed it on the inner side of my cloak next to my heart. The cloak gave a strange feeling that felt like curiosity before settling down.

"Marvelous. Truly an amazing creation," Astra whispered. When I looked up, she stood inches away and nearly made me jump back.

"Huh? What is?"

Her eyes trailed down to my legs before roaming back up to my face. When she saw my confused expression, she winked.

She pulled out another piece of vellum. Her fingers quickly dipped the quill into the inkwell and began sketching at an incredible speed. Before my eyes, a very realistic rendition of my cloak appeared on the paper, line by line.

She quickly blew on the page and set it next to other drawings.

"Your cloak—receiving a fully intact soul cloak is a rarity. Most of us usually piece together scraps from the Reds. Only a fortunate few have a complete cloak. Devon, when's the last time you saw the system offer someone a soul cloak?"

Devon was silent for over a minute before walking to the door. "The last person to get one... was Elias."

"Oh..."

The heavy atmosphere made me squirm, and I got up to follow. Astra tapped my shoulders and handed me two scrolls. One had a bright red string tied around the vellum, while the other had a black string.

"Take these. Open the red one when you have some free time. Only open the black one if you're ever alone and in need of protection. Devon's taking you to the armory, so keep these safe and store them in your pack when you get one, all right?"

"Thank you!"

I accepted the scrolls and waved goodbye while catching up to Devon.

After a few minutes, I cleared my throat and probed a question. "We're going on a hunt, right? What are we hunting?"

"Don't know."

What? Why?

"What do you mean?"

"We've gotten reports sent to us by one of the scouting teams— suspicious activity inside the world of Orynx. A village in the Felstrad kingdom has had several *accidents*. Too many to be pure coincidence."

I stopped.

World of Orynx? He mentioned the Nexus, but we're going to a different world? What the hell have you gotten yourself into, Cain?

"You mentioned the Nexus and my world integrating... I didn't really understand what you meant, but you said that like there are many worlds. Does that mean Grimms are interdimensional monster Hunters?"

He stopped.

"I forgot you wouldn't know the history of Grimms. Most pups have to study basic Lore about the organization before joining. We hold jurisdiction over six worlds. Originally nine, but things happened, and now it's six. Orynx, the world we're going to, is on the smaller side with only two continents. Felstrad is a minor kingdom on the western continent, but we keep watch over it due to certain resources."

Another massive Lore dump struggled to settle into my mind. The concept of multiworlds felt foreign to my Earther beliefs.

There might be a chance of going back to Earth someday... No, don't think about that; focus on what you need to do.

We journeyed on for about ten more minutes, delving further into the cave system until we came upon a staircase leading to a massive metal door. When Devon placed his hand in the center, black lines lit up, and it swung open.

Deep, brassy chimes rang through the air. After looking around for the source of the sound and finding none, I took in the room before us.

Weapons of every shape and size lined the walls. Daggers, shortswords, and claymores hung from mounted racks to the west. Axes, halberds, and spears hung in the east wing.

Several wooden stands displayed full suits of armor while crates overflowed with a mismatched assortment of gear.

It feels like I've walked into a medieval fair's replica shop.

"Have you ever used a weapon before? Any experience or training?" Devon asked.

My eyes roamed across the shiny metal and leather before shaking my head. "Not really, no. I've fought with wooden sticks as a kid, but using Elias' axe to kill the granny was my first time using a weapon."

"No swords, then." He moved to the east. "Your strength isn't high enough for the heavier stuff, so we'll keep it light."

He unhooked an axe about the length of my arm. I recognized it as a bearded axe: a curved handle made of ashwood wrapped in black leather.

After placing it on the table beside him, he grabbed a spear that was nearly my height.

"Axe or spear. Try them both on the training dummy over there. I'll collect the rest of the supplies while you pick a weapon," he said. Devon walked away, and I turned to the two very *real* weapons in front of me.

Chapter 13

Iron vs Straw

Am I expected not to injure myself? Who gives sharp weaponry to someone who admitted to only using wooden sticks?

I picked up the spear. It weighed less than I expected, but the wood felt too thick in my hands. My fingers rested uncomfortably around the leather wrapping.

I don't know why I expected it to have a hollow core. This whole thing just feels unwieldy.

I walked over to a straw dummy. Someone had painted monster teeth and three eyes on the face while drawing a big red bullseye in the center of its chest.

Here goes nothing.

I stabbed, and the blade pushed deep into the wood behind it. When I let go, the spear remained stuck.

That was... interesting.

I felt ridiculous trying to attack a wooden dummy. A quick glance told me Devon hadn't watched as he grabbed a leather belt from a small crate.

After removing the spear from the wood, I placed it back on the table and picked up the axe. It felt surprisingly light but still had a weight to its head that felt good in my hand. I tried to twirl it around, only to come dangerously close to biting into my shoulder.

Let's not do that again. I doubt it'd look good if I maimed myself.

Despite my self-warning, I tried to maneuver it around my body, using quick chops at an invisible enemy. The weapon felt good in my hands, better than the spear.

I approached the dummy and raised the axe. My target was the neck, but the blade cut into its upper jaw. As I pulled, the dummy's fabric restitched before my eyes; the six-inch cut disappeared, leaving the target undamaged.

Enchanted training dummies, of course. How silly of me to think something would be normal around here.

The strangeness of everything felt like needle pricks when I least expected it. In my mind, I was swinging an axe. But I had to remind myself that I was doing so in a vast tunnel system peppered with magical doors and inhabited by werewolves.

Some things would take time to get used to. Perhaps, a long, long time to get used to.

A knot built in my stomach, and I forced myself to relax by exhaling slowly. I shimmied and loosened my limbs before turning to the dummy.

I moved my hand closer to the head of the axe and kept my knuckles behind the beard. I tried a series of punches and flicks that left me feeling awkward, but I found the first notable difference to my body since my stats leveled.

The movement felt good; my hand kept track of everything, and I made micro-adjustments with each strike. It took a minute, but I lowered my hand and tried to swing again, aiming for the seam around the neck.

My arm swung sharply, and the blade sliced right through the side of the cloth. My strike continued as the axe pushed into the wooden stand before stopping near the middle of the neck.

Aha! I did it!

"Good strike. Next time, widen your stance until your feet are shoulder-width apart. Keep one foot slightly ahead," Devon instructed.

He observed with his arms crossed. His tone had an authoritative edge, prompting me to retrieve the axe from the dummy. At least, I tried to. The axe-head lodged firmly into the wood, and there I was, looking foolish as I struggled to pull it free.

I choked the dummy and gripped the stand while yanking the weapon. The enchanted dummy fixed itself, and I got into position.

Feet apart... Shoulder relaxed. Let's not look like an idiot.

I breathed in and held. With my axe raised, on the exhale, I chopped in one fluid movement, my torso turning with the swing.

The axe-head cut straight through, but at a wonky angle. I adjusted at the last second, and the blade separated the dummy's neck from its shoulders. As I watched it repair itself, I looked at the axe and smiled at my reflection in the polished metal.

That was pretty damn cool.

I gave Devon a thumbs-up. "Thank you! That felt good."

"Don't thank me. If we did things properly, you'd have several years of experience with the weapon before we sent you on a hunt," he said. His eyes narrowed, and he looked toward me but not at me. He shook his head and motioned to the table. "It'll do for now. Come, grab your things. I'll show you how the belt works, and then I got one last thing to show you before we go to Neina."

The items were relatively simple. Apparently, most of what he wanted me to take was part of a standard traveling kit for Grimms. Outside of a few vials filled with different colored liquids, it all seemed rather mundane.

He gave me a leather belt with several loops to store the vials. Each had its own use: one was a healing salve, another was a smoke bomb, and the third remained a mystery.

"What's the third one do?" I asked as I adjusted the belt to the clean pair of pants that came with it.

"Scent eraser. A lot of beasts track through scent. Pull out the stopper, channel mana into the vial, and wait for the potion to change color. Once it's no longer clear, douse yourself with the liquid, and you'll have a scent blocker for the next few hours."

All right, magical potions now, too. I wonder if they'll teach me how to make these.

The rest of the gear included a leather satchel, a knife, and sheath straps. Carrying the knife felt odd, especially given the other weaponry. But Devon insisted that a backup was always a necessity.

I adjusted the belt, strapped the axe onto my hip, and tried to move around. The knife brushed my leg, so I had to readjust. The second movement test went perfectly, with nothing obstructing my body.

"So, I understand we need a backup weapon and all, but why a knife if you can turn into werewolves? I've seen several people grow claws, and Garret transformed pretty quickly. If whatever we're hunting won't fall to an axe or spear, wouldn't the dagger be even more useless?"

"Usually, the rite forces your first transformation. It helps the new Hunter learn what shapeshifting feels like and helps them tap into their Lore Strain. You, on the other hand, don't have that experience. When the new moon arrives, we can have you temporarily induce the shift. Until then, you'll have to wai—"

He stopped and glared at me as his eyes glowed red. A low growl exited his throat, and I instinctively backed up. For a moment, he looked ready to snap at me, literally.

What the hell?

He looked away and pinched the bridge of his nose. "Sorry. I forgot your Lore Strain isn't one of ours. We'll have to do something different to force the shift. We'll deal with that later, though. For now, follow me."

I kept silent and hesitantly followed him toward the back wall. A single torch burned, illuminating the dark corner.

"Do you have your emblem on?" Devon asked.

I patted my chest and felt the metal push into my shirt. "Yes. Why?"

"Good. Follow."

Okay?

He then stepped through the wall.

Chapter 14

TO THE VILLAGE

After my initial shock, I slapped the wall—except my hand went through it. A moment later, I met Devon on the other side.

Something about the torch-lit tunnel felt ominous, but I wasn't entirely sure what.

"One of the perks of the emblem is access to the Whisper Tunnels. Keep close. I don't want to waste time trying to find you if you get lost," he said.

I blinked a few times and jogged along behind him. When I caught up, he muttered something and picked up the pace. The air felt heavy, my feet slid against the slick ground with each step.

The muttering picked up in volume, and I was so focused on the sound that I barely registered that our pace nearly came to a halt.

Peeking from behind Devon's back, I saw a dead end. "What just happened?"

There definitely wasn't a wall at the end of the tunnel.

"Whisper Tunnels. They use old magic from the Paths. Whisper where you need to go and then head forward. You need to keep a clear image in mind when you do, but it helps many of the older Grimms get around. We try to restrict access to the tunnels even with the emblems; there are too many stories of Grimms getting lost in these tunnels. And if you're especially *unlucky*, you'll find yourself in a random place, not inside the Warren."

He approached the dead end. Like the previous wall, he phased through without resistance.

As I passed through a moment later, I found Neina sitting in her chair, her legs propped up and a leather-bound tome in one hand.

"Neina, please. It's been a long few days," Devon pleaded.

When Neina didn't answer, Devon pushed the book down. Bored green eyes stared back at him, and she sighed exaggeratedly.

If her goal is to annoy Devon, then she's succeeding, considering the twitch in his eye.

"So you showed the pup the tunnels and raided Maro's armory. I hope you logged what you took, Devon. You know how uppity she gets," Neina teased. She turned and sniffed the air. "You smell like ointment and ash. Did you burn yourself learning a new spell?"

Is her nose psychic?

She grinned and strutted over to the raised circle in the center of the room. "You're not using your senses, pup. I suggest you start before Devon gets you killed."

If Devon seemed grumpy before, he now looked ready to snap. "Neina, open the portal."

She waved her hand and spoke aloud, the strange chant stirring something in my chest. "*Ek kalla til slóða fyrir hjálp.*"

An unseen wind picked up and swirled between her fingers. Nine prismatic orbs appeared before she flicked her hand, sending them flying. Much like the last time I saw the portal, thick roots grew from cracks in the stone floor and expanded outwards.

The portal archway formed as the lights latched onto the roots. The orbs stretched into a black plane that fit across the archway. In a dozen heartbeats, the black gave way to a torch-lit village bathed in moonlight. Gnarly trees with purple leaves were wrapped around the village wall.

Neina lowered her hand and skipped to her chair. As she picked up her book and snuggled in, she winked, and her face disappeared behind the pages.

Devon rubbed his temple and stepped closer to the portal. "Same as last time, exhale before passing through."

He didn't wait, a rather annoying habit of his. With a sharp exhale, he stepped through and disappeared.

I was about to do the same when a knock rang through the room. I turned around to see Neina lower her fist.

"Is everything okay?" I asked.

She rested the book against her chest and tossed me a small brown pouch. "Don't trust him, Cain. He may seem like the dependable type, but he has his own motives. Remember that."

That's not ominous at all... Okay, then.

"Thanks for the warning."

After exhaling slowly, I stepped through the portal. Again, my cloak did something strange during transit; it expanded into a protective shell around my body. Now that I understood the energy around me as mana, I felt it whip chaotically, swirling in random patterns.

For a second, I thought I felt something beside me, but my feet crunched into loose gravel, tearing me back to reality.

"What's that in your hand?" Devon asked.

Huh?

I looked at the pouch and shrugged. "I don't know. Neina gave it to me. She..." I shook my head. "Never mind. Should I open it?"

"Leave it for now. She wouldn't actively cause you harm, so it's at least safe."

That's not the most confident answer, but all right. Free magical stuff is free magical stuff.

After pocketing the pouch, I followed Devon. Moonlight shone, providing enough light to see the village clearly. Around us, the trees stood eerily, but the surrounding woods were thankfully silent.

The village wasn't far. The gates came into view along with two guards clutching tightly onto their spears.

"They look scared," I said.

"Because they are. Tell me, have you noticed it yet?" Devon replied.

Notice what? Everything's normal, and the forest is silent. What am I mis—

"Oh. The forest is silent at night."

He nodded, and I reduced the distance between us, keeping a hand on my new axe. The cold iron already felt comforting against my skin. Its presence provided reassurance against the suddenly all-too-long shadows.

The guards must have spotted us approaching because one ran inside the gate while the other looked relieved before his expression turned to worry. He had a line of sweat dripping down his forehead, and his eyes darted around.

"Is he scared of us? But... why?"

"Because we're Grimms."

Well, duh! But why does that scare him? Aren't we the good guys?

"H-hello, sirs. May I ask your reason for entry?" the guard stammered.

Devon stopped a few feet away. "On a hunt."

The guard swallowed. For a moment, he tried to say something but closed his mouth and nodded instead. "Good luck, sirs."

We slid past him and into the village. It looked exactly like what I expected a fantasy hamlet would look like—straw roofs crowned clusters of wooden houses. Metal lanterns hung from posts like streetlights back on Earth.

Following Devon, I continued to observe the citizens, who watched from their windows. Much like the guards, they were both relieved and scared when they saw our red cloaks.

Starting to feel like the boogeyman. That woman is pale as a ghost.

Eventually, we stopped at a well-lit building full of chatter. It smelled clean, aside from a hint of vomit. Sure enough, I spotted glistening brown chunks in the grass. Given that and the boisterous shouting coming from behind the door, I knew it was a pub.

Devon pushed through, and the chatter stopped. Wide-eyed patrons stared at Devon's cloak.

The Hunter ignored them and pushed through to the bar. The barkeep behind the counter was a short man covered in scars. He gripped the edge of the counter and fixed his one good eye on Devon.

"What can I do for you, Grimm?"

Devon sat on the nearest stool, and I joined him, feeling like an awkward shadow. He tossed a silver coin on the counter. The barkeep made it disappear so fast I couldn't see where he'd stashed it.

He grabbed two clean glasses along with a brown bottle, poured until each was half full, and set them in front of us with more force than needed. For a second, his eyebrows twitched, but when Devon picked up his glass, he grunted and excused himself.

I stared at my drink with some hesitation. The smell reminded me of beer, but it had a sharp undertone that made me think it tasted bitter. After looking around and seeing a couple people glance my way, I lowered my shoulders and raised the glass to my lips.

Oh, that's disgusting.

I placed the cup on the counter and kept it between my hands. Devon kept drinking while looking bored. Eventually, I couldn't take the lack of information.

"What are we doing?"

Devon took another swig. He smacked his lips and frowned at the cup before placing it to the side. "Waiting."

It's like pulling teeth. He wasn't this tight-lipped when we met. What gives?

"Waiting for what?"

"Give it a few clicks."

I tried the drink again, but it tasted as awful as the first sip. The barkeep side-eyed us but went back to polishing the counter. From his stiff shoulders and awkward posture, he seemed on edge. What for, I didn't know.

If only Devon would just tell me what's going on...

Before I could ask another question, Devon stood, silencing the whispers. I hopped off the stool and waited as he stared at the door.

"An old saying my mentor told me on my first hunt: 'a smart Hunter does enough to catch the prey, not impress the crowd.' It's a good rule to follow in villages like these."

I didn't have time to ask him what he meant when the door opened. A guard entered, followed by a large, portly man with the world's curliest mustache. He almost looked cartoony with his pale skin marred with sweat.

The patrons cleared a direct line from the guard to us. The stout man wrung his hands beside his jacket pocket. He scanned the room, and he shared a look with the barkeep that disappeared as quickly as it came.

He cleared his throat and met Devon's eyes. "I believe we have business, Sir Grimm."

Chapter 15

A Simple Talk

We introduced ourselves and then followed the man and his escort outside. From there, we slowly walked toward the center of town, passing through the dimly lit streets. It didn't surprise me when the houses near the heart of the village were two-story manors with sturdy stone walls and billowing smokestacks. Every city had its place where the richer folk lived; a small village wasn't that different.

The guard's head swiveled, as though he was expecting someone to jump out at any moment. Devon walked calmly, his eyes lazily scanning the surroundings.

If he's not freaked out, then I won't be either.

They led us to one of the largest buildings, with a knee-high brick fence outlining manicured gardens leading up to porch steps.

He pulled out a set of silver keys and unlocked the door. The guard remained outside, his spear raised.

We entered a living room connected to a kitchen and dining room. Our escort took a seat in a nearby chair, sinking into the wide cushion. For a moment, he seemed to forget that Devon and I existed, standing and waiting for an explanation.

His eyes widened, and he sat up while motioning to the other chairs. "My apologies, Grimms. Sit, sit. I'm afraid I'm rather rattled at the moment."

I chose the chair to the man's right while Devon sat in the one directly opposite. He didn't melt into his chair the way the man did. His back stayed straight, and he rested his hands on his lap.

"I assume you are the village master?" Devon asked.

"Ah, yes. The city lord appointed me six years ago. For the most part, it's been a relatively peaceful position. Occasionally, we get the bad egg who causes problems, but the winters have been kind, and the villagers remain happy," he answered. His smile cracked, and he glanced out the nearest window before turning back to Devon. "But my apologies for the disrespectful delay. My name is Carter Prelus. It's an honor to meet you."

Devon's silence further cracked Carter's smile.

He's very good at the whole silent and intimidating thing. I'm glad I'm not receiving it.

Carter squirmed in his seat. He glanced toward me, but I had nothing to offer. This whole trip had been me following Devon around like a little kid. If he thought I'd be able to save him, he was out of luck.

Devon finally spoke, his words calm but with an iron that brooked no argument. "You know why we're here."

Carter nodded slowly. "I do. I'm sorry for the delay. It's just..."

He exhaled. "Two weeks ago, a group of adventurers came to our village. They said they had been tracking a stag for several days. They caused numerous problems. And it didn't help that the lot of them looked noble-born, so there was only so much I could do."

"They entered the deep woods, didn't they?"

Carter looked up in surprise. "Yes! How did you know?"

"Explain the rest of the story."

"Oh. Yes, all right," Carter replied. "After drinking for a night, they continued their hunt the next morning. Five men and their three retainers entered, but only one young man returned. He was injured. The boy shouldn't have survived long enough to collapse at the village gate, but he did."

Carter finally lost his polite smile and used a small cloth to pat his sweating brow, a haunted look in his eyes.

"What kind of injuries did he have, and where is the boy now?"

"He succumbed within the night. We have no resident mage here—only our alchemist, Regis, and his remedies. Those injuries the boy had... they were too much. He had bite marks up and down his limbs and cracked bones."

That sounds horrible.

A memory of that night trapped in a cage played in my mind. The ribbon of flesh missing from my arm, blood splattering the bars, and a snarling wolf watching me from the shadows.

I gripped the wood so hard the armrest creaked. The sound drew stares from Devon and Carter. Somehow, seeing Devon's blunt facade shift to offer comfort helped ground me.

Calm down, Cain. It won't end like last time. I'm not helpless anymore.

I cleared my throat. "Sorry. Please continue."

"Right, yes." Carter wiped his sweat again. "We had an emergency town meeting. The adventurers are obviously dead, but they were goldbloods; we can't leave them without angering the houses. Even if we knew it was pointless, we created a small group of ten men—mostly our guards—to help explore the woods for other bodies. If we could at least bring back proof of their deaths, we'd satisfy the city lord."

"How many of your men survived?"

"Half. It's... a terrible loss." Carter sighed and locked his fingers. "The village is on edge; we keep seeing glowing eyes through the trees. We're afraid something will happen soon, but we don't know what to do."

Devon stood up. "We'll take care of it. Can your guard lead us to Regis? It's best if we examine the body." He continued once Carter nodded. "Good. You know our price. Have it prepared."

Devon walked out of the manor, but it felt awkward to leave abruptly.

"I'm sorry for your loss."

I didn't know what else to say, so I joined Devon outside. He looked away without a word.

Right. He probably heard that.

The guard quickly dipped into the house and exited with a resigned look on his face. He nodded to both of us and led us past a few wooden buildings.

"Hey, Devon. What's the usual price?"

"Twenty-six silver is our standard for a simple hunt, plus whatever meat and supplies we need for the Warren."

The question drew the guard's attention, and he nearly clipped the edge of a wall. His movements became much more rigid, and I wanted to laugh as he did his best impression of a tin soldier.

"Is that low or high? I can't tell if that's a good deal for monster hunting or not nearly enough."

Devon chuckled. His laugh made the guard speed up. "Usually not. But we can already negotiate the price depending on the danger. And most kingdoms know not to short a Grimm for their work. They generally have an amount set aside for problems like this."

"And if they don't pay up?" I asked. I had a sneaking suspicion in my gut that the solution wouldn't be peaceful.

Devon stopped and let the guard get further away. "Then a new hunt begins."

We caught up to the guard. He led us to a wide shack made of mismatched and stained wood. The faint tinge of herbs and mint grew stronger the closer we came.

The guard knocked and stepped back while covering his nose—the reason became apparent when the door swung open, unleashing the unfiltered assault of pungent herbs. Strangely, Devon didn't react and stared passively at the man who answered.

He wore a grass-stained outfit and leather gloves. Judging by the twigs adorning his gray hair, we had found the alchemist.

"What is it? If Carter is sending another round to their deaths then—" The alchemist paused when he saw our cloaks. "Oh. The Grimms are here."

The guard motioned for us to enter. "Sorry to disturb you, Regis. The Grimms need to examine the body and ask a couple of questions. Mr. Prelus' orders."

Regis pulled out brass-rimmed spectacles. "You'll have to ignore the smell. Usually, I can mitigate it, but I had to create more salves."

He led us down a flight of steps into the basement. "I'm not sure what Carter told you, but the boy's a mess. His fingers were missing most of their flesh. Chewed clean off. Whatever got to him avoided his central organs but made sure his death was slow."

He tugged at his collar when he received no reply. I didn't blame him. Devon's silence was maddening.

We left the stairwell and pushed past a smaller door. Inside was a vast underground room lit by several lanterns. Outside their direct light, parchment and wrapped packages sat bundled on tables. On the far side, drying herbs and various liquids littered the room.

Regis moved to a door with an iron lock. It led into a room the size of a walk-in closet.

The long table at the center held a brown sheet dipped in wax. A clinical odor that reeked of antiseptic permeated the room and singed my nose hairs. I quickly covered my nose with my hoodie sleeve, but that did little to help.

Regis shrugged. "I've done what I can to preserve the corpse, but we'll have to burn it soon."

Devon turned to the alchemist. "Remove the sheet. If there is any remnant mana, we'll be able to track it."

"All right. You might want to cover your nose."

He then tugged the sheet, revealing the corpse underneath.

Chapter 16

Into the Woods

The corpse could hardly be called a man. The torso had dime-sized holes of missing flesh and large, blackened hoof marks on his upper ribs. The fingerless hands had their meat stripped away, but whatever did it did so in a messy manner. Decaying tendons dripped from pale flesh, and black veins crisscrossed throughout his claw-marked body, predominantly on his arms and legs.

Thankfully, Regis had covered the man's privates with a smaller sheet, but the sight of it all made me queasy. Still, it didn't strike me with as much fear as I thought it would, which disturbed me.

I've never seen a body like this before. I don't think I ever want to again.

Regis grabbed metal tongs from his apron pocket and pried open one of the jagged claw marks, exposing squishy, gray meat underneath.

"Four marks—two reached the bone. I found strands of dense fur. If I had to guess the culprit, it'd be a forest wolf. They're common enough in these parts but tend to stay far away."

"It's obviously not just a wolf, right?" I asked. "Those are hoofprints."

Devon raised his eyebrow, and I became unsure if I had stepped out of line. He nodded a second later, and I took that as a sign that I hadn't.

Regis shook his head. "No, and I could pass off a hoofprint or two as a boar trampling him, but there are far too many and too close together. It looks deliberate. Whatever happened to him in the woods, the beasts worked together to maim him."

"And those wounds?" I pointed to the dime-sized holes. "They don't look like tooth marks and claw wounds."

"Because they're not. I'm not a wildlife expert, but they are likely puncture marks from some kind of bird. Perhaps a raven or a crow."

What is going on? That's a lot of creatures that shouldn't be working together.

I looked at Devon, but his face revealed nothing.

Why are you being unhelpful now? Is it because I spoke up?

"Detect any mana?" Regis asked.

Devon shook his head. "Thank you. We have enough information," he said.

"Ah, all right then." Regis placed the sheet back over the corpse. "You know the way out. Good luck on your hunt, Sirs Grimm."

Regis stayed behind, watching us leave. I snuck a glance at the sheet and bit my lip. The image of a disfigured corpse would be haunting my dreams for a few nights.

* * *

"What do we do now? Do you know what's attacking people?" I asked as I stared into the eerie forest.

We were outside the village. The guard who had escorted us had returned to his post. The look of fear in his eyes had lessened, but a healthy amount remained.

I rubbed my bandaged hand. The injury had long healed, and I felt the skin on my palm flex like normal. Deciding the salve-coated cloth held no purpose, I took it off. Before I could toss it inside my backpack, Devon grabbed my wrist.

He scowled. "Burn it. Try never to leave things with your blood behind. Hexers will use it to curse you. Be. Careful."

He released me, and I massaged my wrist. His grip hadn't hurt, but it definitely cut off my circulation.

You don't need a fireball, just enough of a flame to burn the bandage.

I tried to create the image of a flame, but Devon's gaze rattled me. I closed my eyes to block him out. In my mind, I built the spark like Astra taught me. Next came the runes, adding to the flame, growing it. I imagined the heat as I watched the fire crackle, its licks repelling the void.

I connected the mana in my chest and tried to limit its flow down my arm. It was under my control, but I knew it would flare up once I finished the incantation.

Not a fireball. I need a flame...

Instead of the chant, I remembered Astra's shortened version. "*Ek kalla heiðarloga.*"

The warm energy in my chest responded like a spooked horse. I growled, a sound foreign to my ears.

No!

Heat formed, wanting release.

Listen to me!

The flames built, and the flow slowed. For a second, I thought I did it, and my eyes shot open, but then the pool in my chest crashed against my will like a tsunami and washed away my control. The flames—a bright orange ball that extended past my fingers—flared into a small torrent that caused me to scream. The bandage became ash, but the smell of burnt copper filled the air.

Devon squeezed my arm. The flow stuttered and reversed back into my chest. He held me up by the limb, and I tried not to squirm.

"You tried to shorten the incantation."

I grimaced. Strangely, a cool sensation invaded my veins. The feeling numbed the pain, and I stopped biting my lip.

"I needed to burn the bandages, not launch a fireball. Astra showed me the incantation when she was explaining what they were. I thought it'd be a better match for my needs."

He sent another burst of what I assumed was his mana over my arm. "It would have been. But incantations are difficult, and failing one can lead to backlash."

"Sorry. I thought I could do it."

He shook his head. "Foolish, but not wrong."

"Huh?"

"You managed the incantation; you just lost control afterwards. I'm assuming your passive skill is why your mana is hot."

"Yeah, I noticed that your mana and hers are cold. Are you saying I actually managed to do the incantation?"

"Yes, but with horrible efficiency. You took the words but not the runes or the proper image. Brute forcing an incantation is possible but extremely stupid. Do it again, and you may lose more than the skin off your fingers."

I stared at my smoking palm. The smell of cooked pork wafted strongly in the breeze, making me crinkle my nose. "Do you know if Elias struggled with his fire magic? There's a feeling in my chest, and it responds whenever I try to complete the incantation."

"No. Whenever we hunted together, he only ever used fire spells. At least now I know why he favored them so."

Devon's voice verged on a growl, genuine anger crossing his face.

"Grab the bandage roll in your pack. Don't use the spell again unless you have no choice." He tossed me a vial, and I caught it. It looked the same as the salve Astra used for my burns.

"Thank you."

"Wrap your wound. Can you use your summon?"

"Yes, but I only tried it once."

"Good. Summon it."

I scrambled to bandage my hand, then closed my eyes and held out my good arm.

This time, the system took over. The mana blossomed out of my chest and down my arm. A spell circle rotated in my head, and I pictured fangs and claws rising from its center.

Summon: Shadow Wolf

A chunk of mana left my body. I opened my eyes to the shadow beast as it sniffed my fingers.

After scratching its head, I commanded it to sink into my shadow, and it did. The sensation that connected it to me felt weird, like an invisible weight.

Remembering how Astra reacted, I watched Devon's face for signs of tension or alarm, but he simply nodded and motioned to the forest.

"Next hunt, use your summon to scout for you. A shadow beast is made for stealth," Devon said.

"Gotcha. I can try that now if you like?" I replied.

"Don't. Have it protect you while we're in the woods. I'll keep you safe, but I won't coddle you. Prepare yourself to use your axe."

Right... This isn't a game. I can die if I'm not careful.

The moon overhead stopped at the tree line, the purple leaves blocking most of the light. I tried not to think about how similar it felt to that night in the cage, but the suffocating feeling of entering the dark woods grabbed my nerves.

We had barely moved past the tree line when the sound of running disturbed the numbing silence. I gripped my axe, waiting behind Devon, his face hidden behind his cloak.

A gray wolf with gleaming claws flashed through the shadows. I swung my weapon, hoping to intercept the blow. My arm extended, cutting a diagonal line.

Blood splattered on my front, and I tumbled to the floor.

Chapter 17

Fanged Foe

I rolled and pushed myself up. The wolf let out a growl that rumbled in my ears, followed by whimpering. Its coat flared, and it bared its teeth as it retreated, and red droplets splashed onto the forest floor.

My shadow wolf circled the bigger beast—its fur a near imitation—with its hackles raised and growled.

Devon cocked his head and turned to me. "I suggest you finish it. There will be more."

I glared daggers.

That thing could have killed me! Don't just stand there looking bored!

I let out a growl, and the wolf made a passing swipe, but my summon partially sunk into the ground. Claws passed through shadows. A streak of black blurred through the air, and a splatter of crimson coated the nearby tree.

Okay, focus. Step in. You can heal now. Just help; your wolf can handle this.

I gritted my teeth. My legs felt like granite. My mental screams did nothing as my limbs betrayed me.

The wolf lunged again, and my summon tried to dodge, but it must have learned its lesson. It snapped and swiped with its claws and teeth in unison.

A sharp command pulled my attention.

"I hear more beasts. Move, Cain."

Iron weighed my arms, but I pushed through. The wolf had backed off, and my summon regarded it warily. I stepped in as my wolf jumped to the side.

I swung, meeting fur and claw, the blade pushing into its skin. My arm rocked with the impact but struck again in a frantic attempt to inflict a lethal blow.

The swing missed, and the wolf sunk its fangs into the space between my pointer finger and thumb.

"Aaagh!"

It dashed to my right, and I turned to track it. Its claws flashed again, and I launched my boot into its paw. I chopped at its leg, but I slipped. Dull, yellow canines overtook my vision, and I screamed.

Before the jaws could rip off my face, something crashed into the wolf's side, and a loud yelp bounced between my ears. Two wolves rolled on the ground, each snarl and growl coming with a sharp pinch.

My summon howled in pain and brought red to my eyes.

I rushed forward, my legs tensing with each step. I waited until the wolf kicked my summon away, launching the magical beast against a tree. My feet pushed off the ground, and I raised my axe.

The wolf scrambled to get to its feet, but my weapon came down first and sank into its chest. A sickening crunch of bones sounded, then the blade sank deeper into the softer meat behind it.

"Awooh!"

A heavy paw slammed into my thigh, knocking me backwards. I fell but kept my eyes glued to the gushing blood pouring out of the wolf's chest. It struggled, writhing on the ground.

"Finish it!" Devon's eyes were furious as he pointed at the wolf. "We do not torture our prey."

"I—I... do—"

My jaw slammed shut as the struggling wolf twitched and then dropped dead. Two pools of swirling darkness dripped down its maw. Shadow teeth tore away at the wolf's broken neck, bits of fur and blood trailing the motion.

"I..."

Devon sighed. "Stop. Reflect on this later. Are you injured?"

I frowned and patted myself. I tried to use my thumb only to realize it struggled to respond. Blood melded into piles of dark purple leaves as shadows blanketed the area.

"Do I need to burn this?" I asked blankly. "I don't know if I can without charring more skin."

"Don't worry about it. Just don't leave it behind. Focus on your surroundings for now. Grab your axe. Don't let go unless you have to."

"All right."

I approached the fresh corpse. Despite watching it die, I waited, hesitant.

It can't breathe. It's dead.

I wiped the blood against my shirt, ignoring the flaring pain from my palm.

My summon cocked its head and rubbed against my leg. It looked back, and I struggled to smile as the final strands of fur stuck between its teeth floated to the ground.

"Thank you. I'm sorry you got hurt."

"Wulf!"

Using my foot as leverage, I gripped the handle of my axe and pulled it out of the wolf's chest. It came away with a wet *schlick*, and I stumbled, pushing my foot deeper into the wolf's belly. Blood gushed out, and I nearly threw up.

Devon glanced my way but returned his focus to the trees. I didn't dare ask another question. I doubted I could keep my voice from shaking.

"To our left, past the tree with the forked trunk. It's hiding in the bushes; watch for it. If it comes closer, tell me."

The tree stood out amongst the others, and as he described, a large bush blocked the view beside it. I squinted but couldn't make out the eyes or body of any beast or critter.

My summon licked my arm. It sank into my shadow, and a strange relief settled in my chest.

No, you know why. It protected you. You feel safer.

I did feel protected. I wouldn't have a face if my summon hadn't knocked the wolf away. That thought chilled me to my core, and I grabbed my cloak.

For the first time in a while, I felt the cloak shift, and the fabric tightened around my shoulders. Blood stained my pant legs, but whatever magic the cloak held forced the substance to slide off.

Another thing that protects me.

Despite the creepy surroundings, the tension in Devon's shoulders eased.

You're safe. Calm down.

Movement near the bush grabbed my attention, and I stared with curiosity. Not a single leaf moved, but I refused to look away.

It took a second, but I spotted it again, creeping in from behind a trunk five feet closer.

"It moved. Three trees closer," I said.

"Good. Keep watching."

I didn't know what Devon was waiting for, but I did as ordered. We remained motionless for what felt like an eternity, watching the creature leap agilely from one tree to the next. Not once did I manage to get a clear view of the beast's form. All I could make out was its small stature as it kept to the shadows, using trunks as a shield.

I sweated. If the thing came at me, the odds of me reacting in time were next to none. I'd be relying on my shadow wolf, my physical capabilities too slow to keep up.

"It's behind that tree. Ten feet to the left. Devon, what are we waiting for?"

He didn't answer. Instead, he released his spear from its holster. What I had thought was smooth, white wood turned out to be bone. The pores had been sanded down, giving it a polished appearance, but the butt of the spear had two bumps resembling a femur.

What kind of creature has a femur that long?

Devon slammed the tail of his spear into the ground, the shaft sinking into the loam. When he let go, the weapon remained upright. "You can come out. Hiding will only delay the inevitable."

Silence met Devon's words.

I looked at the spot where the creature had last moved, and I rolled my wrist, feeling the weight of the axe-head as it moved.

Devon turned in place and crossed his arms. "If you don't, I'll sniff you out. And when I find you, I won't be willing to talk."

More silence followed. He cracked his neck and reached for his spear, but a low hiss stopped him.

"Hunter..."

The voice crawled down my spine with its guttural warble. It was as if a kid was speaking through a cheap microphone.

"What need? You murder. Thrall," said the creature.

Each syllable crawled up my skin and nestled into my ear. Despite my discomfort, Devon remained stoic, his body a statue in the night.

"You attacked us unprovoked. We were within our rights to slay the wolf," he answered.

"Entered my forest! Trespasser! Trespasser!"

I covered my ears, the pitch rising to a whistle. Something clawed at a nearby trunk, splintering the wood. A *thump, thump, thump* beat in a steady staccato.

"These are not your woods."

"Lies! Mine! Mine! My woods!" the creature shrieked.

"You are but one of many." Devon reached for his spear. "A child cannot claim the seat of an ancient."

"Stop! No!"

Devon stopped and pointed at the tree. "Enough games! Reveal yourself!"

"No! Trespassers. Killers. Murderers."

Devon waited, his fingers nearly touching his spear. Then, the thumping and scratching faded, leaving only a low hiss.

"Fine. I reveal. Talk, then go away!"

"I make no promises."

The creature growled. Another thump. Silence.

There was movement, and a final long, slow scratch.

"Hunters!"

Chapter 18

The Hunt Begins

The monster rushed at Devon. Its form blurred, slick brown fur and leathery skin matching the forest floor. It launched itself like a bullet.

Except Devon moved just as fast, if not faster.

His arm shot out and grabbed the thing by its throat before slamming it onto the ground, where he put his boot squarely on its neck. It struggled, hissing like a feral beast. Devon pressed harder until it choked, creating a muffled hum.

"Cease," Devon commanded.

It did not listen.

In one swift motion, he grabbed his spear and spun it around until the iron spearhead pressed against its neck.

The creature stopped moving.

With it frozen in midair, I finally got a proper look at it. It had a body resembling a mountain lion, blended with some sort of lizard. A large patch of fur covered its back, transitioning to wrinkled, leathery skin. Its scaly tail ended in a fluffy bob. Its pawed limbs were short. The creature's face resembled a furless cat with gray irises and slit pupils.

Devon kept his spear pushed into his prey's neck, the sharpened iron offering a swift death if the monster sought freedom. He raised his boot, allowing the creature to suck in a deep breath. "Speak now. Tell me your name."

When it didn't answer immediately, he twisted the spear.

"I have no name. No more," it replied with a strangled growl.

"What did you do to the Hunters? Why did you attack the villagers afterwards?"

Pure rage overtook the creature. Its tail thumped, and it strained its neck upwards in a snarl despite the tip of Devon's spear drawing a line of blood.

"Trespassers! Evil! Murderers! Murder!"

Devon frowned and looked at me. "Most creatures born with mana or from a Lore Strain start as less than intelligent. Most can talk, but it's harder to break from the chains of their Lore. Take the Reds: they start as little girls who speak in simple rhymes. If they mature, they learn to push past those chains and can speak normally." He motioned to the snarling monster. "Not foolproof, but it's a good indicator that the creature is new, not an aged or ancient beast."

"Get out! No more! Leave! Murderers!"

The creature continued its rant as it struggled, ignoring the spear pushing into its skin. Devon stomped hard, causing the air to leave its lungs. After being allowed to suck in a deep breath, it stopped moving and watched Devon coldly.

"I'll ask one last time. What did you do?"

"M-murder them. Revenge. Remove trespassers. Remove. Murderers."

"Revenge for what?"

It thumped its tail but remained silent.

"Are the humans dead?"

Another thump. "Yes!"

Devon sighed. "We are Hunters, mercenaries, guardians—Grimms. But we do not owe allegiance to humans. If a village invades the home of an ancient one, we only intervene if the killings are unjust." He leaned down and met the creature's eyes. "These are not your woods. You cannot claim revenge on the villagers."

"Murderers! All murderers! They kill! They invade!"

That's a new word. If the villagers weren't trespassers, what did they invade?

"Will you leave these woods? Swear to a pact?"

I glared at Devon. *What is he doing?* The creature had confessed to killing the villagers; to let it go seemed foolish. What prevented a monster from continuing to be a monster?

"Never! Won't! Can't leave. Him!" The creature roared, speech turning inhuman.

"If you don't, we'll find you. You'll die."

"Won't leave!"

Devon stood up straight. His eyes gave nothing away as he kept his expression blank. "Cain. Prepare yourself."

My eyes widened. "What? Why?"

He ignored me, continuing to stare at the thrashing monster, its tail knocking into Devon's legs.

He raised his hand. "*Reka.*"

The creature screamed. As it spasmed, its two eyes served as flashlights, burning brighter with every second. "Nooough! Nrghouooo!"

It spasmed again, and the light faded from its eyes, leaving behind bloodshot veins across the sclerae. It stopped moving and a lone bird released a loud caw.

"Don't try to copy what I just did. The backlash would melt your brain," Devon said as he removed his foot.

It twitched again and released a hiss, void of the haunting echo of the child's voice. Devon thrust his spear into its neck, and the hissing ceased. He withdrew his spear, deftly flicking the weapon to shed the blood from the metal.

"What happened? Is it dead?" I asked.

"No." Devon pointed deeper into the woods. "What we're actually hunting is still alive. I merely released its control over this beast. The puppet master used it as a host. Judging by the fact it can control multiple, it uses one creature as the central conduit of its powers."

"So it's still alive... And that thing was a puppet? What about the wolf?"

"A thrall, but not a host. Let's go. It'll reestablish a new host soon. Be prepared to fend off more beasts."

What kind of beginner quest is this?

I didn't voice my thoughts; I simply played the good little apprentice and followed behind. He could take the brunt of the danger if he wanted to drag me into the evil woods with mind-controlling monsters.

"More wolves?"

"Maybe. You remember the wounds on the corpse: birds, wolves, and boars. Watch the branches for anything small."

I nodded and kept my axe ready. My summon hid in my shadow, waiting to be released.

You're protected. You're not alone. I killed a wolf. What's one more?

My words must have tempted fate because soon after, something small and black came rushing out of the trees. It came at an angle, crossing through a large thicket of branches.

I reflexively swung and managed to clip its wing. My summon raised its head and snapped its jaws around the bird, and the winged foe disappeared in a wet crunch. I stopped to stare at my shadow, but Devon tapped my leg with the end of his spear.

"Keep moving."

We continued our trek. More beasts called from beyond sight, but none attacked. The moonlight became spottier as the canopies grew denser. Devon held out his arm when we came across a thin brook.

"Follow this to its source. Stay alive, and I'll come find you."

"Why are we splitting up?"

He ignored me and twirled his spear. "If the puppet master shows up in its real form, do not hesitate. It will kill you if you do."

Devon raised his head and howled. My heart thumped as the sound continued like a shockwave that pushed back fallen leaves, creating a breeze against my skin. A new sensation flooded my veins. It wasn't the cold of his mana, nor the heat of my own.

Instead, my pulse quickened, and something called to me from within. I joined his howl.

It felt good.

I felt hot and bared my teeth. I licked my canines as I raised my axe.

Hunt! Seek the prey!

The words came unbidden, painting themselves in my mind in blood-splattered letters.

Move! The hunt begins!

Devon looked at me, a chilling smile on his face. When he spoke, his words sounded as though he were whispering into my ears. "Survive, pup."

I couldn't hold back the energy and ran, chasing the stream. A deep growl snapped the branches behind me, but I couldn't look. My heart pounded, each pulse propelling me forward. A fiery-hot drive surged within, demanding to burn.

Something piqued my senses. A musky scent reminiscent of wet fur wafted through, but an unknown aroma lingered beneath.

There!

Something burst from the nearest bush. It reached around my stomach. Without knowing what it was, I swung my axe and tumbled forward, but I kept moving. The creature crashed to the ground as two objects hit the floor.

Before I could think, I raised my wrist, now coated in blood, and ran it across my tongue.

Corrupted prey. Cull the herd.

It tasted like much more than blood alone. It was salty and coppery, yet it carried hints of gaminess and the tang of berries. And then it soured, ruined at the height of savoring the taste.

I spat out the blood and kept running. The foreign thoughts were correct. The blood was corrupt.

I skipped over a fallen log and continued along the stream. The air buffeted my face, filling my nose with the scent of the forest. My thoughts narrowed in on one goal—get to the end.

Chapter 19

Tusk Trouble

I kept running deeper into the woods, scattered moonlight providing the only reprieve from the blinding darkness.

My blood ran hot, and I yearned to act.

I gotta keep moving; I need to find the source.

Rattling hounded my steps like something heavy knocking aside branches. It matched my speed, and then it gained on me.

The smell hit me—a rich scent of sweat and dirt.

Another creature approached, and I raised my axe, aiming to deliver a finishing blow without slowing down. I had to keep moving, and this beast blocked my path.

It barreled through the trees, a muscular, hulking beast with two arm-length tusks.

Eliminate... Must kill!

When it came within striking distance, I aimed for its neck. The gray-skinned boar met my blade and knocked me away, sending me rolling across the stream.

Water dripped down my face, and I evaded the beast as it tried to gore me. I swung again, managing to slice into its flank. The blade sank an inch, a shallow wound at best.

With all its weight on its front legs, the boar kicked me. I rolled out of the way, and my summon left my shadow. I tried to stand. My foot slipped in the mud.

My shadow wolf attacked, sinking its jaws into the boar's leg, but the boar flung it away. The animal snorted and stomped at the ground. Its hoof created a divot in the dirt, and it stared at me with beady, black eyes.

Carefully, I braced myself. It huffed and kicked off. I rolled, my legs clearing its charge. It swerved and boomeranged around, attacking once more.

My summon sank into the shadows after being launched, so I knew what to expect. When the boar came closer, my wolf rose from the nearest shadow cast by a lone tree. His teeth pulled at its back leg, causing the boar to fall flat and drag my wolf along.

Now!

I leaped forward as it sprayed dirt in its slide. A small rock grazed my ear, but I continued.

I chopped downwards. My axe tore into the boar's tough hide. It was so thick that I barely did any damage.

The boar pushed itself off the ground and knocked its head to the side, cutting a deep gash into my pants. I shouted and fell. It tried to get up again, but my wolf yanked it down.

It squealed as it played tug-of-war with my summon.

I crawled away, my leg throbbing.

I have to kill, but I can't get close.

Only one thing came to mind. My axe wasn't good for fighting something that could spear me with a casual turn of its head. I had to move. I needed to survive. And to do that, I needed to win.

I lifted my injured arm and saw blood seeping through the bandages. Mana surged from my chest. My heart pounded, each pulse sending a stream down my arm.

Fire. Conjure the flame.

The spark erupted, and I tried to create the runes. I nearly completed the first line when another squeal disrupted my concentration.

I threw my axe at the boar's eye. Instead of embedding in with a nice *thunk*, the handle hit its brow, forcing its head back without damaging it.

Damnit!

My brain recreated the spark, connecting the magma in my chest to the flame.

Burn bright, blaze with heat. Bathe the void in light.

The boar crashed to the ground, sending vibrations up my legs. I ignored it, created the first line, then two, and then made the rune. The spark became a bonfire, and I screamed the words.

"Heita'k á hyrupp heiðarloga; um mér at orna!"

My hand sizzled as fire erupted from my palm and shot out like a cannonball. My wolf released the boar's leg and sunk into the shadows before impact. The fireball whistled through the air, and I turned away as the bright orange flames created spots in my vision.

The boar met the incoming projectile with renewed fury, smashing its tusk into the flame. Except the flame was only semi-physical. The fireball exploded point-blank, the flames erupting into a blinding nova. The beast squealed, but heat jettisoned down its throat, suffocating its lungs and flash-frying the soft meat within.

The fire expanded like a raging tide, engulfing the beast as it crawled into every open orifice. The force of the explosion pushed me to the ground, but I felt invigorated.

It scrambled to move but collapsed into a charred heap.

Now it's dead.

The cold press of my shadow wolf's nose nuzzled into my neck, and it licked my skin. I reached with my good hand to pet it and stared at my smoking right hand.

Black streaks had expanded down my wrist, and bleeding cracks shifted around with each twitch. I expected the damage, but the aftermath disturbed me. Yet, the heat that flowed through my veins continued to burn.

I needed to get up; there could be more beasts coming.

I used my summon to help me stand. My legs shook, forcing me to limp. I had more injuries, but that didn't stop me.

"Grab my axe, please," I asked.

After reclaiming my weapon with the help of my summon, I kept moving. I had to stick to the trees as leverage. Each step hurt, but it didn't matter. Get to the destination and wait for Devon: that's all I needed to do.

Thankfully, whatever mystical force the puppet master used to command the forest was absent as I stumbled deeper into the woods.

Heh... So much for the no-blood-left-behind rule.

The sticky substance coated my legs.

I wasn't in great condition, but Astra assured me we could heal most damage. It was one of the perks of being a Grimm, after all.

I'm putting more than one point in Constitution next level. I can't keep getting crippled.

The concept of leveling my body like some video game character refused to normalize in my mind. Then again, I stumbled through a cursed forest, interrogated a cat-lizard, and threw a fireball at a mind-controlled boar.

Normal was a made-up word at the moment.

* * *

Eventually, the canopy opened to moonlight, and the trees gave way. I inched toward the ethereal blue glow, one unsure footstep at a time.

That's not right. Why is it blue?

Something stirred in my gut, but I was nearly there. Whatever energy was still thrumming in my veins that demanded I reach the destination would have to settle with getting past the tree line.

As I approached the glowing light, the bubbling sound of water filled my ears.

The brook widened and wound past a large rock. Water splashed against a shallow ditch past it and opened into a pool where further streams trailed deeper into the forest.

I limped past the rock and scanned the surroundings. The blue glow intensified, and I accidentally kicked a pebble into the water, creating a small splash.

The water droplets that hit the mud around it glowed a bright azure, sending up a stream of light particles that drifted into the air.

The strange blue tones made sense now. I found it odd that the moonlight didn't create a purple hue, thanks to the colored leaves. Whether the water was actually *water*, I didn't know. It reminded me of the fountain inside the Warren—the one that showed me my reflection for the first time after a night of horrors.

I shelved that memory and pushed on. As I got near the ditch, the particles dispersed, and I was finally at the source of the stream.

Chapter 20

BLOODY MAJESTY

Lying on a stone dais in the middle of the pond was a bloodied stag. My summon growled, but the creature was truly dead.

I sniffed the air and had to cover my nose. The coppery scent penetrated deep, and I could taste it on my tongue.

Corrupt!

The thoughts were right. I couldn't even savor the blood this time; nothing about it smelled good. I could only describe it as rancid meat and battery acid blended together.

Droplets of blood dripped into the glowing water, creating more particles before fading away, consumed by the ethereal blue.

The dead stag stared off into the distance with clouded eyes. The milky film made it hard to tell, but the irises were bright green underneath.

I stared at the strip of pink flesh dangling from its antlers.

It must have killed one of the Hunters before it succumbed.

The stag's white fur rippled in the soft breeze, creating the illusion of the beast breathing. I looked away and focused on the cause of death.

An arrow with white fletching penetrated deep into its shoulder. On its back and sides, two more arrows marred its hide.

The sight felt wrong, and I couldn't understand why. I tentatively sniffed the air and immediately covered my nose.

Still wrong. Is it the corpse? Is it rotting meat?

Except, the corpse wasn't mangled or decayed. I wasn't an expert on dead animals, but most things decomposed.

For something killed several days ago, it was remarkably intact.

Corpses bloat, right? Gasses expand, and maggots should be covering the body. Unless this is magical and nothing makes sense...

It was probably magic, and I was very much out of my depth.

I accomplished my goal. I came to the source of the stream where a magical corpse lay dead. The adrenaline-fueled need to purge the corruption faded, leaving me with a hollow thumping in my chest.

What now?

I walked to the water's edge and looked around. The forest offered silence and not much more. At any moment, I expected another beast to come rampaging through, hellbent on crushing my skull.

Nothing happened.

I wasn't sure, but I mentally counted over a minute where I stood in relative peace. My wolf nudged my leg, and I stroked its fur.

"Right. What do we do now?" I asked my wolf.

"Hunter..."

Ahh, I should have kept my big mouth shut.

Goosebumps blossomed across my skin.

"Hunter!" the creepy voice repeated.

"Is this what happened? Is this why you killed the villagers?"

"Murderer! Trespasser! Leave! Leave!"

I'm going to haunt you if I die, Devon. Where the heck are you?

"Is the stag important to you?"

"Kinslayer, get out! Go!"

"I didn't kill the stag. You're the one who attacked me."

Scratching sounds from behind made me spin around. I brought up my axe to intercept an attack, but none came. It was only a fox staring at me.

Its fur stood up; its tail pointed straight.

The fox stepped forward. "Leave! Leave! Get away from my brother!"

My wolf moved in front of me, and I finally noticed how much smaller it was. When I had originally summoned it, its head met my navel. Now it barely reached my thigh.

This isn't good. It's disappearing.

The fox ignored my summon and moved closer. "Kill. Kill Hunter. Revenge!"

In a fight, I figured my summon could take the fox, but it was potentially one of many hosts to come.

I wasn't in fighting condition, and apparently, my wolf could only last so long. Still, I gripped the shaft of my weapon harder and lowered my body with my feet wide apart.

My leg prevented me from moving fast, so I'd have to take the hit if it came. Every blow counted.

I can do this.

The creature hissed, and a wave of pressure pushed the pool's light particles away. My axe nearly slipped from my hands as the particles condensed and formed into a snarling maw.

The floating jaws snapped once, then dispersed. The creature let out another hiss, creating another maw.

This repeated as I slowly backed up, legs shaking, my wolf in tow.

Possessed beasts were still beasts. They were real—normal in a way. But this? This wasn't normal.

This wasn't something I could fight with an axe.

My foot splashed into the water, and I slipped. The fox yelped and charged forward. Two ethereal maws floating above its head sailed forth.

The shadow wolf intercepted the charge, but the maws came down. My summon managed to avoid the first one, but the second maw caught its neck, dragging it to the ground.

I heard a loud crunch, and a shooting pain shot into my chest. My head throbbed, causing me to slip further into the pond. Blinking away tears, I saw the dust maw disperse, revealing the fading shadow puddle of my wolf.

"Yip!" my wolf said.

I swung forward, forcing the fox back; however, it darted around the blow and jumped at my face. It knocked me over, and I rolled, using my failed attack to wrap around the fox's body as it bit into my cheek. I continued moving, slamming the creature against the ground.

Sharpened claws tore into my skin, but my cloak deflected hits that landed on its fabric, the material somehow cushioning the blows.

I grabbed the fox's neck, digging my fingers into its fur. The axe stopped me from securing a good grip, so I let go of the weapon.

I tried to pry the animal away from my face, but it sunk its sharp teeth into my flesh.

"Arrgh! Let go!" I yelled.

I tried again, and it scratched me. Without another option, I bellyflopped, crushing the fox. It yelped, blending the bestial cries with the distorted microphone effect.

Even as I struggled, it clung to me. My legs wobbled, slipping deeper into the pond. Another sharp sting on my neck snapped the terror inside me, and I roared.

"Aaaargggh!"

I jammed my fingers into the creature's eye and dug deep. It rocked backwards, trying to escape. With my flesh freed from its fangs, I yanked hard and hurled it away.

It rolled but shot to its feet and yipped, forming another maw from the thickened cloud. "Die, Hunter!"

In desperation, I grabbed my axe and swung it around, stopping inches away from slicing into the stag's neck. "Back off now!"

The fox shook, its tongue dancing between its teeth. A deep, demonic growl rumbled from its throat. "Get away!"

"No," I said. I lowered the axe an inch further, and the fox snapped at the air, another maw beginning to form.

"Cut it out, or I take off its head."

The fox snarled, but it took a step back, and the maws disappeared.

It watched me, its gray eyes locked onto my hand. Sweat covered my palm. I wasn't sure how much longer I could stay standing in the freezing water. I lost a lot of blood, and even the heat inside my chest struggled to warm me up.

"Get out. Leave. Leave!" the fox growled.

I'm not moving an inch, psycho.

I spat blood into the water and tried to rein in my ragged breathing. "Where's Devon, the other Hunter?"

Another snarl and a thumping of a tail, the creature bit at the air but said nothing. The little fox looked rabid, blood dripping down its snout.

I kicked at the water. "Answer. Now!"

"Dead. Gone. No help. Leave now!" it snarled back.

I don't believe that for a second.

"Destroy the connection. Leave the fox, and I'll go." My blade rested on the stag's white fur, the sharp edge splitting a few hairs. "Now."

The fox's body became eerily still. Its eyes stayed fixed on the axe. With each second it spent unmoving, the more I considered making a break for it. But that would be foolish. I could barely walk. The fire in my chest was on its last embers.

It took everything I had to stay still without moving. My teeth threatened to rattle the more the cold seeped into my limbs.

My cloak tightened around my shoulders, and my eyes widened. The fox's eyes lit up like a lantern, similar to when Devon banished the last host.

Holy crap... It's complying?

That illusion shattered the moment it twisted, and a strong wind battered my back. The axe slipped, landing on the stag's neck. The axe blade sliced through the pelt and cut into its flesh.

The wind picked up, and the blue particles moved with it. Three maws larger than my head formed from the cloud, each snapping once. The echoes sounded like rattling bones, sending a chill down my spine.

"Die!" the fox screamed.

One maw veered left, another darted right, and the third lunged straight for my face. My heart raced, and my foot slipped, causing me to stumble.

Something hit the ground before I did.

I raised my hand as the maws crumbled to dust that smashed against my chest. They felt heavy. I dropped to one knee, and pain jolted up my leg.

Grunting, I clenched my teeth and looked up.

Chapter 21

The Woods Have Eyes, and They Weep

Sticking out of the ground was a spear. The head had punctured the fox's skull and protruded from the base of the jaw, impaling the corpse to the earth.

"Devon? Please tell me that's you," I shouted. I waited for a reply, but none came. "Devon, I'm serious. I'm going to die from hypothermia."

More silence.

Okay, this isn't funny.

I opened my mouth to shout again, but footsteps made me turn my head. Devon walked out of the woods and stepped into the pond's light. His hair looked ruffled, and there were a few scratches along his legs, but he seemed in good health.

In fact, he looked completely fine.

"What the hell?"

He quirked his eyebrow. "Something wrong?"

My eye twitched. "Yes! Do you see what I look like right now?"

I must have been a pitiful sight—soaking, shaking, and bleeding. I used the dais to stand. With the magical fox dead and my mentor here, I tucked my axe back into its sheath.

He moved steadily to the fox and pulled out his spear. Ignoring my glare, he dipped it into the pond and swirled it around. His eyes roamed over the stag's still-bleeding corpse. "Looks like I was right."

I snapped. "What do you mean? You knew this would be here, right? That's why you sent me this way. Why did you send me alone if you knew where to find trouble?"

His eyes met mine; they looked human. "Because you needed to feel the call of the hunt. An untested pup always dies."

I punched him, but the blow was so weak I mostly hurt my own hand against his steel chest. "Ow! Ugh. Screw you. You're insane!"

"Maybe," he responded. He wrapped his arm around my back and slipped his hand under my shoulders. He then lifted me out of the pond and dragged me to the dirt. "Or maybe I want to ensure that Elias's legacy can survive what's to come. You chose this life, after all; let's not waste it."

And having me nearly killed is the best way to go about that? I hope Astra lays into you.

"You said you were right." I stopped to wring out my hair before sighing. "What did you mean? I didn't think about it at first, but how is the stag still bleeding? There can't be that much blood in its body. And it's not rotting."

"You must have tasted the blood. What do you think?"

Corrupted.

I gritted my teeth and glared again. "I don't know. It's magic? Nothing makes sense here. And that weird voice in my head keeps saying 'corrupted.' Whatever that means."

"The puppet master's Lore Matrix is corrupting the beasts it possesses. It has deviated from its Lore and mutated into something different."

"That means almost nothing to me."

"Monsters aren't born from nothing. You'll see that for yourself."

If you're going to be that cryptic, why bother talking at all?

I sighed. "It said something about a kinslayer. This stag and the puppet master were related, right? That's why it wants revenge?"

"Mhm."

Instead of explaining further, he bent down and grabbed the stag's horns.

"What are—"

Riiiip!

The head came free from its shoulders, dripping a torrent of blood onto the stone dais before spilling into the water below.

Damn.

Devon tossed the head, and it landed in front of me with its milky eyes staring into mine. My jaw dropped, and Devon lifted the massive beast's body onto his shoulders. His footsteps sent up pockets of blue dust, but he ignored them as he stopped beside me. "Pick up the head. We got one final task to accomplish."

"Huh?"

"The hunt isn't over, Cain. Get up."

I looked down and tested my muscles. They moved, but I felt the protest screaming in my head. "I can barely move."

"The water will speed your recovery. Let's go."

Numbly, I forced myself to stand and stared at the stag head. The dead eyes gave me the creeps, but Devon left no room for arguments.

I gripped the top of the horns with hesitation, not wanting to let the thing touch my chest—not if I could help it.

Yep, this is cursed. I need gloves; this is crazy.

Devon showed no signs of struggling with the beast on his back. With my face scrunched in a scowl, I jogged after him, catching up to match his steps.

I had several questions, but I kept them to myself. My body ached, clearly drained of energy. If I collapsed and slept for a few days straight, I wouldn't be surprised.

* * *

In a clearing sat a rickety wooden cabin. It was a small dwelling, smaller than most of the houses in the village. There were no lights, but moonlight bathed the area.

Past the overgrown moss and shabby wood, faded paint and a simple design outlined the doorframe.

It probably looked cozy when it was first constructed.

We got within twenty yards, and Devon dropped the stag's corpse. It hit the ground with a thud, coating the grass in red. Then, an animalistic scream came from within the cabin.

"No! No! Defiler!"

The door rattled, and Devon unhooked his spear. "Come out. There's nowhere to run."

A powerful bang smacked into the door, followed by another screech. I slowly lowered the stag's head to the ground and moved behind Devon.

He glanced at me, and I shook my head. "This is all you. I'm all tapped out."

The door burst open, the hinges creaking. The house was pitch-black inside.

"Hunters..."

A single foot emerged from the darkness. It was slender, pale, and childlike. Next came a hand: long black nails—longer than my fingers—gouged the wood. Although the ring finger was missing, the hand and arm weren't deformed. They were small and human.

Devon nudged the stag with his foot, and the creature twitched. A guttural scream made me clamp my hands over my ears, and I watched in horror as it exited the cabin.

A little girl stepped into the light, exposing her cloth sack dress, ragged hair, and puffy eyes.

She looked to be around nine years old.

"Devon... Is that the puppet master?"

"Yes."

Oh.

Up until now, I had been ready to watch gleefully as we slayed monsters and saved the day—I wanted to get out of here and find a comfortable bed to nap in. But the puppet master's true form made me pause.

She wouldn't have been the first demon child I killed, but after so much talk of Lore and corruption... I needed to know what this monster truly was.

The girl's red hair covered her face, but she brushed it out of the way. Her eyes were bloodshot. Tears streamed into her mouth, revealing perfectly normal teeth.

That detail broke me even further—even though I knew it shouldn't have I had expected monster teeth sharpened like daggers. The Reds could shift their appearance too. But the more I thought about it, I didn't really know what they were either.

"Leave... my brother... alone!"

The girl charged, aiming her sharpened nails at Devon.

She didn't make it more than a few steps.

Devon hurtled toward her, stabbing her in the chest. Her body rocked back, and she clawed at his spear.

To my horror, she didn't die the moment her heart turned to mush.

"Hu-rgh... Hunter! Re-venge! Must... sto..."

Her hands pounded against the spear, but her fury waned, leaving her arms dangling limply by her side. Her legs failed next, and she slid to the ground, her hair covering her face in a curtain of red.

I just stared, unsure how to feel.

Devon sighed and raised his head to the sky. After a long silence, he turned and waited for me to look away from the girl's body. "In the future, there will be many times you'll face enemies who look like this. Not all prey will be terrifying monsters of the night that you can behead and feel good about. Sometimes, the monsters are humans who stumbled onto the wrong path—even little children who met a terrible fate."

"When she said kin... Her brother's the stag? How doe—" I shook my head. "Never mind. Is it over? Did we finish the hunt?"

He nodded.

Good.

I peeked into the cabin; the pitch-black darkness had receded.

The place had no furniture, save for a straw bed. In the corner, a small collection of shiny stones sat around a small threadbare doll.

Biting my lip, I turned around and stood beside the stag head. Devon gently picked up the girl's corpse.

I refused to look into her eyes.

He entered the building, placed the girl on the straw bed, and covered her with a blanket before returning to the fallen stag. With the same ease as before, he placed it next to the child.

I held the stag's head, expecting him to take it, but he closed the cabin door.

He stepped back to join me and raised his arm. *"Ek kalla heiðarloga."*

A fireball shot out of his hand, and the cabin became an inferno, lighting the night in a blaze. Smoke rose, and the breeze carried it away.

There weren't words to say, and I didn't want to say any if there were. In a way, I felt good to have silenced the enraged monster. Hopefully, in death, the siblings would know peace.

We stayed until the crackling wood turned to ash, and the winds carried it away. For a moment, I thought I saw the fire shift into a ghostly blue, but the roof collapsed and buried it under the rubble.

Devon pulled a blanket from his pack and wrapped the stag head tight. He tied it like a bindle onto his spear, and we carried on. If he felt annoyed by my limping, he didn't mention it.

We retraced our path, passing by the glowing pond. Several trees lay uprooted, while others bore deep scratch marks or had gaping chunks torn from their trunks. The farther we went, the worse the damage.

Once we neared where we split, I took note of three dead bodies. Two of the corpses were brown bears. One had its hide riddled with holes, its once beautiful pelt now a sticky mess of dried blood and dirt.

The other no longer had a head on its shoulders.

The third beast had large antlers bigger than the stag's. It looked like a hybrid between a deer and a moose. Its death was just as brutal as the others, one of its broken antlers shoved into its eye—penetrating through the base of its skull.

"Devon..." I swallowed. "H-How strong are you?"

He kept walking, answering without turning his head. "Not strong enough."

Chapter 22

Unveiling the Real Monsters

When we exited the forest, I hadn't noticed the light change; it felt like crossing over from nighttime to early morning. The sun peeked from the horizon.

"Wow. We were in there a lot longer than I thought," I said.

Devon shook his head. "Step back into the forest."

Okay?

I shuffled a few steps back and blinked. It was night again.

What?

I exited the forest, and the early morning sun lit the sky. Devon stood there with a smile, one of the first I had seen in ages.

"Right. Magical forest. Magical, creepy forest that's permanently nighttime. Who the hell would willingly set up a village around this? That's just asking to be eaten by a monster."

We moved toward the road. "You assume they had a choice in the matter."

"They're not being magically compelled to live here, are they?"

"No," he replied. "The royal family understands that places like these need people around them to keep the magic in check. And they have a higher chance of receiving wizards and sorcerers this way."

"Wait. Are you implying humans are like sponges, and them being here somehow absorbs mana or something? How does that work?"

"Yes and no. Most monsters and magical creatures stay away from people. Every beast learns to fear the mob. But yes, places like the forest are steeped in magic, and the ambient mana slowly spreads and is absorbed by the villagers."

"And that's a good thing?"

"Most humans lack the aptitude to control mana. So, it's absorbed and helps keep the body healthier; that's it. On the other hand, if a child grows in an environment with higher mana, the odds of them adapting to the mana is higher, which means a better chance for the kingdom to acquire someone who can wield that power."

That explanation ticked me off. To willingly put your people in harm's way to profit off them sounded too calculating and cold. But I couldn't think of an appropriate response. If the village kept the monsters from spreading, the kingdom would be safer unless I misunderstood everything Devon said.

"I'm not sure I agree with the policy, but I don't know enough to offer a solution."

"Good. It's not our place, either way. We hunt, we grow, we protect the pack and the Nexus. That is all. Anything else is secondary to that."

That doesn't sound fulfilling in the slightest.

The conversation died, and we made our way to the gate. The guard saluted. "Welcome back, Sirs Grimm. Was the hunt successful?"

Devon pointed to the sack hanging off his spear. "It was. Will Carter be expecting us?"

"Yes, sir." The guard pointed into town. "My companion set off to inform him of your return."

Devon nodded and entered the village.

Once we were out of earshot and alone on the village road, I dropped my smile. "Okay, what gives? I thought the people were afraid of us, which, frankly, I don't understand why we have such a negative reputation."

"We're monsters who hunt monsters. To think otherwise would be foolish."

"But he sounded happy? Respectful?"

"He was. Not everyone sees a monster and only feels fear. You didn't, after all."

I sighed. "Touché."

* * *

We arrived at Carter's house in relative peace. A couple of early risers were out and about, and Devon was right. Only one out of seven people waved hello. The rest kept their distance.

Carter stood outside his house with a guard in tow. His eyes narrowed on the cloth package behind Devon's back. "Greetings, Hunters. I take it your hunt went well?"

"Indeed."

The village leader wrung his hands and seemed antsy.

"Is something wrong?" I asked.

Carter clenched his fist before smiling. "No, nothing's wrong. But uh, would you happen to have any proof of the beast?"

He's so antsy. And the guard looks ready to run.

I expected Devon to drop the stag head on the ground and demand payment. It seemed the correct thing to do, but no—he reached into his vest pocket and pulled out a small threadbare doll.

Carter signaled for the guard to take it. The guard complied, fear and disgust in his eyes.

"I assume you recognize this," Devon said coldly.

"Ah... I do," Carter replied. He clenched his fist, his anxiety gone. His mouth was set into a hard line when he looked away from the doll. "This is, unfortunately, very familiar... Did the *monster* have a missing finger?"

"Yes, the ring finger."

Carter exhaled slowly and raised his chin while straightening his shoulders and back. He turned to the guard. "Signal the morning bell, please. After doing so, I'd like you to take a few men and apprehend Darren and his wife. Bring them to the square right away."

"Yes, sir!"

Nicholas, the guard, took off, leaving the three of us standing there. Devon looked bored again while Carter fumed underneath his stiff shoulders.

"Will you be staying for the trial, Sir Grimm?"

"We will. But we'll take our payment now," Devon replied.

"Right. Give me a moment."

Carter entered his house, leaving the door open.

I turned to Devon. "I'm assuming the people he mentioned are the parents. Will they be thrown in jail?"

"There will be a public trial. Grimms do not interfere with the town's justice, but you need to see what most of the worlds we protect are like. I get the feeling your world is radically different."

I didn't get a chance to respond since Carter returned a second later with a large sack and a small pouch. The sack looked heavy, considering his shaking arms.

"The silver price is inside the pouch, all twenty-six," Carter explained as he handed over the pouch first. After Devon counted the coins, he offered the larger sack. "Inside is smoked venison and fish. I included some jams, preserves, and fresher parcels of meat wrapped in wax paper. Is it satisfactory?"

I took a whiff. It smelled salty but delicious.

Devon tossed the sack to me. I shuffled to catch it and nearly dropped it.

"This'll do. The contract has officially ended."

Carter nodded. "Thank you. Now, let's get this over with. I do ask that you refrain from interfering. This is now village business, and we'll take care of it ourselves."

* * *

The village bells rang, piercing my eardrums and adding to the grim mood. Birds soared into the sky, their screeches filling the air with a cacophony of sound.

I doubt anyone could sleep through that.

When we arrived at the square, a large crowd had already formed, and they stood next to a stage. Two guards held their spears over a couple bound in rope. The woman sobbed, her tears splashing the pillory. The man looked on with dead eyes.

The crowd spotted us, which sparked a surge of whispers. They parted a path toward the stage, and Carter carried on while we stopped near the front. Villagers moved away, treating us like lepers.

This is getting old real quick.

Devon was unbothered as usual, so I stood alone in my grumpiness.

When Carter got on the platform, the woman turned to him. "Mr. Prelus, please! Let us go!"

The crowd's eyes glued to the stage like it was a drama meant for them.

Righteous fury filled Carter's eyes. "Viviene. Silence yourself, or I will have you gagged."

She choked back a sob while her lips quivered. Carter ignored her and cleared his throat. He scanned the villagers and nodded.

"Good. Enough people are here," he said. He then cleared his throat and nodded to the guard, who slammed the end of his weapon on the stage, creating a loud bang. When the crowd grew silent, he spoke. "Everyone, I'm sure you've seen or heard of the Grimms entering our village late last night."

Whispers started up again.

"Grimms? Where?"

Seriously? We're the only ones not dressed in drab shades of gray. How do you miss us standing ten feet to your left, lady?

"They entered the Mracker's pub. I was there."

"Did they have glowing eyes and fangs?"

"Shhh! They're right there; they can hear you."

The guard shouted, "Everyone be silent!"

The crowd complied.

Carter held out the little girl's doll. "We know hardship. We are a village near the outskirts. It is not uncommon to lose people and suffer tragedy amongst our numbers."

His words carried over the square, and stragglers who had only just arrived stopped in place.

"Last summer, Darren and his wife Viviene reported their children had a grave accident. All they found was a single finger from their little girl."

"We searched those woods!"

"Did they find them?"

"I knew it was suspicious!"

Viviene squirmed. "They died, I swear. The wolves got them! Darren, tell them!"

She bumped into her husband, but he ignored her. Her jaw hung open as Darren raised his head to the sky. Tears streamed down his face.

"I'm so sorry..." he whispered.

Viviene dropped to the ground, her face falling into despair.

The whole situation made me feel sick. These people were obviously monsters, but public displays like these felt... *savage.*

I don't like this.

"The Grimms have gone into the forest on our behalf. We have lost too many villagers to some unknown beast, and the nobles will be breathing down our necks. We needed to get rid of this monster."

More eyes tried to pierce my hood, but I did my best to ignore them. My cloak tightened around my shoulders, and I smirked.

Thanks, uh, buddy.

The cloak didn't respond, but something resonated from the fabric. The pressure lessened, providing a thin bastion against the scrutiny.

The woman on trial shook in fear and squirmed in her bindings.

"We all know the deep woods. The monsters that come from within have always struck fear into our hearts, and we know not to meddle in their woods. But these two have. The monster who slayed some of our best guards was none other than the daughter of Darren and Viviene."

Gasps and shouts erupted from the crowd, and a few spat on the ground. The whole room erupted in chaos at the reveal. Everything felt surreal, like this was something out of a movie script.

The guard banged his spear again and then twice. The crowd returned to audible whispers but nothing more.

"Darren, will you deny these claims?" Carter asked as he leaned down toward the father.

Darren closed his eyes and turned away. "No..."

Carter nodded and then moved to Viviene. "And you, Vi—"

"I claim innocence! It was all Darren's idea. I... I had to play along. Please! Let me go!"

"Shut up!" someone shouted.

"Monsters! They're monsters."

"Poor children."

I shifted closer to Devon and whispered, "Is it always like this? This is insanity."

His eye flickered over. "Yes. For one of their own to murder children... the crowd is reasonably angry. Carter is just making it easier for what comes next."

"Next?"

"For abandoning their children and for causing the indirect deaths of several villagers, I declare these two guilty. Their actions filled the ground with blood and fed the mother. If anyone objects to this declaration, speak up now."

No one did.

Carter motioned to the guards, who moved to stand directly behind the father and mother. "The penalty for such actions means death. Guards."

Wait! What?!

The guards stepped forward in sync. Their spears entered the prisoners' backs and exited their fronts. Blood coated the spearheads, and they were ripped out in one clean motion. The crowd roared, and the prisoners sank to the boards.

I took a step forward, but Devon gripped my shoulder, squeezing tight enough that I felt my bone creak.

"No. Let's go."

I tried to resist, but his hand was iron and refused to budge.

"Let's go, Cain. We're done."

Chapter 23

Haven Four

We traveled out of the village in silence. I felt angry, and I didn't know why. It just felt... wrong. No other words described it better.

I glared at Devon's back. He wasn't to blame. What would he have even done? The people were dead, and jumping on stage like a madman helped nobody.

Yet why was I so mad?

We were at the spot where we had arrived from the portal. Devon still hadn't said a word, and knowing him, he wouldn't.

He reached for something under his shirt and pulled out a necklace. The chain was a simple string, while the medallion between his fingers was made of shiny metal. I caught white lines on one side and black ones on the other.

He held up the necklace and then bit his lip hard enough to draw blood. He wiped a drop on his glove and then smeared it on the white line of the medallion.

Afterwards, he slipped the necklace back under his shirt. I raised an eyebrow, but I got my answer before I could ask—a single black root sprouted from the ground and then several more.

Like the archways from the portal spell, the roots grew into their familiar form, and rainbow lights appeared in its center. The portal back to the Warren had arrived, and Devon wasted no time in stepping through.

As before, my cloak shifted around my body, and I sank into its embrace. A moment later, my feet touched the Warren's stone flooring, and I searched for Devon only to see that he was nowhere to be found.

Neina sat in her chair, her book covering her face.

"Did he—"

"Yep. Took the Whisper Tunnels. He'll be back if you want to wait," Neina interrupted.

"Ah. Did he say where he was going?"

"Yes, but I suggest you wait or go somewhere on your own. He went to deliver the moon elk to someone you don't want to meet right now. Trust me."

"Okay."

This is so damn awkward.

"Any suggestions on what to do with this?" I asked as I held up the sack full of food.

Neina lowered her book. "That is for you. For the raw meat, grab a room with a cooking pot and a fireplace."

"Oh." I lowered the sack and sighed. "How did you know what's inside?"

Neina sighed and set her book down. Her legs shifted off the armrest, and she crossed them. She placed her chin in her hands and stared. "Did you really ask what to do with a mysterious sack expecting me to know the answer?"

"Well, I—"

"Devon needs to force your shift already. You're practically blind. Use your nose. I smelled the meat the moment you appeared."

"I'm sorry."

"Don't be. Stop being sorry for being a pup. Get over yourself. This place is as much your home as it is mine. You belong here, Cain."

That's a relief, even if I don't feel like I belong.

"Thanks. Last question, I swear."

"Hmm?"

"Do I have a room? I'm not really sure what the living situation is like."

"Take the Whisper Tunnels. Whisper 'Haven Four.' Just imagine a black stone door with a golden knocker."

"Don't I need a clearer image?"

She picked up her book.

Right, I did say it was the last question.

I smiled and walked toward the hidden wall. I stepped through and entered the Whisper Tunnel.

Welp, let's hope Neina isn't messing with me.

"Haven Four…" I whispered.

I imagined a big black door with a golden knocker. The image was rather plain, but Neina didn't provide other details. I just had to trust her.

My feet carried me into a jog down the tunnel. It seemed endless; within seconds, the wall behind me vanished. To stay focused, I kept whispering the location's name, reinforcing the door in my mind.

The journey didn't take long; it felt as smooth as breathing. One moment, there was an endless passage. The next, the tunnel ended at a tall, black door.

It was twice as wide as I was, and the knocker looked gigantic. Its metal shone in polished gold.

Glancing back the way I came, everything looked normal. With a shrug, I grabbed the gigantic knocker.

Bang! Bang! Bang!

The door swung open silently. Only the void greeted me, and I stepped back.

I debated going back and asking Neina if I found the right place but decided not to.

She might bite my head off if I keep disturbing her peace.

That thought got me to chuckle.

Damn, you're scared.

I was. The strange void left me with an uneasy feeling. However, tiredness won in the end; I wanted to take a nap more than I feared a magic doorway.

Bracing myself, I placed one foot inside. The darkness was absolute, but as I pulled it out a second later, my limb remained undamaged. Taking that as a good sign, I pushed through the void wall.

I expected another cave room, maybe even a small closet. But an open clearing in the middle of a forest never crossed my mind.

The trees were dark and rich, the bark smooth. The tall trunks continued high and fanned out into bushy canopies. Their leaves were a royal blue—almost like sapphires. Above the trees, a bright sun conquered the sky.

On ground level, a stone-lined campfire pit sat front and center. Patches of soft grass grew around it. A trickling stream flowed nearby.

I whistled softly. This wasn't exactly what I meant by needing a room, but this was so much better. It felt like camping but all to myself in what looked like a perfectly safe and peaceful forest.

After a quick walk by the stream, I found a pond that bubbled beautifully. Another pathway on the opposite end led to a deep cave. Clean blankets lined the floor.

At least I have a bed.

I returned to the fire pit and plopped my butt atop the grass. It felt as soft as it looked, and I relaxed. Feeling peace for the first time in ages, I placed my arms behind my head.

Except when I did, my limbs flared in pain. Inflamed red scabs crisscrossed up my arm. My hand was similarly swollen, but it looked more healed than the cuts.

I don't remember getting these... Did I just not notice?

My face felt hot and tender: more injuries I had forgotten about. As a last check, I pulled up my pant leg and found the area where the boar stabbed me in the same state.

That didn't seem right; none of the injuries should have been this healed. It all felt too fast—even with magic. Yet, here I sat, alive and breathing.

I should be in the emergency room... But here I am relaxing in a magical forest ... Just how strange can my life get?

I slowly exhaled and sank to the ground. For a moment, I feared I cursed myself and tempted fate. It wasn't entirely out of the realm of existence; luck existed as a stat, after all.

I stared at the leafy canopy, ignoring the deeper thoughts simmering beneath the surface. If I pushed them out of my mind, I could relax, and that's all I needed.

A single moment to spend as me—by myself.

A loud rumbling interrupted my silent contemplation, and I patted my stomach.

So much for sleeping. Does fish jerky taste good?

Chapter 24

Restful Days, Bright Flames

Earth and moss smell strong, mixed with sweet berries and sharp mint.
Old-young one lies. Teeth long, like mine, but sharper.

Don't trust the hand; smells wrong.

Star moves away, can't chase now.

Hand stays. Want to bite. Rip and tear! No—show teeth instead.

Must take deal.

I shot up and reached for my axe. I started to pull the metal from its sheath, but then my panic faded.

The sky looked as bright as when I entered.

I removed some grass from my skin but stopped when my finger met my cheek.

What the?

I patted my face with both hands, feeling smooth skin instead of the expected scabs. Then I stopped to look at my palms, which no longer hurt and appeared in perfect condition.

I rolled up my sleeve to reveal normal, healthy skin without a single scratch or claw mark.

Even my leg felt fine when I flexed it.

Just how long have I been sleeping?

I stood and brushed crumbs of jerky off my chest. My food sack lay nearby, noticeably emptier than before my nap.

My previous hunger returned, so I kept snacking on the jerky. At one point, I wasn't even sure if I chewed. I must've looked savage, but no one was around to judge.

It seems I passed out after eating.

Now I felt hungry again. I picked up the sack, noticing its lighter weight.

I bypassed the smaller packages of smoked meat and grabbed three thick cuts. Unraveling the wax paper, I found the meat surprisingly juicy and fresh despite its age.

I lacked the tools to cook.

That's a problem.

A quick search in the cave led me to a box I missed. It contained cups, plates, and cooking ware atop a small pile of wood—everything I needed.

I returned to the fire pit, arranged the logs, and set the largest pan on top.

Another check of the box revealed no firestarter or flint. The idea of cooking meat suddenly lost its appeal, but my growling stomach disagreed.

You just ate, you bastard!

I glared at the pile of wood. There was another way to start a fire.

I can heal now. A bit of temporary pain, and then you're done. You got this.

Ruining my body's hard work would be a shame. Another protest from my guts declared its lack of care.

Sighing, I closed my eyes. I flexed my fingers and began the visual exercise.

Grow the spark. Picture the flame and all the details surrounding it. Let the light push the dark away. Feel the heat between your fingers. Slowly, steadily, cup the flame and make it grow. Bathe in its radiance.

It went from a spark to a big inferno, and I let the imagery drop. My eyes opened, and I stuck out my tongue.

All right, let's try not to set ourselves on fire.

The flame came to life once more—a tiny, flickering light. I pictured adding just a small puff of air to fan the flames and stroke it bigger. It grew, and energy stirred in my chest.

No, not yet.

I dropped the image again and restarted. This time, I lessened the puff of air to a light whisper. The flames barely grew, but that was fine. I needed to learn to regulate the spell if I wanted to keep my hand in working condition.

Time meant nothing to me inside this unmoving world. Each time I opened my eyes, the sun stayed the same, and the trees stood motionless. All that motivated me was the same thing disturbing the peace by growling.

After another dozen tries, I felt good.

Okay, this is the one. You got this!

I started the incantation sequence. The spark grew steadily, and I kept it controlled, my will forcing the flames to grow at the pace I demanded. It felt a lot like meditation, and I cleared my head of all thoughts.

The first rune line appeared, and then more, one by one. The energy in my chest pulsed, ready to race out from the center. I let it, the magma sliding down my arm and pooling at the center of my palm.

Flames wavered, but nothing more.

I'm in control.

I finished the rune, and the flame became larger, but I filtered the energy fueling the fire. So far, my mind had complied and followed my will. The mana in my chest no longer battled me for dominance like before.

I breathed. In and out. Repeat.

"*Ek kalla heiðarloga,*" I said, the sound perfectly moderated in tone and volume.

I opened my eyes to see bright orange fire trailing up my fingers. I smiled as the flames built.

I kept still, not ready to declare the incantation a success.

When it didn't flare up or explode, I relaxed—but only a little. Slowly, I leaned closer to the stack of logs.

Release.

The flame shot out, and heat reached my face. I winced, ready to roll away, but the fire settled inside the wood. I curled my fingers into a fist, and the energy inside my chest retracted its tendril.

The wood blazed with a steady roar, creating the perfect campfire.

I only found my hand slightly damaged; the skin at the center had charred marks while the ring around it looked red.

Holy crap! I did it!

"Yes! Haha! I did it!"

My shout pierced the silence.

The hour I spent practicing felt so worth it, even if I wanted to tear into the raw meat right then and there.

I picked up the three slabs and placed them on the pan. It took a few seconds, but the meat started to sizzle and fill the air with its scent. I didn't have any salt or pepper, so I grabbed a few pieces of jerky and very aggressively rubbed them along the top.

My cloak pulsed and grew heavier on my shoulders. When the weight faded away, I rubbed the material, its silky surface nice and cool.

"Thanks. I don't think I've ever been this hungry before."

No reply.

I shrugged and cracked my neck. Hopefully, Devon could explain the whole magic cloak thing to me better. Whatever a soul cloak was, it felt like a part of me, and I wanted to know exactly what it could do.

With the meat cooking, I decided to fill the pitcher with water and wash my hands. I grabbed what I needed from the box and approached the pond. My eyes lingered on the white streaking my bangs before moving on and examining the poor state of my clothing. My hoodie sported several holes, and the black fabric had dried blood stains near my neck and arms.

I'll wash these after eating. Maybe Astra can help me fix this.

If anyone knew how to handle fine threads, it'd probably be her. Her control with her silver reminded me of a puppeteer controlling string.

Setting aside the sad state of my clothing, I washed the plates and jug, using the water and my fingers to scrub at the polished wood. If the lack of soap was destined to kill me, so be it.

Before leaving, I filled the pitcher to the top with cool water and carried everything back to camp. The salty smell caused another growl from my stomach, and I flipped the meat over.

The steaks had a nice golden brown, and the juices dripped off the sides.

Screw it. It's not even bloody, you're fine.

I held out for only a minute longer before I slid the hot steaks onto the plate.

I lifted one to my mouth and bit down. The salty juices filled my throat, and I groaned. There wasn't much flavor, but it tasted amazing.

I took large bites and chewed fast. The savage hunger came, and I relinquished control. I tore into the meat, blood running down my face as I used my sharpened canines to rip and tear.

The last piece of meat entered my stomach. I bit at nothing and growled. I reached for another, but forcefully calmed myself.

"This is insane. Who decided that werewolves needed to be this damn hungry?" I shouted.

My tongue lapped at the juice on my face, and I felt the urge to eat more claw its way back into the forefront of my mind. I sighed and fought against the desire.

I leaned back, letting my head hit the cushioned ground.

The bright blue of the leaves certainly looked pretty.

"You overcooked your meat, pup," said a deep, raspy voice behind me.

Chapter 25

A Grim Conversation

I leaped to my feet and turned around, grabbing my axe.

The voice belonged to a tall man wearing basic black clothing. He was barefoot and flexed his toes in the dirt. On his shoulders was a familiar red cloak—one beyond the definition of torn. Each strand threatened to lose its thread with every minor movement he made.

He raised an amused eyebrow and ran his fingers through his short hair. The snow-white locks stood out against his tanned skin. He had a handsome face, young—probably in his thirties—but his eyes spoke of an age beyond mortal scope.

Most of the Hunters had either amber or red eyes when they showed strong emotions. But the man before me had eyes that blazed like the sun. He blinked slowly, the gold in his irises shifting like living flames.

"You're welcome to try attacking me, pup. It wouldn't do much," he spoke again.

I eased my hand away from the axe. "Sorry. Things have been a little crazy lately. Sorta jumpy right now," I replied.

"Not uncommon when faced with life-or-death situations." He looked at the remaining steaks still steaming with heat. "Mind if I have one?"

"Oh, yeah, go right ahead."

He sat next to the fire on his own patch of grass. He stared at the flames, and for a moment, a blaze reflected in his pupils.

A smirk crossed his face as he grabbed one of the steaks. He used his bare hand and pinched the meat between his fingers.

He sniffed it before cocking his head and taking a bite. He chewed the meat slowly while I stood there awkwardly staring.

Is this his home? Did Neina send me into someone's room?

I decided to stop being a creep and sat back down. I tried my best not to stare and kept my head glued toward the fire, but it proved difficult. Eventually, he slid the whole steak into his mouth.

My jaw dropped at the sight. The meat wasn't small by any normal standards, and he had swallowed the whole thing. With an exaggerated gulp, the meat slid down his throat and disappeared deeper inside him.

His smirk dropped, and he glared at the remaining steak. "Way overcooked."

The hell it is!

The steaks were medium, pink in the middle. And somehow, I had a strong feeling that medium rare would still be overcooked.

"Sorry?"

He laughed, a deep bellow that filled the air.

This guy is starting to freak me out.

He smiled. "Sorry. It's been a while since I've had to interact with someone who doesn't know me. It's a nice change."

"Oh. Well, I'm glad I can help? My name's Cain."

I stuck my hand out, and he stared at it. My smile cracked a little, but I kept my arm extended. After six seconds too long, he clasped my wrist. It surprised me, but I grabbed his in return, and we shook.

"You may call me…" he paused. "Just call me Grim."

"Like Grimm the Grimm?"

"Sure, but my name has one 'm' instead of two."

Ain't no way that's your real name.

"Sure. Uh, am I intruding? Is this your room?"

Grim shook his head. "Not really. I do favor this room, though. What do you think?"

I scanned the surroundings; the place smelled nice, looked as bright as ever, and was peaceful. My eyes trailed the tree trunks and reached the swaying blue leaves.

Wait...

It wasn't my imagination; the leaves were moving as if a breeze gently rocked the branches. None of the expected noise reached my ears, and when I tried to listen, all I heard was the crackle of the fire.

More alert now, I scanned the room further but couldn't find anything different.

Except for the swaying leaves...

I glanced toward the room's new occupant. He watched the fire with unblinking eyes, his body posture relaxed. I didn't notice at first, but I realized he sat eerily still.

Despite the lack of movement, his cloak moved in an unfelt wind.

Who are you?

"Do you mind passing over the other steak? You can have half if you want."

Grim handed over the plate. "I'm good. Would you mind sharing some of the meat in the sack?"

I blinked. "Sure. Feel free."

His long canines poked out from beneath his lips. When he opened the sack, he sniffed again. After rummaging for a couple of seconds, he pulled out exactly what I expected.

Four wax paper-wrapped packages of meat plopped to the ground, and he set the sack aside. Without waiting, he slid a finger under the knot of strings; it snapped.

Butcher's twine fell. The red and raw flank sat in the middle of the paper, and he picked it up.

"*Skál*," he said before taking a massive bite.

Blood dripped down his chin. He took another bite, causing more juice to spill onto the dirt.

The sight looked rather monstrous, but at least he didn't wild out. Once he consumed the chunk, he grabbed another. This process was repeated until only brown paper and broken strings remained. Without asking, he poured the pitcher of water over his face. He sighed deeply and leaned back, his two arms supporting him.

"Delicious. They gave you good cuts—probably too afraid to insult a Grimm with something lower quality," he stated.

"Did that... taste good? Usually, I have seasoning to help flavor the meat."

"Hmm," he remarked. "I suppose to many it may not. What about you? Care to give it a go?"

"Ah, no thanks. Raw meat doesn't really agree with my stomach."

He tisked. "Pity."

He picked up a log and prodded the flames. The wood caved in and sent up a small torrent of ash and embers.

Minutes passed, and I started to feel awkward. I didn't know what to say. I always had a select group of friends that I kept very small for reasons like this. It was hard to feel awkward when you had an extrovert who loved the sound of their own voice.

Damn, Jory would have loved to be here.

The thoughts of my best friend hurt something deep inside, and I shook my head. Something about his face stung my brain.

Nope, not now. I'll deal with it later.

Something poked at my senses, and I felt a shift in the room. I looked to the trees and watched the leaves continue to sway, then back to the fire.

Aha! There!

The fire popped, and I caught the flames moving an inch. Barely perceptible, but after waiting for another sign, the movement repeated. A slight breeze blew, and when I stuck my hand out, it caressed my fingers.

I looked around, but I couldn't spot anything else. Grim never looked away from the flames, his golden eyes matching the intensity of the fire.

"Hey, mind if I ask a question?"

He didn't look away. "Ask."

"Who are you?"

"I told you; I'm Grim the Grimm."

"Okay. But like, who are you really?"

"Does my answer not satisfy your question?"

No, obviously not. I'm getting tired of all the mysteriousness.

"I'm sorry, but you have a claim to a magical forest room, and your eyes look like flames. Nobody has eyes like that... not like yours. It's like I'm staring at an ancient beast."

My words sounded stupid to my ears, but they were all true. The odds of this guy being some average Hunter were zero to none. And the longer I spent in the haven with him, the more inhuman he seemed.

He bellowed. His laugh roared through the trees, his broad smile revealing his sharpened canines in their full glory. As he continued, something pricked at my skin. Nothing physically assaulted me, but it was like his laugh carried a pressure that washed over me.

Almost like... Devon.

My cloak tightened, but a blur in my peripherals made me look up.

Staring from only inches away was Grim. His eyes felt like the sun, each swirl an explosion that drew me in. And the void in the center of it all? Complete and utter darkness.

I couldn't move. His eyes paralyzed me.

"Tell me, pup, do you really want to know who I am?"

Chapter 26

Awaken the Beast

"Well? Ask. I might answer," Grim taunted.

I didn't reply. I couldn't.

He turned his head, his eyes rotating with him. The sight made my head spin, pain pulsing across my skull. He stared, unblinking.

Slowly, he pulled back, and I regained my senses. My lungs sputtered, and I gulped for air.

Grim's lips twitched upwards before his mouth dipped into a frown. "Pity. I expected more spine. Perhaps I misjudged you."

Something about that statement made me furious. The energy in my chest stirred, riling up like an arching cat.

"I... I was taken by surprise. That's all," I declared.

His frown deepened. "Surprises are deadly for us Grimms. You learn to handle it or die."

The needle of discomfort poked deeper, and the lava in my chest churned.

"That's exactly what I have been doing. From one nightmare to another. It hasn't stopped."

A log in the fire pit fell apart, sending an eruption of ash into the sky. The flames blazed high, bathing the area in heat.

Grim took a step closer. "It never will."

His eyes threatened to freeze my limbs, but my cloak resisted.

"The nightmare never ends. It's a hunt—the endless hunt!"

His voice intensified. Again, the air vibrated with his words, and I felt the pinpricks against my skin.

The leaves above shimmied as a strong breeze made them dance erratically.

I stepped back but stopped, my feet glued in place. Something about this man demanded I respond.

"And I will. I'll handle it."

My eyes met his, and I stared defiantly. The lava bubbled, and I let out a growl through clenched teeth.

His smile reappeared.

"Good. You'll need the backbone."

What?

Blood splattered between us. Bright red droplets seeped into the black of his clothes. His arm extended toward me, but I didn't see where his hand stopped.

I looked at the hole in my chest.

Oh.

I expected pain, but strangely, I felt nothing—only little, teeny-tiny pokes.

My eyes rose to meet his again. "Wh—What?"

More blood left my body, and I grabbed his arm, but it wouldn't budge. My legs grew weak, and I collapsed, but he caught me by the waist. I fell forward.

His fingers wrapped around my ribcage, forcing me to stay where I was.

He pushed his face into mine. "Did you know that the real reason for forcing pups to transform has nothing to do with tapping into our bestial *nature?*"

"Wh—I don't..."

"Mmm. You'll see. Don't die now; I might crush your heart if you keep moving."

"Why are—"

Rainbow lights flickered at the bottom of my vision.

The lights intensified until I saw nothing else.

"Ah, there we go," Grim muttered; his words sounded far away.

Rainbow gave way to gold. Each dot and sparkle solidified together and vibrated at a rapid pace.

Then it stopped, and words appeared—the kind that branded my mind with their content.

[ALERT] LORE MATRIX INSTABILITY
ERROR% LORE STRAIN TAMPERING
ERROR% LORE STRAIN EROSION ERROR%

The words flickered. System notifications continued to scroll back into place, but another shift from Grim's hand forced the notifications away.

"So stubborn. Stop resisting."

But I'm not. I can't resist.

"Ahh. That boy really messed up the transfer."

[ALERT] Changes to Lore Strain have been made.
System Identification: Changes made by Dea.

Grim growled, a deep sound that shook my bones. "No, you don't. Don't make me break you. I have, and I will again if you try to reveal that information."

I didn't understand why he kept trying to speak to me. His words barely registered in my ears. The entire time he fiddled around with his hand in my chest, I kept losing my train of thought. All that remained was the slow creep of frost around my heart and the branding of the system text inside my mind.

[ALERT] Changes to the Lore Matrix accepted.

The words blipped away. Grim raised me up like a puppet. "Sorry, pup. I warned you. It never stops."

Please...

A heat hotter than I had ever felt melted the ice inside. The pool of magma at my core couldn't compare. Flames like the sun's surface torched my heart. It pumped, sending the burning blood through my veins. My senses homed in on the mechanism that kept me alive.

Pitch black became crystal clear, and my vision returned.

"Arggh! W-What's going on?!" I screamed.

Grim opened his mouth, revealing a blinding light shining deep within his throat. "Don't stop running. Whatever you do, the chase never ends."

He braced as he ripped his arm out of my ribcage. A searing pain crawled across my flesh, but my skin regenerated. Bones snapped back into place, and I fell to one knee.

I looked up, but there was no sight of Grim.

I tried to stand but crashed with a painful thud. My fingers traced the hole in my hoodie, and I pressed.

Whatever I did set off a chain reaction. My bones tingled amongst the molten lead traveling in my veins, my entire skeletal structure coming to life. It gave way to a flare-up of discomfort that made me want to thrash.

Then it started.

My spine *shifted*, and my back straightened. "Aaagh!"

Fireworks continued to explode along my spine. I fell forward, barely catching myself from kissing dirt. I pushed through the pain, vacuuming air. I raised my head and a piece of white ash fell onto my nose.

My eyes darted toward the fire. Through all the pain, I had forgotten about it, but it continued to blaze, extending into the trees.

A beautiful golden flame kissed the leaves. Fire met nature, and there was an explosion of purple light.

It was dazzling.

My jaw clenched, and my arms snapped to my sides. My skull landed on the ash-covered grass, and the blades tickled my eyelids.

Bone after bone, each one snapped and shifted. The tingles were icepicks, hole punches that forced the burning energy into each pore.

"Graaaggh!"

A primordial scream exited my vocal cords, and I pushed up with new arms. I raised myself higher off the ground than I thought possible. My eyes flitted to my arms where I expected to see a bleeding mess. Instead, thick, fur-covered muscles flexed and rippled. Long, curved claws sunk into the dirt.

My heart pumped a final time, and I shot to my feet.

Flames. Burning... Red... Heat!

A scent entered my nose. I dove, sprinting on all fours. It felt wrong, yet so *right*.

Old... Strong. Delicious meat... Must have!

I dodged the trees. They were in my way. I jumped and landed on one, sinking my claws into its bark. My arms swelled, and I pushed off, flying through the air until I reached the soil.

The scent grew stronger, but it kept shifting.

Stop running!

My prey didn't listen and moved further away—faster than I could catch up. That didn't sit well with me. I howled and cut a line diagonally through the trees.

I exhaled a hot steam that trailed behind me. Powerful muscles propelled me forward, the distance between me and my target shrinking every second.

I'll get you. Mine! Mine!

A sharp turn caused my tail to smash into the side of a tree, so I turned and swiped at its trunk. Chunks of wood shrapnel went flying, and my claws came away wet with sap. I wanted to claw at it again, but the scent called.

Continue the hunt! Follow the prey! There!

Ahead stood a stone wall. I stopped and sniffed. The trail led to this spot.

Where is it? Where's the prey?

I snapped at the air, and the unsatisfying clack of my teeth enraged me.

It's here. I know it! I smell it!

Yet nothing but stone and dirt met my eyes. I sniffed, following the trail of blood and warm meat. I kept pushing forward until my nose touched the wall—except it didn't, and my snout pushed through.

I raised a claw to the stone, only for it to similarly cross the illusion.

Lies!

The pads on my feet touched cold flooring instead of dirt. The narrow hallway extended far, but I knew what I wanted.

Find the prey.

I kept running, and even when my fur felt a disturbance run against it, I pushed past and moved on. The tunnel came to a fork, but I turned without hesitation. The smell only came from one direction.

I heard a sound—voices off in the distance. The distorted words bounced off the walls, but I couldn't understand them until I crept closer.

"Stop lying... Devon!"

"You... see him. What will... do?"

I inhaled, tasting the powerful blood on my tongue. It came with a hint of sweat and mint. Another scent mixed in, but I ignored it.

Not my prey.

My blood called to me, and the hunger inside demanded an answer. I let out a deep howl rumbling from my chest.

I rushed forward, taking in the sight of two humans on the other end of the tunnel. One had blonde hair—shorter than the other—and she stared with icy-blue eyes wide in surprise.

I ignored her.

"Devon!" she shouted.

My mentor turned, his eyes in a similar state. But he moved—quicker to react—stepping in front of the woman.

It didn't matter.

"Prey!" I roared as I splayed my claws in a final leap.

Chapter 27

FUR AND CLAWS

I readied my claws to sink into tender flesh, but instead, Devon grabbed my wrist and swung me into the wall. My back met stone, and I yelped.

The claws on my feet found purchase on his legs, and I kicked him away. He slid back as I fell to all fours and propelled off the wall.

Something grabbed my limbs, and I crashed to the floor, pulling the person behind me.

"Devon! What's happening?" the woman shouted.

Let go!

I twisted and knocked her away. I grabbed her side and heard something snap. She went flying, so I jumped to my target.

He rolled and kicked me in the ribs. It launched me back; something cracked inside my chest.

The pain didn't matter.

I swung at his boot and tore into the leather.

"Alice! Grab Astra. Now!" Devon yelled.

I rushed at him as he dodged my attempts to maul him.

Stay still!

My claws dug into his calf. In return, the same boot that broke a rib smashed into my nose. I reeled and let go. The stars in my eyes blinded my vision.

A vice-like grip snatched my wrist, wrenching it behind me. Desperation surged as I fought to break loose, but a swift jerk pinned both arms, driving them hard against my spine.

"Listen, pup. Release the transformation. Now!"

I slammed my head backwards. *Crunch*! My skull met something solid. Even as my vision blurred, I reveled in the action. Feeling his grip loosen, I turned to chomp on the first thing I could find, biting into his leg.

Blood gushed into my mouth, the delicious iron satiating the hunger inside my stomach. It felt warm. The energy in my core boiled the blood, ready to consume the liquid in its fire—but something changed.

It flared into an icy chill that sizzled inside my throat. The lava reacted to the liquid ice and exploded, making me hack up blood. I growled, swiping away at the small puddle.

A shadow flickered in my peripherals. My head snapped around, and a thick arm clotheslined my throat. I tried to snap at the free meat, but thick claws wrapped around the roof of my snout and yanked upwards. Devon reached my neck and crushed it, cutting off my airway.

I met glowing crimson eyes.

They didn't paralyze me the way Grim's had.

"Enough! Settle down!" he growled.

His long blond hair formed a wild mane, and his lower face projected into a snarling muzzle.

I shoved my hand into his mouth while he instinctively snapped down. Sharp teeth sank into my flesh, mangling the meat. Finger bones snapped, but I curled my claws around his fangs and yanked downwards. He resisted, but having leverage on his lower jaw meant I won in the power struggle. His large wolf head met mine, and I snapped at his neck.

A crushing weight on my chest kept me from biting down, holding me just an inch shy. I strained against it, but his leg held absolute.

Devon tensed his shoulders, releasing a deep howl that pushed itself past the flow of fire inside my veins. My bones rattled while my thoughts churned to a slow stream.

Two heavy paws pressed my arms to the floor. I tried to resist but could barely think as the howl commanded me to stop.

No... No!

My thoughts cleared, and I found the same red eyes glaring down.

"Astra, bind him."

"Fine, don't move."

I sucked in a deep breath. Devon reacted by crushing my arms. I ignored the break to hook my leg around his, causing him to tumble forward.

Now free, I raked my claws across his front. I didn't feel the same call to hunt prey, not like before. But a new feral urge slid into my mind.

You won't subdue me!

I pulled, trying to drag him closer, but the engine inside my chest sputtered. As a switch flipped, the strength that filled my limbs gave out, and I faltered. A large foot smashed into my face. My jaw creaked, and my skull hit the stone wall.

My body sank to the floor, and as I pushed up, silver chains snaked around me. They slid across my muscles and fur—up and down my limbs, across my chest, and around my neck. Another chain circled my mouth, the links snagging onto my fangs.

I squirmed, but the chains constricted. Arms and legs bound tight, and my jaw clamped shut. I toppled over. Desperately, I wriggled—trying to break free—but my fleeting strength left me floundering helplessly on the cold floor.

My eyes caught a gleam of movement, and I watched as the woman Devon called Alice raised a giant axe. She hoisted it high. Before she swung, Devon's hand settled on her shoulder, and she stopped.

"Stop. He's one of us," Devon said.

She frowned and looked at me with fury in her eyes. "I wasn't going to. Only if he moved."

Devon shook his head. "I don't care how angry you are; we don't need Astra to chain up two."

Her frown deepened, but she stayed silent. Before my eyes, Devon reverted back into his human form. Fur disappeared, and clothes took its place. As he changed, Astra approached me, her dress swaying with each step.

She leaned down and held out a closed fist. "See you when you're awake, Cain."

As she uncurled her fingers, she blew gently, sending a shimmery pink powder into the air. I flopped but couldn't escape the chains. I smelled something sweet. I inhaled deeply—the scent intoxicating—but my lips went numb.

I blinked, and Astra waved, the motion blurry. I closed my eyes and let the void take me.

* * *

My head rolled to the side. Both eyelids felt heavy, but I managed to crack open my right eye. Blue light filtered through the room, but a blurry spot in my vision made everything hard to see.

I raised my hand and winced as my arm ached with a dull pain. I rubbed my lids. They felt puffy.

What happened to me?

Then came the flood of memories; the smell of blood and meat hit my nose, and I recoiled. At the time, I felt drawn to it. Now that the frenzy didn't consume me, the only thing I felt was... *revulsion.*

More memories hammered in. Scenes of me running through an endless forest and to a wall and a tunnel smashed into the forefront of my mind.

Next came the sight of humans.

No. Not humans. Grimms. They were Grimms I recognized.

Next came the flashing sequence of attacking Devon and launching the girl, Alice, away. I winced as the memory played.

I'm pretty sure I heard the sound of one of her bones breaking.

After that, most of the following memories were fragments of thoughts and senses that flooded my mind. I gripped the side of my head and groaned. Devon did something, but I felt the beast inside me rage.

The memories slowed and stopped when I recalled silver chains tying my limbs together.

I groaned again and massaged my temples.

Ugh, something happened... Grim did something to me.

I tried to remember, but I only had fleeting memories of him before the transformation.

Something clinked, and a small puff of cool air brushed my cheek. I squinted at a cup hanging in front of my eyes. It steamed with a dark green liquid. Inside rested a metal spoon with small white chunks floating around it.

I looked up and met Astra's bright smile as she dangled the soup. "Take it. It'll help get rid of the aftereffects."

"Thanks," I said as I took the warm cup.

I stared at the unappetizing green liquid and chunks, but Astra tapped my forehead and motioned for me to drink. I sighed and scooped up a sip's worth into my mouth. The liquid felt grainy, but it tasted like vegetable broth. I sipped some more and hummed at the surprisingly hearty-tasting soup.

"Not as bad as it looks."

"Well, that's a little rude. I make potions; why couldn't I cook some good soup?" Astra asked, her words carrying little bite for how offended she acted.

In response, I made a visible show of slurping. She squinted but smiled and sat on the couch.

"*Ah.* That's good," I said. I lowered my cup into my lap. "Is... Devon okay?"

She patted me on the leg. "He's fine, don't worry. As feisty as you were, you're a few decades away from being able to take down someone like Devon."

Jeez, you didn't have to knock me down that much.

"And the girl. What abo—"

"Alice, no. Stop," Devon said from outside the wall.

We turned, and I shrunk back as the very angry-looking huntress stomped through the illusion the moment it dispersed. She approached, ignoring Astra as she stood. Devon trailed behind her.

"You!" she said as she pointed an accusatory finger.

Uh-oh!

She grabbed me by the collar.

"Look, I'm sor—"

She reared back her left arm and delivered a fierce hook, smashing into my cheek.

Chapter 28

Burning Explanation

My head rocked back, and I swiftly cupped my cheek. Alice released my collar, so I fell back onto the couch, sinking into the cushions.

"Uuggh! What the hell?"

I glared at her as I felt heat rise in my face. She looked at me with a satisfied smirk. "Now we're even."

"Wha—"

"You broke a rib."

My protest died on my tongue; it was a fair argument.

I lowered my head. "Ahh, yeah. Sorry."

She tsked and walked to the other side of the bar, staring menacingly at Devon.

Wait, why are you mad at him? Shouldn't she be mad at me?

Devon sighed. "Alice, keep yourself contained. If you insist on being here, keep silent while he explains things."

Her mouth tilted into a snarl before she busied herself with pouring a drink.

I was curious, but not that curious. Instead of examining her, I inspected the holes torn into Devon's pants.

My tongue brushed across my canines.

Did I do that?

I shook my head and met his eyes. "Are you okay?"

He gave me an annoyed stare. "I'm fine. But I need you to explain what happened. How did you induce the shift?"

It was subtle, but Alice stopped pretending to be interested in her water and stared directly at me. Her eyes were homed in on my face, and I didn't want to look over.

"Well, that's the thing. I didn't induce it. Not willingly, at least."

He squinted. "I see. Explain."

"After you disappeared, Neina directed me to a room called Haven Four."

I paused, waiting for Devon to react. Either he had remarkable control over his facial cues, or the room's name meant nothing suspicious.

"And?" he asked slowly.

"Well, I relaxed, napped, and cooked food." His eyebrows furrowed after I paused, so I continued, "And then I met another Grimm. But, uh, he was weird."

Astra leaned forward. "Who did you meet? Someone who can force a shift is dangerous."

"Right. It gets fuzzy, but I remember him being weird and asking for food. He called himself Grim—Grim the Grimm. And I remember how strange he looked. White hair and an extremely torn cloak. But his eyes— that I remember clearly. They burned like the sun."

A shudder overtook me. Those eyes weren't scary, but they looked otherworldly. Even if the interaction afterwards made my head roar with static, those eyes had seared themselves into my mind.

Astra and Devon shared an intense, silent stare-off.

"Is there something wrong?"

Ten long seconds passed, and Astra huffed. "Fine. I won't."

"Anyone want to explain what's happening?" I asked.

"No."

What?

Devon sighed. "Cain, I need you to make another promise. You can't share information on who you met."

A thump rang out. Alice raised her fist off the counter. "That's idiotic. Just tell us who he met. Stop hiding things, Devon."

"Alice, calm down. I want to share information as well, but we can't," Astra soothed.

"Tell me why. We're Grimms; why are we hiding things from each other?" Alice demanded.

The silver chains adorning Astra's dress clinked as they slowly writhed in the air like angry snakes. "We. Can't."

"What do... Oh, it's an Absolute."

I turned, looking between the three. "Anyone wanna fill me in? What's an Absolute?"

Alice's face scrunched. "An Absolute is a hard rule that we can't go against. It's built into our system. We swear to a couple of them during the rite."

Wait a second... Was Devon making me agree to one of these when I explained my system notifications?

"Devon. Did you make me swear to one of these?"

Devon sighed deeply. "No. Not an official one. I would if I could, but we can't make those rules."

Okay, that's good, then. Still, this whole thing feels awkward without knowing why it's so terrible for others to find out.

"I guess I promise then? It's not like I remember too much of what happened."

It really wasn't an issue. If whoever I met gave them such a problem, I could at least minimize the issue. Besides, I barely knew anyone else. I didn't have a lot of people clamoring to ask me questions.

I glanced at Astra, who was massaging the back of her neck while stretching. She flexed her fingers and limbered up.

"Does the Absolute do something to your body? You guys look tense."

Astra sighed. "Not if you're just talking about it, but this one in particular is... rough."

She clamped her mouth shut.

Okay... then.

I lifted my cup to finish the last of the soup, but then a sharp pain poked at my chest.

"Uurk! What the—"

"Cain?" Astra asked.

I clutched my chest, my hand sliding underneath my shirt. *Thump! Thump!* My skin felt boiling hot, and the pain increased.

The cup slipped from my fingers and dropped to the floor. Soup spilled across the stone as the cup rolled away. It came to a stop by Devon's boot.

Astra knelt beside me. I met her eyes, and she rested her hand on my forehead.

"He's burning up. Cain, what's happening? What does it feel like?"

"It..." I struggled to open my jaw. The pain intensified and spread up my neck. "Sharp... Heart attack."

Feels like... one.

Astra forced my head onto the armrest. Devon lifted my feet onto the cushions.

I shut my eyes but not before seeing the concerned look on Astra's face. *Ugh.*

The heat spread, going higher. I tried to think coherent thoughts, but the raging wave pressed at my mind. Astra said something; I could make out her voice, and then Devon replied, but I couldn't understand it.

Someone touched my chest, and I tried to squirm away as the sudden disturbance sent another rippling wave upwards. They grabbed my hand and pried it off.

Le—Let... go!

Two strong arms pushed back my shoulders while another two held mine to my side. I tried to struggle free, but then a blistering cold spiked my sternum.

The rush of ice hurt like pins and needles, and my heat retracted.

But only for a second.

The pain ramped up and pushed past my neck and up the back of my head. It reached my spine and then doubled back like a missile. Flames crawled deep into my chest and then continued into my bowels.

I tried to open my mouth, but the assault was too much. Fingers pressed into the sides of my skull and something heavy pushed on my stomach.

"Ca—"

I rolled to the side, but strong arms forced me back.

"Op—your ey—"

Fingers clawed at my face. I tried to shake them off, but they wouldn't let go. They pulled at my eyelids.

Stop!

The fire rose, and the heat peaked to where my skin felt like it was melting off my bones.

Crack!

Like a vacuum, the heat retracted. It pooled in my gut and then crawled up my chest until I felt it settle around my heart.

"Cain. Open your eyes."

I tried to flutter them open, but they felt heavy. "Mmmmng..."

"Don't move, okay?"

Freezing cold fingers pressed against my brows and pulled at my eyelids. One pushed down too hard, and I groaned again. They retracted but came back with a lighter touch.

My vision was blurry, but I saw the yellow irises of Astra's eyes. "Hey... How are you feeling?"

"Mmm. Not too great. What did you do to make the heat go away?"

She shook her head. "We tried to inject you with our mana, but whatever overtook your body destroyed it. If the energy has settled, it wasn't us."

"Oh. Okay."

I turned my head and looked at Alice. Her eyes widened, but she smirked.

"What's funny?" I asked.

Astra winced.

Why? What did I say?

Alice's look morphed into one of anger, rage, and then hurt. It reminded me of the way Garret looked at me.

What did I do?

She balled her hands into fists. For a second, she looked ready to punch me again. "Your eyes... They're glowing like you shifted."

Oh? That's not too bad. So why does she look mad?

"Alice. I'm sorry," Devon whispered.

She flinched, the anger turning into genuine pain as if she felt betrayed by his words.

Seriously, what's happening?

"Am I missing something? What's wrong with my eyes?" I demanded.

She glared back at me and then looked away. "Your eyes... They're the same as my brother's."

Chapter 29

CONFESSION SYSTEM

I didn't know what to say.

Sorry I got your brother killed? Oh, uh, hello, your brother gave me super-secret werewolf powers and then died in my lap?

I had to look away; I couldn't meet her eyes.

The movement caused Astra to slip, losing her grip on my eyelids.

"Hey, be careful," she admonished.

Why would you bring her here? I can't face this—not right now.

"Sit still for a second. Can you try to open your eyes slowly?" Astra said.

I tried to open them and found that they almost complied. The few tries exhausted me, so I shook my head. "Not yet... Still heavy."

"All right. Let's give it a moment."

Honestly, not seeing Alice's reaction was terrifying. She could be furious, shocked—anything—and I wouldn't know it. And to make it worse, I was stuck looking like an idiot.

The only good thing about not being able to open my eyes was the tiny bit of relaxation. My body felt exhausted, and it was becoming an all-too-frequent state of being.

"Devon," I grumbled.

"What? What's wrong?" he replied.

"Uh, everything. You're not going to force me on another hunt, are you?"

Silence.

I swear I'll bite him if he says yes.

"Devon?"

"Devon, answer the pup," Astra cut in.

He growled a low, non-threatening sound. "Fine, I'll answer. We will, but you deserve some rest first. For now, let's figure out what's going on."

Sounds reasonable enough.

"What did you do with the stag head? Why did we keep it but not the rest of the body? Don't tell me you mounted it."

I wouldn't be comfortable mounting something that used to be a child.

"He gave it to me. I help with alchemy around here, and moon elk horns are very useful," Astra said.

"Like brewing potions in some big iron cauldron?"

A light smack hit my upper arm, and I winced.

"We are not barbaric witches. We have alchemy equipment."

"Ooh, sorry."

"It's fine, just be careful. Witchcraft alchemy is very different from modern alchemy. And more than a few Grimms would be upset hearing that."

I decided to keep my mouth shut. Shuffling sounds made me curious, but my eyelids still wouldn't work. I passed the time by imagining all the cool things I could do with magic.

There has to be a lightning spell. I just know it.

My thoughts were interrupted by a chime ringing in my mind, and a buildup of liquid squeezed my heart.

"Cain? What's wrong?"

The squeeze happened twice more before another chime rang. *Ding!* My eyes shot open, and I blinked away the tears. "Oh, that smarts."

I continued blinking, and my eyesight finally came back to me. After running through a quick series of tests, I had full function of my eyes.

"Are my irises still weird?" I asked as I focused on Astra's face.

She shook her head. "They are green again. How are you feeling?"

I frowned and flexed my fingers.

Functional. My shoulders are a little stiff, but the endless hellfire is gone.

"I guess I'm all right?" I ventured.

She nodded slowly. "Okay, good. Try sitting up."

I complied. Alice stared from behind the bar. She neither smiled nor frowned, so I couldn't tell what was going through her head.

My gaze focused back on Astra, who made me follow her finger. "I'm fine, I swear."

"Good then. It looks like your body finally settled."

A small prismatic dot appeared in the corner of my vision, blinking once then swirling slowly.

A system notification? Huh.

I expanded the dot, allowing the colors to stretch across my vision. It turned into golden text lines hovering midair.

[ALERT] System functions have been restored to full capacity.

[ALERT] You have slain Corrupted Beasts x3, Sister Host V11.

Rolling Reward:

Applying Strain-Modifier: -25%...

[ALERT] Diverted to Lore Matrix...

Title Granted: [First Hunt]

Bonus Stats Gained: Luck +2

The screen blipped out of existence, leaving me staring confused at the air.

I brought up my status screen, and the plus sign to my stat was back.

Name: Cain Veldman

Title: Crimson Hunter

Level: 2

Stats

        STR: 13

        AGI: 13

        CON: 15

> **INT: 14**
> **WIS: 13**
> **LUK: 13 (+2)**

Skills

> **Summon Shadow Wolf**

Passives

> **Ember Soul**

So I'm luckier now? Why did it give me luck? I thought it was nearly impossible to get stats to that.

I willed the status screen away. "So, apparently, my system is back to being functional? I just got my notifications for the hunt. Is it always like this?"

"No," Devon said slowly. "What do you mean you just got your notification for the hunt?"

"Oh... Is this okay to share?"

Alice stared with suspicion at Devon while Astra scrutinized me closer.

He sighed. "It's fine. Just explain what you mean. You should have gotten it the moment we left the forest."

"Definitely did not get a notification until now. Are we being watched? The system is rating our every move and dishing out points?"

This world is more like a game than I thought. I guess I shouldn't be surprised.

Astra narrowed her eyes at Devon before turning to me. "The system is an intricate piece of magic older than we can possibly understand. It knows when you are on a hunt—it's our entire system's purpose. Beyond that, it's a mystery. Grimms have tried for ages to figure out how it calculates things, but there is not enough consistent data to tell us. If you killed ten monsters on one hunt, it might not reward the same thing to another Hunter who repeats the exact same mission."

She exhaled. "But we can usually place a pup's next level up within the first three to five hunts. You're a bit different since you're already level one."

A fist smacked the countertop, and we all turned to face Alice, who ignored the spilled water in front of her. "What do you mean he's already level one? He's only been on one hunt. How is that possible?"

An awkward silence filled the room. Alice glowered between the three of us until she settled on Devon. "I'm sick of you hiding things. Explain. I already heard about someone joining us without going through the rite. I didn't even know my brother could do that! If he could, why didn't he..." She gripped the edge of the counter. "Why didn't he turn me? Why is Cain so special?"

Screw you too!

I was ready to defend myself, but Astra squeezed my leg. A growl threatened to escape my throat, but I reined it in.

Fine! It's not like I don't understand why she's upset.

Devon stood up.

"Alice. You knew your brother best. He was always the kind of man who would help others. You know this." Devon's words were sharp, and he enunciated every word.

"Apparently not. It seems Elias liked to hide things from me. Things that you seemed to know about."

Devon shook his head. "No, I didn't. We all have secrets, and there are many that we can't tell anyone. You know this."

She growled. "He is... was my brother. Just because you like to lie doesn't mean he did. Or at least, that's what I thought."

Her voice dropped to a whisper. The whole scene made me feel uncomfortable. It felt private; it made the huntress too vulnerable for a stranger like me to see. And Devon looked awkward. For the first time, he looked unsure of himself.

It's like watching steel bend; I don't like it.

Something changed in Alice's expression. Her eyes hardened, but her chin raised.

"Fine. Keep the secrets, but I want something in return." Alice pointed in my direction. "I wanna go with you two on the next hunt."

Chapter 30

Argument Bystander

"Why? Adeline has been working with you for months now. She—"

"You plan on going on another hunt soon. I want in," Alice interjected.

Devon stood up straight. "You can ask Adeline to take you on one. You need time to—"

Alice slammed her fist again. "You're the one who keeps reminding people to prepare. That as Grimms, we should do whatever we can to stay alive."

"You don't need my guidance, pup."

The escalating argument halted, giving way to an intense staring contest. I glanced at Astra, silently mouthing a question. She responded with pursed lips and a subtle head shake.

I decided to throw back my hood and close my eyes. The cloak gave off a slight tingling sensation, and I chose to think of it as a happy reaction.

Pseudo-sentient cloak or not, I'm glad I got you on my side. Thank you for protecting me during the hunt.

I waited, but the cloak remained silent.

I sighed and tried to tune out the low sounds of snarling from the other side of the room.

The peace didn't last long.

"Fine," Devon spat.

"Really? That's it?"

Another low growl reverberated around the room. "If you're ill fit for the hunt, I'll leave you behind. Is that understood?"

"Yes."

"You follow my orders—whatever they are."

"Yes, unless they'll get me killed. You were the one who told me that a Grimm learns to listen to themselves first."

"I swear..." He groaned and dragged his hand down his face. "Fine, but you will respect me as an elder."

"Yes."

Devon cracked his neck and looked at me. "Rest for today. Go to the mess hall; you need food. Astra, can you stay with him?"

"I will," Astra replied.

He placed his hand on the far wall and disappeared without saying another word.

And now we're down to three.

"Hey, you," Alice called out.

"Yeah?" I asked.

She held out her wrist. I stared at it and then at her face. Her brows furrowed, but she kept her smile thin.

Huh.

I reached out tentatively, shaking her hand. She flinched yet didn't pull away. A look of confusion crossed her face. Releasing her hand, I glanced at Astra, who raised an amused eyebrow.

"What? What did I do wrong?"

"Ah, Cain. Is that how you shake in your world?"

Yeah?

I looked at Alice, but she had already retracted her arm.

"It's customary to grasp each other's wrists when you shake. Grabbing someone's hand is usually seen as dangerous and potentially a threat," Astra explained.

Right. I think they used to do that in the old days.

"Sorry, I'll remember next time."

"I'm going to go prepare my things," Alice replied.

She went to the room's exit wall. "*Afhjúpa.*"

The wall faded away, and the stone reappeared behind her.

I relaxed and slumped backwards. "Please don't tell me I'm about to get murdered in my sleep or something."

Astra chuckled. "No. Despite her rough edges, Alice wouldn't murder a fellow Grimm."

Images flashed in my mind of a large axe held to my face. I shivered as I remembered how the dim torchlight made the edge shine in the dark tunnels.

I'm not convinced that's true.

"So what now? What do I do?"

"Relax. You should relax. We should get you food soon, but we can spend a few clicks in here if you'd like."

I sat up and shook my head. "No, it's all right. I think I can feel the hunger coming." I hesitated but decided to ask anyway. "Can you tell me exactly what I did? I still only have the vaguest idea of what happened."

Astra's eyes looked sad, but I couldn't tell why. "I wasn't there for the initial encounter, but from what Devon told me, you came barreling down the hall in your shifted form. You sent Alice flying, broke her rib, and cracked another while you desperately tried to get at Devon. Honestly, you were stronger than you should have been for your first shift. Pups usually don't have the kind of strength you displayed."

"Wait, what do you mean? I have seen what Devon can do. That doesn't seem right."

She shrugged. "He held back. Otherwise, you'd be missing a few limbs, but you still struggled more than should have been possible. At least now we know *why*."

I waited, but she said nothing. Reluctant to press her further, I stood up and stretched. Only after I raised my arms did I realize just how bad my clothes were. I stared down at my hole-ridden hoodie.

"Hey, Astra..."

"Yes?"

"Why do I have my clothes on? Shouldn't they be in tatters somewhere?"

She burst out into deep laughter. She placed a finger on her lips and smiled. "You know, we used to have an old betting board. Every time we got asked that question, the person who guessed the correct amount of time before the next question would win. I may have to find it again; it's been a few years."

It seems like a perfectly valid question to me. What gives?

She guided me to the wall. "Sorry, we know of transformations that do just that. You transform your body, grow, and goodbye clothes. Thankfully, our strain doesn't have those issues."

I stopped behind her. "You're saying that our clothes... What? Poof away and come back when we're done?"

That's ridiculous.

"The real nitty-gritty details of the shift are a little confusing. But yes, our clothes poof and come back. I don't know why people want our clothes torn to shreds. I've heard that complaint from a few Hunters before, and I'll never understand it. I like my dresses too much for that."

She placed her hand on the wall, and it opened without a word. Together, we walked down the hallway.

When we got to the mess hall, several people were sitting down for food and conversation.

I suddenly didn't feel like dealing with the crowd, so I stopped in place.

Astra gracefully turned me around. "How about we have some food in the archives?"

"Yeah, that sounds great. Do you mind if we make a stop somewhere first?"

"Oh?" she asked. "Where would that be?"

"I think I want to revisit Haven Four."

* * *

I stared at the suspiciously clean fire pit. My cooking supplies sat inside the wooden box in the cave just like I first found them.

After scratching my head, I looked at the sack of dried food and my axe resting on the ground on one of the grass squares. Astra returned from the pond and joined me.

"I've checked, but I can't go further into the woods. A wall of trees blocks deeper access," she said.

"I swear I remember running through the forest. I'm sure of it. And this fire pit definitely had a fire in it," I replied.

"Don't worry, I believe you. Haven Four is one of the numbered rooms. I only have information in the archives for the six to ten. Numbers one to five are completely unknown to us."

My foot nudged the sack, but it didn't react.

Probably for the best.

If my food sack came to life, I'd start pinching myself. There was only so much of this fever dream I could handle.

I hoisted the sack over my shoulder after sliding my axe back into its sheath. To my relief, none of the jars of preserves broke during my absence. But suspiciously, all the fresh meat was gone.

"All right. I'm ready."

"Oh, we can discuss more about incantations if you like. With your aptitude for pyromancy, you might be able to shorten it soon," Astra replied as she hooked her arm in mine.

A chuckle escaped my lips. "Oh, yeah. About that."

Chapter 31

Taming the Hunger

When I woke up this time, it was to the sight of a nice and very empty room.

I breathed in deep and let my thoughts settle.

No dreams. I wonder why?

I half-expected some vague memory of running through forests, but my exhaustion must have been more extensive than I thought.

Yawning, I sat up and tugged at the itchy fabric around my neck. The shirt Astra had given me felt fine, except for the collar. The collar itched at my skin until I nearly tore it off after the first twenty minutes.

Hopefully, one of the worlds will have more modern clothing materials. I refuse to accept that scratchy underwear will be a permanent fixture in my life.

The mention of life triggered a flood of old memories—primarily feelings of happiness—surrounded by people. I understood what the sinking feeling in my chest meant. But those memories carried blank faces—faces I knew belonged to people I cared about.

It didn't occur to me before, but I couldn't recall anything from the last several years—snippets, maybe, but nothing more.

And yet, I don't remember enough to know if that's wrong or not.

The hollow sensation turned sharp, and my heartbeat sped up. I gripped the thin, stuffed mattress and slowly stood.

Ahh, let's go see if I can survive a trip to the mess hall this time.

I exited the room and took in the familiar hallway. The place felt like a maze, but I knew my way to the cafeteria; it was the one thing I made sure to remember before saying goodnight to Astra.

My footsteps echoed loudly, but no one was there to hear them. For how large the place felt, it appeared relatively empty.

When I crossed into the wider tunnel, the smell of meat hit my nose. It smelled amazing.

When I neared the entryway, the smell intensified, and I wiped drool from my chin. The realization stopped me, but it only slowed the struggle.

Wow, okay. Get a grip. It's just food.

My body didn't agree. My stomach felt decidedly empty, and it demanded to be filled.

I stepped into the room and ignored the groups of diners. My eyes homed in on the sizzling pork cutlets in a large pan. I took a few steps before a shiny piece of metal flashed before my face.

"Woah there, pup! Back, you beast!" a large bald man said as he shook his knife.

I came out of my stupor. "Sorry. I smelled the food." I cleared my throat. "Still getting the hang of this. I'm Cain."

He slowly retracted the knife. "So you're the new pup I've been warned about."

My mouth opened and then closed. "Volto? Devon mentioned you, I think."

"Aye. Now, back away from the meat, or I'll gut you. Give me a minute, and I'll have your plate ready."

I quickly did as he asked and found a seat nearby. The placement of the tables forced me to sit either far away or uncomfortably close to the other groups. The former felt like the best option for a quick eat and dip.

As I sat, I noticed a boy from the larger table watching me like a hawk. He looked vaguely familiar, but so did most faces.

I think he was at the speech.

He turned and left me alone when another boy pulled his attention back to their conversation.

With the scrutiny of the others evaded, I had a couple of minutes to myself. Every second, I smelled something new in the room. It threatened to overwhelm my senses, but the experience felt amazing.

And with every new intake of air, I wanted to get up and tackle Volto. Thankfully, my agony ended when a plate landed on my table, piled with a mound of food. Eggs, pork cutlets dripping with sauce, a few loaves of bread, and even a large bowl of porridge with bits of golden meat sticking out of the rich gravy. To finish off the meal, a large mug of apple juice clanged down on the wooden table set next to the plate.

"Eat up. Don't waste it. Don't make a mess," Volto ordered.

"Thank you."

He grunted and lumbered back to his station. With the menacing chef out of the way, I picked up one of the rolls and tore into it. It tasted sweet, glazed with honey. Each bite failed to satisfy my hunger, so I tried another.

I came close to growling at that final roll but caught myself and turned my attention to the eggs. I might've once thought about savoring each bite, but the food vanished off my plate almost as quickly as I could shovel it into my mouth.

My fingers twitched to grab another, but something hard smacked into the back of my head. The impact drew me out of my feasting frenzy, and I looked down to see a wooden cup roll across the floor.

Slowly, I raised my head, and my eyes met the disgruntled chef staring menacingly from across the room. "Eat. Slower."

I nodded and gently grabbed the cup off the ground. I pulled up my hood so the red fabric blocked the sight of the chef and speared a cutlet.

The juice ran down from the crust and tasted salty on my tongue. Every instinct told me to rip into the meat. Instead, I took a single bite. The flavor exploded across my tongue.

I can't ever be a vegetarian. This is way too good.

I still finished the cutlet within three bites, but that was progress. Progress I sorely needed. After a few almost desperate moments, I finished my meal without losing control and pushed the plate away.

Only the drink and a single roll remained, and I nursed the cup between my palms, sipping as I leaned back in my chair.

Sizzling pork filled my nostrils, but the scent didn't inspire the same rabid desire the way it had before.

I sighed. Before I could relax, a woman slid into the chair. Her long blonde hair crept out of her hood, and she stared at me with cold blue eyes.

"Alice? If you're here to punch me again, I might throw up on you," I said.

Her face contorted into a confused expression. "What? Why would I punch you?"

Does she have amnesia? What the heck?

"You know what? Never mind. Is there something you need?"

"Yes." Her face returned to being serious. "Let's fight."

I nearly spit out my drink. It went down the wrong pipe, causing a coughing fit. After smacking my chest, I sucked in a breath and stared at the crazy girl. "And why would you want to do that?"

"Because we are going on a hunt."

Ah yes, that explains everything—not!

"And how does that tie in with wanting to fight me?"

She scowled and looked as if I had grown three heads. "We have to rely on each other during a hunt. How could we if we don't know what each other can do?"

Her words came out quickly but in a recited manner. It sounded like a rote memory she had drilled into her head.

Yet, surely Devon would have mentioned this. Or he already knows what I can do, so it doesn't matter.

Alice sat upright with her shoulders squared. I ignored her, needing time to process the request.

Okay, let's try to avoid confrontation.

"Right, I'm sure that's a valid concern, but we'll have Devon with us. And if I'm being honest, I don't think he needs to worry or care about what either of us can do."

The frown lines on her face deepened. "Are you scared? We can heal, and we use training weapons for the fight. What's the issue?"

The issue is, I don't feel like trying to get into dangerous combat with you!

"I'm just not into being a masochist."

Her face scrunched up. "Maso-kist? What's that?"

I officially hate this conversation. Just let me eat in peace.

"Can we... just not right now? I just ate. I need to go see Astra anyways."

"Then I'll join you."

I groaned.

She can't be too bad. We're going to be working together. Let's just roll with it.

"Fine. Do you mind if I uh..." I held up my last remaining roll and waved it. "Did you already eat?"

"Yes. I'll wait for you to finish."

Okay...

I politely but quickly scarfed down the last roll and drained my cup. I brought the dishes up to Volto, and he cracked a smile.

"Over there, pup." As I went to the basin, I heard him mumbling. "Finally, someone who's civilized."

Grumbling chef aside, I headed for the archives. Alice joined me, her steps silent as she kept within an arm's length.

As we turned a corner, she grasped my wrist and placed a hand over my mouth. Before I could scream out in protest, she pushed me through the wall.

Chapter 32

STALKERS AND HOODIES

"What the hell?" I asked as she released her hold over my mouth. I spat out the taste of leather on my lips. "I'll swing if you try attacking me."

She ignored me. Her stance lowered, and she held up both hands as if ready to tackle someone.

"Hey! What are you doing?"

Ignored again, I moved to confront her. When I did, I found her face set in a deeply serious expression.

I didn't like the way she looked. Instinctively, my hand moved to my axe.

Ten seconds.

An arm pushed through the wall, entering the Whisper Tunnel. Like a viper, Alice lunged forward, grabbing the person by the collar. She swung him around and hooked her fingers under their belt.

He tried to shout, but she lifted him over her shoulder and slammed him into the ground.

Thud!

Alice gripped his throat while pinning down his arm. Her knee pressed on his chest, and she growled.

"Why are you following us, Proltus?" she demanded.

She loosened her grip enough for him to swallow audibly. He stared up with bewildered eyes. "Alice, what... are you doing?"

A quick knee brought toward his crotch made him panic.

"Answer. Now."

"All right, all right! I was passing through, and—"

"Cut the lies. You're terrible at it. Last chance, Proltus."

I stood on the sidelines feeling uncomfortable. While I felt bad for the Grimm, I disliked the idea of someone tailing me even more.

Eh, screw it. If he wants to play the creep, he deserves the consequences.

"Okay! Stop. I was curious about what you two were doing," he shouted before Alice pressed down.

"Stop lying."

"I... Fine. I was making sure he didn't do anything weird!"

I stepped forward. "Well, screw you too."

He rolled his head my way and glared. "Why should we trust someone like you? The other survivor is a broken mess. And yet you're here—suddenly one of us—acting like nothing's wrong! How is that anything but weird?!"

I readied myself to snap back a retort, but Alice's knee in Proltus' gut forced him to exhale.

Alice slid her hand under his chin, and he met her gaze.

"A Grimm is a Grimm. We don't question our own," she said.

A pup is pack; we are one.

For the first time in a while, the strange thoughts made themselves known, resonating with Alice's words. A frown crept onto my face due to the unexpected intrusion, but the sensation vanished just as quickly.

I shook my head as Alice backed away.

Proltus got up. "Grimm or not, watch him. Devon is hiding something, and it's not right."

I winced. Speaking of keeping secrets, I caught Alice's eyes flickering for a split second. She pressed her lips thin.

"I can take care of myself, Proltus. Don't follow us again."

He balled his hands into fists and stepped forward. I tensed.

Don't do it. I'll bite.

He took one last look in my direction before walking through the wall.

"If there's a problem, I can just head to archives alone," I offered.

"Did you hear nothing of what I said? I don't care about Proltus' paranoia. His fears are not my own," she responded.

"Yeah, sorry. How did you know he was coming?"

"The better question is, how did you not? I smelled him getting closer. You should have, too."

Right, super senses. Let me tell my nose to stop focusing on food for a second; I'm sure it'll comply.

I kept my thoughts to myself and gestured to the wall.

"Still coming with?"

"Yes."

This is going to be a long day.

* * *

"All right, tell me what you think. It took me a hot minute, but I convinced one of the kids to head into town and bring me back some cloth. It's not exactly the same material, but it's as close as I can get. Whatever fabric your original clothes are made from is of decent quality; maybe one of your hunts will take you into a kingdom proper, and you can buy material from there," Astra explained.

I pulled up the zipper of my hoodie, noting the absence of the previous holes. The new material matched the rest of the jacket flawlessly. With a big smile, I flashed Astra two thumbs-up. "Thank you! It's perfect; I barely notice the difference."

That's a lie; it's not as smooth. But hey, whatever. It's practically as good as new.

"And you fixed the pants, too. Awesome. Thanks, Astra."

"You should learn how to mend clothes yourself. Holes in your clothes are never fun, even if we get used to it."

I looked down at the many folds in her dress. "Really?"

Her eyes flashed yellow, and she smiled. "Oh yes. Woman or not, you don't stop to ask the ghouls to give you a second to cover up."

"Right. My bad. So, I have two questions because I never really stopped to think about it before. We got paid in money—silver coins to be exact—but there are different worlds and kingdoms; what use is the currency? And two, can we just leave whenever? Could I ask Neina to portal me somewhere?"

She raised an eyebrow. "Got somewhere you want to go? Are we that terrible?"

"What? No. I'm just curious where everybody is. I've seen so many rooms, but they're all empty."

"I'm only kidding," Astra teased. "In truth, most of us are out on hunts—long hunts. Rarely do we come back to the Warren between hunts. Some people prefer roaming a kingdom for a time. And nobody is keeping you here, not really. Pups are monitored, but once you're a Grimm, you're allowed to go wherever you want. But that means you do so without the guidance and protection of an older Hunter. And sometimes, it's not the monsters that come for you at night."

That's... rather dark. Okay. No complaining about being chaperoned. Got it.

"And the currency? How does it help us, and do we get paid? What if I wanted to buy something for myself?"

Astra gestured to Alice. "Want to explain? You guys could probably head into town before Devon takes you. It'd be good to explore and introduce him to the residents."

Alice looked annoyed at first, but her eyebrows settled, and she regarded me with curiosity. "Very well. We can visit the armory. Maro should be awake."

Astra giggled and settled into her chair, picking up a book.

"Have fun now! And remember, if Maro accuses you of anything, use Devon as an excuse."

Is it just me, or was there a hint of amusement in her voice?

We said our goodbyes to Astra and exited into the Whisper Tunnel.

"Why would she say that? Is there a problem with Maro? What am I walking into?" I asked.

"Hmm. Maro is... Well, Maro. Everybody learns not to touch things in the armory without logging it first. I don't know all the stories, but more than a few fights have been started because of improperly logged equipment. And in every one, Maro has never lost."

My eye twitched.

I'm throwing you under the bus immediately, Devon. I didn't see you log anything.

Despite my hesitation to see this terrifying figure, I followed along.

"Okay, what about money? Are we paid?"

"Yes, given an allowance every month. I don't think many have issues with currency. We're allowed to keep eighty percent of what we get from hunts. I think only Devon gives everything to Maro."

I quickly rubbed my face to shake away another twitch and kept going. Alice whispered the armory's name and broke into a jog down the tunnel. I matched her pace, and soon enough, we reached the end where the familiar blank stone wall greeted us.

We arrived at the top of the steps. It felt like, with all the hype to Maro's terror, I'd be better off facing another wolf.

"Stop stalling. Maro isn't a problem if you did nothing wrong," Alice called out as she descended.

I followed, albeit reluctantly, down into the jaws awaiting me. We walked into the armory, and Alice pushed past the rows of tables and stands. There was a clink of metal behind a mountain of crates.

"Maro? We've come to collect our stipend," Alice called out.

Something heavy smacked the floor, followed by another.

"You bloody vultures, is it so difficult to come say hello without wanting something?" a husky voice shouted from behind the boxes.

Wait a second...

The owner of the voice stepped into the torchlight.

She stood like a mountain of a woman, taller than Devon. Her muscles bulged as she stood, threatening to rip out of their confining shirt. Her fiery red hair bobbed behind her head in a tight ponytail. Her eyes met mine—a green brighter than my own.

Her eyes dipped to my waist, then widened. The calm look on her face morphed into one of rage.

"So you're the one who ransacked my armory." Her eyes flashed crimson. "Explain yourself."

Chapter 33

Maro's Armory

"Devon did it!" I exclaimed.

Oh no, I'm not going to die for you, Devon!

She stepped closer. "Really now? Are you sure?"

"Yes! I just followed along. I swear."

And just like that, the crimson faded from her eyes, and she smiled while patting my head. "Good pup. You're safe for now."

She walked back to the mountain of crates and ripped the lid off one of the larger ones. I was awestruck by how effortless she made it look, her muscles barely tightening as she tore through dozens of steel nails.

It probably is that easy for her. Wow, that's terrifying.

I ignored how the head pat from the giant of a woman made me feel.

"So I'm good? *We're* good?"

"Yes, you didn't lie. So you're good." She rifled through the crate's contents and shifted the packing hay. "Aha! Found you."

As she pulled out a large sack, it bulged at the seams, its contents threatening to burst out as she set it on a nearby table. From it, she retrieved a clay sphere roughly the size of my fist.

Considering the look she gave, she did not seem impressed.

"What's wrong?" Alice asked as she curiously peered at the sphere.

"There are hairline cracks on the explosive," Maro replied.

I took a step back. "Should we leave?"

Despite the revelation of a cracked bomb in her hand, Alice made no move to step further away. In fact, she leaned in closer to inspect the damage.

Maro set the clay sphere aside and pulled out another one, rotating it slowly. "Also cracked. Bah! Useless idiots. Who stores loaded clay with thin shells in a sack?"

With cautious steps, I moved forward to see what she was talking about. It was nearly impossible to see, but tiny spiderweb lines broke the smooth surface of the clay. The damage seemed superficial, but those cracks could perilously compromise the bombs.

The giantess grumbled and returned the spheres to the sack. She looked over with confusion. "Pup, why are you standing around like a meek kitten? It won't kill you."

You just said it was a bomb!

I put on a strained smile. "You called it a bomb. Those are pretty dangerous."

"You're a Grimm, boy. Act like it. It's not even a real bomb. At most, you might snap a finger or burn your hand a little. It's a chalk dumper. Used only for specific monsters."

"Huh. Okay."

Now that I understood what the *bomb* was about, I felt more at ease. Chalk bombs? Intriguing. I racked my brain but couldn't come up with a single monster that would meet its end via a chalk explosion.

Speaking of which, I never asked an important question about the whole being-a-werewolf thing.

"Hey, potentially dumb question, but I never thought about it before. Are we weak to silver? Astra uses silver chains, so I didn't think much of it, but back in my world, that was the legend of werewolves—a weakness to silver."

Both Alice and Maro sneered. Their reaction made me shy away.

Maro sighed. "I'll forgive you because you're new. But we don't like to joke about silver being our weakness here."

"Oh…" I said carefully. "Why's that?"

"Because that rumor spread a century ago led to Grimms being ambushed with silver weapons. And while we would normally embrace the false assumption, it became problematic when they kept trying to associate us with the cursed werewolves who are weak to silver. A few kingdoms tried to kill any Grimm on sight. And you can guess why that's a problem."

"Yeah, I can. What did we do as retaliation?"

Maro's face turned dark. "Two of the kingdoms no longer exist, and another is now an abandoned continent. The monsters that infest the land hold dominion over it, and no human has set foot on its shores."

Attempting move on, I asked, "So there are other werewolves? Do we treat them like other monsters?"

Her thumb wavered up and down. "Depends. Very few manage to get enough control over their curse to be around other humans. Most werewolves we meet are rabid and need to be put down. They've long lost the ability to shift back into human form—if they ever could in the first place. Thankfully, our Lore Strain is specialized to prevent that."

Alice cleared her throat. "So, we're heading to town. I'd like to collect my stipend. Cain, too."

"Right," Maro grunted. We followed her, and she tugged a black metal chest out of its hidey-hole and plopped it on the sturdy table with a loud crack.

"Standard stipend for Hunters is around twelve silver. It's neither a lot nor a little. Prices in the town are fair, and most shopkeepers will give you a discount, so don't worry about it."

Her meaty finger pushed into the keyhole, and she rotated it to the right. A resounding click echoed as the lid sprang open.

I glanced at Alice, but she looked as stoic as usual.

Figures. She must not think much of a finger key. All things considered, it's hardly the weirdest thing I've seen.

"The usual?" Maro asked while grabbing coins.

"Yes, please," Alice replied.

She accepted a stack of eleven silver coins and ten thinner copper ones.

"What's the currency? Like, what does each denomination represent?" I asked as Alice stored her money in a hidden pouch tucked behind her belt.

"You should probably get the same thing. It's better to have copper for smaller purchases."

A sack of coins hit me in the chest, and I grabbed it before it fell to the floor.

Maro closed the chest. "I agree. Currency is tricky with there being multiple worlds. It's generally the same value, but there are a few variations. Don't put too much thought into it. Don't pay more than a few coppers for drinks or food. And don't feel bad about spending silver for higher-quality items."

I tucked the pouch into my belt satchel.

I should look into getting a hidden pocket sewn in—might need those sewing lessons sooner than I thought.

"Hey, am I able to get a sewing kit?"

Maro held up a finger and opened a different crate not too far away. She came back with a small bundle of rolled-up leather. "Here you go. I'm glad you're learning. Too many pups try to forgo the skill. Idiots. And they usually suffer for it until they stop being stubborn."

I quickly unrolled the bundle and saw several needles and small metal tools. Inside the bottom of the roll, a few spools of black thread were tucked into a pocket.

Full kit, nice. Surely, it can't be too hard to sew something.

It fit into my satchel, but it took up a lot of room.

I'm starting to understand why we traveled light.

"If that's all, then scram. I got to reorganize since a certain someone ransacked my stuff," Maro said icily.

She's totally not staring at me. No, not at all.

We bid our goodbyes and entered the same wall Devon used to lead us to Neina.

I glanced at Alice. "Okay, first question. Is she human? And second, why didn't we come through here to get to the armory? Would have saved us the trip down the stairs."

Alice shrugged. "She's human, as far as we know. From the Third World. Her village was known for its size. And the armory has enchantments to protect it. If you had tried to break in without going through the main entrance, an alarm would have gone off."

"Huh, thanks."

"Why are you thanking me for basic information? Come on, let's go."

The wall to the armory disappeared behind us. How long we ran, I couldn't be sure. At one point, it felt like I restarted my count halfway through.

"I'll never get used to that," I complained as we came to a stop at a dead end.

"Few do. Some Hunters actively avoid using the Whisper Tunnels," she replied.

"That seems shortsighted."

"Very. But it's not my decision; it's theirs."

When we pushed through the wall and exited out the other side, I found myself staring at a smaller room with a massive stone door.

Alice walked up, and the stone shifted. Daylight slipped through the opening, and I had to cover my eyes as the light threatened to overwhelm my senses.

"You coming or not?"

I squinted and moved further into the light.

Somehow, I expected something amazing and magical—not... this.

Chapter 34

Trip to Town

We were in a forest.

Why would I ever think otherwise?

Alice caught my disappointed look. "What's wrong?"

"Oh, nothing... It's just I expected something cool—not, you know, more trees."

She shook her head and walked deeper into the forest. I followed, stowing away my disappointment. Nothing I'd seen so far suggested anything magically awesome, not the kind that would make my eyebrows recede into my hairline.

For all that I knew about Grimms—and it wasn't much—I expected to find we lived on some mysterious island shrouded in mist.

Yet here we were, hiking through a typical forest.

I kept my sigh internal. The trees were dense, but there was enough space for us to walk without having to squeeze together. Strangely, I noticed the ground curve into a decline as we moved.

"How far are we going?" I called out.

"A few more minutes. Just wait."

"Okay."

As we continued, the forest grew denser. There was a final wall of foliage so thick it made it impossible to see the other side.

Alice smiled. "Come on. It's through here."

She didn't wait for my reply and rushed through the greenery, parting the flora.

Why does nobody like to explain things first? It's not that hard.

I walked at a slower pace. Branches tried to scrape my arms, but my cloak rippled and glided through.

Thanks, buddy.

I pulled apart the vines and parted the darkness. With slow movements, I crept closer to Alice to stand beside her. Together, we looked down the steep cliff between the mountains.

Below us, along the shore, sat a medieval town out of a storybook. Stone buildings stood tall, built into the rugged slopes. Ornate friezes ran like ribbons beneath balconies and dormers. Chimney smoke wafted from gable roofs, and the coastal breeze carried it into the sky.

A beautiful fountain stood in the town square. Water bubbled in the basin and shot as high as the tallest tower while people—young and old— basked in its soothing mist.

Boats sailed by the eastern coast, and the waves bobbed with the calm tide. I inhaled deeply and smelled the salt.

For all the gloom and mystery I'd seen in the last few days, this place looked cozy. Peaceful, despite hosting a mountain full of werewolves.

"It's breathtaking," I whispered.

"I used to come here every day before I became a Grimm. Eli showed me this spot, and we'd sit here for hours," Alice said.

The confession stung, and my stomach sank. I... didn't know what to say.

I cleared my throat. "He sounds like an amazing big brother. I'm sorry."

Her leather gloves crinkled as she balled her hands into fists. "I... I don't blame you. I'm livid, angry, and want to punch something, but it's not you. I need you to know that."

I... yeah.

I nodded. Her fists relaxed, but just enough that the leather stopped creaking. "Come on, let's go."

The trip down the mountain was awkward. I kept silent, and so did she. Thankfully, the journey itself was short. The forest lacked roads or paths, but Alice guided us to an unofficial one with wider spacing between the trees. It cut straight to the edge of the town, saving us a lot of time spent navigating the terrain.

As we arrived, we saw there was a lack of walls or guards. The lax security surprised me. A few people spotted us approaching, but they waved with bright smiles and then returned to their conversations.

"Okay, this is weird. Weirder than the last village. Those two smiled and waved."

"Not everyone hates Grimms. Some of the folks living here are family members of other Hunters," Alice replied.

"Fair, but everything looks so nice for once. No snarling, growls, mean looks... Literally, it's a peaceful atmosphere. I think I'm feeling whiplash."

"Whiplash?"

I shook my head. "Never mind, uh, is that person approaching us?"

"Yes." Alice walked ahead and embraced the small woman dressed in a white blouse. "Hello, Maggie. It's nice to see you."

"And it's nice to see you, too!" Maggie said as she rested her chin on Alice's shoulder. "I heard the news, Firebrand. I'm so sorry."

Maggie squeezed tighter and rubbed at Alice's back. Sad eyes met mine. Maggie's gaze roamed up and down my body before she lifted her head and held Alice at arm's length.

"Is there anything I can do for you? I know you're as sturdy as steel, but that doesn't mean you need to stay strong right now. I'm here for you— whatever you need, okay?"

"Thank you, Mags. I'm fine. I'll handle it as I always do. I'm a Grimm, after all."

"And a fine one you'll continue to be. Now, enough of that. How about you introduce me to your friend over there? I don't think I've seen him in town before."

Maggie hooked her arm into Alice's and dragged the huntress along. She came to a stop within polite distance and looked at Alice expectantly.

"He's our newest member, joined only a few days ago. Cain, this is Maggie: an amazing woman who has watched over me since I came to this place. And Mags, this is Cain."

I held out my hand. "Pleasure to meet you."

Maggie unhooked her arm and grasped my wrist while forming an 'O' with her mouth. "My, how formal."

She stopped shaking my hand and plastered on a dazzling smile. "Well, I wish you safety on your hunts, Sir Grimm."

She's nice. Overly so. I feel like an ass for feeling awkward about this.

"Thank you."

Maggie turned to Alice. "So, what brings you to town? Are you looking for something in particular?"

Alice shook her head. "Not for myself, but I wanted to try some sweets. I know with the fall festival coming soon, there are bound to be some pastries."

"Oh, you and your sweet tooth. You didn't hear this from me, but Balen just got a fresh shipment of squash he's making into his famous sweet pies. Maybe if you go bat an eyelash or two, he'll cook something special for you," Maggie whispered conspiratorially.

"Mags. No," Alice said firmly.

"Don't be tense. You know he has a soft spot for you."

Maggie was like a whirlwind and swept Alice away further into town, chatting her head off.

I just stood and watched. With my guide lost to the wind, I looked around awkwardly as passersby kept waving hello.

So that just happened. Right. Okay, town exploration time.

I popped up my hood and felt a small boop along my arms.

The cloak made me feel safer, and I relied on that while smiling back at townsfolk. Nobody questioned my axe or bright red apparel.

My feet took me down the road. I had no destination in mind and didn't feel like stopping a random passerby for directions. Eventually, my nose picked up a delightful scent.

Stalls lined the market streets, each one manned by a person hawking wares. Each had signs, and I could read all but one. The last sign had handwriting so awful it took me over a minute of staring to figure out it spelled 'Body Scentorizer.'

Based on the fact that it stood by its lonesome, a few dozen feet from anyone else, the sprays must have been strong.

My focus remained on the delightful scent.

Must have!

I stopped.

That was a strong reaction; the thoughts spilled into the forefront of my mind with the grace of a charging bull. It smelled savory and sweet. The aroma was indescribable yet enticing.

That was enough for me.

I acknowledged a beautiful lady selling hand-painted pottery before I took another turn between a row of houses.

The scent nearly blinded my other senses to the point where I tasted it on my tongue.

Want!

Sliding sideways to make it through the end, I stumbled upon a cart overflowing with peculiar trinkets and baubles. Glistening crystals on vibrant ribbons sat in stockpiles across the counter while bundles of dried herbs dangled atop.

Behind the counter, an old woman with wrinkly skin slowly ground something with a mortar and pestle. The rusty orange-red paste caught the sunlight and reflected an almost metallic sheen.

The old lady looked up, her eyes pure black. "So, a new pup has come to visit Old Hildegrim, hmm? Have you come to trade, dearest Cain?"

Chapter 35

Do Granny a Favor

"**N**o."

She blinked slowly, mouth agape. Then she cackled like a wicked witch. Her fragile frame wheezed and coughed, but she kept her maddening cackle going until she breathed deep.

Her arms clutched her staff, clinging desperately as her body struggled to stand. She grinned a gap-toothed smile. "My, my, out of all the youths to come to my cart, you are by far the boldest! What a delight."

Never before had my warning signals for a crazy witch flared so drastically. Every detail about her practically oozed, 'I'm a witch!' At any moment, I was either ready to run and find Alice or throw myself into a desperate bid before I got cursed with a nasty hex.

Yeah, no. I like myself too much to want to be turned into a frog or lose all my teeth.

"I'm sorry, Ms. Hildegrim. I didn't mean to disturb you. I'll be on my way," I said slowly.

The old bat held up a gnarled hand. "Wait! Don't leave so soon, pup."

Nope!

I leaned into a light bow and took a step back. "You have a great day, ma'am."

Her voice carried on the wind and shouted into my ears with force. "Calm down, pup! I will not hurt you."

A growl rumbled in my chest, but my cloak pulsed. It didn't restrict around my shoulders; it merely alerted me to its presence. The safety of it was enough for me to stop.

"I have zero reason to believe that."

She leaned forward as her bony fingers grabbed the edge of her cart. "I'm in your territory, pup. To hurt one of your own here would be the height of folly."

Not pack!

The voice was right; she wasn't pack. Her calling me pup poked at my sides and brought the warm energy inside my chest to a boil.

"Stop calling me pup."

Her eyes twinkled, and she smacked open her lips before settling on a crooked grin. "You're right. My apologies, Cain."

A snarl escaped my throat. "How do you know my name?"

The cloying scent of cloves mixed with oranges filled the air, bringing a sharp contrast to the geriatric woman in front of me.

Now that I wasn't about to bolt, she eased her grip on the counter and stood up straight—as straight as she could with her hunched back. "I heard your name on the wind. When you came into town, you introduced yourself to someone."

That sounds like a lie, but I have no way to verify it.

I relaxed, but only a little. "What do you want? I don't have anything to trade."

"Oh, but you do, dear boy. You certainly do."

"Listen, whatever it is, I'm good. And I should go."

"Stop your cowering. I said I wouldn't hurt you. Sit. Hear out my offer."

Her thin white hair escaped the confines of her hood. She brushed it aside and ran her hands across the assortment of crystals. "How about this: you hear me out, and I'll give you a trinket. You don't even have to agree to anything yet."

I don't feel like getting cursed, lady.

Her eyebrow raised. "How about I swear to it? Hmmm, would that satisfy your paranoia?"

She didn't wait for an answer before she looked to the sky, the sunlight draping itself across her weathered face. "Oh system, by the rules that bind and the powers that be, I solemnly vow not to strike against the one before me during our discourse. Let my intentions remain true and unswayed, pledging harm only if betrayed or provoked. Let this oath stand as testament to my words."

Accepted. Safe. Oathbound.

Her arms dropped to her side, but her staff remained standing. The sickly-sweet scent intensified, and I covered my nose. This time, my cloak did react, and it stretched around me. I looked around, but it did not physically change. Yet, I knew it provided a shell of unseen energy against the wave of pressure that emitted from her staff.

The noise of the bustling town behind me fell away until only a low buzz zipped between my ears. I couldn't see it, but something poked at my chest. It bounced off the shell and squirmed. Another poke and prod followed every shift in position.

The old lady snapped her head in my direction and opened her mouth in rage.

Her mouth was black as tar.

I shifted my hand to my axe, but she bent forward in a position that threatened to break her spine.

She clawed at the staff until she found purchase on a burled knot. She stood up and breathed ragged breaths.

She narrowed her eyes. "An astounding cloak. You don't know how lucky you are."

Her tone lacked the politeness from before.

I slipped my hand under the beard of my axe. She wasn't human; every instinct inside me screamed that fact. "Did you just try to attack me? What was that? What did you do?!" I demanded.

Her staff smacked into the wooden bed of the cart. "I already swore; you felt it. Even a stripling as fresh as you could feel the promise made to the system."

She was right. The energy in the air remained, but I felt it centered around the old woman. It felt heavy, in the metaphysical sense—like chains that weighed above her.

I moved my hand away from my axe, but I kept it near my belt just in case.

"Tell me what you want already."

She waved me off. "Yes, yes. Give me a moment."

Her eyes flickered to the sky before leaning her staff against the counter. She placed both hands behind her back. In slow movements, she stretched until something popped.

"Aaahh. Much better." She coughed up sticky phlegm, which she spat out before bringing her staff close to her chest. "Very well. My favor is simple."

"Go on," I said.

"On the eve of the solstice, I only ask that if you see me, you protect me."

That's way too vague, Grandma.

"Hard pass."

She blinked slowly. "Why not? I do not ask much."

I crossed my arms. "Find someone else. I'm nowhere near equipped to protect you."

"Even if I offer up important knowledge? The kind of information that would make you reconsider everything you know?" she asked smugly.

I blinked. "No. I don't know what you think you know about me, but I have zero interest in that."

A purplish tongue slipped between her lips before receding back inside the abyss she called a mouth. "Even if I promised that the information is something you would want to know? Desperately so?"

I turned to walk away.

"Even if the information is important to the girl you came with? Even if Alice would kill for this knowledge?" Hildegrim teased.

I hesitated.

What kind of devil's bargain is this?

"I..." I shook my head. "No, thanks. Not for something that vague."

To my surprise, Hildegrim didn't complain. Instead, she smiled and tapped her staff three times. The movement rocked the cart and sent the trinkets jingling. Melodic clinks filled the air, and she gestured to her wares.

"Very well, Cain. I won't push, but know I may approach you to reconsider." She waved her hand to the dangling items. "Now, as I promised, pick something."

"Why? I didn't agree to anything."

"I keep my word, boy. I promised you an item even if you did not accept my deal. Now pick one."

Colorful charms and trinkets bobbed on hooks. The sunlight had shifted from behind the cloud cover and shone directly on some of the prettier jewelry, painting the nearby ground with a rainbow.

I couldn't help but ask.

"And these things aren't cursed, are they?"

A weary sigh left Hildegrim. "It's part of the deal that I do no harm. Since we are still conversing, willingly giving you such an item would constitute harm."

I don't fully trust that, but the weird thoughts in my head aren't yelling at me to be careful.

As I approached, Hildegrim remained still, only her eyes shifting to track my actions. I ignored the scrutiny as best as I could.

I didn't know what to look for. Some items were pretty and intricate; others were dull and barely more than a burnt stick tied to some gray string.

I think that's a rabbit's foot. Do they usually have six toes?

There wasn't anything for me to go off. I closed my eyes and counted for three seconds before opening them. They landed on something red, and I pointed to the necklace sitting on a black pillow.

"I'll take that one then."

"Hmm. Interesting."

And that makes me regret everything.

She grabbed the necklace and tossed it over. "Remember my favor. You'll want to help me. I know it."

Instead of arguing, I nodded and walked away. This time, she didn't call for me to stop or wait and instead waved her bony fingers as I left. Not wanting to spend another second in her presence, I squeezed between the two houses and forced my way through until I was back on the main street.

A sigh didn't ease the tension in my shoulders, but it helped me relax. My cloak's shell faded, and it adjusted subtly against my back. Smirking, I tapped the fabric covering my chest and then opened my hand to stare at the necklace.

I sniffed and caught a new scent. I raised the red stone up to my nose and inhaled deeply. The smell made me sneeze.

That's a weird smell for a piece of stone.

Chapter 36

Seaside Chat

I hesitated to wear the necklace. The red crystal smelled like crisp fruit, but only if I put it right up to my nose.

It's not the worst smell in the world. I can't place the fruit, though.

Even if it did smell nice, I tucked it into my pocket and decided to wait until I could, at the least, ask Alice questions regarding the creepy old lady.

Promises, even those made to the mystical system, did not provide me enough confidence.

I shook my head and exited the merchant street.

Out of everything I expected from a town near a den of werewolves... some crazy witch trying to bind me into a deal wasn't my first thought. Yet, it seemed I couldn't just relax. Not even for a day.

Insanity at every corner... I need to get out of here.

Eventually, my feet carried me to patches of reeds and warm sand, and I smelled the sea breeze spilling from the shore. The sound of human hustle and bustle fell away in favor of crashing waves.

The shoreline stretched for a few miles, its dark stones slick from the waves.

I scanned the horizon and found I wasn't alone.

There sat a woman with long, dark hair that fluttered over her shoulder as the breeze blew through it. She hunched, her knees drawn to her chest, but I couldn't see her face.

I slowly approached, not wanting to startle her. My feet crunched against the gravel and stone, and I purposely stepped down harder to create enough noise.

She didn't react.

When I got close enough, I stopped, and my eyes widened. She held a sharp knife. I made no sudden movements and kept my hands jammed in my hoodie pockets.

"Woah. Uh, hey there. You doing okay?"

My words made me cringe, but I didn't know what else to say.

Her eyes flickered my way, but she stayed rigid. The knife reflected the crashing waves.

Okay, let's take this easy.

"*You... You're that kid,*" she said. "*The other one they rescued.*"

It took a moment to jog my memory. Then it all came at once: the cage, my captors' cackles, and unending dread. I wasn't the only one who survived.

"*From the Reds...*"

She flinched and looked at me with haunted eyes. She searched my own—for what, I didn't know.

"You don't look that much older than me. Kinda rude to call me a kid. I'm Cain."

My piss-poor attempt at levity didn't land. I expected something—anything really—but she looked back to the sea.

Right...

"Do you mind if I join you?"

No response.

Waves crashed loudly against the beach, the foam nearly reaching our feet before it receded.

My eyes drifted to the knife in her hand. She held it steady, pressed against her breast. The folds of her shirt caught its edge, fraying the thread.

Sharp knife. Now, what do you plan on doing with it?

"I'm going to be upfront here. If you want me to leave, I can. I just wanted to know what you plan on doing with that knife."

She looked down but not away. Not to the knife, either.

"I can also just sit here in silence if you want."

Her feet wiggled, and she tapped the ground with her toes. She didn't reply but nodded slowly.

It's not exactly a direct answer, but I'll take it.

Slowly, I brought my hand to my chest, and heat radiated off my skin. Even through the thick hoodie, I felt it. The cold breeze didn't bother me in the slightest. I rubbed my fingers and grazed the wet stone.

Unlike me, the woman wore a scratchy pants and shirt combo like the one given to me the night before. I knew what the fabric felt like, how thin it was, and she must have been freezing.

Yet, she didn't shiver.

My leather shoes took the hit of the next wave, but the woman's feet got coated in the sea-foam. Again, she did not flinch.

"How?" she asked after the wave receded.

"How what?"

Another wave rolled in, followed by a gust that sent her hair spilling across her face. She brushed the stray strands aside once the wind settled.

"How are you okay?"

I kept my eyes on the distant birds. They looked free, gliding in a sea of clouds.

"What makes you think I am?"

She breathed deep. "Your shoulders—your posture—you don't carry the weight you should."

I blinked. "Or maybe I'm good at hiding it?"

Her lips twitched. "No. Your eyes lack the haunted look. Your shoulders are too relaxed. You walk with ease."

It sounded like an accusation, but I didn't think she meant to blame me for anything.

It hasn't been all roses and sunshine, lady.

"I... huh. If you said that to me a day ago, I might have screamed at you. I don't know what you've been going through these last few days, but it's been a nightmare for me."

Her fingers tightened around the handle.

I hunched forward. White bangs fell over my eyes, and I stared at the stark color mixed in with my brown hair. "Do you remember things from before? From Earth?"

This time, she looked. Her face turned to inspect mine. "Yes. All of it. Why?"

"I don't. At least, I think I don't. I'm not entirely sure. Some things are hazy, but I try not to dwell on that. Focusing on what's ahead of me these past few days has been easier. It gives me less time to think about what I know is missing from my head."

Her eyes met mine, and I smiled. When she turned back to the ocean, my smile turned into a frown.

"I have all my memories. Every single one. I wish I didn't."

A part of me expected to feel angry at her response, but I felt nothing. "Yeah, well, I didn't forget everything. I still have some memories, probably a lot. But if I think too hard about it, the fuzzy details start to show."

"Lucky," she whispered.

Yeah, I don't think so...

"To each their own. At least it helps with my new reality."

"You're dressed like the Hunters."

"Yeah, I am."

"Do you regret it?" she tapped her wrist holding the knife. "You don't want to go back?"

I shook my head. "No. I made my choice. I'll live up to it. It's not all bad: cool magic, awesome perks, new family—that sort of stuff."

There's no point in telling her I can't go home. Not when I don't even know how to feel about it.

"Can't be that easy."

"No. Not at all."

"I see."

A cloud drifted overhead, blocking out the sun. Her shoulders relaxed, and she raised her chin. My eyes focused on the hand holding the knife. She slowly extended it, her thumb lightly sliding over the blade's spine.

"Hey..." I said carefully.

She exhaled, flipped the knife around, and extended her arm. She pushed the handle toward me. "Do you mind if I ask for some help?"

"Help with what?" I asked, tentatively accepting the knife.

"I came here to cut my hair. Can you do it? I don't have a mirror."

Oh.

"Yeah, sure. I might screw it up more than you could, though."

A fragile smile played on her lips. "That's fine. It can always grow back."

Well, this beats what I originally thought you were going to do.

"All right, just don't blame me."

I moved into position behind her back, and she lowered her head, exposing her neck. She took her hair and ran her fingers through it to just above her shoulders.

"Don't worry about making it even."

I gently placed the knife against the bundle of hair and applied pressure. The blade had such a sharp edge that strands fell away with the lightest touch. Once I made the first cut, I paused and waited for confirmation.

She nodded, so I continued. I angled it and kept it as close to the length as she wanted. As the blade came out the other side, she released her hair to smooth it out.

It was... decent. Not pretty, but not bad either.

"I can, uh, fix that edge for you?"

She held out her palm, and I gave her the knife. She held it up to inspect her new look. "Honestly, not that bad. A little jagged toward the middle, but better than what I could have done."

"If you're fine with it," I said with a shrug.

After combing her hair, she picked up the fallen strands. Her eyes held melancholy as she rubbed the hair. When she approached the edge, she let the breeze carry it into the water.

She nodded. "Thank you. I'm Kierra, by the way."

Chapter 37

Teatime Talk

"No problem. Are you okay now?" I asked.

"Yeah, I'm going to head back to town. One of the Grimms is waiting for me," Kierra replied.

"All right. I'll join you then."

As I walked behind her, I noticed her entire demeanor had changed. There was... confidence in her step. One that hadn't been there before.

Good for her. She deserves some peace of mind.

When we entered the town, I tagged along, curious to see who the Hunter was. At some point, I needed to go looking for Alice. The huntress might have abandoned me, but it would be rude to leave without her.

Kierra led me to a small building near the central fountain. Rich tea wafted from inside, and shouting came from within.

She carefully peeked around the corner. "Looks like she's busy."

I quirked an eyebrow and peeked inside.

The tea shop's sole occupants were two familiar huntresses. I looked around, but not even a shopkeeper or café owner sat behind the desk.

Red-tinted eyes glowered from across the room. They looked past me before moving on to their original target.

"Explain yourself," Adeline ordered.

Alice stared defiantly. "I need to go on a hunt."

"Then you should have come to me. Not demand Devon to take you!"

While the Grimms had a showdown, I whispered to Kierra, "Do you want to go somewhere else? We can probably leave them to it."

She shook her head and walked past me. The two briefly stopped to watch Kierra pull out a chair and sit down.

Adeline grimaced. "Why? Why do you need to go on a hunt so badly? We've worked well together all year."

"Because I am tired of taking it slow. I'm ready to hunt," Alice replied.

"And you will, just not now. Give it a while; you still need time to—"

The sound of creaking irritated my ears. Alice brought a closed fist toward her lap. "I don't need to be told how to handle *my* loss."

After a moment, Adeline narrowed her eyes. "No. No, you don't."

"Thank you."

"Don't mistake my acknowledgment as acceptance of your foolhardiness. Rushing to throw yourself into danger is not the answer to your problems."

Alice kept her cool and forced her expression blank. "I will decide that for myself. You trained me well. Trust that."

"Ahhh. You're just as stubborn as both of them, you know."

"What do you mean?"

"You're kidding." Adeline shook her head. "Of course you're not. Listen to yourself. Devon and Elias are stubborn asses, especially Devon. You're just like them."

"There's nothing wrong with that."

"Except none of you realize how stubborn you are. Whatever. Go on the hunt, come back stronger, gain a level, and grow, Alice. Just don't die. You understand?"

Alice nodded. "I do. I won't."

"Good." Adeline turned to me. "Will you come sit down, Cain? Standing around awkwardly isn't helping anyone."

"Are you sure? I can return at another time," I replied.

"Get in here already."

Adeline faced me as I sat. Her eyes danced across Kierra's hair. "So you went through with it. Do you want me to fix up the back?"

Kierra nodded. "That'd be lovely, thank you."

"Is this the person you were waiting for?" Alice asked.

"I'm sorry for the wait. I needed some time to myself."

Alice shrugged. "Nothing wrong with that. I'm Alice."

"Kierra."

I waited, expecting the conversation to continue, but Alice didn't ask a follow-up question. Kierra kept silent.

How am I the extroverted one? Just how?

Alice sniffed the air and cocked her head. "Where did you go? You smell strange."

I reached into my pocket. Remembering that I had a necklace stashed away, I pulled it out.

"So, I met a crazy old lady. Wrinkles, giant cart. Hilde-something. She looked like a witch. We made a deal for me to hear her out, and in return, I got this necklace. Any idea if it's safe to wear?"

Adeline rushed off her chair and snatched the necklace from my hands.

The three of us watched as she held it up to the light and closed her eyes.

I glanced at Alice, but she looked just as confused.

"Adeline?"

She grunted and let the red crystal dangle. "The necklace is fine. There are no enchantments on it."

"Then why do you look so angry?" Alice asked.

Adeline handed me the necklace. "Because it means she's back. And she targeted Cain. Tell me the exact terms of her deal."

"Uh, that for the duration of our conversation, she swears not to harm me—intentionally or not?"

"She made a system promise? Really?"

"Who are we talking about?" Alice asked. "I didn't know any of the townsfolk had access to the system."

"Because they don't," Adeline said, shaking her head. "And you wouldn't know. Hildegrim hasn't been here for over six years."

"Six years? That's when..."

"Yes. When you and Elias came to the Warren."

Tension stirred in the room. "If it's any consolation, whatever she tried to do to me, she failed."

"What do you mean?"

I grabbed the base of my cloak. "I'm pretty sure this protected me somehow. She didn't look happy afterwards—I know that much."

Three sets of eyes fell upon my cloak, and it flared up.

Thanks again.

"Good. That's something. What did she want from you?"

I hesitated.

I can't say what she offered as a reward. Not while Alice is here.

"Just to grant her a favor. To protect or something if I see her."

Adeline growled. "That's too vague. All of this. I'm getting really tired of all the secrets."

She looked away before sighing. "You didn't agree to anything, did you?"

"No. I'm not that stupid."

"Stay away from Hildegrim for now. Astra would know more, but she hasn't caused us harm—not directly. I don't want that to change."

I didn't plan on it. So that works out.

I nodded and stared at the necklace. After some deliberation, I put it on. It looked surprisingly good with the red cloak.

When I looked up, I found Kierra staring at the crystal. "Are you okay?"

She turned to the older huntress. "Magic, werewolves, iron weapons... What exactly do you guys do?"

"We do a lot of things, but essentially, we're monster Hunters. Some view us as mercenaries; others view us as guardians. However noble you want to think our work is, that's what we do: we hunt down and slay monsters."

"I see..."

Kierra turned to me. "You said you don't regret it. Were you telling the truth?"

I shook my head. "I wasn't lying. Despite all the craziness, I don't think so."

She remained calm.

What's going through your head right now? You're so collected.

I rubbed the crystal. It felt cool but not cold. The string, while corded, felt soft against my skin.

I hope it can hold up to physical activity.

My inner musings came to an end when Kierra stood up. "I want to become a Grimm."

Chapter 38

Are You Sure?

If the statement surprised Adeline, she hid it well. Instead of shock, she held a critical gaze focused on Kierra's face. "And what about home? Do you not want to return to your world?"

"No," Kierra stated. Her eyes lost their glimmer. "My world holds nothing for me. Not anymore."

"You understand you could die. Our lives are not pretty."

"I accept that truth."

"You won't be human, not truly. You'll be a monster in kind, even if you learn to hide it well. Can you accept that?"

"Yes."

Adeline broke out into a wide grin. "Then I'll introduce you to Astra tomorrow. She'll help explain some things about our world. But I warn you, it'll be grueling. You'll hate me or love me by the time you're ready for the rite."

Kierra smiled and bowed. "I won't fail you."

"Then let's go. Might as well head back now and begin."

Adeline stood and tucked in her chair, followed by Alice and me.

Kierra rushed ahead, and once out of earshot, Alice asked, "What made you think she would want to join us?"

"She's strong, never flinched—a survivor," Adeline said. "She may be unknown and new, but I'll stake my reputation on her. I know she'll be a good one. And we could use the help."

I felt angry. Heat bubbled in my chest. My cloak flapped against my back despite there being no wind. The action drew my attention back to the two beside me.

"Cain, I'm sorry. You're all those things, too," Adeline said.

"I... Thanks? Do you think she'll be okay?" I replied.

"Yeah. I do," Adeline said, giving me an uncomfortable smile. "At least now that my protégé is abandoning me, I'll have time to help her learn the basics of combat."

That's completely unfair.

"What gives? She gets training, and Devon offers me a crumb of wisdom. That's so dumb."

"Didn't he take you on a hunt already?" Alice interjected.

"Yeah, and?"

"You got first-hand experience. Way better than training drills."

My eye twitched. Adeline snickered. "Listen, Devon... he's many things. A good teacher is not one of them. Not unless you're someone like Alice."

"What's that supposed to mean?" Alice asked.

No, she's right. I get it. Alice's personality is starting to make a lot of sense.

"Nothing. Just know that Devon is weird, but he'll make you into a better Hunter than all of us. If you survive his methods."

I said nothing as we continued. Eventually, we turned down a different street, and I recognized the two buildings I squeezed through.

"Over there, I started smelling something amazing by the stalls, and it led me through that small space," I said.

"Is there any reason you didn't go around?"

"Well..." I scratched the back of my head. "I didn't really have much control over myself other than I wanted whatever I smelled."

"Right. You're still a pup. I don't envy you. Those days sucked."

"Wasn't too bad," Alice remarked. "Got to eat more of Volto's food."

Never mind, I don't understand you.

Maybe it was how we met, but the more she talked, the less I understood. Blunt described her best, but in my head, all I could think of was the hazy memory of her threatening to chop my head off.

Adeline clapped. "All right, I don't smell anything—nor do I see anything. It looks like she's gone. When we get back, I'll report this to Devon and tell the others to keep a lookout for Hildegrim if she shows up. You especially, Cain."

I nodded, stealing one last glance at the alleyway before following Adeline.

Hopefully, I never see her again.

We made it back to the Warren, and Adeline said her goodbyes while leading Kierra deeper into the tunnels. While the outside trip had been nice, it wasn't enough time to suddenly get over the awkwardness I felt around Alice—especially when she wouldn't stop staring.

"Hey, listen. I think I'm going to go find Astra."

I didn't even buy anything in the village. Though, I don't think anyone could blame me.

"I'll join you."

I grimaced. "You don't have to. I think I'm fine."

Her mask slipped, and I caught disappointment in her eyes. "All right. I'll see you tomorrow then."

"Look. I get that you're serious about us getting to know each other and all that, but like, I just want to relax a little, you know?"

"I understand. I'll see you tomorrow."

And why are we seeing each other at all tomorrow?

"Yeah," I said. "Maybe I'll be up for some training then."

Her eyes brightened. "Sure. It's good that you use an axe. We don't have the same weapons, but there are some drills you should learn if you want to get better."

That didn't seem too bad. And honestly, I could use some practice. My wild swings had kept me alive so far, but I couldn't stop thinking about how poorly I had done against the wolf and boar.

And then Elias' face popped into my head. My fists tightened, and I felt my chest constrict.

Pack. Kin.

"Hey? What's wrong?"

I met Alice's blue eyes and recoiled. "Uh, yeah, I'm fine. Sorry."

Get ahold of yourself, Cain.

"You sure?"

"Yeah... I, uh." *In, out. Relax.* "There wasn't a good time to tell you this, but I ... well. Before your brother *passed away*, he wanted me to deliver a message."

Anger flashed across her face, then sadness.

"What did he say?" Her voice came as a whisper.

"To my sister, tell her I'm sorry. And not to blame the others. She'll make a great Hunter, greater than I had ever been."

My eyes didn't meet hers.

"Thank you."

Her footsteps echoed down the hallway as I stood there.

You have nothing to thank me for. Not for this.

"Wow, that sucks," I whispered.

Now that the words had left my mouth, I felt hollow—more so than I thought possible.

Yeah, magic can wait another day.

The sky still held daylight, but I wanted a nap. Hopefully, come tomorrow, things would stay normal.

Well, as normal as things could be around here.

When I got to my room, I slid back the curtain and stared into the darkness: bare and empty, save for a bed in the corner with messy sheets. I stepped in and closed the covering behind me. The darkness enveloped the room, and I sighed, letting the tension in my shoulders fall away.

The pillow welcomed me into the world of dreams.

* * *

"Cain."

My eyes fluttered open. Shadows greeted me, save for the dim light coming from the curtain.

I plopped my head back onto the pillow.

Stupid dreams and dumb voi—

"Cain."

I bolted upright and jumped to my feet. I reached for my waist but found only my belt.

"Who's there?!"

"Pup," came the voice again. This time, my brain was alert enough to recognize it.

"Devon?" I searched around and spotted a shadowy figure sitting in the corner.

Dim light caught the crimson of his irises. "What did you do to Alice?"

Chapter 39

Disturbing the Sleep

"What?" I asked.

"You did something. What was it?" Devon repeated.

I slowly lowered myself back onto the bed. His red eyes tracked my movements, unblinking.

"I told her what Elias wanted me to tell her. That's all."

What game are you playing, Devon?

"What message? You never mentioned that."

Oh... yeah. I guess I didn't.

"Sorry. I guess I forgot about it." I waited for him to blink, but he didn't. I blew out a puff of air before continuing. "Before he died, he wanted me to tell her that he's sorry. She'll be an amazing Hunter. And not to blame the others."

Finally, his eyes closed. The sudden lack of glowing crimson made the room feel even darker. When he opened them again, they lacked the intensity of before.

"Is there anything else that you failed to mention? Or are the surprises over?" he said gruffly.

"Hey. That's unfair." The wood creaked beneath my fingers. "I'm lucky I remember anything at all! Or did you forget what I've gone through!"

I stood and my cloak constricted, the ends hugging around my body.

"All I did was deliver a message. I almost didn't even do it! Do you know how awkward it is to blurt out a message from someone's dead brother?

What was I supposed to do, Devon? It's not like I'm prepared for anything. You keep leaving me alone!"

Shouting turned into a near growl, and I forced myself back onto the mattress. I seethed. The energy in my chest boiled.

"Cain."

"What?!"

"Go get some food. We're leaving within the next few hours."

You...

As he stood up and pushed back the curtain, my jaw dropped open. I couldn't believe it. He exited without looking my way. No apology, nothing.

The bed shook as the rage built to a breaking point.

Calm down. Don—

I punched the bed frame; the hard wood splintered against my knuckles. The pain shot up my hand and left a throbbing pulse in its wake.

I didn't care.

"Aaargh!"

The throbbing aligned with my heartbeat; every heavy thump in my chest came with another flare-up. It didn't hurt, not really. But it stung and helped douse the anger. Not by much, and I still felt like punching something in the face, but it helped.

My cloak hugged tighter and the growl that had built in my throat died.

I stared at the curtain and then crashed my head against the pillow.

The ceiling irritated me, so I flopped around and groaned as the hunger in my stomach made itself known.

* * *

When I stalked into the mess hall, I ignored the lone Hunter in the corner sipping on a steaming mug. Volto slowly stirred a pot. Not wanting to make a scene, I sat toward a wall and threw up my hood.

Another grumble exited my stomach, and I sank deeper into my chair. The hunger battered at the gates, demanding satisfaction, but I didn't care.

"Pup. If you want to eat, either ask or get yourself a plate. Nobody wants to hear your bellowing," Volto grumbled.

I sighed and stood up. "Sorry. I'll grab a plate."

"No need. Just sit. I can practically hear your teeth grinding. Don't come over and taint my soup. It should bring you happiness, not rage."

That's... ridiculous.

I chuckled mirthlessly. Doing as Volto said, I sat and waited. When he approached, I smelled something new—something sweet.

The hunger bucked and demanded I run to the source of the smell. Instead, I dug my nails into my palm and waited.

Cut the crap. You'll be fed soon enough.

The weirdness of talking to my stomach was not lost on me.

A heavy bowl laden with soup slid underneath my chin, along with another plate topped high with dark meat and loaves of rustic bread. Beside that was a bowl of what looked like five cupcakes slathered in rich honey.

"Eat up, and don't waste a drop," Volto ordered.

I nodded and picked up the first loaf, breaking it in two. It smelled simple. I dipped it into the soup, and it soaked it up like a sponge. I tossed it into my mouth, enjoying the crunch paired with the hearty broth.

After swallowing, I used the larger half of the loaf as a spoon to shovel more soup. I tasted onions and garlic—a dash of rosemary and sage. The bread collected chunks of potato and carrots and prevented the liquid from dripping back into the bowl. When I added a cut of meat, I nearly scarfed the whole thing down without chewing.

A loud thump brought me out of my food craze, and I smiled sheepishly at Volto. He glared and then returned to his pot, watching the rotating liquid like a hawk.

The soup, bread, and the rest of the meat disappeared within minutes. Once gone, I shifted the empty plate away and replaced it with the stack of cakes.

I was about to grab one of the desserts before a large figure slid into the opposite chair. For a brief second, I thought about chipmunking the cakes and walking out of the room, but I preferred keeping the saint of a chef happy, so I couldn't leave without finishing my food. It wouldn't feel right.

Red fabric blocked my sight of the person's face. But I recognized the leather gloves resting on the table.

"Devon."

I just want to enjoy my meal alone. Why is that impossible?

"I'm sorry."

I breathed in and then out. "Okay."

He said nothing else as he got up to grab his own plate from Volto.

I still want to punch you. You can't hear this, but ooh, I still want to punch you. Too bad your body is made of friggin steel.

He came back with a plate, and I watched him eat. He said nothing else, so I grabbed one of the honey-slathered cakes and bit into it.

By the time Devon finished off his eggs, I was wiping away crumbs from my mouth.

"Is Alice okay? After I delivered the message, she thanked me and left."

He sipped his drink. "For now. She's fit to join us for the hunt."

That's not what I was worried about, but okay.

I wanted to ask him why he decided to wake me up menacingly, but I held my tongue. No point in creating drama if I didn't have to.

"Did Adeline tell you about Kierra and the crazy old lady?"

"Yes. If she wants to bring a new pup into the fold, she'll handle it. I trust her. And regarding Hildegrim, don't accept any deal from her. She's stronger than she looks."

"Didn't plan on it," I replied. I pulled the necklace out from under my shirt and held it up. "She said it was safe, but is it? When I picked it out, she had a strange look in her eyes."

His eyes fixed on the red crystal. His face made it impossible to decipher how he felt about it. The only response he gave was to sip more of his drink.

"I think..." he started slowly. "You'll be fine. Elias had a similar encounter six years ago. As far as I know, there wasn't any issue that spawned from it."

We finished our meals, and I dumped our dishes in the sink. Volto nodded stiffly, and we left the mess hall. Devon led us toward Neina.

I shrugged and followed along. "Shouldn't we grab Alice first?"

"No." He turned the corner and pointed. "She's already waiting."

I peeked from behind him and saw Alice's blonde hair. She stood at the entrance to the portal area with her arms crossed.

She spotted us coming, and she reached over to grab her axe leaning on the wall. Like Devon, she strapped it to her back.

"Finally. Are we ready?"

"We are," Devon replied. He turned to Neina. "Can you create the portal?"

I ignored Neina's reluctance to get up and searched Alice's face. Despite my concerns, she looked perfectly normal. Her shoulders were relaxed, and she seemed almost eager.

The roots crawled out of the stone and formed the familiar archway. The rainbow lights gave way to a portal of bright daylight leading deeper into a forested path.

Alice crossed over first, and then Devon. Neina waved from the sidelines. "Don't die yet, pup."

I sucked in a breath and walked through.

Chapter 40

ENTERING THE SEALED CITY

Surprisingly, the first thing that hit my nose was the smell of roses. I looked over to the source of the floral scent to see a steaming pile of animal droppings.

No... No!

To my horror, Alice produced a glass vial and used a stick to scoop up the gray pellets. Once done, she capped it and tossed it over to Devon.

"W-why? Why did we just collect that?" I asked.

With a serious expression, Alice pointed to the air. "The droppings are used in a few potions. Whenever we come to this world, we try to collect them."

If I found I'd been slathering on rosy animal dung, I'm gonna flip.

"And where exactly are we? I didn't get much of an explanation."

Devon motioned for us to move onto the path. "Fourth World. Veridomis. We're near one of its major cities. This continent only has one kingdom, and for the most part, the city and the surrounding villages live in peace."

"Then why are we here? What resources do we care about in this forest?"

"Alice?"

"This is the Malkar's forest, right?" Alice asked.

"Correct."

"Is it a Sealed One?"

"A what?" I cut in.

"Before, on the last hunt, I talked about elder beings who hold dominion over the forest."

"Yeah?"

"Sometimes one of those beings doesn't play nice. And while we boast of our ability to hunt monsters, sometimes they like to come back. To prevent that, we seal them away. We check those seals every half-century to make sure they are intact."

"So, we're doing a routine inspection?"

Devon shook his head. "No, the seal isn't due for inspection for another twenty years."

"Then there's another reason?"

"We got sent a letter from another Grimm currently investigating another incident nearby. A report came in last week about the disappearance of women and children from the village. Supposedly lured off by a dark figure."

"That's not a lot to go on."

"Better information than most. Now come, the village is a few hours away."

Conversation ceased after that. I questioned why we didn't portal directly to the village, and apparently, the answer was simple. The Nexus point that we use to anchor the incantation is the only one nearby.

After that last question, Devon clammed up, even when Alice asked. It wasn't directly obvious, but he seemed tense.

By the time we reached the outskirts of the village, the sun stood high. Like the last village, stone walls guarded the homes within, but this time, spires loomed over the hamlet.

They sported gray brickwork that narrowed as it reached the top. It gave off a strange castle feel to the otherwise plain-looking village.

Devon pointed to the spires. "Those are the anchors to the seal. Do you remember my words, pup?"

I frowned at the usage of 'pup' when Alice got called by her name.

"Yeah. Do enough to catch the prey, not show off," I answered.

"Good. We'll be heading to the church."

The gates were open despite the large walls. We continued, but no guard came to greet us. I looked to Devon, but he didn't stop.

Devon sniffed the air, and his expression turned dark. I started to pick up the sound of grunts accompanied by something slapping together. Alice also scrunched her nose and stared at our leader.

He shook his head and moved to a small shed attached to the wall. It had no windows but a single door, currently shut. The sounds grew louder, and I made out the pounding of rhythmic grunts followed by moans.

The smell of sweat and body fluids hit me like a brick, and I recoiled. I covered my nose, but not before a mixture of leather and grease shoved its way into the olfactory barrage.

Aagh! I did not need to smell that!

Devon gripped the door handle, and the metal shrieked under the force. When he let go, the door sat tilted on its hinges, a nail threatening to fall out.

The intimate couple inside screamed and jumped apart. While the woman covered herself with the dress bunched around her hips, the man had a look of pure horror and screeched until he reached a shrill pitch.

Devon stood menacingly in the doorway, silently staring at the man, unamused.

Busty, bless her heart, smacked the man on the head. His mouth slammed shut.

"Inform the village leader that we've arrived," Devon commanded, his voice like sharpened steel.

The man saluted, and the rest of his clothes slipped to the floor. He glanced down in terror, but he kept the salute, both from above and below.

Devon walked away, leaving full view of the covered woman and the shaking guard.

"Does he even know who we are? Do all villages know what Grimms are?" I asked as I heard the start of an argument coming from the shed behind us.

"If he doesn't, the village leader should."

"They should get a new guard," Alice added.

Agreed. Only one person, and he left the village wide open to three mysterious strangers. Not a good look for a place in charge of a monster's prison.

Villagers walked through the streets and set up stalls for the day's hustle and bustle. When they spotted us, they'd have the same reaction: to stare, but they lacked the fearful responses I expected.

A few kids turned and pointed at our cloaks. Parents held tightly onto the back of their children's shirts, while others openly smiled as we passed through.

"Devon, is this one of the friendly places that like us?"

"Yes. To them, we're living legends. Only the church will react differently."

I wanted to ask more, but he stared ahead, ignoring the peaceful crowd of villagers. His constant flux of being willing to talk and not frustrated me to no end, but right now, he was the leader on the hunt.

The church wasn't far, maybe another ten minutes of walking through the busy streets. Unlike most of the wooden buildings, the church boasted smooth white stone that stood tall. The entrance and road looked well-maintained and clean of debris.

I noted the long line of runes etched into the archway. I recognized none of them, but they looked familiar, script-wise.

The sound of rustling cloth pulled my attention, and I saw a shaking priestess staring at our group. She clutched tightly onto the amulet around her neck before she bowed and raced off.

That's... not good.

A few villagers were seated inside the grand hall, conversing in low whispers as they sat on benches. Everything looked normal, except for the visibly spooked clergy scrambling about.

An old priestess wearing green robes came rushing out of the side hallway. She looked around her fifties, aged but not ancient. Her auburn hair lacked the same youthful luster as the priestess chasing her skirt.

As she neared, she slowed and grimaced. "Hunters, you've arrived."

"We have. I take it you know why?" Devon asked.

She nodded, the younger priestess behind her looking like a frightened child. It made her appear more petite than she really was, even as she stood about a head taller.

"Indeed. I'm afraid we did not realize it at first. The first disappearances were written off as bad luck." She sighed and grabbed the amulet with the picture of a carved tree dangling from her neck. "Then we caught wind of someone who saw the creatures."

Discussion in the hall ceased, and the villagers shushed themselves. The head priestess noticed this and motioned for the hallway. "Please, it's best not to scare the masses."

Alice glanced around the room and pointed to the seven murals on the ceiling. While preoccupied, I failed to notice the intricate paintings above. The artists preferred bright colors and simple silhouettes with detailed backgrounds.

Seven women wearing thorns and flowers looked to a taller woman. She stood up straight, her silhouette full-bodied with swirling roots wrapping around her limbs. Behind her stood a tree similar to the one on the priestess' amulet. On her head, sticking out from behind her ears, was a set of antlers close to a stag's.

Plant people? Dryads?

My thoughts churned, but I couldn't recall any stories from Earth involving them. All I remembered was people who bonded with trees and stood as champions of nature.

But this is a church, so do they worship them? Is that tall lady a god?

My eyes tore away from the designs as we crossed the hallway. The pair led us to a heavyset door.

The older priestess turned around to face her assistant. "Felana, dear. Go fetch the journal in my study, please." She unhooked her necklace and placed it into the girl's hands. "Be swift, dear, but do not run."

Felana nodded solemnly and, not quite sprinting, moved swiftly down the hall.

The head priestess opened the door and led us inside.

We sat next to a table that had steaming tea and thin-looking cookies.

She gestured to the table. "Please, partake of our food. I'm sure you could use some refreshments."

Devon remained seated, but Alice took a stack of cookies. I glanced between the two and decided to join Alice. Unlike her, I accepted a teacup from the older lady and smiled.

"Thank you," I said.

She didn't smile but nodded before sitting. Her breath came in slow, rhythmic beats that I could hear clearly over the crunching of cookies.

Her eyes sank, and she lowered her head into a stiff bow. "Please... Hunters. Save my grandchild."

Chapter 41

No Promises

"Do you have the required price?" Devon asked. His reaction felt so mercenary. Cold.

It was heartless.

Alice stopped chewing and watched the exchange neutrally. That reaction pissed me off even further.

What the hell, Devon?

"I do. And I'll offer more if need be."

He shook his head. "I make no promises. We shall wait for the girl to return."

The priestess' fingers curled into a ball. She kept her bent posture, and Devon said nothing to correct it. With more anger than necessary, I bit down on the cookie.

What a shame.

Before Devon continued, I placed the cup and saucer down. "My apologies. I'm Cain, and your cookies are fantastic."

Alice side-eyed me, but Devon remained expressionless.

All right, statue man. At least learn her name.

She looked surprised but quickly smiled, a genuine one. "Thank you, Cain. I'm glad you enjoyed them. Please have some more. And I apologize as well; my surprise is no excuse to lose my manners. My name is Thelassa, head priestess of our church."

Her smile remained until she returned to looking at Devon's unreadable face. She lowered her head and ran her fingers along a journal's spine. Her thumb ran down the fore edge till she stopped midway through and opened the book.

Silently, she handed over the journal. Devon read the page and then turned to another.

Throughout it all, Thelassa stared nervously at the journal in his hands. Devon shut the journal and handed it back.

"Has there been anyone affected by the flare-ups?"

Thelassa shook her head. "Not permanently. Three of the noted cases suffered a mild fever for an hour that receded on its own. From daily talks, we know of no obvious problems."

"And you noticed the south anchor had a cut link a week ago?"

"Yes," she said hesitantly. "From our best guess, the chain was tampered with over a month ago."

He paused and watched her. She fidgeted in her chair but kept her shoulders squared.

"The townspeople are uninformed," he stated.

Her head lowered further, but I saw anger flash across her face. "No. The village leader thought it best for the information to be kept from the people."

He didn't respond and instead stood up. He moved to the door.

What are you doing?

Alice sniffed the air and frowned.

"Do you need us to get ready?" she asked.

Devon shook his head.

Okay.

"Sir, please... It's... busy!"

The voice sounded female: young and panicked.

"Get out of my way!"

"Sir, please wait—"

The door slammed open, and a short, muscular man barged through. He caught sight of Alice and me. He had enough time to run through a series of increasingly shocked and frightened expressions before Devon grabbed him by the neck.

The man let out a screech before Devon lifted him into the air. He desperately clawed at the manacle around his neck, but Devon's fingers refused to budge.

"Should've let your bodyguard go first."

Devon stepped to the side as another man—one dressed in black leather and twice as muscular—rushed in. Devon grabbed him by the skull, lifting him to join the other fool.

He kicked, but Devon slammed him face-first onto the ground. A wet crunch rang through the room, and a loud moan followed.

The bodyguard had enough time to windmill his arms before Devon's boot launched him into the wall. His back met stone, and a resounding thud accompanied the spray of blood that splattered the floor.

As the muscular bodyguard groaned, curled into a bleeding mess on the floor, the man in Devon's grip ceased struggling and stared in horror. His eyes switched to Devon, who looked disinterested.

"I apologize for the blood," Devon said.

Thelassa's lips thinned, and she stared furiously at the man in his hand. "It's of no bother, Sir Hunter. Mr. Albrus is the one who owes the apology."

Devon nodded. "Alice, guard the outside. Stop the priestess from running away screaming, please. Cain, keep the bodyguard down."

Alice nodded and then bolted out the door. A shriek pierced the air, sharp and sudden, before it silenced just as quickly. I hadn't even noticed Felana running down the hall, but Devon seemed to have eyes everywhere.

Not wanting to fail a simple order, I found the bodyguard slowly bracing himself.

Sorry.

I placed my boot on his back and whispered, "Don't move."

He stilled. I couldn't see his face, but he reeked of sweat and blood. The copper of his blood smelled foul to my senses but not in a corrupt way.

The beast inside me felt zero interest in tasting his flesh.

Alice came back—half dragging, half coaxing Felana. She stared at Albrus in terror and then rushed into Thelassa's arms. Thelassa immediately comforted the girl while whispering soothing tones.

I looked at Alice, and she watched them before turning to the bodyguard underneath my shoe. She nodded and then blocked the door.

Devon held Albrus up by the collar. "Are you foolish, or do you have a death wish?"

"I... I d-don't. I—" Albrus stammered.

"You failed your duty as steward of this town. The report we received came not from you—the one person whose job was to alert us to changes in the seal."

The town leader went bug-eyed, and he stared daggers at Thelassa. She met his eyes defiantly, and Albrus shouted, only for Devon to force his jaw shut.

"Under the treaty forged between this kingdom and us, your death would not only be justified—it would be expected. Mind your tongue."

Devon released his collar. The town leader shook. He opened his mouth, but no words came out.

When Devon reached for him a second time, Albrus did the unexpected and crashed to the floor like a stiff corpse. The room went silent.

The bodyguard turned his head and saw his boss on the ground, unmoving. He tried to shift, and I pushed my boot down further.

"Oomph!"

Devon placed his hand on Albrus' chest and shook his head. "Pathetic. He's alive but unconscious."

I think that's pretty obvious, Devon.

"What do I do with this guy?" I asked.

"Knock him out if he tries something stupid."

I waited, but the bodyguard refused to move.

Good.

"Priestess, do you have your half of the key?" Devon asked.

Thelassa patted Felana's arm, forcing the girl to sit down while she got up. She held out her hand. "My necklace, dear."

Felana unhooked the necklace around her neck and returned it to Thelassa.

Thelassa tossed it to Devon. "Do you require anything else?"

He shook his head.

"Very well," she said. She walked over to the unconscious town leader and bent down. "Always the fool, Albrus."

She slipped past Devon, poked her head into the hallway, and let loose a shrill whistle. The echo of running feet bounced down the corridor. She then stepped aside, gesturing toward the bodyguard pinned under my boot.

A string of priestesses entered the room. They held sharpened daggers of black metal that reminded me of a thorn.

"Ladies, the Grimms have business to attend to. Please take Mr. Albrus and his bodyguard to the confinement room."

Chapter 42

Seal Inspection

The priestesses pulled out dark green thread from inside their robes. *Uhh...*

"Release him, Cain," Devon said.

I removed my boot and stepped back. Two of the women tied the bodyguard's legs together, while the other bound his hands behind his back. His eyes tracked the priestesses, and when they finished tying him up, he strained at his bindings.

The thread held while his muscles flexed, failing to produce the result he wanted.

Devon raised an eyebrow. "Plant fiber. Made from the flowers that grow around the seal?"

Thelassa nodded. "Yes. One of your kin showed us a method to soften the plant and process the fibers into thread. We tried not to reveal the discovery."

The priestesses dragged Albrus away and forced the bodyguard to his feet. For a moment, he looked ready to fight back, but he met Devon's eyes and kept his gaze on the floor. Blood left a trail as he walked.

Devon turned to Thelassa. "We'll take our leave."

Her face drooped. "I understand. Good luck on your hunt."

He exited the room, and I followed suit. Alice took up the rear, and we left the church. Once we were outside, he led us down a vacant alleyway.

"I can hear you grinding your teeth, pup."

I relaxed my jaw. "That was cold, Devon."

"And? Do you think I should have done differently?"

"Maybe with more tact? I understood the guards, I understood the alchemist, and the village leader from the last hunt. But her? She is a grandmother worried for her grandchild."

He leaned in close, and his hot breath tickled my face. "And what do you think happens when all you have to show is a dead monster and the bones of a child? Most of the time, you won't even find that, maybe a few scraps of cloth or a ragged toy dropped in mud. We are Hunters, not heroes. We do not provide hope. We do our job."

I glared, and he scowled. His eyes were tinted red, and I saw myself in his reflection. The white of my bangs fell into my face, and I looked away.

Damnit!

"Let's go."

My pulse quickened, but I reined in my temper.

I hate that you're right!

I kept my mouth shut, unable to argue a better viewpoint.

"I think," Alice started, "Devon's right. We shouldn't offer false hope. Not when we can't guarantee it. But I think we could have guaranteed we'd try our best."

"And when our best isn't good enough? Has Adeline been teaching you that?"

She shrugged. "No, she hasn't. And if our best isn't good enough, that's on her. We tried, and whether we succeed or fail, we move on."

He said nothing, and we resumed our walk. He led us toward the southwest spire. The closer we got to the structure, the more I realized how much I underestimated the scale. It stood at a massive height, easily dwarfing the church.

When Devon hopped over the small metal railing sectioning off the spire from the public, I already felt a strange energy in the air. It was cold and came as a soft buzz to my senses. My cloak expanded.

"Is it supposed to feel like this?"

"No," Devon answered.

He pointed to the long black chain jutting from the wall. It looked embedded into the stone and sealed shut with no lock. Along the chain, several links had missing pieces of metal.

"Someone sabotaged the chain," Alice commented.

"Does that mean the monster escaped?"

"No," Devon said. "That'd require all four spires to be destroyed."

"Just how powerful is this thing?"

"Records are hazy. Most information was passed down orally back then. Few people wrote of details this dangerous. As far as Astra was able to recover from the snippets in the archives, the Sealed One is immortal."

"How are you supposed to fight it?"

"By whittling it down: exhausting its powers until it has nothing left. Secure and cage it. Trap it within a ritual. One of the details points to the Sealed One's ability to replicate, sending out pieces of itself as avatars."

He lifted the chain, running his finger along one of the broken links. "This metal holds foreign mana. Eroded—not cut. Whoever did this was powerful enough to fight through the enchantments."

"This is ancient, right? How strong would they have to be?" Alice asked.

He shook his head. "I don't know. There's a good chance that they had help in some way."

He dropped the chain and moved to the middle of the structure, running his hand along the stone until he came to a stop just above the center links. He pulled out Thelassa's amulet, flipping it over so that the tree faced us. He pulled back, and the necklace stayed—embedded into the spire.

A series of long, curling lines appeared stroke by stroke.

The cool energy increased in pressure, and the temperature dropped. My cloak expanded further, and I threw up my hood.

When the lines appeared in their entirety, my eyes stung. "Aagh! What the hell?"

Strong fingers gripped my shoulders and guided me forward. My legs hit the chain, and I stopped.

"Step over," Devon commanded.

I did, and he pushed me further. Alice growled as Devon guided her past the chains.

Instead of meeting a wall, we continued, and I finally opened my eyes to find myself inside a cramped space.

Sticking out of the ground in the center of the room was a giant crystal just shy of Devon in height. It pulsed with purple light every five beats.

By my side, Alice stood, staring at the crystal while rubbing her temples. Devon was already across the other side of the room, looking at the opposite wall.

"What is this?"

"Mana quartz. Some of the largest you'll ever see."

"It's pretty."

No reply.

I sighed and moved closer to Alice. "Are you okay?"

"Yes," she replied.

And again, I'm somehow the social one.

I exhaled, and my breath fogged the air. I ran so naturally hot that I didn't feel the chill.

"Let's go. We need to check the other spires." He pushed through the solid wall, leaving Alice and me staring at each other. She shrugged and followed while I stole a glance at the wall Devon had been inspecting.

There wasn't much: four small crystals embedded into a black metal panel. Several rune lines swirled around it, containing the square piece within a circle. Three of the four crystals lit up, but one flickered.

That doesn't look good. I hope we're not too late to fix things.

I joined the others, and we moved on. Two of the spires were fine; the chains had intact links, and the crystals were just as bright.

But at the fourth spire—the northern one—the chain's links had the same eroded cut as before.

The giant mana quartz did not glow.

The only source of light was the three small blinking crystals in the back panel.

Devon stayed silent as he forced us out and then ushered us back to the church. He looked... annoyed.

"What's the plan?" I asked.

"To ask for the records of any mana users in the town," he answered.

We made it back to the church in no time, but something was wrong. Devon's head perked up, and he hurried his steps, forcing Alice and me to jog along to keep up.

When we entered the church, it was to the scene of Thelassa comforting the busty woman from the gate guard encounter. Felana was busy drawing rapidly on a piece of paper.

Thelassa stood, but before she could reach us, the crying woman rushed toward Devon. She grabbed his cloak and looked up into his eyes with tears streaking down her face.

"Please. You have to save my daughter! Please, Sirs Grimm. Please!"

Chapter 43

Compromised Child

He quietly removed her hands from his cloak. She shook in place. Ignoring the woman, Devon turned to Thelassa.

She grabbed onto the mother's shoulders. "We'll pay the amount—whatever it is. Please, Hunters. The disappearance is still fresh."

Devon nodded. "Cain, summon your wolf."

All right.

I backed up a few steps and held out my hand. Before I closed my eyes, Alice raised an eyebrow.

Okay. No distractions.

Not that it mattered. The system-guided skill came as easily as breathing. I pulled up the runic circle in my mind: conjuring the image of fangs, teeth, and claws. I let my energy rise into the spell lines, empowering the runes within. The cold of the void flared up as the runes burned a bright orange.

"Wulf!"

I felt a cold tendril lick my palm, and I smiled. Crouching low, I ran my fingers through the pseudo-fur of my summon.

"Hello, fella. I'm Cain. I need you to help me find someone, okay?"

"Wulf!"

I spun around as I felt someone behind me. Alice leaned on my shoulder. "That's a shadow wolf. Like the Reds—their familiar," she stated.

Ah, crap. Forgot about that.

"Yeah," I replied carefully, waiting for the angry reaction.

Instead, she nodded approvingly. "So that's your first kill reward."

Huh.

"Yeah, cool skill."

"I'm glad you got Elias' revenge."

She joined Devon, leaving me with a concerned shadow beast prodding my palm with its icy snout. I reflexively scratched behind its ears.

I guess we're still good.

Thelassa led the mother away while Felana handed Devon a dirt-stained purple scarf.

"Here you go, sir. It's the only article of clothing the mother found," she said.

Devon sniffed the scarf and then handed it to Alice. She inhaled deeply. When she did, she held it away.

"Putrid."

Devon motioned for me to take it, and I raised it to my nose. I sniffed once and gagged. "What the hell? That's not a healthy smell for a child."

"It wasn't the child," Devon corrected.

"Then what? That's pretty sharp and smoky."

"Let's be off. Have your wolf join your shadow. Once we're out of the city, have it search the woods ahead of you."

He didn't wait to see if I understood what he meant and set off. We followed behind him, moving at a brisk pace. Several townsfolk pointed and stared, but one look at our faces and hurried steps made most hesitant to greet us.

It's almost like things are back to normal...

We reached the city gate and found it manned by two guardsmen. They shared a glance before promptly stepping aside and saluting while diverting their eyes.

Yeah, definitely back to normal.

Once outside the gate and far enough away from the wall that the guardsmen couldn't hear us, I had my summon emerge from my shadow, and he released a brief howl.

"Close your eyes—probe the connection you have with the summon. Access the mental link," Devon instructed.

I did as he said and felt around. Once I thought about it, my active brain took over.

"Done."

"Picture the skill; let the system guide you. Connect to it. Try to see through your summon's eyes."

The spell circle in my head spun, and the void in between rippled. The rotation continued until I felt a tug on my senses.

"Don't fight it, Cain."

His voice sounded distant, yet loud and clear.

I let the black hole pull me in and felt my consciousness zip down the connection. It wasn't as if I suddenly took over the summon's perspective. It was more akin to having music play in the background while watching something. I listened to the lyrics and understood what was being said, but it wasn't my main focus.

I had the distinct out-of-body experience of looking at myself from the perspective of a creature only hip-level in height. I twitched, and I saw my fingers move through the mental feed.

Devon grabbed me by the shoulder and shook. I nearly tumbled forward. The connection recoiled, and my thoughts returned to normal.

"Remember that you're vulnerable to physical disturbances in that state. Learn to peek and nothing more. If you want to stay alive."

"Got it."

"From here on out, you two are to scout the forest and track down the monsters that took the girl. Use common sense; if you think you'll die, don't. Retreat," he commanded.

"And if that means leaving the child behind?"

I met Devon's eyes, the irises stark crimson. Something came over me, and I felt a challenge inside my chest. The lake of magma that rested in my core flared up, and the world became a little brighter in color. It felt like every detail sharpened.

Alice became stiff while Devon snarled.

"It means you leave them behind. If you die, others die. There are no second chances, Grimm."

I growled and felt the energy sputter as my vision returned to normal. The realization of what happened hit me, and I clutched my head as the foreign thoughts returned.

Leader!

"W-What was that? What just happened?"

Devon shook his head, his eyes now normal. "Focus on it later. Begin the hunt."

Alice took off, and I joined her while commanding my summon to run ahead. My shadow wolf overtook me quickly and bounded between the trees.

Damnit, Devon. Not everything has to be a lesson!

Unsure of what to look for, I directed my summon down a carved path. The forest was filled with bright colors and thick flora, but I watched my steps and jumped over the roots as I saw them.

I connected to my wolf. Through its eyes, I saw it moving through the trees at a much faster pace. It darted and weaved, running deeper until the thick canopy overhead shaded out the sun. At a narrow stream, the wolf stopped and sniffed the ground before pivoting upriver—following the bank.

I opened my eyes and continued, remembering Devon's words not to spend long in that state. After a couple of minutes of running, I stopped and dropped low.

Something rustled in the grass, and I silently removed my axe from its sheath. I nestled deeper into the lush bush covering my side.

The creature moved closer; a small rock bounced past my head, rolling to a stop a few feet away.

I inhaled. Just out of view, I heard heavy breathing. Something solid hit the ground.

One more step.

The creature shifted in place, and hot breath blasted across my skin, smelling like berries and alfalfa mixed with damp earth.

Not prey.

I carefully rose above the bush to meet the curious gaze of a three-eyed deer. Its antlers were small nubs in the middle of two sets of ears. It chuffed again, and the yellow spots of fur on its backside stood up.

I stared into its deep black eyes, the irises nonexistent and alien.

My hand slid behind the beard of my axe, but I kept it at my side, not wanting to spook the deer. It didn't attack. Instead, it lowered its snout to chomp on the bright red flower growing on the bush.

Friendly, alien deer. Of course, they exist in an alien world.

It wasn't my prey. It wasn't a monster—merely a forest beast foraging for food.

I took careful steps back and kept my eyes trained on its legs. It looked at me for only a moment before grazing again.

Once several feet out, I relaxed and regulated my breathing.

Not even a week in, and you're already a savage who swings axes at deer— Hell of a change, Cain.

The deer turned my way before moving on to the next set of flowers. As I watched it swallow a colorful cluster of petals, a buzz in the connection to my summon sped up my heart rate.

A deep howl blasted through the trees, and the deer bolted away.

I closed my eyes and sank into the connection.

Come on, come on...

My brain struggled to understand what happened; the movements were too fast. But then a crude weapon sank into the ground, missing my wolf's paw by only an inch. When it looked up, the foreign thoughts came to life.

Prey!

My wolf found the target of our hunt.

Prey!

My wolf found the target of our hunt.

Chapter 44

Enter the Brimstone Cavern

It took me a second to understand my summon's surroundings, but the monster that attacked clambered over the ashes of its fallen companions.

My wolf rushed from the creatures made of burning embers and coal. Their eyes were pits of hot flames as they raised their picks into the air.

The connection didn't transfer sound, but I imagined them screeching, the sounds as creepy as the monsters looked.

My summon jumped for the shadows. My vision turned muted and gray, like the world but in negative.

A long tunnel eventually led into a narrow opening that broke away into an expanse of trees. Through the rush of black and white, a lone spot of grass nestled next to a bent trunk looked lighter than the rest. I saw my wolf leap back into the normal world. Color returned, and I closed the connection.

The vision told me my summon was near a crevice in the mountains, so I sprinted in that direction.

I kept moving until my wolf popped out of the underbrush and came to a stop by my feet. It had taken damage; its size diminished by a few inches. I rubbed its snout and then turned to find a figure in red hopping out of the trees.

Alice glanced at the wolf. "He's smaller. Did you find our prey?"

I shook my head at the directness she displayed. "I think so. The strange voice in my head said 'prey'... I don't know what they are, but think of humanoids made of burning coal."

She frowned. "Elementals? That's unusual, especially a fire-based one in a forest."

"Know what they are?"

"No," she shook her head. "Most elementals I've encountered were the friendlier wind variety."

Well, now what?

"Do we find Devon?"

"Why would we do that?" she asked. The look she gave me was one of disbelief. "He sent us on a hunt. Let's complete it."

"And we're looking for a child."

Her face lost the eager, almost bloodthirsty look and morphed into one of deadly seriousness. "What incantations do you know? Astra must have taught you one."

I chuckled darkly. "A fire incantation."

If she felt a certain kind of way about me using fire sorcery, she didn't show it. "I only know a concussive one. But I have an ice-based system skill."

Now that I want to see.

I commanded my wolf to guide us, and we followed. As we ran, I turned to Alice. "Effects?"

"Short range—cone where I aim. Freezes most things solid in a wave of frost."

A part of me recoiled at the amount of excitement I felt at the thought of seeing cool magic despite the dire situation. For all we knew, we could find a roasted child's corpse.

The realization dimmed my exhilaration, but the heat in my chest spread down my limbs; it was a listless feeling.

Damn. I'm eager for the hunt.

I bit my lip. The taste of pennies hit my mouth, and I let it douse some of the giddiness inside my head.

Only one thing to focus on. Cut the crap, Cain.

Following my summon, we stopped next to a crack in the earth on the side of a mountain. The way forward was blindingly dark, the sunlight failing to reach through the crevice.

Alice pulled out two glass vials. They contained muted blue fluid and what looked like a wad of spiderwebs.

She handed me one and pulled at the cork of her vial. It came loose, and the wad fell into the liquid. She quickly re-stopped the vial and shook it. The vial glowed.

With the fantasy equivalent of a glow stick lit, she placed it around her belt.

"Do what I did," she instructed.

I repeated her actions and had my own light source.

She pulled out her axe and nodded. I let my summon sink into my shadow, ready to protect me while we dove into the cave. She went first. I wanted to argue against it, but she had the ice skill.

I conceded and stayed close behind. Whatever attacked us, I would be ready.

The tunnel led us deep into the mountain and widened until we could comfortably walk two abreast. As we moved deeper, the air grew steadily warmer.

When our light revealed an open expanse, we slowed and prepared ourselves.

I lowered my voice to a whisper. "From what I saw, this should be the spot. I don't see anything, though."

We spread further apart; she went right, and I went left. I crept close to a large chunk of stalagmites that rose over six feet.

The long, pointy spires weren't smooth; the necks of the spikes were lumpy.

I placed my gloved hand on the stone and slowly lowered it toward the base.

Hot... I can feel it through my glove. They have to be nearby, but where?

Alice hugged the wall and paused at a slab of stone. I backed away. The way we came was the only way out as far as I could tell.

I gazed at the ceiling to a thick stalactite that had a particularly strange tip. Unlike the rest of the spires, it bulged around the base and thinned until it expanded into a clubbed end. Now that I noticed the strange design, I spotted more clusters—each coming in pairs.

"Hey, Alice. Look up. Does that look strange to you?" I asked as I pointed.

She trailed my finger to another pair of chunky stalactites. "Strange. Different from the others."

"Yeah, you notice how warm everything is? Think that's related?"

"It has to be. I don't see where they could have gone though. If what you described was a fire elemental, they shouldn't be able to move through stone."

Move through stone? Yeah, how the hell would we fight that?

She walked deeper, and my cloak smacked the back of my leg. I glanced down.

No wind.

I looked up, and my heart skipped a beat.

The stalactite pair was no longer mere stone. The black veins glowed orange and dull red. Blazing embers in the shape of two eyeholes glared from above.

"Alice!"

She rolled away as the stalactite shot to the ground, stirring a layer of dust that blocked my sight. A few smaller rocks hit my chest, and I raised my arms for protection.

The pile of burning stone rose into the facsimile of a humanoid. The cave lit up with fire gleaming between the chunks of stone flesh.

"Alice!"

No reply.

I gritted my teeth and held my axe tight as the creature took a single step. Its knee bent at an odd angle before realigning into place. The elemental opened its mouth, revealing a glowing hell pit lined with jagged teeth.

Its eye glowed malevolently and then turned. I heard the sound before I saw it. A shockwave of cool air blew apart the dust cloud in a wide arc. Like a surging tide, a layer of ice crystals coated the two monsters. The orange glow dimmed, and the cave darkened.

I didn't get a chance to look for Alice as she came rushing toward the nearest monster. She swung her heavy axe, using the flat side of her blade. She hit the legs and blew the rocks away in a shower of sparks and broken crystals. Liquid fire oozed from the stubs as the frozen half crashed to the ground.

She turned to attack the other, but a spinning object flew from the left. It clipped her cloak, but she bent backwards and embedded itself in the ground.

Alice hopped away and came to my side as we felt more impacts beneath our feet. Clouds of dust rose, and nearly a dozen creatures shambled into view.

When one approached the steaming elemental, still frozen like a statue, it placed two red-hot hands against the ice. The frost melted away, and the monster's coal orbs lit up.

"What now?" I asked.

She smiled. "We fight!"

Chapter 45

BRIMSTONE BATTLE

I glanced at Alice's hand but noticed her glove looked fine. *That was effective. But we'll need more than that.*

"Wrong weapons to fight these things. How do you want to do this?!" I shouted over the avalanche of grinding stone.

"Cover me!" she yelled back.

My cloak wrapped itself tightly around my shoulders.

I couldn't help it. I grinned.

The cave's temperature rose dramatically in a burst of heat, and I shifted away. Alice glanced over but kept tracking the mob.

"On one."

I pushed forward on the balls of my feet.

Ready.

"Three."

I exposed my canines.

"Two."

The monsters ran, their rusty pickaxes held high.

"One."

The rush of cold air sent dust out in a cone as the flash freeze overtook the monsters. Only the first three were frozen solid while several others hissed, and their veins of fire sputtered.

I was ready to move, but Alice wasn't finished. I sensed a wave of mana, but it felt different. Unlike the freezing pinpricks, this new mana lacked pointedness; it felt *raw*.

A distortion in the air rocketed toward the group. One of the monsters swung at the hard-to-trace projectile, and before its pickaxe could block, the sphere exploded.

The monsters tumbled away. The one that tried to intercept the force ball had its arms blasted off, and a hole exploded out of its chest. The remnant energy whipped more debris our way.

One of the three frozen monsters shattered and splashed the ground with rapidly cooling blood. Alice stumbled, but she caught herself.

I rushed ahead, aiming for one of the fallen monsters. The energy in me bubbled, and I let the rush of adrenaline take over.

The back end of my axe swung into the leg of the downed elemental. The hit jarred my arm, sending a jolt up to my shoulder, but the leg went flying. I hopped away before the burning blood sprayed my boots.

Something swung from behind, but my summon emerged.

The monster's arm was wrenched downwards, the pickaxe dropping to the floor. I swiftly grabbed it and swung underhanded. The pick embedded into the monster's neck. I kicked it, and the monster let out a terrible grinding noise that made me flinch. It tried to get up, but my wolf tugged the stone limb.

I kicked again, and pop went the head.

Another explosion of air turned the surrounding ground into an ice rink—the frost built on itself, thickening the existing coat. But one monster flared, and its body became an inferno. Steam knocked back my hood, but my cloak tightened.

A second pick came swinging for my head, and I rolled away.

"Get the pickaxe!"

My wolf released the arm and snatched the heavy metal tool. With my summon on its way, I whipped my head around to find Alice turning one of the monsters into a spray of pebbles.

Crap. Not keeping up.

I scrambled to my feet and accepted the pickaxe. My wolf growled at the approaching monsters, the once intimidating crowd now reduced to a much more manageable amount.

"Can you do the force thing again?"

Alice shook her head and retreated as two elementals swung wildly, missing by a mile.

Fine.

The steam fogged up the air, making it humid. It drenched my clothes.

"Fight together?"

"No. You'll get in the way of my swings."

My eye twitched, but I contained the growl inside my chest. I had nothing else to suggest.

She sprinted to where two monsters tried to free their frozen companions.

Two pickaxes swung her way, trying to impede her charge. She dodged one while knocking away the other. The momentum of her swing carried her into the nearest elemental, which melted away the ice. The blow shoved it aside as her axe clipped it in the hip.

The steam stopped, but the ice kept melting. She paused as if stilling, only to shuffle out of the way of another monster's pick. Metal pickaxe met rock and crushed the chest of the frozen elemental.

"Wuulf!"

I whirled around just in time to see my wolf phase through an attack while a prick against the connection stirred the bubbling heat in my chest. The monster moved with tense, sluggish motions.

Gripping the pickaxe tightly, I struck its arm at the wrist. Stone shattered, and the monster's weapon clattered to the ground.

Unfortunately, my attack pulled me too far forward, and when I tried to swing again, the monster quickly smashed into my arm, knocking it away.

Fuu—

A roar of blaze erupted from the monster's body, singeing my hand. The heat was instantaneous, and I shut my eyes. I swung again wildly, but the blow bounced off the stone.

I waited for another hit, but then a rush of frigid air scraped at my skin, and a sheet of cold crawled up my front.

My eyes opened to a hail of rubble as Alice's wide swing demolished the frozen statue. The monster's blood landed on my cloak but slid right off.

Alice jumped back and joined me, panting heavily while clutching her arm tight to her chest. A coat of ice crystals covered her skin up to the elbow, letting off streams of fog as the room's hot air melted it away.

"I'm sorry," I said.

She glanced over and frowned. "No. Focus. Aim for the joints. Make them drop their weapons."

Only six remained. During the absolute destruction of Alice's rampage, I took out a measly two and downed another.

I sheathed my axe. Two weapons sounded cool in my head, but I'd die if I continued fighting the way I did.

Two elementals broke free from the crowd to bullrush us, so I moved aside and yelled. They swerved away from Alice to come at me. They were in sync, their movements jerky. My summon met their charge, hopping up and receiving a pickaxe through the chest. The metal phased through, and my wolf's form visibly shrunk.

Still, the weight of my summon was heavy enough to knock the monster down, leaving only a single foe coming my way.

It swung. I slid my leg backwards, letting the metal bounce off the floor with a clang. My swing met the arm at its elbow, and the form broke apart. I kicked at its leg, and it tumbled forward but remained standing.

That's fine.

I raised my pick and hooked its leg, pulling it off-balance. The leverage was in my favor, and it toppled over. Another swing aimed at the back of its neck rewarded me with a dead monster spewing fire.

Its corpse scorched the ground, but I ignored it to rush to my summon, who took another hit. Now the size of an average dog, it sank into the ground as I stepped nearby. It dipped into my shadow, and I raised my arms for an overhead swing.

Instead of rising to meet my attack, the elemental collapsed to the floor. Spinning out from the cloud of steam, one of the monsters' pickaxes came flying for my head. I tried to move, but it arced and smashed into my ribs. Bone broke, and I crumpled to the wet ground.

My broken ribs caused a wave of agony across my side, and I struggled to breathe.

I looked for Alice, but she was slowly backing away from a pair of elementals while her arm dripped a trail of blood.

I met the coal-fire eyes of the new duo that came for me. One stood tall, its mouth burning with flames.

With steady nerves, I extended my arm. My mana rushed into the center of my palm. The elementals paused but then ran forward.

My gaze looked past them and toward Alice, where she backed away.

I'm not the threat here. Just need a distraction.

I dropped the tight control of my core and let it surge forth, rushing down my limb. In my head, I completed the rune and conjured the spark.

I don't need control.

The last line etched itself into the flame, and the runes flared to life, sucking in the mana.

"Ek kalla heiðarloga!"

The flames engulfed my palm and crawled up my arm, each flicker biting at flesh. I winced in pain, but the fire pooled and zipped across the cavern. The monsters stopped and turned—all too slowly as the fireball soared through the air.

Crack!

Chapter 46

Fiery Finish

Alice glanced up in surprise, but she never stopped moving. When the fireball crashed into the stalactites, she jumped out of the way as the explosion cracked the stone. The monsters cornering her looked up as an avalanche fell on their heads.

The elementals went down in a scattering of rocks. Their burning blood spewed, but judging from the hissing and popping noises—as well as the twitching limbs—they were alive.

Not for long.

Alice was upon them before they could shift a pebble. She leveraged her axe and popped off their heads. More fire met the air and splashed onto a sheet of ice that sizzled.

That only left the two monsters ahead of me. I grunted but rolled in time to avoid a pickaxe. The metal head bounced off the ground before tumbling to a stop several feet away.

Need to distract them.

I rushed over to the pickaxe and snatched it up. Spinning around, I lobbed it at the nearest monster, who smacked it aside. The hit did nothing, and my broken ribs screamed.

It didn't matter. They had forgotten about the huntress behind them.

My feet pivoted, and I held out my arm—the same one that barely responded to my demands. The elementals stopped, and I smiled devilishly.

"Hey!"

Rocks shifted, and flames blazed as they both turned igneous.

A massive axe smashed one elemental into another, sending them rolling. Alice went to work on one, who fought back, but she dismantled its limbs. While she handled that, I slowly limped over to the other and unsheathed my axe.

My wolf rose from the ground and grabbed the elemental's back leg, forcing it to fall. The back of my axe met the joint toward the shoulder and blew apart the limb. It twisted, hitting my leg and causing me to crash to my knee.

Screw you!

My good hand grabbed its arm and held it taut. It struggled, but I removed its limb with another chop. The monster tried to spray fire, and my wolf yipped—the connection buzzing. I powered through despite the heat and cracked the side of its head.

It sprawled to the floor, unable to brace itself with no arms. It rolled, spitting its last flames before sputtering out.

A tap on my shoulder made me snap my head around. Alice offered me a metal shaft, unbothered by the snarl that escaped my lips.

I grabbed it and wedged it between the monster's neck. With the weight of my body, I braced and pulled backwards. Elemental blood coated the stone, and I continued.

One more... Pull!

The stopper came off, and blood left the body. The head rolled away and came to a rest, staring at me with dimming eyes. Red-hot ash turned black. Veins of fire pulsed then faded away as the monster's body lost whatever magic kept it together.

My strength finally failed me, and I flopped onto my back. A groan left my body that continued for too long.

Alice joined me and released her own groan of relief and pain as she bunched up her cloak's hood to use as a cushion.

Her arm bled. The poor limb, covered in dust and rock shards, was in a terrible state—not that I could boast any different.

"How's the arm?" I asked through shallow breaths.

"Cold. How's yours?" she replied.

"Cold," I chuckled, then stopped when I nearly whimpered. I blinked and found her watching me. "What?"

"You've adapted remarkably well. Seems like you're a natural for this life."

Huh?

"What are you talking about? What brought this on?"

She shook her head. "You rush into battle; you fight. Sloppy, but you do not flail. You've embraced pain the way a true Grimm does to ensure victory. Are you the same you from before?"

It was an easy answer.

"No."

A comfortable pause followed, then she chuckled. "Good decision with the stalactites."

Blood oozed out of the wounds in my arm. "Yeah. I need more incantations. Fire won't cut it forever."

She said nothing, and that was fine with me. I turned as I felt a strikingly cold snoot bump into my cheek.

"Hey, you did good work. Thank you," I said as I scratched its fur.

"You should feed it more mana as a gift," Alice muttered.

"I can do that?"

She shrugged. "It was in the tome I researched when I thought about doing a summoning ritual. Generally, familiars will stick around—especially if they like your mana. It's food, but some are tastier than others. Offer it more."

I do have mana to spare. All right, let's try it.

I held out my hand, palm-side up. I let the mana running through me condense around my palm. My summon stared at it, sniffed, but then cocked its head.

Frowning, I dropped my palm. I closed my eyes and felt the connection settle around my core. It felt like a string attached to my sternum.

Have I been doing summonings wrong? Do I even need my hand?

This time, I imagined the connection like a straw. A low, constant suction of mana fed into my summon. With the means of transfer open, I simply nudged it.

The reaction from my summon was immediate; its form started to unspool and lose cohesion. I nearly stopped, but then its tail wagged.

My jaw fell open as the wolf grew in size. A strange and almost hesitant tug came from the connection, and I explored it. It came again, and I understood. I nodded, and the wolf nodded back.

I fed more mana, and the strain sent my chest spasming in new pain, disturbing the broken rib. Still, I kept the flow running until my wolf regained its full size and loomed over me with pitch-black eyes.

The void drew me in, and I couldn't see my reflection. The flow of mana stopped—not by my doing but by the wolf. I blinked, and a cold, wet tongue pressed against my cheek.

"Hey! Woah, cold. Too cold!"

It kept licking me before lowering its head. It bowed and then sank into the floor, its shadow joining mine.

A strange feeling settled in my chest but then disappeared.

Rest well, buddy.

I could have dismissed my summon, but we weren't done.

Crap, still need to find the kid.

"Hey, Alice. Can you still pick up the kid's scent at all?"

She pointed to the far wall, a slab of stone like any other.

"I see nothing but a wall?"

"Look again; the color is off."

I squinted and slowly saw what she meant. It was a dark, ruddy brown rather than soot black.

"The smell gets stronger near the wall."

Alice got up first. Her arm had stopped bleeding. The werewolf perk of regeneration was already kicking in.

She offered me a hand, and I took it, embracing the pain.

Together, we stepped past the elemental corpses and approached the wall. It looked rough and uneven. Alice tapped her axe to the stone, and the sound that came back sounded off.

Hollow?

"Can you break it down?"

She nodded and bent her knees. With a big windup, she hit the wall, and it crumbled. The stench that wafted out hit us like a truck. I nearly vomited right there before regaining control of myself and covering my nose.

"Inside, look," Alice coughed, her voice muffled by her hand.

I peered into the darkness and saw a small, sprawled-out form. Alice moved aside, and I stepped in. I picked the girl up as gently as possible, ignoring the sharp discomfort.

Slipping her over my shoulder, I walked far enough away to breathe without needing to cover my mouth. Despite a relatively dirty appearance, the child looked unharmed. No obvious cuts or injuries marred her skin.

I felt the shallow breaths and frowned.

"Hey, Alice. We should get out of here. She can't breathe."

Instead of replying with an affirmative, Alice paused. I gave her a questioning look.

And then, the rainbow-colored blip appeared at the bottom of my vision.

Chapter 47

TRIUMPHANT RETURN

The notification was damn tempting, but I wanted to get out of the cavern. Steamy, humid, and filled with dust, I was concerned for the child and her already labored breathing.

Thankfully, Alice didn't stop for long before quickly moving to the piles of corpses scattered around the cavern floor. She kicked away the rubble and bent down. She repeated this while I moved to the exit.

When she joined me, she held out her hand, displaying a small—almost marble-like object—made of black, smooth stone, with glowing orange lines that reminded me of a rune.

"What's that?" I asked.

"Most elementals have a heart stone. They become fragile after they die, but a few were intact," she explained.

She pocketed the marble.

"Cool. What are they used for?"

"Several things. Alchemy mostly, but they are sometimes used as components for spells and rituals."

My chest still hurt, but some of the pain lessened by the time we made it out. The tunnel gave way to a bright sky, and I inhaled the forest air.

Oh, I'm so glad to be out.

Alice stopped to check the child on my shoulder. When I met her eyes, she shrugged. "Breathing is improving but still struggling. Mild fever."

The child's dirt-stained blonde hair ran down my back in rivulets. I brushed it aside and wiped off some of the gunk around her eyes. Despite touching her face, she remained unconscious.

It worried me, but I wasn't a doctor. Hopefully, one of the priestesses would know what to do.

Alice took the lead, and we set off. I kept searching the trees, half expecting Devon to pop out with a monster head impaled on his spear, but when we reached the gate with no sign of him, I started to worry.

I voiced my concerns to Alice, and she fixed me with a deadpan stare.

Right. He should be able to handle anything.

The guard—a new one this time—caught sight of our arrival as we neared the gate. His eyes widened, and he quickly backed off when he spotted the child.

We ignored him and continued down the streets. Fewer villagers were out, so we had an easier time marching to the church. Those who passed us moved back in shock. More than a few parents covered their children's eyes.

It's just a little blood; we can't look that bad.

In truth, I already knew. My arm did not make for a pretty sight, especially with dried blood and bits of crispy skin flakes.

Thelassa and Felana met us in the courtyard as we arrived at the church. Two other priestesses held the mother back.

"Seyenna! What's wrong with her?" the mother asked desperately.

She pushed against the arms restraining her, but the priestesses held firm.

"Come, lay her down here," Thelassa instructed as she motioned toward one of the stone benches.

I laid her flat on the bench while Felana placed a folded cloth beneath her head.

Thelassa examined her—but not before looking at our arms. "Will you need assistance, Hunters?"

Another flake of blackened skin dropped to the floor. "No, but do you have bandages and some clean water?"

She nodded, and Felana rushed inside. Thelassa went through a series of checks over the child's body. By the time she sighed, Felana returned with a bowl and some rags, along with a roll of bandages.

I momentarily tuned out the near-meltdown of questions the mother inflicted on Thelassa.

She ignored the barrage and addressed Felana again. "Dear, was there no warm water left in the basin? I suppose we'll have to make do. Go fetch me the Tilly root and some sarcor extract."

Staring at the cold bowl of water, I couldn't help but sigh.

Werewolf regeneration aside, it's probably best not to risk it.

With my left hand, I pictured the rune in my head.

Creating the spark was easy, and I whispered the words, letting my voice remain clear but soft. The mana inside me wanted to rampage, but I forced it to bend to my will and power the rune just enough to conjure flames in the center of my palm.

Instead of letting the mana fire off, I placed my hand in the water bowl, and flames sputtered out. My mana reacted and shot into my palm with enough force that I nearly lost control. At the last second, I reined it back in and watched as the water bubbled.

Much better.

It drained my mana immensely, but I was safely inside the city, so it didn't matter if I ran myself a little dry.

"You shortened the incantation," Alice commented. "You're using Astra's version."

"Oh. Yeah. I practiced a little before the whole, you know, incident in Haven Four. Makes lighting campfires a hell of a lot easier."

I handed the bowl to Alice. It was a bit tricky tying the bandages, but I managed to do it as well as she did.

Thankfully, Alice helped tie the wrap of bandages around my torso without issues. My rib was already recovering, but pain rattled through my bones.

Thelassa approached. "Where is your pack leader?"

"Uh, I think he's still out there."

She looked worried but nodded. "Is there anything we can do for you while you wait?"

"No, thanks. Will the kid be okay, though?"

"She will recover with some rest," Thelassa replied, leaning out of the way to reveal a confused-looking child squeezed to death in her mother's arms. "Beyond the damage to her lungs, she will be fine. May I ask where you found her?"

"Inside a cave on the side of a mountain," Alice answered.

"Very well. I shall leave you two alone for now. Please, ask any member of the church if you need help with something."

With that, Thelassa left, and I finally relaxed, settling into a nearby bench.

"I'm going to open my notification now. Did you already do yours?"

Alice shook her head. "Not yet. Go ahead."

Rainbow lights swirled, and I focused on the spinning circle. It expanded across my vision, and I waited for golden text to appear, but then the notification blinked out of existence. I opened my mouth to protest, but the notification returned, and the rainbow gave way to written lines.

[ALERT] You have slain Enthralled Kobolds EvCf x12

Calculating hunt reward...

Applying Strain-Modifier: -25%

Calculation complete.

Hunt Reward: Level up!

You are now level 3.

Chapter 48

PROGRESS MADE

I blinked, and the system notification closed.
That... doesn't seem right.

Beside me, Alice grinned. Her eyes held a red tint.

"Good news?" I asked.

"Yes! I leveled up. I knew I was close. This is why I needed to go with Devon," she answered.

I put on a convincing smile. "How many hunts have you been on?"

"With this new one, it marks my fifteenth."

Maybe it's the first hunt messing with things?

I pulled up my status sheet.

Name: Cain Veldman
Title: Crimson Hunter
Level: 2 (+1)
Stats
    STR: 13
    AGI: 13
    CON: 15
    INT: 14
    WIS: 13
    LUK: 15
Skills

Summon: Shadow Wolf
Passives
  Ember Soul

After enabling the level-up, the plus five next to my stats came up.

Now, where to put you…

In truth, I already knew I needed to improve significantly in a few areas. And as impressive as magic was, I needed the physical capabilities to keep up. The decision came easy, and I added two in STR and AGI and placed the final point into CON.

I closed out of the status and found Alice staring. She asked, "Did something change?"

Ahh. Lie or no? Will she be mad if I tell her I leveled up?

I sighed. "Yes, I leveled up."

Her eyes became flinty. "How?"

"As if I knew. Astra was surprised I leveled up to two already."

She searched my face, and I waited. It wasn't quite anger in her eyes, but she definitely looked like she wanted an answer. Then she stopped, and her face lightened.

"Your first kill. It was a Red, right?"

"An Elder Red, according to the system. It's how I got the summon and my soul cloak."

"I see."

"Okay?"

"The older ones—the grannies—have more to their Lore Matrix. It should have provided you enough to gain a few levels." Her face grew dark once more. "I'm surprised you're only just now getting to level three. You should have reached that already."

Thankfully, she dropped the act and returned to relaxing on the bench. The whiplash of being confronted and then not almost forced a nervous chuckle.

Maybe I can find some normal people on my next trip to the town.

We didn't wait long. Alice sniffed the air. I smelled it too. It stirred the foreign voice inside me.

Blood and savory scents mixed in with the musk of sweat and the tinge of berries. It hit me in full force, and I wasn't surprised to find Devon approaching from the side street.

His shoulder was bloodstained, and his pants sported several small tears near the shins. He scanned our condition, sizing us up the same way we did him. When he found Alice's cradled arm, his eyes hardened—subtle, but the red showed through.

He stopped beside the bench, and I looked around to see if he had brought anything.

"Pup, what are you doing?" he asked, unamused.

"I half expected you to come back dragging a corpse behind you."

Not finding that funny, eh?

"We saved the child. Got ambushed by a dozen creatures called kobolds."

Alice handed him one of the glowing marbles. He palmed it and rolled it between his fingers before handing it back.

"The creature I chased was a mana-corrupted bear," he stated casually.

I stared at the state of his clothing.

Doesn't look like it did too much damage.

"Did you shift?"

He nodded.

"So, does whatever broke the links have the ability to recruit elemental monsters? Or was the kid's kidnapping a coincidence?"

Alice subtly shook her head. "There isn't a lot of information to go on. What do you know about fire kobolds, Devon?"

I scooted over to give Devon room as he sat beside Alice and me.

"There are different variations. Kobolds are known for being mostly earth-aligned. It's rare to see a fire elemental, but it happens."

"Should we be concerned about that?" I asked.

"We are."

"Then why aren't we doing something?"

He looked at me this time, but his eyes were fully red.

"And what exactly do you think we should be doing right now while you both have injuries?"

Almost as if summoned by his words, my arm pulsed in dull pain before it itched.

Fine, you're right. It still feels like there's something we can do.

* * *

For over an hour, we relaxed, but then I felt the call. My stomach growled loud enough to echo.

I sat up and found a few priestesses staring. Not wanting to deal with the embarrassment, I threw up a hood, and Felana moved closer.

"Hunters, if you are hungry, I can show you to the feasting room."

Feasting room?

Devon placed a hand on my shoulder. "As a word of caution, we will require a lot of food."

Felana smiled. "That will be no problem. We have food in abundance."

She wasn't exaggerating. A long table sat at the center of the feasting room, wide enough to seat dozens at once. I had my doubts about what they'd cook up, but when plate after plate of steaming hot food came, I dropped my concerns.

It wasn't just vegetables, as I expected, but several cuts of meat topped with rich gravy. Large pitchers flowed with sweet juice as well as water. I tried to keep my hunger reined in, but the food practically melted on my tongue.

Only several minutes later did I finally leave my feasting frenzy and settle into my chair. If Alice or Devon disapproved, they didn't show it, and Felana only smiled encouragingly.

"I'm glad you enjoyed our cooking."

I resisted the urge to rub my very full stomach. "Thank you. I'm a little surprised you have meat to serve."

She cocked her head. "Why is that?"

"Uh, sorry. I kind of thought with the murals that you guys were vegetarians. There is a lot of pro-flora imagery."

"Oh!" she chuckled. "We worship our goddess Yjana. She is part of nature as a whole, not just the plants. Beasts eat beasts, so we also partake in the consumption of meat."

Felana seemed happy to be talking about her goddess, so I asked a few follow-up questions until Devon cut in and made us leave. Unlike finding an inn like I thought, he brought us outside the village walls and near the forest.

We continued until he declared our search complete and sat. Alice walked off and gathered sticks, soon having a small bundle.

No...

"Settle in, pup. Start collecting more wood and dried leaves to start the fire," Devon commanded.

"We're not staying out here, are we? I don't even have a sleeping roll or a tent."

He remained silent.

Of course, we are. Why would I ever think anything easy from you?

"Do we have to worry about monster attacks? Or more ambushes? Anything?"

"Remember the saying?"

I ground my teeth. "Yes. I do."

"Good. Get to it."

Chapter 49

A Child's Tale

Safe, warm, protected.

I hunt, but not the star. New prey, new task.

Must keep promise, must protect my kin.

Howl, call, begin the endless hunt!

When I woke up, I smelled the remnants of campfire smoke. The fire itself had dimmed considerably, barely more than a few flickering flames poking out beneath the logs. A small gust stirred the embers, sending the smoke wafting away into the canopy.

I blinked and noticed Devon staring at me from across the fire, his back pressed against a tree.

"Nothing came?" I asked.

"No," he answered.

Alice slept against her own tree.

At least one of us is getting some good rest.

My back popped as I stretched. "I don't understand how you think this is normal. Why not bring something you can sleep on, at least?"

"Why does it matter if you'll be fine within the hour?"

Because it still sucks to wake up with a kinked neck.

I said nothing, enjoying the chill wind against my cheek. The woods smelled fresh—like nature, neither bad nor good. And unlike the silent forest from my first mission, birds and insects filled the night with their calls.

I met Devon's eyes again. "Is she asleep?"

"Yes."

"Then answer me this. Would you have really said no to saving the child?"

"I already answered you."

A rumble built, and I clawed at the dirt. "If you could—if you could actually save the child and there wasn't payment—would you have said no?"

Another gust blew, timed to the rising tension. The fire pit smoldered before the wind let up, and flames flickered back to life.

Answer me, Devon.

He grabbed a stick and stuck it in the fire; the leaf attached to the broken branch caught light instantly, adding a modicum of fuel to the struggling flame.

"Yes."

My muscles tensed. I opened my mouth to speak, but he shook his head and tossed in another stick.

"I would have said no. It doesn't mean I wouldn't have tried." His eyes were crimson: bright and ethereal in the fire's dim light. "I owe only two people my life and no one else. What I do or decide to do is my own choice. I'm not a protector, Cain. I'm a Hunter with only one task."

To find the prey!

"To continue the endless hunt?"

His eyes narrowed. "Yes."

There was a lot more I wanted to say, but the calm on Alice's face made me choose to enjoy the silence instead.

Anger. You looked ready to burn the world, Devon.

I let that fall to the back of my mind while I enjoyed the smell of bark and ash.

The rest of the hour was spent trying unsuccessfully to fall back asleep. Eventually, I gave up and stretched. My stomach took the opportunity to growl, and I exhaled exasperatedly.

"How long am I supposed to go through this?"

"It lasts a few weeks. It'll keep extending when you go through massive stat changes."

I froze. "How did you know?"

"You leveled yesterday?"

"Yes, actually," I answered. I motioned toward Alice. "Her too. Apparently, it might be because of the Granny."

Honestly, I half expected him to react to the news of her leveling, but he showed no outwards reaction. Instead, he pulled up his hood, covering his long hair with a sheet of red.

"You're moving differently. You must have gained stats in agility."

"You sure she's asleep?"

"Yes. Why?"

"You already know my Lore Strain is different. Did Elias ever tell you that he could assign his stats directly? That he can choose where to allocate them?"

The stone beneath his hand reduced to bits of powder.

Yeah. I thought you'd react like that.

"No," he bit out.

A part of me wanted to admit the extent of the stat changes, but I decided to keep it close to the chest for now. If he never asked, I had no reason to potentially alienate myself further. Despite Neina's warning, I trusted him. Maybe not with my life, but he had shown a willingness to at least care—whether for me as a pup or just because he felt obligated to the pack. I didn't know, and frankly, I didn't care.

"We heading back to the city?"

"Yes. But food first."

Hmm?

He stood and pulled on a piece of rope attached to the trunk nearby. A deer corpse strung up by its feet dropped and swung above the dirt.

Devon untied the knots and rested the deer on top of a pile of leaves, its three eyes gazing lifelessly. He slung it over his shoulder. It looked heavy—smaller than the moon elk—but bulky enough.

He walked to where Alice slept and lightly prodded her with his boot. When she sprung up like a cat ready to attack, he swiftly grabbed her by the wrist.

She whirled around ready to pounce but stopped when she noticed the two of us staring. Devon wore a neutral mask while I leaned away. Her shoulders relaxed.

"Oh, you hunted breakfast. Are we heading out?" she asked.

"Yes. Back to the church."

Alice quickly went to work and doused the fire. She stomped it down, leaving nothing but a dirt-covered pit.

Together, they set off, leaving me behind.

Hopefully, the priestess can do something with the deer.

* * *

The deer barely fazed the church residents. If anything, they looked excited to have a bunch of fresh meat. I ate my fill and then some.

Devon gifted them the rest of the deer, and we were once again in Thelassa's chambers. Except this time, the busty lady and her daughter joined. The daughter, in particular, stared at the three of us with wide eyes that glimmered with excitement.

"Okay, dear, can you please explain to these heroic Hunters what happened?" Thelassa asked.

Seyenna smiled and nodded.

"I was playing with Do'lby. We stayed near the walls! I promise," she began.

Thelassa nodded for her to continue while lightly patting the girl's arm. "And then what happened?"

"We were looking for a bug, but then he decided to scare me," she continued. She puffed out her cheeks.

"Then Do'lby scared me, and that was mean, so I chased him. He ran fast, but I was faster! So I caught him and tackled him!"

It would have been a cute retelling of a child's playdate if it weren't for the heavy breaths she took between each sentence. Her teary-eyed mother rubbed her back but managed a smile when Seyenna looked at her for approval.

"Good job, honey! Can you explain what happened next? Did your chase take you away from the walls?"

Her bright smile turned downtrodden, and she raised her shoulders in a guilty expression. "Yes. I'm sorry."

Her mother sighed and hugged her shoulders. "It's okay. Just keep telling these kind people your story, and we'll talk about it later. I promise I'm not mad."

With those magic words, she brightened and nodded. "So I won, and Do'lby was defeated. I said he had to find the prettiest flower as my prize, and then he went deeper into the woods. He then came back with a bright pink one! But he said there's more, and I needed a crown because I'm the winner."

Thelassa and the mother shared a look. Eventually, Thelassa lowered to meet eye-to-eye with the girl. "Dear, are you sure? Do'lby made you follow him deeper into the forest?"

For a second, she looked scared again but regained her smile.

"No," she said while shaking her head. "He didn't make me. He's my friend."

"Right, dearie. And then what happened when you went searching for the flowers?"

"Well. He acted strangely, and when the wall disappeared, I got scared and said we should go back, but he didn't want to go back and grabbed my arm. I'm... sorry. I told him to stop, but he wouldn't."

She sank, her face scrunching up. "I remember smelling more pretty flowers, and he stopped pulling. I... I don't remember after that. I'm sorry."

The mother wrapped her arms around the child and gently shushed her. Nobody said a word as she led her out of the room, leaving the three of us once again alone with Thelassa.

"What she isn't able to tell you in that story is that Do'lby, her friend, never did such things. In fact, he went back to his parents when he couldn't find the girl," she said wearily, her body drooping into her chair.

Chapter 50

One More Night in the Woods

We were back in the forest, sitting and waiting for Devon to tell us what to do next. He stood with his eyes closed, leaning against a tree, his hood up. No matter how many questions I asked, he remained dead silent.

"Devon, seriously. What's the game plan?" I demanded.

"The plan is to wait," he grumbled.

"You don't think that's silly? All things considered? Especially with what happened yesterday?"

"Have you paid zero attention to what I've been saying?"

I knocked my head against the trunk behind me. "Maybe I'd prefer not having to rescue another literal child from the clutches of some monsters."

"Alice. Explain."

She sat up. "It's because of the cores. They're too small. And there's the corrupted bear you fought yesterday." Devon remained silent, so she shrugged and continued. "The cores are small—too small. That means the elementals are new. The bear wouldn't last for long; its body would break down. That means the mana leaking from the seals is only starting to affect the area."

I looked between them both and eventually settled on Alice. "Okay, I get that. But why wait, then? Wouldn't it be better to search for the monster now while it doesn't have other mobs to back it up?"

"Where would you search?" Devon interrupted. "Where would you look—for a creature you know almost nothing about—who has the ability to create more monsters?"

"I... don't know. I sort of thought you would."

"This isn't the last hunt where the creature responded to anything entering its territory. If it's related to the seal, that means whatever is kidnapping people will be looking to break its prison open."

"Oh. Ooh. And getting a horde of monsters is a good way to do that?"

"Possibly. Now, silence. If nothing comes to mess with us in the next few hours, we'll head back."

And just like that, Devon went silent, and we headed back to town.

The whole wait felt useless, as if we sat out there specifically to do nothing, even if Devon said it was for a reason.

Once we were back in the church, sitting alone in the feasting room, I stood up and sat in front of Devon. "You've been tight-lipped, and I want answers. One, and I really should have asked this, but how do I induce the shift? I already did it once. Can I do it again? Two, are we going to sit here all day?"

"For a pup who was little more than a traumatized kid less than a week ago, you sure changed a lot."

I growled. "That's not the point."

Or maybe it's because I'm getting too exhausted to be shocked by everything anymore.

"No to the first. When you can bring out your claws, you'll know how to proceed from there. It's instinct. Don't bother asking me to teach you instinct," he said calmly. "And yes, we will sit here if that's what's required."

My head sank until it rested on the table.

I don't know why I'm feeling so antsy, but I am. It just feels wrong to sit here.

A glance at Alice, mimicking Devon perfectly, only pissed me off further, so I switched my focus to munching on another piece of venison.

At least I'm getting fed gloriously.

* * *

The crackle of fire woke me up, and I blinked my drowsiness away to stare at the stable flames.

Right. Forest.

Another wasted day. Yesterday, despite all of our waiting, nothing happened: no monsters came, no kidnappings, no terrifying screeches of the damned clawing at innocent souls.

Nothing.

I should have been happy about the peace the town received, but knowing something so dangerous stalked the forest did not sit well with me.

Yet, no matter how much I protested, Devon stood firm in his reasoning. What could we do? Even if we combed the forest for the creature, it guaranteed nothing.

If only talking to them didn't feel like pulling teeth. I might relax a little.

Speaking of the living abrasives, Devon was in rare form. His head hung low, and his hood covered his eyes while he sat motionless. Alice slept as she did the last time: back straight, leaning against a tree, with her hand hovering near her axe.

I waited, but Devon didn't speak up. Standing up slowly, I paused again, but he remained asleep.

I guess he has to nap sometime.

I added another stick to the fire and walked away from the camp. With their insane sense of smell, I had to go a fair bit away. When I finally reached a nice secluded spot, I relieved my bladder and watched the night sky.

The moon stayed hidden behind the clouds, but enough light shone down that I could just barely see myself in the dark. The coverage from the clouds must have been nice for all the nocturnal denizens of the forest.

After finishing up, I headed back to the camp. My boots crunched loudly on some leaves, but if Devon hadn't woken up when I left, I doubted it would be a problem now.

When I returned to the campsite, the two were still sleeping, so I sat back down by my trunk and resumed resting. The silent night was comforting, punctuated only by the steady crackling of the fire.

I've never been outdoors this much. Hooray for new experiences.

My sarcasm was rewarded with a mirthless chuckle that I barely managed to muster. Surprisingly, alone time sucked. I didn't want it.

Pop!

A small fleck of ash shot across the ground and landed next to my boot. The ash mixed with dirt as a gentle breeze blew it off the leather. It was a mundane thing, entirely dull.

Screw it, get some sleep.

I closed my eyes, only to open them again before they fully shut.

I waited and listened. But I only heard the campfire. A breeze shook the leaves overhead, yet no sound of rustling reached my ears.

My axe slid from its sheath, and I slowly stood up while scanning the surrounding trees. Alice continued to rest, her chest rising and falling rhythmically. Yet, my fingers tightened their grip when I looked toward Devon's resting form.

He no longer breathed.

"Devon. Tell me you're awake," I said calmly.

No response.

My heart rate quickened as the hairs on my neck stood.

"Alice, get up. Now."

I kicked a rock her way, but it bounced off her leg.

I called for my wolf, but again, no reaction. I didn't even feel a stir through the connection.

"Get up—both of you. Get. Up."

A strong gust howled through the forest, and the orange blaze cooled before winking out. The area was bathed in shadows that the moonlight struggled to banish.

I summoned the rune in my head, calling to the mana in my chest. It bubbled and stirred, rising to my demand. But as I pictured the void filling with teeth and claws, the rune sputtered and tugged at my core.

The strange recoil made me cough. The lava that kept me perpetually warm burned like acid reflux. I growled and powered through the discomfort. There was something there; I felt the connection, but it blipped out of my senses before I could trace it.

Another gust, and my cloak wrapped around my sides. The protection from the sharp wind abated, and I tossed my hood up, feeling it ripple around me.

The familiarity of my cloak anchored me back to reality, and I took a step back while raising my axe. Alice was gone.

Across the now cold fire—hidden beneath a cascade of shadows—stood the tall, looming form of Devon. His hood covered his eyes, but his hands slowly flexed, each finger clawing at the air.

I didn't know what to say, so I did the only thing I could. "Cut the games. Can you speak?"

The creature pretending to be my mentor flashed a bright smile, the white shining like the moonlight.

Chapter 51

Shady Deals

Screw this.

My arm extended, and the fire crawled along my palm. Runic lines blazed to life, fueled by the heat flowing through my veins.

The fire clamored for release, but then the shadows swarmed. They rose like a tide, blocking out the light, consuming it whole.

"Ek kalla heiðarloga!"

Fire shot out, and instead of punching through the darkness, the shadow tide folded over the blazing ball, wrapping around it like cloth. The flames exploded, pushing back the leaves and rustling the edges of my hood, but the shadows swallowed them.

They receded until it was once again just me and the creature standing, staring at each other across the fire pit.

It opened its mouth, and a warble of words screeched out. I covered my ears as the sound scratched at my brain, like nails on a chalkboard. Flames emerged from my palm again, but the creature stopped and closed its mouth, hiding the pearly white smile.

When it opened its jaw a second time, I braced myself, but instead of wailing like a dying cat, a smooth, almost buttery voice tickled my ears.

"Hmm. Can you understand me now?" the creature asked.

Sounds male, deep, polite. Not a young creature.

I kept the flames ready and waiting, the fire building in the center of my palm but not breaking through the skin.

"I can, but I don't think it matters," I replied.

"I think it does, Grimm. Hmm." His voice carried through the air as if designed to deliver itself into my ears at the perfect volume. "Are you really a Grimm?"

Pack! Kin! I am a Hunter!

The flames brightened, coating my fingers in a wave. My chest tightened, and I flashed my canines. "Watch your words."

Even though a chill ran down my spine, heat seared through my body in a riot.

"Am I wrong? I can sense it—your Lore. It tastes different."

In the corner of my eye, a few of the trees started to disappear, being covered in a blanket of black void.

The smell of burning skin reached my nose, but I didn't care. Fire illuminated my face, and I reveled in watching the shadows recede. "Did you touch the others?"

In response, it broke its stiffness.

"Unharmed," it answered. Its bright smile glared from the depths of its hood. "For now."

"Ek kalla heiðarloga."

Flames shot forward in a whoosh! Another wave rose to consume it, but this time, I caught a twitch in the creature's smile: subtle and nearly impossible to notice if I hadn't been forced to stare at its teeth.

"Why? Why stay with them? You're not the same. You may call them kin, but I know it's untrue."

Smoke rose from my hand, and a line of black snaked around my digits.

Silence! Liar! Am pack!

A flicker in my core caused my eyes to drift downwards. The sensation vanished before I could pinpoint the disturbance in my mana pool. Realizing my lapse, I quickly looked up, but it was too late.

A cold hand grabbed my wrist, searing my flesh with ice. My skin sizzled with the dueling temperatures. I tried to yank my arm away, but the shadowy limb holding my wrist in place bulged like a balloon.

"I can sense it—taste it even—the difference between you three. It's still there, slowly burning away piece by piece. Until you have nothing left. The system is careful about that."

Iron rushed for the creature's head, but it stopped my arm, holding me at bay. My leg flew out, but more shadows rose to grab my ankle.

"How about a real offer? No games, no tricks. A real, genuine offer?"

Lies! Prey! Hunt! No Dea—

"What?" I ground out, silencing the voice in my head.

It must have been what the creature was looking for because its dazzling smile grew a few extra teeth, brighter and bigger. "It's still there, even with the inferno in your chest. The Nexus isn't closed to you, not yet."

My muscles stopped straining. Like a flipped switch, the world became brighter. I blinked slowly. "What... do you mean?"

"Oh, it's simple. Help get me free, and I'll open the pathway to your old world."

Instead of responding, I snapped at the creature's arm, aiming to sink my canines into its shadowy flesh.

Shadows tried to constrict around my throat, but my cloak flared, and they fell away. The devilish grin it maintained twitched, and instead, something solid and freezing cold pushed against my chest, holding me back.

"Why? Why react so aggressively to such an offer? Don't you want to go home—return to your friends and loved ones?" it continued, sounding hurt.

Like I'd ever believe an offer like that!

"Let go of me!" I exclaimed.

"Oh? Is it something I said? I feel as if I've been very cordial," the creature remarked.

I stopped struggling, standing still just enough to peer into the void that rested inside the hood. Another flare in my core brought a surge of fury, urging me to rip and tear the creature to pieces.

Slowly, I got out every word, struggling to chew the bile at the back of my throat. "A monster that kidnaps children cannot be reasoned with!"

It leaned closer, just out of reach of my teeth. "And if I returned the child? Promised not to touch a single hair on their head?"

I froze.

The creature, ignoring my stiffness, continued talking. "If you're willing to help free me, then I would have no need for the child. I'll even throw in the portal back home. It's a good deal. All I want is my freedom. What do you say?"

"Would you..." I began slowly. The colors brightened even more, and I saw orange reflect off the white of its teeth. "Swear to the system?"

Almost as if it was waiting for that very question, I felt the force against my chest ease by a fraction. "Ooh. Yes, I can make a system promise. I'm surprised someone as new as you knows what that is. Hmm... yes. But you understand you must complete your end of the bargain?"

Get away. Liar. Decei—

"Yes. I do. If you agree to return the child, I'll do it."

Prey! Hunt!

I drowned out the voice, letting the lava cool my wrists and sizzle beneath my skin.

The creature's tone shifted to a higher-pitched thrumming that tickled my ears. "Oh good, good! So many Grimms... All savage folk who know not the power of a deal. You understand you'll have to speak the first words?"

The connection blazed to life, lasting longer than a mere flicker, and I felt an anger different from my own come through it.

I smiled. "I do. You're right, I want to go home."

It paused to study me, and its smile extended beyond the confines of its hood, over the facsimile of Devon's jaw and stretching into the strands of his hair, superimposed as if it were drawn on.

"Then speak the words, and I shall follow." It paused and shifted closer. "Once done, I'll release you. I do apologize for the rough treatment, but I had to protect myself. None of it will matter. Once we have the promise in place, we can both rest easy knowing we won't betray each other."

I didn't react, simply nodding. I looked at the shell of darkness that had risen around us.

Waiting longer than I should have, I carefully lowered my face until the orange glow of my eyes glared back. The fear slithering across my spine faded away, and I let the heat swim upwards, warming my bones. The tug at the center of my chest filled my voice with steel.

"Oh system, by the rules that bind and the powers that be, I solemnly vow…"

The creature cocked its head. "To try my best to free the shadow sealed in stone. I shall not sabotage or betray the monster before me."

So even you recognize yourself as a monster. How fitting.

"Oh, System, by the rules that bind and the powers that be, I solemnly vow…" I trailed off, letting my voice drop. I squared my shoulders and exhaled. "To absolutely nothing."

Chapter 52

Shade's Temptation

The connection blazed so brightly in my mind that I could hear the sound of the beast clawing at the gates.

Even as shadows rose like a devouring swarm to consume me whole, I smiled savagely and raised my head to howl.

Darkness overcame the moonlight, and my vision faded.

"Wuulf!"

Talons shredded black curtains, creating a gleam of white in between. The negative lines tore the wave into strips that splashed against my body. My cloak absorbed the brunt of the freezing chill, and I accepted the rest as it invaded my muscles and sparked against my bones.

The world distorted, vibrating hard enough to send me to my knees as the bulging limbs holding me released their grip.

"No! Nooo! NOOUGGHH!"

Each rejection rose in pitch, losing the smooth baritone. My ears rang, and my vision swam.

Fire, burn, and blaze. Create the heat. Push the void away!

"Ek kalla heiðarloga."

Power surged, and I let it engulf my arm until the last of the bandages burned away. The flames pooled and formed a blazing sphere that warmed my face. When it shot out, it whistled.

The creature released me fully, and the shadows pulled away. Before my flames reached it, it zipped like a bullet, pulling away the blanket of black.

When the surrounding forest reappeared, a red cloak flapped against the breeze, then spun around following an iron axe.

"Cain, duck!"

I dropped to the ground as Alice lunged. A choked scream was cut off, and blood splattered the ground. It sizzled and popped, releasing a cloyingly sweet scent that turned sharply putrid.

Corrupted!

I kicked up and rolled, turning around to see a three-eyed deer. Its massive antlers jutted at odd angles, some bending around to pierce its own skull. Dried black blood crusted the punctures, and when it blinked, each eye vibrated.

My arm was nothing more than an unresponsive piece of charcoal. As the deer smashed its head against a trunk—trying to skewer Alice—I leaped.

It happened too fast. I managed to bring my axe down just in time before I impaled myself. The air left my chest, and I dragged the thick beast down with me to the earth. It released a haunting screech and kicked. One hoof cut a line across my pants, the razor-sharp edge drawing blood.

It released another cry, and a hoof came for my face, but my wolf rose from my shadow and crunched down. Shadows blinded me, but I raised my axe anyway and swung.

Iron met rough fur and thick muscle, so I swung again. The beast shuddered and stopped moving.

Once the corpse coated me in a shower of corrupted blood, I got to my feet. My wolf followed, standing in front with its tail pressed against my pants, its head rotating on a swivel.

I looked around, ready for another fight, but Alice stood nearby, her axe resting on the ground.

Her eyebrow raised, she stared at my arm. "What happened?"

My eye twitched.

That's what I should be asking you!

"I got trapped by a shapeshifter in some nightmare realm. It kept asking me to make a deal to free it. I think it might have been the Sealed One," I said.

"What?!" she replied. "How could it have—Ugh. Devon needs to tell us what's going on."

I looked around, taking in the changes to our small campsite. Firstly, two trees lay uprooted, their trunks shattered. Nearby, a deer corpse protruded from a bush, and close by, three wolves—each with scorpion-like tails—lay with their heads cleanly severed.

Behind Alice was a giant bunny with a massive horn jutting from the center of its forehead. Its paws had sharpened claws longer than my hand and two elongated fangs. The pale red eyes stared lifelessly, and it rested on the ground with a massive chunk missing from its neck.

It's nearly the size of my wolf, holy hell.

"Devon?" I asked. "Where did he go?"

She twisted and swiped hair out of her face, smearing blood across the blonde strands. "When your illusion faded, something zipped through the trees, and Devon gave chase."

"So, wait here or head back to the church again?"

She shrugged and examined the dead rabbit. With ease, she flipped it onto its back and pulled out a knife. Expertly, she made an incision beneath the paw and circled around before sliding it down the hind leg. She connected it to the belly before repeating.

The sound was highly unpleasant, but her knife glided through the connective tissue as she worked the pelt off the beast. By the time she finished, a disturbingly skinned animal corpse stared at me with dead eyes, which Alice ignored in favor of rolling up the hide and bundling it with some string.

"I thought we don't touch corrupted animals. Devon never showed any interest," I commented, securing my hood to block out the horrific sight.

"The meat is toxic to most humans; even most forest animals know to avoid these corpses. But the pelt is safe—probably enhanced from the mana to be sturdier."

I stared at the deer corpse, noticing the wild slashes cut deep into its hide.

Yeah, don't think this one is worth saving.

"You going to do the wolves or bear?"

She shook her head. "Bears roll around in carrion, and the wolves have venom on their fur. Look at the yellow tint that connects from their tails."

I followed her finger and noticed what she meant. It was hard to tell, but a drop of yellow moved from one hair to another, the surface of the coat oily enough for the dirt to soak up each drop.

Snorting, I lowered my head and met my summon's gaze. The swirling black eyes greeted mine, and I accepted the press of its cold tongue against my cheek.

"Hey. Thanks for saving me. Would have been a goner without you."

"Wulf!"

I wrapped my arm around the wolf's belly and gave it a firm squeeze before joining Alice in sniffing the air. It smelled familiar, and we were not surprised when Devon came crashing through the brush.

He examined the surroundings, lingering on the skinned rabbit and the pelt in Alice's arms before focusing on my toasted limb.

"Cain said the creature spoke to him before it fled," Alice explained. "It claims it's the Sealed One."

Devon's eyes flashed red. "You met with the Sealed One?"

I let out a mirthless chuckle. "Yeah. I got trapped in some shadow realm. I didn't notice at first and went to relieve myself. When I got back, I almost went to bed, but then I noticed how silent the forest was."

"And how it shouldn't be," he stated.

I nodded. "Yeah. Then Alice was gone, and it pretended to be you: keeping your body, clothes, and hair but no face. Just a bright white smile."

"Then?"

"Well… It kept trying to ask me to betray you two. Told me I wasn't a Grimm, not like you. And it even tried to get me to swear to the system."

Devon's eyes narrowed. "And?"

I flipped him off. He blinked, staring at the finger before shifting back to my face. "What do you take me for, Devon? I played along and told it to piss off. My wolf came in, tore through whatever it was doing to keep me separated from you two, and then it fled."

"That's it?"

"Yes. That's it."

He sat on the bear's corpse, and blood oozed as he pressed down. "I tried to give chase, but it was too fast—even when shifted. It led me around in circles and got away."

"So, we're back where we started," Alice said. "We'll have to wait for another attack or kidnapping."

"If we have something belonging to it, I could set up a ritual to bind it, but without that, we'll have to wait for another chance," Devon replied.

"And I'm to play bait again? Because I doubt it'll try the same tactic twice—not now when I've already made it clear it can't tempt me to its side," I said.

"What did it offer?" he asked coolly.

That sounds more like a command than a question, but fine.

"A way home. Something about there being enough of a spark for it to create a pathway through the Nexus. And freeing all of the children."

Devon said nothing, and a tense silence filled the campsite.

Of course, Alice possessed zero social hesitation and cut through the tension with the question. "And you didn't take it?"

"No," I growled. "No, I didn't take the shady deal from a monster that kidnaps kids."

She simply nodded and turned to Devon, who looked up blankly.

He stood. "Let's go. Nothing for us here, and you'll be hungry soon."

All the tension in my body fell away, and I barely contained my sigh.

Yeah, just another day on the hunt. So fun.

Of course, just as I got ready to move, a tug at the connection between me and my summon drew my eyes toward the wolf. Another tug followed, and then it opened its jaw wide before spitting out a piece of what looked like swirling shadows. The shadows moved and shifted away from the brighter beam of light.

I smiled at Devon. "Looks like my wolf did your job for you."

Chapter 53

Last Minute Prep

The system notification came.

[ALERT] You have slain Corrupted Beasts x2
Calculating hunt reward...
Applying Strain Modifier: -25%
Calculation complete.

After the notification appeared, it blinked out. Apparently, I wasn't lucky enough to be rewarded every time I hunted.

When I asked Devon why the number count was so low, he shrugged. The system had its own method of deciding whether or not I deserved to share experience for a kill.

Frustrating, but fair. I shouldn't have gotten a lot of kobold kills, but I did, so I can't really complain.

We headed back to the church for several reasons. One was to bathe in a place that had some crude but better-than-nothing soaps. The second reason was to satisfy the insane appetite that showed no signs of calming.

Every time Felana served what must have been a smörgåsbord of food, I felt bad. But when I expressed my concern, I'd receive a chuckle and a hand wave.

Now that our civilized needs were settled, we were once again with Thelassa. She regarded the contained piece of shadow cloth with apprehension.

"You want me to close the gates and tell the town to hide away in their homes. Is that right?"

"Correct," Devon answered.

Lines in her brow furrowed deeply. "If that's what you think is best, Hunters. I will do so. Will this guarantee an end to our problem?"

"The ritual will bind the creature. Once done, we'll be able to track it and then dispatch the monster."

"And..." she swallowed. Hesitantly, she cleared her throat. "And what about the... captured women and children?"

Devon might as well have been the Grim Reaper with the look he gave her. "If they survive the hunt, then we'll secure their safety."

She nodded and stood. "Give us an hour. We'll have everything prepared."

We watched her leave and shut the door. Devon pulled out a small vial filled with almost glittery yellow liquid. After placing it on the table along with a small cloth sack and several other small pouches, he looked between the two of us.

"Once I start the ritual, you two will have to defend me," he began. He pulled out the contained piece of shadow cloth. "The creature will panic and throw everything at us. If the ritual is disrupted, we waste the ingredients. If we're lucky, we get two chances."

That's not good. You're our strongest member.

"Why not have one of us do the ritual? You're the strongest one here. Wouldn't it be safer to just have you do it?" I asked.

"Because you don't know the runes needed. And you barely know any runes whatsoever," he said, holding up a hand to forestall the obvious question. "And neither does Alice. Even if she did know the right runes, you both don't have enough mana to support it."

That shut me up.

"Fine, so we have to fend off waves of monsters? That's crazy and insane. And why do you plan on doing it outside the town—the town with nice big walls to protect it?"

"Cain," he stated coolly.

"What?"

"Is that a serious question?"

You know what?

"Yes, it is a serious question. We have the means to defend ourselves. Why not use it?" I insisted.

"You're still angry over the missing child, so tell me, what happens when the monsters break down the walls and start ravaging the city in a mad scramble? Will the sacrifice of innocent lives be morally acceptable to you then? Is this what needs to happen for you to get over the shackles of your old world?" he asked, his tone edged with severity.

My blood ran cold. "No, I understand," I conceded.

"I'm glad we're in agreement then," he said. As we resumed our walk, he paused. "Remember, those four spires are all that's keeping the Sealed One's body locked away. If we're forced to fight the full form, our mission fails. Considering what will happen if we don't take the brunt of the danger, we can only perform the ritual away from the city."

That's a much more reasonable definition... Still, I see your point, even if you're a jerk about it.

From there, Devon outlined the plans. We would be heading toward a spot, coincidentally near the campsite we had used for the past two nights. I vaguely recalled the area: it was densely forested, providing ample protection. Additionally, a river on one side of the area limited what types of creatures could approach.

Glancing at Alice, I found her smiling.

Her skill was versatile, making me somewhat jealous of her ability to send out a literal wave of frost.

A slight nudge from my chest made me look down and see the blurry form of a wolf snout poking out.

Yeah, yeah. You're great too, I promise.

We waited for the hour allotted to the church. Once that passed, loud bells rang, each thrum vibrating the walls.

Devon stood and collected the concoction he was preparing. "It's time."

We followed him out of the room and into the hallway. As we reached the main room, a third ring drowned out the rush of hushed whispers. A baby cried only to be shushed by its mother.

Turning the corner, the usually roomy church was packed to the brim with people. Mothers, fathers, teenagers, and other townsfolk took up the benches and stood in groups.

As one, they turned and cleared a path out of the building. Bodies pressed together, and eyes watched our every step. Some looked angry. Others looked hopeful, and plenty looked afraid.

As we crossed the room, a new kind of smell assaulted me. It reeked of sweat—a sour scent that caused anger to well up—as well as another emotion that disgusted me.

Why does this make me wanna smile?

It brought an excited feeling to the energy within, as if my nerves wanted to fire up and force my legs to pounce.

Turning my head, I noticed the smell came from a man to my right. When I met the eyes of a skinny bloke sweating through his shirt, the excitement faded away and gave rise to disgust.

He glanced up, then whimpered before looking away and rubbing his scarred arms. Five lines of off-colored pale flesh ran from his shoulder to his elbow. A tug on my sleeve made me turn my focus to Alice. Nodding apologetically, I followed, and we left the church, turning down a side street.

Even outside, people gathered and made their way toward the building.

"You'll get used to the smells," Devon said.

"Huh?" I shook my head. "What did you say?"

"Back in the church, your eyes briefly shifted, and you stopped to smell a man who nearly pissed himself. The face you made, excitement turned to revulsion. That's because you smelled his fear," he explained.

Fear? Then why did I get excited?

"Why... did I feel—"

"Excited? Ready to hunt?"

"Yeah."

"You're a predator, Cain. A rabbit to a fox is a fun chase. If you realize that your prey is none of those things, the excitement will die."

"I don't like looking at scared humans and calling them prey," I stated.

Alice cocked her head. "You called them humans. Do you accept that you're not one of them?"

I didn't know what to say. I hadn't even meant it that way, but now that the thought was implanted in my head, I couldn't help but feel that she was right.

Like Adeline said, you won't be human—no matter how well you hide it.

"Sorry, I'm ready."

The two of them said nothing, and we continued our way out of the gate. More than ten guards stood tall with their shoulders tensed. Those who whispered under their breaths stopped when the rest of their company turned to face us.

Again, the guards saluted—not all, but most. They had grim looks, dark enough to color the sky. Over eighty percent of them had spears, gripped in tight fists.

The last two, the ones with swords, stepped up and nodded at Devon. "We're ready, sir. Is there anything you need of us?" one asked.

Devon stood, unfazed by the guardsmen.

"Just be prepared. There's no guarantee of monsters showing up, but if they do, protect the walls. If that fails, protect the spires. The chains cannot be broken," Devon ordered.

One guard looked pissed, but a silencing glare prevented him from responding.

"It will be done. Good luck on your hunt."

The guards shut the gate behind us, and I looked up at the towering walls. Bands of metal reinforced the door frames, preparing them for the siege.

"Do you really think there are enough monsters to swarm the city?"

"No, not even close," Devon responded. "But it only takes a few to slip through to do enough damage."

"And the chains? The seals? Do you think normal monsters can destroy them?"

"Maybe."

He went silent and moved through the trees.

Chapter 54

PROTECT THE CIRCLE

Devon had us clear the ground of every stray rock. With the stones removed, leaving a grassy circle, he had everyone step out.

"Cain. Burn the grass; do not disturb the ground."

I raised my arm and closed my eyes, conjuring the spark. I kept the flame low and restarted when it grew too big. A new flame took its place: small, barely a match's worth of light.

Runic lines appeared and blazed once settled in. My mana came to life, flowing down my arm but forced to crawl as it neared my palm. I let it connect to the rune in my head, and the flame grew larger but still well within control.

"Ek kalla heiðarloga."

Flames shot out and landed on the grass. It lit up like a wildfire, and bright green turned black instantly. I smelled burnt dew, but the flames didn't mind the liquid as they turned the grass into ash.

I lowered my palm and rubbed at the skin: smooth, not bleeding or cracked, and only a little dry.

I'm getting better at this. Maybe after another dozen tries, I'll stop self-immolating.

"Do we need to clear the ash?" I asked.

He shook his head and pulled out a different vial. The liquid had changed from a bright yellow to a crimson red, but I recognized the stem from a plant he used.

After pulling off the stopper, he poured the contents onto the ash, dyeing it pink. When he stepped back, the liquid moved on its own, spreading out to cover the circle.

"That's not right. Liquids shouldn't come to life."

Devon ignored me and pulled out another vial, this one a murky gray. He repeated the process, and the circle looked dusty.

"What exactly are you doing?"

"Preparing the spell circle. The ash will be the binding while the liquid primes it," he answered.

He pulled out a third vial, and the circle became a muted black. Devon didn't look worried, but he never smiled to begin with.

Alice, for her part, had her axe out and a small cloth soaked in oil.

I adjusted my cloak. It tightened, squeezing onto my shoulders before relaxing.

That, at least, brought a genuine smirk to my face.

Devon clapped and rubbed his hands together. Something crumbled between his palms and started to flake to the ground. The particles joined the ash and faded. But a change took place and created a buzz in the air.

He stepped inside, his feet leaving the ground undisturbed until he reached the middle. As he stood in the center, the buzzing grew louder, which triggered my cloak to envelop me in an energy shell. The buzzing subsided, and I rubbed my aching jawbone.

Alice's mouth twitched. She hastily wrapped the rag into a bundle of leather and shoved it into her satchel.

Devon shouted, but his words came out distorted, as if he were speaking from inside a bubble. "I'll be starting in the next click. Ready yourself. Do not let anything disturb the circle."

He placed both hands on the ground, and they sank to his elbows—far deeper than they should have. The buzzing intensified even with my cloak protecting me.

Alice's eyes were no longer human. They glowed bright red, her fangs exposed in a vicious snarl. She swept her head around and saw me staring. She squinted and pulled up her hood.

Her face partially relaxed, looking strained but no longer savagely angry.

I moved closer so I didn't have to yell. "Are you okay?"

She gritted her teeth. "I'll be fine. My cloak is enough to protect me from the effects as long as my hood is up."

I rubbed the red fabric draped behind me.

Thanks again for the protection.

The sudden feeling of my wolf leaving my shadow forced me to whip around, bringing up my axe.

A loud cry trilled out as my wolf leaped and latched its black fangs onto the side of a creature's neck. They crashed to the ground, sliding forward, while my summon melded into the shadows. Despite the fall, the deer kept its momentum, gliding across the grass and sending up a spray of dirt in its wake.

"Protect the circle!"

Alice swung her axe, cleanly cutting through the creature's neck. The deer hit her legs—bowing her over—but it stopped the corpse from sliding. I held out my arms.

Small clumps of dirt smacked into me, and my cloak flared, intercepting another.

With the circle protected, Alice dragged the corpse away. "No more talking. Focus."

I let out the breath and tightened my grip on my axe. My summon raised its head from the ground, and I flashed a smile.

"Good job. Let out a warning if you sense more; don't worry about protecting me right now."

It barked and rose, solidifying. It sniffed the air and walked out of the clearing. Through our connection, I could track its position even after the wolf vanished among the thick trees.

Minutes passed, and nothing else attacked. Then the connection flared, and I tensed. "Alice! Incoming!"

I closed my eyes and let the void pull me in. I gained my wolf's sight.

Damn. That's a lot.

They resembled kobolds, crafted not from burning coal but from green grass and thick brown roots. Eight charged through the trees—mouths agape—revealing jagged rock chunks. They brandished wooden picks, each twice as thick as those from the cave.

"Earth kobolds!"

She nodded, and that savage smile reappeared. It transformed my anxiety into an excited energy that surged through my limbs.

Hunt! Hunt! Crush the prey!

I shook my head and awaited my summon's return. Its blurry form emerged from the trees, and I joined Alice.

Once the sound of thumping reached our ears, she set off. We sprinted, and the sound became a vibration beneath our feet.

My shadow wolf kept up, but I ordered it to stay behind.

Can't *leave the circle unguarded.*

When the first of the monsters came, Alice raised her arm, and I readied myself.

I expected frost, but instead, the air around her palm hummed, and I braced myself for the impact.

The monsters swung, but she thrust her arm forward, releasing the accumulated mana. A wave of energy rippled through the air. Roots and stone collided with the projectile, only to be scattered by an explosive force.

Rocky forms tumbled. Alice was upon them, her heavy axe crashing into the legs of those who still stood.

I swung my axe, clipping the beard behind another's arm and dragging the teetering elemental to the ground.

The explosion devastated the kobolds, and I shoved the handle of my axe into one's neck. An ear-scratching creak filled the air, and I ground my teeth as it took everything I had to decapitate the monster.

Its head popped off, and a spurt of putrid brown liquid splashed. I nearly vomited from the smell but forced it down and moved on to the next prey.

The creature attempted to swing its massive pickaxe, but I stomped on its arm, driving it into the dirt and causing the weapon to drop.

I lifted the pickaxe, surprised by its lightness. It descended, tearing the monster's arm off at the shoulder. As I raised it again, a rough grip seized my leg, pulling me backwards.

My chin hit the dirt.

"Aargh!"

The stone grip on my ankle tightened, eliciting a protest from my bones.

No!

I swung the pickaxe and smashed it into the arm. I swung again and again. Each hit sent more splatters of the putrid liquid across my clothes, but I kept swinging.

I stood. Only one limb remained on the monster's body.

Die already!

I jammed the pickaxe into the gap between its chin and neck. Stone crumbled and wood splintered as both monster and axe shattered. The dim brown-yellow glow in its eyes faded to black.

My breath came out ragged, and I turned to see Alice dodging the wide swings of the last standing elemental. The one I had disarmed struggled to rock itself off the ground.

It turned. I lifted the pickaxe. Screeching gravel and vibrating stone pierced my eardrums, and I screamed in unison.

The heavy pickaxe met its shoulder, and it crashed to the floor. I raised it again and let it fall. The head broke off and went flying away. That didn't stop me.

I climbed over it, grabbing its eye sockets and hooking my fingers in place. One foot stomped on its upper back, and I pulled.

It screeched again, and I pulled harder.

With a final twist, the head came off in a shower of goop, and I tossed it away. A heavy thump blew some fallen leaves into the air, and Alice wedged the shaft of her axe into the final monster's neck.

Her smile made me realize how wide my own stretched across my face.

"Good job. Let's return to the circle."

Yeah. I guess we should.

A loud wolf howl rang through the trees, and our eyes widened. I grabbed another pickaxe and rushed back to the circle, where I felt my wolf take a hit.

Chapter 55

Blunt Force Damage

We raced back, and the entire time, my blood boiled.

Another buzz forced the connection to waver.

Come on!

I sent mana flowing through the connection, hoping to keep my wolf alive.

I kept up with Alice as we burst through the trees.

Another paw swiped at my wolf. It moved out of the way, but the spray of rocks clipped its hide and sent a salvo of flare-ups through the connection. Luckily, the summon had aimed the monster away from the circle, where Devon's blurry form vibrated through the static.

The massive bear roared. Its muscles bulged, and it lunged for my wolf, but the summon sunk into the ground and popped up a foot away.

I let the pickaxe trail behind me. As the bear reared, ready to squash the pesky shadow summon, I planted pressure on the ball of my foot and swung the pickaxe in a wide arc.

The pickaxe rotated end over end before the head impacted the bear's jaw and tore across its eye. Spit flew from the beast's snout as it recoiled from the surprise attack.

Like an idiot, I stopped to watch my wolf dig its claws into the bear's belly. It roared again and stumbled, but Alice capitalized on its confusion.

Iron met stomach; her weapon slid across the fat and skin before the beast reacted. Its fur puffed up, and her axe stopped its momentum. A heavy claw swung for her shoulder, but she ducked.

"Graagh!"

"Cain!" she called out.

My wolf jumped onto the bear's back and bit its throat, but fur bulged and covered the beast's neck like a thick scarf.

Fire sprung to life in my arm, and the rune connected to my mana.

"Step back!" I yelled.

Alice rolled away from another wild swing, and my wolf leaped, landing beside me.

Burn, Blaze, Incinerate!

"Ek kalla heiðarloga!"

Lava flowed through my veins, sputtering before pooling again at the center of my hand. I squeezed the flow shut, forcing it steady.

The fireball zipped through the air and exploded. Flames burst in its eyes and burned fur as the blaze spread down its neck. The bear smashed its head into the ground and desperately pawed at its face. The fur around its stomach loosened and retracted. Alice reached for the heavy pickaxe and clubbed the bear's skull.

A sickening crunch rang out, and she leaned back. Her arms blurred, and she swung the pick end into the bear's eye.

It roared a final time as the fire rapidly consumed its body in an inferno before it dropped dead.

"Help me," Alice commanded as she quickly poured a flask over the grass around the bear.

Oh crap!

I rushed over and stomped on the patches that burned. The flask helped, but the flames continued to spread from the fur.

"Move back," she commanded.

A layer of frost coated her hand before sending out a wave that doused both the bear and the ground. Spots on its fur continued to burn, but they were quickly extinguished as steam rose.

A breeze carried the acrid smell of burnt hair and roasted meat. It was awful, and I used my shirt to screen out the scent.

"Ugh. This isn't going well," I groaned.

She pointed to her ears.

Right. The static.

She stared at the smoking corpse. The circle remained unscathed, and the corpse now served as a makeshift barricade, but I didn't like how close it was to the line.

"Leave it. It's too heavy to lift," she declared.

"All right, then. I'll send my—"

I tackled Alice away from the corpse. Her eyes widened, but my cloak screamed in warning, and we dove to the ground with me over her.

Her eyes glanced at mine, but then the world shook.

A force rippled at my back and squashed me against Alice as we were bombarded. My cloak dulled the blows, but the fourth hit smashed into my shoulder, and I groaned.

Buzzing filled my ears, and my head swam. For a moment, I forgot where I was, but something squirmed beneath me.

A rough hand gripped my shoulder and lifted me. Alice reached for my face, and I leaned back, but she lunged and pulled my hood over my head.

I hadn't noticed it had slipped off.

Once the hood was back, some of the disorientation faded away, and the subtle ringing stopped. My cloak shifted, but weakly. I patted my chest, and it tightened again.

Huh.

I raised my head and met Devon's eyes as he grabbed the side of my skull, forcing me to be still.

He snapped his fingers in my face.

"Hey!" I yelled.

Then his hands turned cold, and it felt like something was squirming across my brain. I jerked out of his grip and rubbed my temples.

"Can you hear me now, pup?" he asked.

"Yeah, I can. Did you just inject mana into my head? What did you do?"

"I broke up the corrupted mana stuck to your skull. Can you stand?"

With a bit of effort, I stood. My back felt worked over, but I could move without yelping. "Yes."

"Good."

Alice had a complicated look on her face that dropped the moment she caught me looking. She nodded before looking toward Devon, who approached the spell circle.

Half the circle was gone, the dirt torn up.

"What happened? It was dead. Why did the bear explode?"

I searched, but the bear's corpse was gone. Rocks and ash mixed with black tar and scattered bone. A crater had taken the place of the corpse.

"The bear had its Lore Strain corrupted. When you two combined your mana types, it created a volatile reaction."

So we messed up...

"Can we still do the ritual?"

He held up a small series of vials in his hand. "We've got one more shot. Help clear the circle."

We helped pull pieces of bone and scraps of fur from the circle while shoveling dirt into the holes and flattening the ground. It looked rough, but Devon didn't comment further.

I grabbed a piece of bone and held it up to the light.

A piece of skull... So this is what clipped me.

Fury overtook me, and I crushed the bone. When the last piece fell from my glove, I took a deep breath.

In. Out. In. Out.

I wasn't sure why I felt so angry seeing the bone fragment, but it made the energy in my chest rage.

"Cain. Focus," Devon commanded.

I snapped to attention and watched him step into the circle. The ground was already pitch black, and he sat. The familiar static returned. The effects were still muted, but they bothered me more than before.

Alice hefted her axe.

"I'm ready," I called out.

Chapter 56

SECOND TIME'S THE CHARM

I sent out my wolf once more. I watched through its eyes, trusting Alice to pull me back if something came.

My wolf made an arc, hopping over the river to scout the other side and then wrapped back.

Nothing's coming. What's going on?

Several minutes passed, and my wolf had completed an entire rotation. I pulled back from my wolf's sight.

"Anything?" Alice asked.

She gripped her axe so tightly that her knuckles showed white.

"Nothing," I said. "Is it possible the monster ran out of creatures to send against us?"

"Doubtful. There has to be something more."

I didn't reply. Instead, I sent my wolf on another round.

Come on. Where are you?

My wolf bolted through the trees, going in and out of the shadow realm. The world lost color, only for it to return each time he exited out of the shadows.

He jumped over the river again and circled around the crevice where we found the kid. I hesitated but sent my wolf inside.

Maybe they'll be in there.

It wasn't a bad place to hide; it was spacious and protected, but the entrance was small enough that a beast like the bear wouldn't have been able to squeeze through.

When my wolf reached the cavern, I held my breath, unsure of what to expect.

I can't tell if I'm hoping for monsters or not.

Yet, inside, all I saw were piles of rocks and stagnant water. The stalactites looked the same—none came in pairs like before.

Damn.

I pulled back from my wolf and tapped Alice's arm. She turned, an expectant look on her face. I shook my head, and she growled.

The static in the air continued to assault my ears, the irritation building even with my cloak cushioning the effects. When my cloak slapped my arm, I looked down. I slid my axe out of its sheath and found my thumb running along the edge of the blade.

My green eyes stared back from a dirt-stained face, and I sighed.

"I don't know what's happening, but this should be good, right?"

Alice didn't respond.

"Hey, I said it's a good th—"

She raised a hand.

Gradually, she pivoted, readying her weapon. I hoisted the heavy pickaxe over my shoulder. Moving to stand beside her, I tilted my head to the side, straining to listen.

Alice tapped her nose, and I understood. I sniffed the air, smelling only burnt hair and dirt.

What's she on about?

"What do you smell?" I yelled.

She glared and shook her head. "You've got dirt covering your nose. Musky and damp. Like wet fur."

I commanded my wolf back to me, but it would still be a few minutes away.

We didn't have to run toward the monsters—not this time. Instead, a single three-eyed deer sprang from the trees. Its coat had several missing patches of fur, and black veins crawled up its neck.

It stomped the ground and charged. Alice ran at full speed. She was slower than the deer, but it lowered its head and rushed at her—ignoring the circle and ignoring me with my pickaxe raised and ready.

Alice swung first, the flat of her axe rushing through the air. Antlers met iron, and her strength overpowered the beast as she smashed its head aside. The deer's body pushed into her shoulder, but she yanked its head downwards and quickly kneed the creature in the jaw.

It reeled, stumbling backwards. In a blur of cold metal, blood gushed out and turned the ground dark red. Its head crashed to the forest floor, and its antlers sunk into the loam.

She breathed in and out, flicking her axe free from blood and meat in the same breath.

That's badass.

I never gave it much thought; I was too busy dealing with the insanity of every new change. Yet, that entire fight lasted a few seconds—her actions precise, well-timed, and deadly to the extreme.

Better than my own flailing.

She sniffed the air. "Incoming on your right."

My attention snapped into focus, and I pushed down on my toes.

A white, whiskered snout pushed out of the trees, and I froze.

One of the giant thumpers came bouncing out of the canopy. I scrambled to meet it, abandoning the idea of being able to catch it in melee like Alice did.

I called the flame into my mind and let the energy go wild.

I yelled, hearing the static distort the sound.

My hand flared with heat—throbbing in pain—but the flames shot out and raced toward the bulky bundle of white fur. But the hare jumped away.

The fireball exploded and knocked away the dirt; the massive horned hare landed a few feet away and raced toward me.

It leaped, closing the distance. I swung low, but it hopped again and barreled into me like a fuzzy cannonball. Powerful legs thumped my chest, and my breath exited my lungs. I spluttered but grabbed the hare with both hands.

I yanked on its ear, but its horns scraped against my leg. My anger rose again, and I punched it. The hare screeched and sunk its fangs into my arm.

Agh! Let go!

I pulled, and its fangs bit down harder, my blood mixing with its wet fur. The hare's coat absorbed the droplets like a sponge.

The world brightened again, and the voice in my head called out, clear as day.

Rip and tear!

I rolled over and trapped the beast beneath me. My jaw opened, and I sank my canines into its neck. Disgusting wet fur hit my tongue, but I bit down harder, going past the fat and tasting delicious blood on my tongue.

Then, the blood soured.

I pulled away, keeping my teeth clenched. A ripping sound cut through the static, and I raised the hare up before slamming it down. It unhooked its fangs and kicked my arm away, struggling to stand. It jumped a few feet and then rolled to a stop. The hare's chest spasmed, and then it sank to the floor.

I stood and wiped the foul-tasting blood off my mouth.

"Cain!"

I turned around just in time as a deer came charging past.

In a scramble, I grabbed the heavy pickaxe and flung it, but the deer skipped away. It continued toward the circle, and I chased after it.

Alice shot a force ball. A distortion in the air tangled the deer's legs, and it tumbled. Its head came down at an odd angle, and a muffled crack echoed through the clearing.

We raced toward the beast, but it didn't move—only twitched. Its chest rose in a labored breath.

Alice said nothing as she pulled out her knife. In a quick jab, the blade slid underneath the skull and through the deer's brain. The creature stilled, and my shoulders relaxed.

"That was close. Too close," I muttered.

I glanced toward the circle. Devon's form was a blur, and the black grass around him wisped and floated into the air, joining a slowly growing mass.

Another pulse created a loud pop.

The smell hit me. We both turned as furry beasts—dripping water across the dirt—strode out of the woods. A dozen wet snouts of different shapes and sizes charged.

I glanced back to the circle.

There's no way.

Yet I ran.

Alice sent out a wave of frost. I shot a fireball at a deer veering toward me, knocking it away, but the wet fur prevented the flames from taking hold.

She swung, but a hare jumped onto her back and launched off her shoulders. It soared, and I swung my pickaxe, clipping its foot.

It didn't matter.

No!

The static roared, drowning out the beating drum of my heart.

Another hare leaped forward. Its furry feet landed, and its body shuddered. I called to the lake of fire in my chest, letting the flames crawl up my arm.

But the hare jumped again, and I felt the world still.

Except it continued past the circle.

My brain stuttered, and even Alice froze as the beasts ran, fleeing the clearing, ignoring Devon and us entirely.

What?

"Alice?"

"I... don't know."

And then three loud gongs pierced the static.

One bell for sighting. Two bells for approaching. Three bells for attack.

I left the pickaxe behind and bolted toward the trees, following the fuzzy tail of a deer that disappeared behind a bush.

Chapter 57

Focus!

"Cain, stop! Focus!"

I hesitated as Alice gripped my shoulder. I paused long enough for her to forcefully turn me around.

"You heard Devon," she yelled. "They have walls and can handle themselves."

"But the people, Alice!" I argued. I stared at the broken branches left in the beast's wake. "What if they break through the gate?"

"Have your wolf check it out. Calm down."

I growled but shut my eyes. The connection was there, and I imagined the void sucking me in. It pulled me through, and my vision split. My wolf veered toward the city.

Come on... Come on!

Through its vision, I saw a mana-corrupted bear crashing through the trees. My summon ignored it and rushed ahead as the bear knocked another trunk out of its way.

The ground shifted, and my wolf exited the forest, coming to a stop as it neared the town gate.

Another bear scratched deep furrows with claws that were way too long. Pieces of its fur shone gray as it carved at the gate. More monsters arrived.

It wasn't just forest critters laying siege to the city. Two groups of kobolds—one made of moss-covered stone, and another made of living dirt—crowded together. One slowly climbed atop another, and more followed.

Hares hopped onto taller animals' shoulders and leaped, only to fall short.

A physical shake brought me back to my body. This time, I tugged my shoulder free from Alice's grip and stepped toward the woods.

"Stop. What did you see?" she demanded.

I gritted my teeth. "There's a lot. A crap ton! They'll be in the city soon. We need to go!"

She shook her head, and I growled. If she cared, she didn't show it and instead grabbed my cloak. It reacted. Her hand came free, and her eyes met mine.

"We need to protect the circle and bind the monster. If we don't, the entire Sealed One will be free."

"And if people die?"

Her eyes flashed red. "Then they die."

I kept the snarl from escaping, and she held my gaze. The sudden flare-up of static ruined the silence. In response, my cloak regrew the shell around my body, but it felt paper-thin.

The static rose to a shrill pitch. Alice covered her ears and shook while I stared beyond the haze as the black blob floating above Devon's head elongated.

Black grass merged with the blob, leaving the earth a lifeless gray. The sphere then morphed into a stake and split into three segments, each rotating slowly.

The spikes spun in a rush of energy, and suddenly, the circle exploded in a shockwave that knocked me over.

I looked up; the spikes had created black streaks as they rocketed away. The lines of the ritual circle lifted into the air before crumbling to ash.

Devon removed his hands from the ground. He wiped away the dust and stood, eyeing the two of us.

On the back of his hand, small inky runes rotated clockwise. In the center, a single black streak stayed still. It pulsed every two seconds.

"Get up," he ordered.

A groan escaped my lips as I stood. Several of my bones popped and cracked. My arm throbbed, but the punctures had already closed.

"Devon. The city. It's under attack," I said.

"They'll handle it. The binding should have disrupted the creature's control."

I bit my lip and closed my eyes, switching my point of view to my summons. Almost all of the forest beasts retreated from the gate.

Only the corrupted bear and elementals continued to bombard it. From the top of the wall, a single soldier stared down with his spear pointed outwards. He shook like a leaf in the wind.

He called back to someone behind the wall.

I exited the double-sight and forced myself through a breathing exercise. Devon waited, but Alice resheathed her axe.

"They'll bust the gate down, Devon. A massive bear and two groups of kobolds. Not to mention other corrupted animals. Can't you just rush over there and get rid of them?" I implored.

He held up his hand with the spinning runes. "This won't hold for long. The guards will have to make do."

The world brightened as colors rushed in vivid detail. But then the mana in my core retracted, and the colors faded away, leaving the world dull.

"Fine," I said.

Whatever fueled the engine in my chest to run hot cooled, leaving grim acceptance behind.

Devon pulled out a bottle filled with light-blue liquid. He downed it, and for the first time, he struggled. His hand shook.

"Are you okay?" I asked. I found him slouching, his breaths mistimed and erratic. "You look like crap."

"Used too much mana. My regeneration is trying to fix a lot of the internal bleeding."

He shifted slightly before pointing across the river. "Let's go."

I reluctantly called my summon back. As much as I wanted to watch the town, I needed it just in case.

"How do you know where to go?" Alice asked as she joined me.

"The ritual created a connection with the binding. As long as the ritual is in effect, I can track it."

"Rough estimate: how far is it?"

Devon didn't reply, and I groaned. But then I noticed him lean to the side to spit muddied blood.

"No more talking. Follow me."

He took off, just barely above a fast jog.

* * *

After crossing the river, we ran for nearly a mile and came to what looked like a hole in the ground. I was honestly surprised I didn't keel over and die, but even more impressive was that Devon never stopped.

His chest heaved, the sound loud enough to mask screeching birds.

Alice panted, heavier than me, but not by much.

I guess the stats are actually doing something.

"Are we really entering the dark pit?" I asked.

Devon glared. "If the entirety of the Sealed One breaks free, the entire town will die. Don't forget that."

"I haven't," I replied with steel in my voice.

"Good. Pull out your weapon. Keep your summon close."

Alice handed me another one of the glowing vials. The vials slotted into our belts, illuminating stone steps.

Devon went first, and Alice followed. It was impossible to see past Devon's broad shoulders, but the stairs didn't continue for long before they leveled out into a stone hallway.

The stone had curving lines carved into its side, but if they formed words or letters, I didn't understand them.

We continued until Devon slowed his steps. I sniffed the air and smelled something sweet.

Prey!

The thoughts came screeching into existence, and I covered my lower face.

"We're here," Devon stated.

Chapter 58

The Prisoner Says 'Hello.'

I pulled out my axe and crossed into the expanded cavern. Dark—endlessly so. It was impossible to see the other side; the shadows acted like a sponge, absorbing the meager light from the vials.

The smell intensified. A burning feeling spread through my chest. The foreign thoughts didn't say anything, but I felt them scratching—readying like a cat prepared to pounce.

Devon moved forward, his spear unhooked from its sheath. When he met the curtain of darkness, he pushed through, unbothered by the shadows.

Alice entered next, and I followed, my steps strangely silent. When the shadows draped over my skin, my cloak created another thinner shell closer to my body.

The shadows couldn't penetrate the barrier—bringing a teeny, tiny sense of relief. That feeling ended the moment my eyesight cleared enough to see the other side.

Devon and Alice stood still. They stared down at a dais hosting a circle filled with sand the color of midnight.

Several tunnels continued off from the far walls, but that wasn't what they stared at.

No.

It was the pulsing black spikes impaling a tall, lanky figure. They protruded from its body and stabbed into the sand underneath.

The being's form writhed, pulling away before being snapped back into place. It was as if the idea of a limb—the idea of a body and blood—made up the Sealed One.

Three horns jutted from its head, wavering into three lines of black smoke. The torso, where the spikes punctured through, shifted into a shadowy haze that threatened to drift away.

When the Sealed One turned its head, that familiar all-too-wide smile stretched across its mouth. Malevolent red eyes pulsed in time with the spikes.

"So, the Grimms have to collect their prey from the trap." It spoke in a voice that tickled against the back of my neck. "I expected better from you, Hunters."

Devon stayed silent and dropped into the arena. Alice went to follow, but Devon held up a hand.

Right. Let Devon handle this.

"Hmm... Red got your tongue?" it taunted.

Devon pushed against the sand. If it wasn't obvious before, it was now: he limped, his foot sliding backwards.

"The little wolf has a maimed leg. The Hunters from before would have never approached me so injured. Has the quality gone down so much since my imprisonment?"

Again, he stayed silent—even as the Sealed One shifted.

"Fine. The elder wants to hold his tongue to keep cool in front of the pups. You hide the crushed organs and snapped bones well. But do they know how fragile your Lore Strain really is?" There was a pause, then it laughed. "What about what's attached? Do they know the danger you pose to them?"

"Enough," Devon commanded.

The smile grew before rubberbanding back into place with a painful screech. It clawed at my eardrums, but the sound morphed into deep, rumbling laughter.

"Ahh, so I've touched a nerve. You need to do better, little wolf. Being exhausted is no excuse to lower your defenses. So, why shouldn't I reveal your dangerous little secret?"

Devon raised his hand, and the spikes flared before rotating. Another screech, and the Sealed One sunk deeper, its limbs falling as the eyes flashed. They grew three sizes before they, too, contracted.

"Torture? You'll have to do better than that."

Another pulse from the rune on Devon's hand, and the spikes pulsated with a wave of energy. It forced me back.

Horrific wailing filled the cavern walls. I raised my hood, but I could still hear it.

Its pitch oscillated from deep to shrill. Once the sound stopped, Devon slumped forward.

In an instant, the Sealed One scratched Devon's pants. Sharp claws penetrated the fabric, but the bindings' restrictions forced them back.

"You could kill me instantly; why haven't you, Grimm?"

Devon held his spear to the Sealed One's throat. Where iron met shadow, they recoiled, and a hissing sound echoed through the cave.

I smelled it again, the disgustingly sweet odor.

A deep revulsion rose from the bottom of my gut and I tasted bile on my tongue. I quickly covered my nose.

What the hell? That's... potent.

Alice shook beside me. Her eyes were fully crimson. Her canines were exposed, and a rumble came from her throat, prompting her to snap her jaw shut.

Like a switch, she nearly collapsed. As she regained her footing, she shook her head. The crimson stayed, but the feral hunger from before faded.

"Alice?" I whispered.

That was a mistake.

Pressure ramped up, smothering me. It felt like a giant's fist, and my cloak flared in response. The pressure eased, but not enough, and a sharp warning came from the red fabric.

Cold bit into my flesh like needles. I gritted my teeth. Nothing physical touched me, but I felt it; I knew something was there.

Then the feeling stopped, and more screeching filled the space.

When it ended, the chuckle returned, and Devon forced the spear closer in a single sweep.

The spikes flared and sank deeper into the sand.

"Disappointing, Cain Veldman. I hoped we could come to a deal—one prisoner to another," it said with enough emotion to win an Oscar.

Not even if hell froze over.

"Oh yeah, as if I'd trust a shapeshifting monster that lures children into the forest. What did you expect?" I replied.

I balled my hand into a fist and exhaled slowly.

That messed with me more than I thought.

I tapped my cloak.

You okay?

It didn't respond, but the strings around my hood tightened, and I smiled. However, the memory of cold pinpricks created a rising explosion in my chest.

The creature chuckled, but its presence shifted away.

"What do you want?" Devon asked.

He moved his spear an inch closer, and the smell came back. I tapped Alice on the shoulder. She snarled, crimson glowing menacingly in the dark.

She nodded once before focusing on the arena below us.

"Who corroded the chains on the anchor stones?" Devon asked.

"Oh? Those? I thi—" Devon cut a sizzling line across its chest. "Hah! Just a mortal looking to change their fate. Nothing more."

Another line cut—this time across its horns. Instead of rebuilding, one horn stayed shattered, bringing the glowing red eyes back into focus. The Sealed One rose and extended its hand, straining even as the spikes spun.

Even as it tried, it couldn't lay a claw on Devon, who slammed his spear through its arm. The limb exploded on contact, and the creature recoiled. Alice shuddered, and I couldn't block out the disgusting, sweet smell.

Kill! Purge the prey!

Fire rushed through my veins. The shadows fell away. Energy surged up my neck and to my face—it triggered a part of the shift.

I reined in the kill drive by pressing my nails against my palm.

If Devon felt the same effects as Alice, he didn't show it. And he really should have. He was much closer than her, yet his shoulders remained still; the only sign of weakness was the twitch in his pinky.

"What did you do with the people you lured away?" Devon demanded.

"Oh. So even a man without a heart can feel for the humans under his maw?" it teased in a strained voice. The smile grew until it curled up the sides of its face.

"Well, if you want to rescue the mortals so badly... I suppose you can speak to them."

From the sand, a single limb—long and pale—emerged. It rose slowly. The midnight grains fell as an elbow appeared—then the biceps, and finally, a shoulder. A sleeveless shirt made of blue fabric extended out as another hand popped into view.

This time, the voice echoed through the screeching, cutting through the double voices, and glided across my thoughts.

"Go on. Say hello."

Chapter 59

FIGHT FIGHT FIGHT!

The last of the risen humans popped out of the sand, the grains rejoining the arena floor. They looked stiff—unnatural. Their eyes were hollow: pure white, without irises or pupils. I counted four women, two men, and a single small child.

That has to be Thelassa's grandson. Holy crap, is he even alive anymore?

His hair looked combed and his skin unblemished. If it weren't for the eyes and rigid stance, I wouldn't have thought anything was wrong with the boy.

My jaw slowly clamped shut. If the creature was hoping for a reaction from Devon, it would be disappointed. The stoic Hunter ignored the human statues and pressed his spear even closer to the Sealed One's neck.

It ignored the blade, its red eyes spinning in the black haze that made up its face. "So cold. Should have known you only care for one thing and one thing only."

"I'll ask again. Who helped you destroy the chains?" Devon demanded.

"Bindings are a funny thing. Even seals as ancient as the one used on my real body. Weaken the link, and energy can slip out. Weaken a few more, and enough can leave the seal to create a sliver, an avatar: a mere *shadow* like me."

Devon stabbed through another limb, but the creature roared with laughter.

"You know not why I'm trapped here nor why I am to be locked away. My name is hidden, and my records are struck clean. I can tell, or you would have come prepared. Simple. Foolish. A Grimm is a prideful being: an apex predator that hunts other predators. Turning monsters into prey. I never understood why a pack of monsters would go through so much effort to pretend to be what they're not."

Shadows rose, and Devon flexed his fingers. Bindings spun and sank deeper into the sand. The Sealed One's body shrank into itself, its form losing cohesion as it wailed. But even as it screeched, the smile only grew, and the two horns extended.

"Ill-prepared runt is all that you are. And for that... I'll make you my... *Prey!*"

Devon stabbed its chest, but it caught the spear by the shaft. He growled.

Where iron met shadowflesh, it sizzled. Yet the limb remained firm and pushed the spear back. Its torso expanded as the creature loomed over Devon.

"Get back!" Devon yelled at us.

The shadows exploded, and the cave turned into an expanse of endless darkness. The void grew and pushed forward like a wave. But then it rebounded, becoming a cocoon that towered into the air.

The shadows repelled Devon. Then, a maddening cackle echoed across the walls as the wisp took form.

Separated from the Sealed One—from shadow itself—a monster five times wider than Devon formed. It expanded. Lanky limbs loomed over him. Shadows became purple flesh with black veins.

The giant squeezed, towering over Devon. He raised his arm in defense, runes flaring. But as the bindings trembled, the monstrous form bore down, mercilessly crushing Devon's ribs.

"You are but a child compared to the Grimms who sealed me," it taunted, its voice filled with malice. It cackled and pulled itself up. "Let me show you a real monster."

The giant flung Devon into the far tunnel and gave chase.

"Devon!" Alice screamed.

She jumped down, and I followed, boots hitting the sand.

The Sealed One's shadow simply snapped its fingers. As one, the human statues charged.

Alice swung her axe, but then the child held out his arms. She stopped, and one of the men tackled her. Sand filled the air; they went flying.

Damnit! Alice!

I rushed over, but three of the women ran at me.

I dodged one, and they slid across the arena floor. The second woman grabbed my wrist, but I kicked. Her grip tightened. "Get off!"

Another push. She stumbled back, and I evaded the grasp of the third woman. I yanked her hair downwards, letting go as her head smashed into the sand.

Agh! Are they possessed or zombies?!

The rest charged at Alice while the child ran toward me.

A roar shook the arena, followed by a wolf's howl. It called to me, exciting the mana in my chest. My heart blasted with every thump, pounding in my ears.

Prey! Hunt! Fight!

A woman came for me, but my summon rose from my shadow and clamped its teeth around her torso. She went down in an explosion of sand, and I jumped away.

"Don't kill her!"

Whether my wolf listened, I had no idea. Flailing limbs assaulted my side, and I struggled to stand. The child crashed into my leg, sending a jolt through my bones that ran up my hip.

Damnit!

I spun around, trying to shake myself free. But the kid stayed attached. Small hands dug into my thigh, and a woman latched onto my arm. She pulled.

My bones creaked under the pressure.

Screw this!

I swung, using the back end of my axe to break her nose. Her head rocked back, but she didn't let go, and then the child tried to crush my thigh but couldn't muster the force.

Behind me, Alice cried out.

Alice!

It wasn't time to be reluctant. I couldn't hold back—not now!

Let... go!

I punched again, landing squarely on the side of the woman's head. Her grip loosened, and I pushed her away. A second woman came at me, but my wolf knocked her to the ground. As the last two tried to rush forward, I grabbed the child's arm.

No more holding back. Sorry.

I yanked at an angle, and something snapped. The child's arm broke in my grip. I ignored the disgust welling up.

With the leverage gained, I pulled the kid's arm away and stomped. Lifting him, I threw him at the others. He crashed into them, and they nosedived to the floor in a crumpled heap of tangled limbs.

Thump! Thump! Thump!

My heart pounded. A series of buzzes made me turn, and my wolf flew through the air. The woman had long scratches down her arm. As my summon landed, it tried to sink into the ground, but my cloak snapped up.

The pressure returned, and shadows extended from above. Light from the vial struck the wall of shifting black, creating a glaring hole in reality.

Blood rushed to my head and my eyes strained at the sight. A crushing headache blossomed across my skull.

Thanks to the distraction, I didn't have time to react as a tug dragged me to the ground. My chin hit the sand, and the impact rattled my skull. Mana flared, and I pushed up. The puppet caught my foot and pulled.

I managed to get on my back just in time as I saw a wave of cold rush at my face. It crept up the woman's body. The frost hit me, but that was fine.

I accepted the thin sheet over my skin and felt my mana respond. It roared in defiance, the heat building till the ice melted away, leaving me drenched.

The wave hadn't stopped; it surged past me, slamming into my wolf. I kicked free, breaking away from the woman's grasp. Turning quickly, I saw Alice in action: she flung off one man clinging to her axe. She shoulder-checked another, sending him sprawling. With a swift whirl, she launched another puppet through the air.

Crack!

The woman landed a few feet away as Alice snarled. She stalked forward.

She raised her arm. But in that split second of distraction, a hand stealthily slipped around my neck, yanking my head back. I tried to pull free, but whoever grabbed me kept squeezing tighter.

I yelled for Alice, but she ignored my struggle. Desperately, I tried to pry, but they wrapped their legs around my waist and pulled me backwards. The motion allowed my shoulder to slip, but not enough to free myself.

Working to wrench my assailant downwards, I couldn't get the leverage needed. My axe reflected my face. The blazing orange irises of my eyes shone through the darkness.

Kill the prey!

I roared and flipped the axe around. One chop, then another. Blood splattered the ground. I kept hacking away, hitting bone as I continued.

After the sixth attempt, air rushed into my lungs. The puppet's arm sank into the sand.

Kill!

Whirling, I rotated and swung. Before I could fully process what I had just done, the iron sliced through pale flesh and emerged out the other side. I had just enough time for my eyes to widen in shock before a fountain of red sprayed.

I rolled to my feet just as a severed head tumbled across the ground. Its owner dropped to the floor.

I... I...

"Cain!"

A massive brown shape flew through the air. Claws dug into the earth and slid across the sand. The werewolf howled, and the thoughts in my head responded, screaming. I raised my axe, seeing only red.

I just...

"Cain!"

My eyes met Devon's crimson gaze, and he whirled around to throw one of the charging puppets out of the arena. Before I could react, he rushed at me.

I froze.

In a swift leap, Devon grabbed me and tossed me away.

Time slowed to a crawl.

I could only watch as I flew through the air and a massive wooden club the size of a tree trunk landed where Devon had been standing.

"Devon!" I screamed.

Chapter 60

Not This Time

My body crashed into the arena floor, and my world became a jumble of my own limbs. A pulse from my cloak helped dampen the blow, and the dark sand cushioned my fall.

I tried to stand, but my side screamed in protest. I raised my hand, and what little light shone through the darkness illuminated the bright red dripping off my fingers.

Cage. Dark shadows. Insane giggling.

I shut my eyes. My heart pounded.

Memories came flooding in.

No!

Red fabric squeezed with enough pressure for my shoulders to ache. The rush of pain made me take a breath, and I sputtered, spitting out the gritty particles of sand.

Must... get up!

Another loud roar called out, closer this time—close enough to send my head spinning. Foreign thoughts screamed in my mind.

I couldn't understand anything. A headache pulsed in sync with my heartbeat.

Have... to get... up.

I tried to stand once more, but my leg gave out almost instantly, and I collapsed.

My mana bubbled, and I couldn't contain it. The world brightened, then dimmed repeatedly. I pushed up and leaned on my other leg.

A swing of my hand created an explosion of sand that pelted my skin. I swung a second and third time until I coughed and waited for the cloud to settle.

What I saw made my stomach plummet deeper. Alice no longer swung her axe. She didn't send out waves of ice or exploding force balls into the crowd of human puppets.

No.

Her axe lay forgotten. She roared with a howl that splattered droplets of blood down the side of her snout. They joined the spittle that crawled across her blonde fur.

Sand fell away as she grabbed one of the men and slammed him into another puppet. A roar drowned out the crunch of bones.

She released her grip and ran toward the giant. It reached for her, and she leaped onto its arm. For a moment, she managed to run up its limb, but then a hand—faster than she could move—smashed her to the floor.

The towering monster's form blurred before re-solidifying.

Alice! No!

It lifted her and hammered her into the ground before casually flicking her away. Her body rolled, bowling into the crowd of puppets. A scream escaped my lips. My vision blazed with colors, and a vague outline formed around the giant. It glowed shades of purple before fading from sight.

I stood; my leg screamed. Nothing else mattered. I had to get up.

Another roar. My blood ran cold.

Devon...

The monster swept its large fist over the sand, but Devon jumped backwards. He leaped onto it, much like Alice had. But he didn't run up. No. He sank his claws into it, sending black ooze fountaining into the air.

The giant blurred once more, and Devon sank to the ground. Like lightning, a leg came down and crushed the wolf beneath its foot.

I wanted to scream again, but sand flew into my mouth.

I screamed anyway.

"You are a pup! A child! Weakling! For all the favor the gods give you, the best you can do is howl at the moon!" The Sealed One's voice echoed through the cavern, blaring into my mind like a war drum.

The giant lifted Devon into the air and squeezed.

"Aaargh!" Devon roared.

My leg collapsed. I dug my elbows in and crawled, inch by inch.

They will die.

My blood burned, and I couldn't see straight. The darkness closed in, leaving only Devon, the giant, and the Sealed One's shadow behind it all, illuminated by a half-buried vial.

I pulled. My elbows splashed sand into my face, but I ignored it.

Another roar, this time from Devon, bloody and furious.

Prey! Ki—They will die!

"When I'm free—when I destroy those chains—I will torture every last Grimm until I swallow each of you whole. Your Lore will grow mine. Be proud!"

A connection in my chest stirred, and the shadows around my arm bent before snapping back into place.

I kept crawling. The Sealed One ignored me. I was nothing to it but a broken pup.

Kill the prey!

Loud stomping shook the sand. Pressure pushed me down and held me still.

"Your Lore, oh heartless one. Do you want to give it willingly? Or shall I take it by force?"

My cloak flared, and the resistance slipped away, but something wet trickled down my stomach.

Almost there...

"Hmm. What if I drain the female pup first? Will you scream then?"

A howl—one that filled my bones with molten lead—resonated. The energy swirled then drained into my chest. My fingers dug deeper into the sand.

It took a few more lunges, flopping my body forward, until I saw it: the three spikes of obsidian impaling the Sealed One's avatar. Two tall horns, longer than my arms, and a torso that bent with each flicker. The outlines of its body were a haze, clouding the air around it.

Kill! Kill! Kill!

My teeth gnashed, and a howl grew. The giant padded over to its master, holding the limp body of Devon and Alice in both hands. It dropped Alice to the floor, uncaring as she sank into the sand.

"Let's keep it slow. I'll feed on that emotion you're feeling. The resentment, the anger, the fury! The loathing in your chest. Scream it out. Give it all to me!"

Fangs scraped my tongue, sending copper down my throat.

They'll die...

I let the heat build. Another inch. More sand collapsed, but I flopped closer. Closer. Closer.

A guttural scream tore across my thoughts. Against the dim light, the Sealed One raised its arms like a conductor. The giant braced one massive, meaty fist against Devon's body, pinched his arm between two fingers, and tugged.

"Aaarghh!"

They'll die!

I extended my arm one last time. The Sealed One was a few feet away.

A long, shadowy limb rose, forcing my chin into the sand. I couldn't breathe; the pressure hurt.

The fire inside my veins grew, pushing toward my neck, and I let it. Another pulse from my cloak stopped the flow, just long enough for blood to rush to my face.

Burn! Blaze, grow the flame into a towering inferno.

My mana responded and shot down my arm, connecting to the image in my mind. It took over, even as I couldn't breathe—the air crushed out of my lungs. I imagined it fueling the flames, bringing the inferno closer to eruption.

Ek.

Kalla.

Another scream and a visceral ripping sound shattered the image.

No!

My core shuddered. The pressure eased, and my head shot up. The dark world around me faded, and I saw the Sealed One—clear as day— surrounded by ethereal chains. They pulsed with white lines so thick that they strobed.

A tether—long, skinny, and oozing with black shards—connected to the Sealed One's head and extended like a fishing line into the sky.

I pictured it all turning to ash.

The sun blazed in my head, and I let it burn the void away.

Incinerate it all!

The giant threw Devon's body to the floor, and blood splashed.

They'll d—

Ek kalla heiðarloga!

A loud whine filled my ears, overpowering the screams, the static, and the laughter.

The world turned into a blazing flash of bright orange.

Time seemed to stop, yet it didn't. The energy in my chest made me feel light, almost giddy. And the only thing in my mind was the need to burn.

I repeated the phrase, and another fireball shot out. A single, deep thud spilled sand over me like a wave, but I forced myself to stand, favoring one leg.

Another explosion blinded the field. My hoodie burned.

It didn't matter.

I took a step forward.

Burn!

Another explosion rocked the arena, and the Sealed One came within reach. A shadowy limb tried to grab my arm, but I let the flames crawl up my skin. Black shards crumbled into motes of white ash that lifted into the sky.

Burn!

Another explosion occurred, and something heavy collapsed to the ground, followed by a distorted screech.

Only a foot apart, I grabbed the binding in the center of the Sealed One's chest.

It tried to reform but failed. This pattern repeated over and over until only the eyes remained—the smile gone.

"Oh, pup! You do have teeth. How ma—"

The flames popped, and its form exploded, only for it to hazily reshape with one eye missing. I willed another fireball, but a hungry call from my core denied me. My anger demanded more! And yet the flames would not come.

A cold, wet nose touched my leg, and I looked down to see my summon with my axe clenched between its teeth.

"Now that's a Grimm."

In a flash, cold iron bisected the Sealed One. The shadow flesh sizzled and splattered onto my face. I inhaled the sweetened air, letting the scent fill my nose.

The haze slipped through my fingers, becoming deflated black leather.

My axe sank into the sand.

"Cain..."

Devon's eyes met mine: human, torn, and bloody.

I smiled.

"Hunt complete."

And then the world blurred as my head hit the sand.

Chapter 61

END OF THE HUNT

I blinked, and my vision started to clear.

As I regained my eyesight, a wave of exhaustion hit me, and my body ached.

"Ugh..."

"See, he's alive," Devon said.

"Are you sure? I don't feel like it."

"Can you get up?"

Can I?

I tried to stand, but my limbs screamed in such agony that I released another groan.

After regaining control, I flopped back onto the sand. "No... Maybe. Give me a minute or two. What about Alice? Is she all right?"

"I'm alive," she said in a flat voice.

A weight lifted off my shoulders. I actively forced myself not to replay the scene of the giant hammering her into the ground. In fact, I forced myself not to replay a lot of what happened.

Ah, crap. The villagers.

Despite my body's protests, I leaned on my good side and slowly sat up. The effort brought me to a wheeze, but I ignored the pain. I turned my head slowly, trying to pierce the darkness.

Damn. All I see is sand.

I tried to stand, but my leg wouldn't budge, so I settled for gently twisting my torso. My ribs creaked, and something wet ran down my side.

"Guys. Alice. Do you think any of the people are alive? The kid, they…"

My voice trailed off when I remembered what I did to one of the puppets. Memories played of my axe cutting through flesh: the feeling of warm human blood hosing me down… I wanted to scream.

"Cain. Stop," Devon said.

I couldn't breathe, and I squeezed my leg, sending a jolt up my spine. It hurt, and that was good. I needed the distraction.

"I'm… fine."

He didn't argue back.

"Alice? Are you able to move?"

"No. Legs shattered. Will take a while for regeneration to kick in."

So we're all broken little things. Man, that boss worked us over.

Something frozen hit my arm, and I flinched. After biting my tongue to keep the scream in, I found my summon sitting with its head cocked.

I hadn't noticed it at first, but it was small—its form barely the size of a golden retriever.

"Hey, buddy. You helped me out back there. Thank you."

Its fur was cold, but I embraced the feeling as it tickled my skin. Its shadowy fur wavered, and my wolf leaned into the scratch before licking my face.

Should probably fix your size.

I willed mana into the connection, but I found something odd. The pool inside my chest—the great lake of fire that kept me warm inside—felt… empty.

Did I use that much? Is this why I feel so weird?

Until I probed the core inside my body, I didn't realize how cool everything felt. I was so used to being permanently warm over the past week that, without it, everything felt much colder.

I still had enough mana to feed to my summon, but it wouldn't be its full size anytime soon.

My wolf pushed its body into mine, allowing me to give it a good hug. As I scratched it, I noticed its feet were stable, standing away from a splotch of darkness on the ground. It was nearly impossible to see due to the sand, but I noticed a pattern of rough-looking bumps on the surface.

What's this?

I grabbed the hide. It felt abrasive but cold—alarmingly so—as if someone had placed ice on its surface. Turning it over, I rubbed it between my fingers and finally realized what it reminded me of.

Oh! This is the Sealed One's avatar...

It sank back into the sand.

The black leather-like material was the remains of the nightmare we faced. I had touched its corpse. My wolf cocked its head.

Does it want it? Is it like a shadow wolf chew toy?

"Hey." I rubbed its ears. "Do you want it? You're staring at it pretty hard."

"Cain? What are you doing?" Devon asked.

"I don't know. The... shadow avatar—whatever it's called—turned into this weird leather. My summon is staring at it."

He didn't respond for the longest time. I was nearly ready to repeat what I said, but then he spoke. "When did you activate your skill?"

"My skill? During the hunt for the missing child. I never had a reason to undo it, and I forgot."

"I see."

And we're back to cryptic Devon. Fine. If he wants to be indirect, then I won't bother asking.

"Well?" I whispered to the wolf. "If you want it, go on. You deserve it."

My wolf's eyes swirled, spinning like the void in my head when I envisioned a spell circle. For a moment, I saw an intelligence that went beyond a loyal dog.

It nodded and licked my face. It sniffed the skin and lowered its head.

I expected it to snap it up, but instead, it gently grabbed it. The long stretch of black hide coiled on the ground in loops, but I noticed something weird around the spots where my wolf's teeth sank into the material. Where it should have been hardened leather—solid to the touch—it softened into wispy shadows.

It released a howl that filled the cavern, and I felt something poke at our connection. It shuddered, I gasped, and then it continued until the discomfort forced me to rock backwards. Sand cushioned my head, but I shut my eyes and focused on the mana inside my chest.

A whirlpool.

The mana drained away and sank into the connection, leaving my body hollow. I tried to breathe but could only cough. Once the last of the mana left, my core dimmed. My limbs spasmed as my teeth clacked together.

Ice entered my chest like a shard of glass. I squeezed my sternum, but the pain continued until I heard a scream escape my lips. My fist banged against the ground until the feeling passed.

The frigid cold turned into fire, swirling inside my core, igniting the inert battery. After the shaking stopped and my limbs regained strength, I noticed something different about the connection between me and my summon.

As I gave mana, it returned some to me: a permanent exchange that favored my wolf, but an exchange nonetheless. I opened my eyes, and my wolf slowly dug furrows into the sand.

"What... was that?"

It didn't answer but looked up, the hide still in its mouth.

Oh.

The void was gone, replaced by two swirling pits of flames raging in a shifting tide.

The piece of the hide disappeared down my wolf's throat with a single chomp.

Whatever magic kept the shadows as fur unspooled. My summon became a cloud, leaving behind a set of glowing eyes that watched me as a thrum built like a staccato. It took me a second to realize it was my own heartbeat.

Bump. Bump. Bump!

An explosion of rainbow colors overtook the void, and I couldn't move as pressure crushed me in an embrace.

The rainbow shimmer gave way and formed into lines of golden text.

[ALERT] You have slain Erlking's Avatar, Enthralled Kobolds EvR x4, Corrupted Beasts.
Calculating hunt reward...
Applying Strain Modifier: -25%
[ALERT] Diverted excess to Lore Matrix...
[ALERT] Excess rerouted to Summon: Shadow Wolf.
[ALERT] Pact has been made. Exchange of Lore accepted.

The lines disappeared, fading away long enough to see that my summon—which had been a black haze—was now an egg. It swirled like a vortex, a pool of darkness so black that it made my eyes water.

A bond is one that entwines the soul. To exchange a piece is to forever spin your thread into their tapestry. Your Lore has been irrevocably changed, as well as your familiar. Grow and thrive.
Continue the Endless Hunt.
[ALERT] Skill changed. New ability granted: Summon Familiar (Freki)

The egg grew, and mana poured into it. I wasn't sure how, but it came in like a waterfall, dripping the energy onto of the shell.

Flames joined the shadows within. A blinding, brilliant fire—one that shone like the sun—swirled into the depths of the egg until it condensed into a core spinning in the middle of the maelstrom.

As the spinning slowed to a crawl, it reversed. The connection stung and tugged until a force knocked me back into the sand.

It didn't hurt. Uncomfortable, but not painful.

The golden text reappeared, and I read the lines as my body adjusted to the influx of foreign energy.

Hunt Reward:
Title Granted: [String Cutter]
Ability Granted: Shadow Bond.
You are now level 4.
[ALERT] Auxiliary title slot unlocked.
Bonus Stats Gained: Agility +1, Intelligence +2, Luck +1.

As the notification disappeared, I rushed to open my status sheet.

Name: Cain Veldman
Title: Crimson Hunter
Auxiliary Title: String Cutter
Level: 3 (+1)
Stats
    STR: 15
    AGI: 15 (+1)
    CON: 16
    INT: 14 (+2)
    WIS: 13
    LUK: 15 (+1)
Skills
    Summon Familiar (Freki)
Passives
    Ember Soul
    Shadow Bond

There was a lot to take in, but I closed the screen as the egg descended to the ground. As it reached the sand, the shell burst.

A wave of heated air rushed toward us, and I closed my eyes as it lingered on my skin. The heat shifted to a cold chill that dug into my pores. As the last of the energy faded, a deep howl filled the silence. When I opened my eyes, a black streak zipped across my face and rushed into my chest. A new feeling settled inside my core; it felt heavier.

I lifted my shirt and stared at a small black tattoo directly above my sternum. It spun with wavering lines that never stilled long enough for me to get a good look at the runes.

Oh, this looks weird.

With the pulsing shadow egg gone, the cavern once again lay shrouded in darkness.

"Cain, when you're able to, check on the humans. If any of them survived, we'll take them to the church."

Crap. Forgot about them. That kid better be alive.

"And if they're dead?"

"We'll burn their corpses before we leave."

You did what you had to do, Cain. Remember that.

* * *

I shoved another skewer into my mouth and tore off the meat from the stick. A few chairs away, the boy sat with his arm in a sling. His parents never left his side, as if they were afraid he'd disappear.

Thelassa looked at me expectantly. I tentatively reached out and accepted another plate. A single crisp cookie made it into my mouth, and I savored the explosion of sugar and berries.

"You know, Hunter, for all that you seem to enjoy traumatizing the townsfolk with the sight of your mangled arm, you have a good heart," she commented.

She watched the young boy talk to his parents as they desperately doted on him.

I finished the cookie and bit into another, letting the sugar melt in my mouth before speaking. "Starting to think that's a detriment in this job."

She chuckled, but it held little mirth. "Perhaps. I won't claim to know best; your life is vastly different from mine, after all. But know that the townsfolk who look at you like heroes do so for a reason."

After wiping the crumbs from my face, I stood. "Maybe. I guess I'll find out after a while. If we ever come back here, I'll give you my answer then."

Thelassa slid a cookie off the plate and bit into one, the sounds of muffled chewing filling the silence.

"You didn't ask, but the other two are fine as well. The young man's family has stayed by his side like hungry hens. They'll be mothering him for days. And the woman has reunited with her husband and child. They'd thank you in person if you wanted to see them."

No way in hell.

I shook my head. "Nah, that's fine. We're heading out in the next few minutes. I just wanted to see how the kid's doing."

"He's doing great. It'll be hard on the parents, but it's good that none of the Erlking's victims remember what happened. Even young Seyenna is up and about, playing with Do'lby in the garden."

If the people we rescued ever remembered what happened, they surely wouldn't have wanted to meet the Grimms who broke their bones. Nightmare or not, being a puppet for some ancient monster would leave a scar on anyone's mind.

For a few more minutes, I enjoyed watching the boy play with his parents, and I reached down to enjoy the last cookie when Thelassa grabbed it. She met my eyes with a wink and reached for something hidden in her robe.

Uh.

She pulled out a wax-paper-wrapped parcel tied together with green thread. As I held it up to sniff, I caught a whiff of sugar and berries topped with hardened cream.

"Cookies?" I asked as I slipped the parcel into my satchel.

"Indeed. It's not much, but I hope they bring you joy," she responded. With grace that belied her age, she clasped her hands together in prayer. "Thank you once more, dear Grimm—for saving our town and my family from heartache."

I put on a polite smile and returned her bow with a shallower one before leaving.

Once in the nave, I dropped the smile.

Adeline's right. We're mercenaries and monster hunters. I'm no hero, lady. A hero would have saved everyone.

My hood drew some looks from several townsfolk inside the church walls. Without turning my head, I strode out. Once the setting sun engulfed me, I continued around the corner and found Devon leaning against the wall with Alice beside him.

"Ready to go?" Alice asked.

"Yeah. I could use a few days relaxing," I replied.

I will actually bite you if I don't, Devon.

Devon said nothing, and we took the side roads toward the village gate. Once we got into view of the entrance to town, I couldn't help but stare at the damage done to its walls. Large chunks were missing, while the entrance sported several splotches of dried blood.

The remaining guards noticed our approach and lined up. More than a few backed away with fear in their eyes. Only the leader greeted us, and he quickly called out for the rest of his men to salute.

Devon nodded once before ignoring the crowd, and we followed behind him, our matching cloaks flowing in the breeze. We didn't look back.

Once in the forest, I finally relaxed enough to lower my hood. I inhaled and enjoyed the smell of nature.

"I never asked, but what do you think will happen with that Albrus guy, the town leader? He's still in the church basement, right?"

"They'll hold him until the new leader arrives. The Grimm in the capital has already informed the city lord of his incarceration," Devon answered.

"Oh? And they're cool with that? I thought we don't deal with that stuff."

"If it concerns a village directly responsible for a Sealed One, we do. And if the city lord demanded his release, the kingdom would need two replacements."

I shook my head and rubbed the spot on my chest that felt cool to the touch.

Let's hope the new guy is smarter than the last.

* * *

We finally reached the spot where the portal had dropped us off. It was an uneventful walk through the woods. Even birds flew the moment we neared.

As we moved into the small clearing, the familiar scent of roses hit my nose, and I grimaced.

"Please tell me we've met our poop collection quota."

"We already have enough, no need for more," Alice responded.

"Silence."

I stuck my tongue out and waited. Devon pulled out his coin necklace and dripped the blood. The ground vibrated, and the roots grew into the familiar shape of the portal archway.

Rainbow lights scattered until it turned into the mirror of Neina's cave. From the other side, the green-haired woman stood with her arms crossed, waiting.

Devon looked back. "Go visit Astra and show her your new skill. She'll want an update for records."

I saluted and joined the two-person line behind him.

Before Devon stepped through, the image distorted and then shattered in a loud wailing that brought me to my knees.

What's going on?!

The sound suddenly stopped. The roots of the archway burned, crumbling to black ash in a torrent of green fire.

"Devon!" I yelled.

He was already watching, standing with a grim expression.

"Damn..." he muttered.

More than anything in the last week, those words filled my stomach with lead.

A bright system notification popped up in the corner of my vision, stretching across my sight.

**[ALERT] EMERGENCY LOCKDOWN OF LOCAL NODES.
NEXUS LEYLINES CLOSED.
URGENT QUEST AUTOMATICALLY ACCEPTED.
[ALERT] NEW QUEST ACQUIRED: HUNT THE MONSTER
THAT THREATENS THE NEXUS! ELIMINATE ALL
THREATS!**

"Devon?" I whispered.

"Damn…"

Thank you for reading a MoonQuill original novel. More exciting stories can be found on our website, www.moonquill.com.

We would greatly appreciate it if you would take a moment to leave a review. Each one helps the author and supports their ability to continue writing fantastic books for everyone to enjoy!

If you're looking for more great books to read, join our mailing list by scanning the QR code or clicking the link below. You'll get a few eBooks for free!